Henry Denker, as well a
ous novels, has had five p
*Far Country* and *A Case of*
pressive awards writing fo
and for ten years he has
*Greatest Story Ever Told*, the
the history of American br
e and his wife,
Edith, live in New York.

Also by Henry Denker

*I'll Be Right Home, Ma*
*My Son the Lawyer*
*Salome: Princess of Galilee*
*That First Easter*
*The Director*
*The Kingmaker*
*A Place for the Mighty*
*The Experiment*
*The Physician*
*The Starmaker*
*The Scofield Diagnosis*

Plays

*The Headhunters*
*Time Limit!*
*A Far Country*
*A Case of Libel*
*Venus at Large*
*What Did We Do Wrong?*
*Second Time Around*

# *Henry Denker*

# The Actress

A MAYFLOWER BOOK

**GRANADA**
London Toronto Sydney New York

Published by Granada Publishing Limited in 1981

ISBN 0 583 13152 2

First published in Great Britain by
W. H. Allen 1979


Granada Publishing Limited
Frogmore, St. Albans, Herts AL2 2NF
and
3 Upper James Street, London W1R 4BP
866 United Nations Plaza, New York, NY 10017, USA
117 York Street, Sydney, NSW 2000, Australia
100 Skyway Avenue, Rexdale, Ontario, M9W 3A6, Canada
PO Box 84165, Greenside, 2034 Johannesburg, South Africa
61 Beach Road, Auckland, New Zealand

Set, printed and bound in Great Britain by
Cox & Wyman Ltd, Reading
Set in Intertype Baskerville

To Edith, my wife

# Part 1

# *One*

The director reached for the police whistle that hung from the leather thong around his neck. He blew one long shrill blast.

Grips, carpenters, the lighting crew up on the scaffold, makeup men and women, extras, even stars became so silent one could hear the humming of the lights. For the director was Jeff Warrener, a man renowned for his vitriolic temper.

'Now, hear me! This morning we begin our ten toughest days of shooting on this film. So I want no "problems." No headaches. No backaches. No menstrual cramps. No interruptions of any kind!

'Starting right now, no sneaking out to make phone calls! No gossipy little chats! No coffee. Except during breaks which I will call myself. No exceptions for anyone! So don't even ask! Understood?'

Jeff Warrener was a man of medium height, but with the powerful build of a middleweight champion. He was considered one of the most physical directors in Hollywood. Not only for his tense and exciting action scenes, but physical in the sense that despite his forty-one years, and the slight gray that peppered his black hair, he could still go three rounds with any professional fighter his weight, or six sets with most of the tennis pros in Beverly Hills.

Yet there were female stars who insisted Jeff Warrener was the most sensitive director with whom they had ever worked.

He was giving his assistant last-minute instructions for the first setup of the day when his secretary came on the stage. With an impatient glance toward her, Warrener commanded, 'Later, Daisy!'

'But, this is an—'

'No "buts"! I said later!' Warrener exploded.

Crew and cast turned to watch. At any other time Daisy Brenner would have left the set immediately, resigned to coping with the emergency somehow.

But this morning Daisy remained adamant. Warrener glared at her, his black eyes furious. That always intimidated her. Today Daisy stubbornly stared back. 'You have a long-distance call. From Connecticut.'

'I don't know anybody in Connecticut. Take a message!'

'They insist on talking to you personally,' she persisted.

'I am shooting a picture!' Warrener shouted.

'He knows that. That's why he tried to call early, before shooting started.'

'Who the hell is "he"?'

'Dr Alvin Ross.'

'I do not know any Dr Ross!' Warrener said, assuming he had disposed of the intrusion.

Softly, because she knew she was venturing into a most sensitive area, Daisy informed him, 'He's Kit Lawrence's doctor.'

'Kit's doctor . . .' Warrener repeated in a whisper. 'Did he say . . . I mean, she hasn't done anything again . . . anything foolish . . .?'

'He only said that he had to talk to you. *Now*.'

'Of course.' Warrener hesitated a moment before asking, 'You think I ought to take it here or back at the office?'

'The way Dr Ross sounded, I'd say the office.'

'Okay,' he agreed, wondering at the same time how his cast and crew would react to this delay after his severe warnings. He camouflaged the interruption by suddenly barking an order to his assistant. 'We can stand more light on the bedroom set! We'll start as soon as it's right.'

Jeff Warrener picked up the phone in his private office,

trying to light a cigarette and talk at the same time. 'Dr Moss?'

'Ross,' the doctor's well-modulated voice corrected.

'Sorry – Ross,' Warrener conceded, not impatient but concerned. 'What about Kit? Did she try it again?'

'No.'

'Good.' Warrener was relieved. 'Look, if it's money, send me the bill. I'll do what I can.'

'It isn't money, Mr Warrener,' the doctor said. 'And if you stop asking irrelevant questions I'll tell you why I'm calling.'

'Okay,' Warrener agreed, his eye on his desk clock. 'Only make it fast.'

'I would like to know when you can be here.'

'Connecticut? Is that what you mean?'

'That's what I mean, Mr Warrener.'

'What the hell . . .' Warrener exploded. 'I am shooting a picture that will go ten more days. Then there is cutting, scoring and a million other postproduction headaches. And you want to know when I can be in Connecticut. That's what I call *chutzpah*! Do you, my dear Dr Ross, know what *chutzpah* is? It is a show-business term meaning nerve, gall! Sheer, unmitigated gall!'

Gently the doctor volunteered, 'In view of the fact that my name was Rosenzweig before it was Ross, you may assume that I know what *chutzpah* is.'

The doctor's tone served to temper Warrener's impatience. 'Doctor, why me in Connecticut? What could I do for Kit?'

'That's what I want to find out,' Ross said thoughtfully. 'But it's too complicated to explain by phone. So I thought I'd ask you and Steven Brooks—'

Warrener interrupted, 'Brooks? If that sonofabitch shows up, I won't! What did he say?'

'I haven't called him yet.'

'Then don't,' Warrener commanded. 'There's nothing he

can do for her. If you ask me, he's the bastard who got her messed up in the first place!'

'Mr Warrener,' Ross explained patiently, 'it wasn't any one man who "got her messed up." Her trouble started long before that.'

'He didn't do her any good,' Warrener insisted.

'I didn't call to discuss Steven Brooks. Only to ask if you could come here.'

'How serious is it?' Warrener asked.

'Enough for me to urge that you make the trip.'

'Would it do any good?'

'Nothing else has,' Ross said. 'That's why I'm calling.'

Warrener was silent for a moment. 'What if you had to wait two weeks?'

'I would understand.'

'Okay, then, I'll try to work it out,' Warrener promised. 'Now, about Steve Brooks . . .'

'It is my opinion,' Ross interrupted sharply, 'my considered opinion, that it would be desirable for both of you to be here.'

Warrener equivocated for a moment, then agreed grudgingly, 'For Kit's sake, okay. But I want you to know that I don't get along too well with that sonofabitch.'

'From what Miss Lawrence told me, I assumed as much.'

'As long as you know,' Warrener warned. 'Now, you'll have to excuse me. I must get back to the stage.'

'Of course.'

Before he hung up, Warrener admitted, 'By the way, Doctor, before I was Jeff Warrener, I was Julie Warshafsky. So we start off even.'

By the time Jeff Warrener was walking his actors through the first shot, the phone rang in Steven Brooks's office in the Creative Arts Building of Mid-West State University. Brooks turned from his typewriter and without waiting to discover who the caller was, he said crisply, 'I know! I'm late! I'll be right there!' He was starting to hang up when he heard a female voice: 'Mr Steven Brooks? Long distance calling.'

'Oh?' Brooks paused, a number of speculations crossing his mind. Was it one of those unsolicited calls from Hollywood about doing a screenplay? Or was Melinda calling with a new idea some publisher was suggesting? Or his present publisher calling to inquire when they might expect the manuscript he was working on right now? Any of them would be welcome. For he had felt cut off from the world ever since he had agreed to do a year as Author-in-Residence.

Originally he had looked upon this voluntary seclusion as the least painful way to readjust to the breakup of his marriage, made doubly difficult by the fact that Melinda was not only his wife but his literary agent as well. But his students were taking more time than he had anticipated. And this morning, like so many other mornings, he had just gotten deep into his novel again when his wrist alarm reminded him he had to teach an eleven-o'clock class in Advanced Playwriting.

He had mistakenly assumed this phone call was a summons to that class. Obviously it was a call from Hollywood or New York.

'This is Brooks!'

'Mr Brooks, Dr Ross.'

'Dr Ross?' Brooks was plainly puzzled.

'Of Silvermine.'

That institution, devoted to the treatment of patients with severe mental difficulties, chose to disguise its function behind that colorful and disarming name. However, it had become so well known as to be instantly recognized.

'Oh, yes,' Steve Brooks acknowledged, wondering if this was another request for a copy of the novel he had written some years ago that was set, in part, in a mental institution.

'I'm calling to ask whether you could come here, say two weeks from now—'

Brooks interrupted. 'Sorry, Doctor, I've given up lecturing. And I have a schedule of writing classes here that won't permit me to leave till spring vacation. In fact, I'm late for my class now. So don't think me rude, but I do have to run.'

'Mr Brooks, if you would listen for just a moment . . .'

'Please, Doctor, I've no time—' Brooks tried to interrupt.

'This relates to Kit Lawrence!'

'Kit? Oh? What happened?' Brooks asked, willing now to listen a long time if necessary.

'Nothing has "happened," ' Ross said. 'In a strange way, that's the trouble. That's why I want to know if it's at all possible for you to come.'

'I'd have to find someone to pinch-hit for me here.'

'Then do that,' Ross urged. 'It's important, Mr Brooks. Very important.'

'I'll do my best.'

'Oh, by the way' – Ross felt impelled to be frank – 'I've already spoken with Jeff Warrener.'

'Oh' was all Brooks said, but his animosity was clearly obvious.

'He's willing to come, willing to meet you.' Ross stretched a point.

'He's no good for her. Never was,' Brooks warned.

'Don't you think I should be the judge of that?'

'I'm warning you. For your own good. And for Kit's.' Suddenly he asked, 'How is she? How does she look?'

'Why don't we let that wait until you get here?' Ross suggested.

'Okay,' Brooks said, relenting.

He had no sooner hung up than his phone rang again. This time his assumption was correct. They were summoning him to class.

Through most of the session, during which he lectured on introducing and integrating characters into the structure of a play, Steve Brooks's mind was constantly seduced from his subject to memories of Kit Lawrence.

To the first time they had ever seen each other. And the last time.

To the days, weeks and months they had lived together. One thing still remained a mystery to him. Had he left Kit? Or had she left him? That part was never clear in his mind.

He forced himself to concentrate on his attentive students. A small, selected group of bearded young men and long-haired young women, they all dressed almost alike, the males among them and the females. But now he was thinking of Kit again because one student with long blond hair and marvelous breasts reminded him of her. Though Kit was not so obviously voluptuous, she was extremely sensuous. Or had been. Leanness used to endow her sculptured cheekbones with graceful yet striking prominence. However, the last time he had seen Kit she was no longer slender. She had allowed herself to become gross, from overindulgence in both alcohol and food.

The present irony of his situation struck him. He was lecturing on integrating characters into a play. But in real life people did not integrate themselves with the same preplanned purpose. In real life, you met people accidentally. Some of them took and stayed on to integrate themselves. Some drifted into and out of your life with none of the preciseness required in a drama.

Kit Lawrence was one who had not followed the rules, either of drama or of real life. She drifted into your life and stayed until you were sure you couldn't live without her. Then she drifted off suddenly. She had an indefinable capacity for making men attach themselves to her and never want to let go. Yet she herself would not be held by any of them.

She had made love the same way. Sometimes with such ecstatic abandon and hunger as to make a man feel this was the way the most sublime love affairs in history must have happened. Other times she seemed completely passive, as if saying, Take me if you wish.

'Mr Brooks ...' The voluptuous blond girl brought him out of his reverie.

'Yes, Ms Vander Zee?'

He constantly strove to maintain an air of academic decorum, addressing his students formally. Especially his female students.

It was unfair, he felt, to exploit their vulnerability. For he had no overmodest illusions about himself. He was handsome, tall, in good physical condition for a man turning forty. His once-blond, now-sandy hair endowed him with a mature distinction that could entice young female students. In addition, he had a reputation unique in their secluded academic world, thanks to several successful Broadway plays, one of which had been revived in a University production to mark his arrival as Author-in-Residence. Two of his novels had been on the best-seller lists for brief stays. So he possessed a certain celebrity that might overwhelm young girls. He was determined not to take advantage of that.

Despite his pious resolution, he was constantly tempted. More than once he had to remind himself, It's only a student's crush, on a professor who bears the glamorous title Author-in-Residence.

He resolved to remain in residence through the rest of the year. At least until his divorce from Melinda had been arranged.

Besides, Dr Ross's call had revived all those thoughts and memories of Kit. No student, no matter how nubile or attractive, could compete with her.

# *Two*

Two weeks later, on Flight 404, New York to Hartford, Jeff Warrener and Steve Brooks met for the first time in almost six years.

Brooks boarded late, and the only empty first-class seat was in the smoking section next to Jeff Warrener. Brooks sank into it, fastened his seat belt in compliance with the lighted sign, and leaned back, a bit tense.

They were both silent until the plane took off. When the No Smoking sign went dark, Warrener asked brusquely, 'Do you mind?'

'Of course not,' Brooks said, though he detested smoke ever since he had given up the habit.

They were silent thereafter, until Warrener asked, 'What are you doing these days?'

'Working on a new novel.'

'Oh,' Warrener said, with the deprecating inflection of Hollywood people when they discover a man is not currently on someone's payroll. However it was worded, it meant they considered the man to be unemployed.

'I'm also Author-in-Residence,' Brooks felt compelled to add.

'Great,' Warrener said, with so little enthusiasm that he had deliberately made it sound even duller than it was.

The plane touched down on a runway banked on both sides with four-foot-high walls of snow. It taxied to a gate. An airline passenger agent, young, bright, and evereager to please, paged, 'Mr Brooks. Mr Warrener, Mr Jeff Warrener.'

When they identified themselves, he led them to an aging man in sheepskin coat, galoshes and fur hat.

'Mr Warrener? Mr Brooks?' the man asked. 'Just follow me.' He made his way to a station wagon, boldly ensconced in the No Parking zone. On its door in small discreet script was the single word *Silvermine.*

They drove through the bleak Connecticut countryside on a wide concrete highway. On either side, the fields were buried by deep snow except where patches of brown earth had been laid bare by the strong winter winds. The driver sensed the oppressive silence and tried to make conversation. Brooks and Warrener did not encourage him.

After almost an hour the wagon passed between two rough-hewn native-stone pillars that announced SILVERMINE on two neat metal plaques.

It pulled up in front of a long fieldstone building accented by the inevitable white trim in true New England custom. Through the wide window Brooks could see what was obviously a comfortable living room. Inside they found a fire blazing in the white-manteled fireplace.

They hadn't realized they were so cold until confronted with the fire. They tried to warm their hands at it. Thus, alone in the room, side by side, they felt forced to talk intimately for the first time.

'What do you think?' Warrener asked. 'What does he want?'

'No idea,' Brooks said. 'Unless it's money.'

'He said no.'

'Maybe it's heavier than he could handle by phone.'

'Such as?'

'She's incurable. So it will take a *lot* of money, and for a long time. You don't broach that to someone on the phone.'

'No, you don't,' Warrener agreed.

Less than ten minutes later a tall, lean, attractive dark-haired man in his early forties, wearing an immaculate white lab coat, entered the room. 'Mr Warrener? Mr Brooks?' he asked.

He led them to his private office, which was decorated as a

warm and pleasantly disarming library. Even his treatment couch was unobtrusive. He invited them to be seated in deep, comfortable leather chairs which flanked his desk.

'I must tell you at the outset this is a highly unconventional meeting. But if I didn't feel it was vitally necessary I would not have asked you to come. On rare occasions I insist on talking to a patient's closest relative.

'But I've never talked to a patient's former lovers. Yet there do come times when, for the patient's sake, an analyst feels forced to exceed the parameters of conventional treatment and seek ancillary help. He might even feel forced to reveal certain matters of confidence between patient and doctor for the patient's best interests. I trust you will respect that. Because in this case there are reasons . . . very special reasons,' Ross stated.

It was obvious to them that the doctor was extremely uncomfortable.

Nevertheless, he continued: 'So this meeting is most unusual. But then, Miss Lawrence is a most unusual patient. A most unusual woman. Or need I tell you two?'

He paused as if awaiting some response. There was none. Suddenly he blurted out, 'Damn it, this is proving even more difficult than I anticipated!'

Warrener smiled. 'If you say the worst part first, the rest is easy, Doctor. At least, that's what my analyst in Beverly Hills used to say.'

Ross flushed slightly. It was impossible to determine whether he was embarrassed or angry.

'Kit's treatment has reached an impasse,' he declared, using her name with a familiarity which was unintentional.

'She's incurable,' Warrener concluded grimly.

'Warrener, we don't deal with curability or incurability,' Ross corrected. 'If the truth be told, we can never *cure*. We are devoted to the concept that there is something of value in every human being. Our work consists of nurturing that value while seeking to control or minimize the patient's destructive tendencies.

'We term that, making the patient functional. I'm asking you to help me do that with Kit. In her case, the challenge is greater than usual. Her enormous talent imposes on us an enormous responsibility. That you both have loved her makes that responsibility much more personal.'

Ross paused before he could admit, 'Kit's case is complicated by a most unfortunate situation. A situation to which I must admit I have been an unwilling contributor.

'No,' Ross corrected himself. 'In the interest of total frankness, I should say a willing contributor.'

With a gesture of determined decision, Ross rose, thrust his hands into the pockets of his white coat and stood before the fireplace to face them as he confessed, 'This is the first time in my career that I have ever become involved with a patient. Sexually involved.'

Furious, Warrener leaped to his feet. 'Are you telling me you dragged me away from my picture, which is right now in the process of being edited, to get you out of a jam over Kit? A jam into which you got yourself? Sonofabitch!'

'Warrener, I'd appreciate it if you withheld any judgment until I've finished.'

'For my money, you're finished right now! You precipitated this situation! Or else weren't a good enough doctor to handle it without getting involved. Now you want me to bail you out.'

'You're making a mistake most laymen make. That analysts are above being human. Well, they're not. Which means they are as susceptible to an attractive woman as other men. As the two of you are. In fact, analysts have a pathology of their own, weaknesses and frailties of their own. It would be better if they didn't. But they do.'

'I still don't see how that becomes my problem!' Warrener shot back.

Steve Brooks felt compelled to intervene lest the other two

become so hostile as to destroy any purpose his journey might have had. 'Warrener, instead of being your delightful sadistic self, give the doctor a chance to explain.'

Before Warrener could reply, Ross took command. 'Gentlemen! We have a problem. The three of us. Because we've all been involved with Kit. We're going to settle it together. Or it won't get settled. With, I must warn, unpredictable and highly dangerous consequences to her.'

Warrener remained seething but silent.

'Now, as to my relationship with the patient. I don't have to tell either of you that she can be a remarkably fascinating woman. She wasn't when she arrived here. She was fat. Her blond hair was a dirty tangle. She was an alcoholic. As well as a heavy smoker. She kept insisting that if she stopped smoking she would gain more weight. So she kept smoking. And she kept gaining weight.

'She was determined to make herself ugly, grotesque. She dressed that way. She made up that way. She was determined to destroy every vestige of Kit Lawrence the actress, the star.

'More than once I was convinced she was a lost cause. Yet there was something about her that wouldn't let me give up.'

Warrener interjected, 'Damn fool! You were already in love with her!'

'Warrener, please!'

Ross continued: 'Something about her made me refuse to concede defeat. It could have been the memory I had of her in a play I saw once in New York. I think the title was *Summer Love* . . .'

'Mine,' Brooks said, a touch of vanity in that single word, for it was his biggest Broadway hit.

'Excellent play,' Ross commented.

Warrener interjected, 'You should have read the damn thing before I got my hands on it. It abused the privilege of being dull!'

Brooks exploded. 'You bastard, because you couldn't

direct my sensitive scenes you called them dull. For you, everything had to go off like skyrockets. Well, just as love isn't all sex, drama isn't all skyrockets!'

'Brooks! For God's sake, give me a chance,' Ross pleaded.

'Sorry,' Brooks said, still furious.

'It doesn't matter why I felt I shouldn't give her up as a patient. The fact is I couldn't. So I worked with her. Slowly, intensively. For she is not only terribly resistant, she has a devilishly adroit mind. She has all the ingenuity of a borderline psychotic, plus the charm and technique of a great actress. That may have been the challenge that kept me so fascinated.'

'Or the need to get her into bed,' Warrener remarked. 'I never met a man who didn't have that urge. And most of them succeeded,' he added bitterly.

Brooks took the moment to explain to Ross, 'He's never forgiven her. He always had to nurse his fantasy that she didn't reject him for just one man, but for all the men in the world. It inflates his ego.'

'I wouldn't get into who she rejected for whom, if I were you,' Warrener shot back.

'That's not the issue,' Ross intervened, then proceeded. 'Gradually – it was a slow process, I must say – I was able to bring her around. In months we had reduced her from one hundred eighty-six to one twenty-four. I weaned her away from alcohol completely. I transformed her from a fat middle-aged woman who looked fifty-five to what she really is – a beautiful woman of thirty-two.

'I can't tell you how many days I've entered our gymnasium to find her working so hard that the perspiration flowed down her like the runoff of a summer storm. It made dark stains on her black leotard. Dark stains . . .' Ross recalled, pausing to savor the memory of it.

Amused at his own thought, he said, 'The strangest thing, that dark damp stain between her breasts was one of the most sexually provocative sights I've ever encountered.

Whether it accented her breasts, which by that time had been restored to the firmness of youth, or whether there is something animally sensual about the look and odor of perspiration, I don't know. But I think that was the moment when I began to look on her not as a professional achievement but as a woman to love.

'And there was the special way she brushed back her hair. As she exercised, a wisp of her golden hair had come loose from the pinned-up mass. It adhered to her damp cheek, covering her left eye. She brushed it back and at the same moment she saw me and smiled. And it . . . it . . . just . . .' Ross could not explain.

Brooks interjected gently, 'Doctor, was this the gesture?' Brooks imitated it.

'Yes, that's it!'

Warrener added nostalgically, 'And at the same time she smiles.' With no animus this time, he turned to Brooks. 'The ninth day of rehearsal. Our first play. Remember when I kept pleading with her, "Kit, baby, it's summertime. Hot. Moistly, sexy hot. But the audience sitting out there is air-conditioned. How are they going to feel it unless you show it? Give me summer. Give me sweat. But keep it interesting, alive, attractive, compelling. I want every man in that audience to fall in love with you. And every woman to admire you, even though they're jealous." '

Brooks nodded, recalling, 'She went off into a corner to do one of those acting exercises Max Kronheim used to teach her. She spent almost fifteen minutes alone. When she came back, she actually was able to make herself perspire. Her face grew damp and began to glisten. Her hair started to cling to her forehead. One strand came down. Then, with great grace and beauty, she brushed it aside. And that did it. Brushing it aside with the back of her hand, her palm turned out, her fingers curled just so. Such economy, such subtlety, so seductive. It was more effective and tantalizing than if she had disrobed and played the scene in the nude.'

'Right, right,' Warrener agreed, as entranced as when he had witnessed her do that for the first time. 'God, if I had one actress in Hollywood with half her instinct, half her inventiveness . . .'

Ross resumed: 'I see it isn't necessary for me to describe how I felt. But what is obvious to me now, wasn't then. That it was a studied technique she was using to seduce me. And I was allowing myself to be seduced. For a time, I found a new arousal with my wife. But I was only sublimating my desire for Kit.

'Finally, there, on that couch, we did make love. God, she is a passionate woman! More woman than I have ever known. Yet you never get enough of her. The more she gives, the more you want. Until she becomes all there is.'

Both Steve Brooks and Jeff Warrener nodded, remembering only too well how it had been for them.

'Kit was never really in love with me,' Ross confessed. 'But borderline cases like her, who hover between neurotic and psychotic, have an uncanny ability to manipulate people. They can even manipulate the analyst. And if, like me, he becomes involved on a personal level, he develops a savior complex, a delusion of omnipotence. I convinced myself that I could succeed where all her other doctors before me had failed. It became a challenge I couldn't resist. So that, in place of the transference in the patient so essential to the treatment, I permitted a countertransference to be created in me. Highly dangerous to doctor as well as patient. We became so interdependent we were no longer doctor and patient, but father and daughter. And, of course, lovers.

'Unfortunately, that destroyed all possibility of success in the treatment. So I recognized that much as I loved her, I had to put an end to it.

'The day after I determined that, she came into this room for her usual hour. She looked radiant. But I did not make love to her. She stared at me, then she laughed. She thought it was some new courting game I was playing, resisting her only to take her more hungrily later.

'She laughed, she joked, she flirted. She brushed back her hair, even though there were no strands hanging down. She used all her million little enticements that had always worked on me before. Until finally her laughter ceased. Her smile drained away. Her blue eyes turned hurt. She stared. Not at me. But off into space. She spoke, her voice flat, totally lacking in animation. Her first words revealed something I should have detected long before.

'She said, "You don't love me. You don't ever want to see me get well."

'Those words can't have the same significance for a layman as they have for an analyst. They are a projection. The patient, harboring certain guilty thoughts, projects them onto the doctor. She did not want to be cured. But she had to pretend it was the doctor who didn't want her to be cured.

'Those words confirmed what I suspected. She was never in love with me. She was in love with the security this place promised. As long as she was here, she wouldn't have to cope with the real world. And what was the best way to make sure she would remain here? To undermine the analysis by making her doctor fall in love with her. And to pretend that she loved him. Though in her own way, she was in love with me. Not because I'm me. But in the course of the transference I became her grandfather, with whom she was always in love.'

He glanced at Brooks. 'As she was in love with you.' He looked to Warrener. 'And with you. We have all, at various times and for her purposes, been her grandfather. Which, I think, imposes on us an obligation.'

'Obligation to do what?' Warrener asked cautiously, his resistance reawakened.

'To help make her functional again,' Ross said.

'Isn't that the doctor's job?' Warrener demanded.

'Usually, yes. In this case, no.'

Brooks asked, 'Obviously you had something specific in mind – else why bring us here?'

'Kit has fond memories of you. And of Warrener. That's why of all . . .' he faltered slightly, then continued, '. . . of all the men she has mentioned, and there have been many, the only two she remembered with strongly affirmative feelings were you. Which means she might respond to you.'

'And if she does respond?' Warrener demanded.

'If she does respond, and that will be the first test,' Ross said, 'then I will want you both to stay on for a few days.'

'To do what?' Warrener asked.

'To help me begin to make her functional again. Otherwise . . .'

'Otherwise?' Brooks insisted.

'We must be resigned to her living out her life in this place, or places like it,' Ross said. 'Unless, of course . . .'

'She wouldn't . . .' Warrener started to ask.

'Yes,' Ross said, 'I'm afraid, one way or another, she would find the means to terminate her confinement.'

Brooks nodded gravely. 'She's had enough practice trying. She'll succeed when she really wants to.'

'I'm afraid so,' Ross confirmed.

'So how can we help make her functional?' Warrener asked.

'Find a role for her to do,' Ross prescribed.

'Just like that? Find a role? Doctor, do you know what the hell you're asking?' Warrener exploded.

Before the friction between Warrener and Ross could harden into hostility, Brooks intervened.

'Dr Ross, what Warrener is trying to say, in his ever-polite and considerate way, is this: Roles, good roles, for women are rare these days. In theater and in film. We have more female stars waiting around than there are roles. So one doesn't simply go out and find a part for a woman star.'

'Especially not for Kit Lawrence,' Warrener added.

Causing Ross to ask, 'What does that mean?'

Overly polite, and in a mocking tone, Warrener turned to Brooks. 'Do you wish to tell the good doctor, or shall I?'

Knowing he would present it in a kinder light, Brooks volunteered. 'Kit has a record, a reputation . . .'

'As being the finest actress in the American theater,' Ross said.

'*When* she shows up,' Warrener corrected pointedly. 'Do you know the number of performances she used to miss? Or the contracts she signed to appear in a play, a film or a TV show and then at the last minute canceled out? No one will take a chance on her again.'

'A woman with her talent?' Ross asked, disbelieving.

'It isn't a matter of talent, Doctor. Economics! Producers, film companies, TV networks just will not gamble the money it takes to mount a production built around her. She is a bad risk!'

'I thought the two of you, with your reputations, could virtually force any producer or company to back any play or picture you wanted. Certainly you, Mr Warrener.'

'I have just finished shooting a picture that is two million four over budget. Unless it turns out to be a box-office smash, that fact will be thrown up to me every time I ask for money to make another film,' Warrener admitted grimly. 'So if you were thinking that I had some fantastic role up my sleeve that I could dangle before our lovely Miss Kit . . . sorry, there's no such part. And if there were, I couldn't sell her to any producer.'

Warrener seemed to have spoken his final word until he reminded himself, 'The first time I've called her that in years. "Our lovely Miss Kit." Except I used to say, "My lovely Miss Kit."

'God, she was beautiful. And her eyes. When she was in love there was a fire in them that was miraculous. You never knew precisely, was it because she was in love, or because someone was in love with her. But she wanted to go onstage and share it with the world. I have seen her do scenes that I had witnessed a hundred times, and she could make me cry every time. If only she'd . . .' He never finished.

But Brooks did. 'If only she'd let her*self* believe it. Believe that the man was truly in love with her. Always it ended the same way. She loved with an all-consuming fire. Always too hot and bright to last. But she couldn't love any other way. She tried, but she could only play it, not live it.

'As she used to play house. Or, should I say, play wife. It was a role she performed with such charm, such love. I remember the time that we . . . well, our affair . . . no, that's a bad word,' Brooks apologized. 'That makes it sound trivial. I don't think she ever made love to any man thinking it was trivial.

'The first time we went to bed was an experience that in retrospect was not good for me. Because from that moment on every woman I have had has suffered by it. I keep making comparisons, and it must be obvious. The last thing Melinda said to me before we agreed to divorce was "I've always felt like the third person in this house." She was right. The memory of Kit has never left me. Nor the need to compare all my days with those days. Those hot, feverish, youthful days.'

Brooks stopped, trying to recall. 'What started me on this?'

'You were saying she liked to "play wife,"' Ross reminded, most curious.

'We had opened in New York,' Brooks resumed. 'Our first big hit together. A dream night. And the same night, our affair started. She was the biggest news in town. Everyone wanted to interview her. Producers offered new plays. Picture companies wanted to screen-test her. But did she give in to any of them? No. What did she choose to do in the days after our opening? She went shopping along Ninth Avenue. At those wonderful markets and Italian bakeries, to prepare supper for me every night after her performance. She wouldn't let my cook do it. She insisted on doing it herself. She wouldn't phone and order food to be sent up. She insisted on selecting it herself.

'She was playing wife, an average middle-class wife, playing it with all the devotion and every nuance that she would have used to play the part on stage. She read cook-books. She wheedled recipes at restaurants we went to. She tried the most exotic and intricate dishes just to please me.'

'Did she succeed?' Ross asked.

'She wouldn't have had to lift a finger to please me,' Brooks said sadly.

Ross asked pointedly, 'I meant did she succeed at cooking?'

Brooks exhaled in a dispirited sigh. 'She produced the worst messes I've ever seen. But I ate them all, rather than hurt her feelings.' He turned to Ross. 'Why did you ask that?'

'Because it's what I've discovered. She cannot function in ordinary life roles. She cannot be a wife. She cannot be a mother. She cannot be an ordinary woman.'

'She can't even be an ordinary lover,' Warrener added, not in criticism but in pity. 'She has the highest highs and the lowest lows of any woman I ever made love to.'

Ross turned to Brooks. 'You might like to know. You never fooled her by eating all that glop she prepared.' He smiled as he continued, 'She confessed to me that once, to test you, she deliberately botched up a recipe to see if you'd say you loved it. And you did. All that night when you two were making love, she would laugh from time to time but never tell you why.'

'Christ,' Brooks said, 'was that it? I never forgot that night. I never knew why she laughed. And at the time I didn't worry. It was enough to be near her. To feel her holding me in an embrace that said, forever, forever. Her favorite word. She would whisper it to me in a way that made my ear tingle. "Forever, Steve, forever," she would say.'

'She always says forever,' Ross explained, 'but actually she means never. Forever is her fantasy. Never her reality.'

'Forever,' Warrener mused in fond recollection. 'Yes, she used to say that to me too. God, how many times I think if she'd married me I could have given her what she needed. Security. Love. A career. Or no career. She didn't have to act to please me. I wanted her as a woman. She could have been a wife with me. And a mother. She could have been anything she wanted. Anything.'

'I doubt it,' Ross said.

'Well, I don't!' Warrener protested.

'Every man she's ever known must have thought that. Right, Brooks?'

'I felt the same way. If only she'd marry me, I could do it. But she would never marry me.'

'It wouldn't have helped,' Ross said. 'She'd have grown tired of that role too. As she did of all the others. She would have failed to show up. She'd have taken to drinking. And overeating. It isn't just security she needs. But constantly *renewed* security. The day would come when she would panic and end up here anyway,' Ross said sadly.

'You see, we are confronted by a quite pitiful spectacle. A most unaverage woman, brilliant in her art, yet seeking desperately to be average, live an average life, have a happy average marriage, an average family, do all the everyday things average women do. And failing.

'When she is trying her best, she is at her worst. Such as with her cooking. Brooks, she may have laughed about playing a joke on you. But I ask you, did she ever cook for you again after that?'

Brooks took a moment to recall, and remembered. 'Why, no. You're right, she never did after that.'

'She had to resort to that childish trick to test you. She wanted your honest reassurance. When she failed to get it, she just gave up. So it is with many of her faults. Most of which are the reverse of what they appear to be.

'They are part of her perpetual seeking and never finding. For example, she lies. But she does not intend to lie. She simply has areas of amnesia. Which are endemic to her condition.

'She seems aggressively promiscuous. Actually she is terrified. She appears faithless. Actually she is desperate. Promiscuity and faithlessness are merely symptoms of the degree of her insecurity. To understand her fully you would have to live your whole life in the same terror in which she has lived hers.

'If I sound like a lawyer pleading a client's case, perhaps I am. But I cannot allow all her potential to go to waste without desperately trying to save it.'

Warrener turned to Ross. 'Doctor, you said you wanted a role for her. What if Brooks and I took a few days to dream up a part? I'm sure between the two of us we could dream up something that would sound good. She'd believe us. I know she would.'

'What if she does believe you?' Ross countered. 'And she feels strong enough to leave here? And go into rehearsal? What happens then?'

'I see,' Warrener realized, his momentary enthusiasm dissipated.

'We can't play tricks on her,' Ross said. 'Whatever you do must be genuine. The slightest hint of fakery would be disastrous. Possibly fatal. I won't let you see her under those circumstances.'

'What if she insists?' Brooks asked.

'She doesn't even know you're here,' Ross said simply. 'And she won't. Unless . . .'

'Unless?' Warrener asked, intrigued.

'Unless you come up with a role that is genuine. And good. Good enough to interest her, to give her that spark again so she can actually go to work. Do you think that's possible?'

'Doctor, great parts are not written to order,' Warrener said.

'Is there some part she's always wanted to play?'

'Saint Joan,' Brooks volunteered. 'She would talk about it when we lay in bed together. After. Always after, she talked about her acting. She often mentioned doing Saint Joan.'

'Is that possible?' Ross asked Warrener.

'You said be realistic. Well, who the hell is going to produce a new Saint Joan on Broadway?'

'Sam Rogers might,' Brooks suggested. 'He'd do anything for Kit.'

'Even with all his money, Sam wouldn't risk it on a Saint Joan in these times.' Warrener began to take a doleful accounting of facts. 'Even if we had the idea, figure it out. Rough draft, revisions, more revisions, final draft. Then we can't be sure it'll get produced. And if it isn't, where does that leave us? More important, that might leave Kit worse off than before. Right, Doctor?'

'This is a desperate measure,' Ross admitted.

Warrener turned to Brooks. 'Don't you see? It isn't for lack of desire on my part. But the odds are bad. Worse than bad!'

'You can't forgive her,' Brooks exploded. 'You never will! No woman ever abandons Jeff Warrener. You must be the one to walk away.'

Brooks turned to Ross. 'Oh, he has ways. Most of them stolen from old scripts. He can pack quietly, without a word, letting the woman watch him all the while. Wondering, staring, sometimes weeping. Then at the door he'll pause, look back and say, "Sorry, kid, it just didn't work." He always has to have the exit line.'

'That's a lie!' Warrener said in a fierce low voice. Then he self-consciously asked, 'Lynne tell you that?'

'Dodie,' Brooks said. 'Three days after it happened I found her alone. At Joe Allen's. Drinking herself into a "cure." '

'Dodie,' Warrener recalled. 'Oh, yeah.'

Brooks turned back to Ross. 'He's a vengeful bastard. He'll never forgive Kit for having the exit.'

'That's not it at all,' Warrener protested. 'Since I left the theater I've discovered if you want to survive in show business you play the odds. Well, in this case, the odds are not only bad, they are prohibitive.'

'This is for Kit,' Brooks reminded.

'That doesn't change the odds.'

'Christ!' Brooks exploded in desperation. 'For once in your life take a risk for someone else! All Dr Ross is asking you to do is go through a cemetery and put a rose on the grave of a woman you once loved. It's a gesture. A single humanitarian gesture.' With a bit of contempt in his voice, Brooks added, 'It's for Kit, you sonofabitch! Let it be your way of forgiving her for whatever wrong you think she did to you. Then maybe you won't have to hate her anymore.'

As he turned to confront Steve Brooks, Warrener's face was tense; his lips moved nervously as if about to give vent to the obscenities which were his refuge in times of anger. Yet when he spoke his voice was soft. In place of obscenities there was only a confession.

'You think I hate her? Why, I can still feel my skin prickle where her naked breasts touched me. I think of her and I feel moist and warm where our hair mingled. If some archeologist digs me up a thousand years from now, he'll find her imprint on me. So, no, I don't hate her. And I haven't forgotten.'

Neither Brooks nor Ross felt able to comment on Warrener's confession, or even to exploit it. They permitted the man to reach his own conclusion.

'Ross, let's be realistic,' Warrener said. 'What can we hope to accomplish? How long will it take? Don't forget I have a film to cut back there in California.'

By now the early-winter evening was beginning to darken the room. In the fireplace the log was dying out, making small crackling explosions in its vain effort to stay alive.

'I would hope you two come up with a story and a character that Kit will find intriguing. You have come here because you feel she's the ideal woman for the role. You want her to get well enough to leave here and go back to work. If she responds, it could be the means of making her functional again.'

'And if she doesn't?' Warrener observed. 'It's a pretty dangerous charade we're engaged in.'

'If it's just a charade, it's worse than dangerous,' Ross warned. 'That's why I want you not to agree with me until you have created a story in which you both have great confidence. Be as tough and professional with yourselves as you can. Because a failure might well kill her.

'No one can stop a compulsive suicide if she really wants to succeed. And this next time, she may,' Ross warned.

# *Three*

Brooks and Warrener checked into the small Colonial-style inn at which Ross had made reservations. It was evening. The ski crowd had returned from the slopes and noisily occupied the lobby and the bar. So Warrener ordered a bottle of Scotch sent up to his room.

They had both been drinking and silent until Warrener began suddenly, 'You know, Steve ...' He stopped, smiled grudgingly. 'That's the first time I've called you Steve in years. I haven't even thought of you as Steve.' Chuckling, he confessed, 'You're always, "Brooks, that sonofabitch." '

Brooks laughed too.

'Steve, what the hell are we getting ourselves into?'

'I don't know.'

'Do you have any story ideas?'

'Not a one.'

'What about the novel you're working on?'

'Wouldn't work. It's the man's story.'

'Could it be switched?' Warrener asked. 'I did that with *Obbligato.* The original was the woman's story. But once Redford said he liked it I had the writers switch it.'

'I know,' Brooks said. 'I was asked to work on the screenplay.'

'And refused,' Warrener said, still resenting the fact. 'What the hell are we going to do?'

'I like to walk when I think. How about you?'

'I didn't bring any boots. And my coat's too light. But I'll walk with you as long as I can.'

The night sky seemed a brighter blue than usual. The entire

sweep of the Milky Way spread across it with a brilliance that made the snow sparkle.

They crunched along. Brooks's Midwestern storm boots made more solid sounds than Warrener's light, costly Gucci moccasins. Breathing was difficult. With each breath the frosty air knifed into their lungs.

'It's my blood,' Warrener said after a few minutes. 'Living in California thins out the blood.'

'Want to quit?'

'Let's keep walking.' Warrener had never been first to admit to any physical limitations. After a while he asked, 'Get any ideas?'

'None.'

They had walked beyond the streets of the town almost to the state highway when Brooks noticed Warrener was shivering. So he volunteered, 'I'm getting too cold, Jeff; I'd like to go back.'

'Okay,' Warrener reluctantly agreed, as if making a concession.

There was a message waiting for Steve Brooks. Melinda. Urgent. He reached her at home. It used to be their home.

'Steven?' she asked, at the sound of his voice. She had grown more formal since he moved out.

'Mel, you called me?'

'Your publisher's been trying to reach you, but at the University. What the hell are you doing up in Connecticut, of all places?'

He was reluctant to tell her. But Melinda was a bright girl. If she had not already pieced it together tonight, she would by morning. He might as well level with her.

'I see' was her first, controlled reaction. He could detect in her voice total determination not to be emotional as she said, 'I wasn't checking up on you. But as your agent, I *am* under pressure from your publisher. They want a delivery date. They have to know whether to put you on their fall list or a year from spring. That's the only reason I called.'

'I'm three-quarters of the way through the first draft. But it's a good draft. Very solid!' he reassured her.

'What happens if you get involved in writing a play?' she asked, most businesslike.

'Well, that would delay everything.'

'For how long?'

'Months,' he conceded.

'If, by any chance, you go into rehearsal, that would mean even more months, wouldn't it?'

'Yes, it would.'

'Then, Steven, speaking as your agent, not your wife, my considered advice would be to continue on your novel and forget about . . .' She ended up saying the one thing she had not wanted to say: 'about *her*.'

'Chances are we won't come up with a story. And that'll be that,' he said, trying to comfort her.

Avoiding any further reference to Kit Lawrence, Melinda asked, 'What shall I tell your publisher?'

'I'll . . . I'll call them in a few days and tell them myself,' he said.

Coolly, she responded, 'At least have the courtesy to let me know what you tell them, so I won't be caught by surprise. There's nothing more embarrassing for an agent than to be in the dark about her client's plans.'

She was scolding him as if he were her young son, not her husband.

'Before I call them, I'll call you.'

'Good!' she said efficiently. Her voice softened. 'Steve, don't reopen that part of your life. You have a great new career as a novelist. Don't endanger it. Not even for her. She doesn't deserve it.'

The bar was empty now that the skiers had retired to get an early start in the morning. Jeff and Steve sat nursing drinks before the fireplace until the huge log burned through and broke in two, sending up a shower of sparks. They had discussed many ideas and liked none. They gave up for the night.

Steve Brooks found one of the twin beds in his room turned down. The room was prepared for sleep; he was not. Nevertheless he slipped into the cold bed, pulled the covers up around him. After a time, he grew restless. He cursed the mattress. He also cursed himself for not remembering to tell the hotel to provide a bed board. Ever since an old tennis injury to his back, he always slept on one. He rolled out of that bed and tried the other. It sagged even more. Eventually, he crawled back into the first one, which he had to warm again with his own body heat.

Between the high cost of energy in New England and the frosty night air, he was colder than he had been in years. He lay in one spot, hoping to warm that sufficiently to enable him to fall asleep.

But he remained awake so long he finally snapped on the lamp on the night table to look at his watch. It felt like five in the morning. It was only quarter after two. He turned over to his left, though his right was his good sleeping side. Finally, he gave up and let his mind drift from story ideas to memories. Memories of years ago.

# Part 2

# Four

The first time Brooks had ever seen Kit Lawrence was twelve years ago, when she was only twenty. She had walked with a sure and determined stride as she came out onto the bare stage for her audition. Slender, she seemed taller than she was. Because she was slender, her young breasts seemed more mature than they were. She appeared unusually secure for a girl so young. Her blond hair hung freely down to her shoulders, and even in the dim glow of the stage work light it shone.

Steve Brooks's instant thought was, My God, she's brought her own halo with her.

'Gloria sent me' were the first words he ever heard Kit Lawrence speak in her slightly husky voice. She was referring to her agent, a woman well enough known in the theater to be identified by her first name. 'I suppose you want me to read the scene that starts on page one-twelve.' She had her script open to the proper place.

Jeff Warrener's vanity and a perverse temptation to test her security caused him to contradict her, 'Not one-twelve. Flip over to two-seven. Where the girl returns home after her weekend away with her lover. You open the door, all bright and dewy-eyed from your first rapturously sexy weekend, but you run smack into your suspicious father, who is breathing fire. Start there.'

Warrener glanced toward Steve Brooks, smiling, as if to say, I'll let her know who's boss right from the start. Up on the stage, young Kit Lawrence sought and finally found page 2-7, read through it, turned the page quietly, then the next page, and the one after that, until she had read the entire scene.

'Ready?' Warrener called out from his seat ten rows back in the dark orchestra.

'Not yet,' Kit said firmly, no hint of apology or trepidation in her voice. She deliberately took even longer to read through the scene a second time. Aware of Jeff Warrener's whispered grumbling in the dark house, she was determined not to be hurried. Eventually, she stared out into the darkness. 'I'll do the best I can on such short notice.'

'Why, thank you,' Warrener called back with sarcastic politeness.

The stage manager came forward to read the father's part with her, but young Kit Lawrence said, 'No, thanks. I'll do this alone.'

Taken aback by her presumptuousness, the stage manager glanced out front, awaiting Warrener's instructions.

'Okay, Charlie, let her do it alone,' the director conceded, his impatience becoming quite obvious. He leaned back in his seat, his belligerent attitude indicating to Steve Brooks that he had already decided against the girl.

Brooks whispered, 'Give her a chance, Jeff. I think she's got something.'

'I do too,' Sam Rogers agreed.

Jeff Warrener was unmoved. If anything, their favorable opinions only served to increase his resentment.

Up on the stage, Kit Lawrence waited confidently until she had secured complete silence. After the last whispers had died out, she walked about the empty stage setting the scene in her mind. She located the door and the major pieces of furniture she intended to use. She was meticulously creating the room in which she would play her scene. That done, she went to the invisible door, opened it, stepped outside. For a long moment she was motionless. Then Steve could see her assume and grow into the role as if she breathed it in from her surroundings. Suddenly, without any cue from her, he knew she was ready.

She fumbled with imaginary keys, found the nonexistent

lock, unlocked the invisible door, all without putting down her script.

She thrust open the door in a burst of happiness that radiated even on that semidark stage. She discovered her father waiting. Her joy was suddenly stifled. Her face, her entire body reflected that change. She spoke her first line of dialogue with no guilt, but with a tender solicitude for her father who condemned her.

To Steve Brooks the miracle of the moment was that he was able to see in her performance not only her every nuance, written and unwritten, but also her father and his response and reactions. For she added words to her own dialogue to create him and his lines. She anticipated what he was supposed to say and said it for him. She needed no one else on that stage to play the scene magnificently. Even Warrener began to become intrigued. He uncrossed his legs, leaned forward, stared. 'Sonofabitch,' he said very softly. 'I'll be a sonofabitch.' The highest praise of which he was capable.

Sam Rogers leaned across Brooks to whisper to Warrener, 'Grab her. Don't let her get out of the theater.'

'Not so fast, Sam,' Warrener said, partly because he made it a rule never to acquiesce too quickly in any suggestion from a producer.

Sam Rogers pleaded in frantic whispers, 'For God's sake, don't let her go! Everybody in town is casting. Someone will grab her before the week is out.'

Jeff Warrener settled back in his seat, contemplating the girl until his silence became intolerable to Brooks and Rogers. Finally he called out, 'Very nice, my dear.'

'Nice?' Brooks contradicted in an angry whisper. 'She's brilliant! When have you ever seen such a first reading?'

As if he had not heard, Warrener casually called out, 'Who did you say your agent is?'

'Gloria,' young Kit Lawrence said, peering into the darkness.

'Gloria who?'

Before Kit could answer, Brooks whispered, 'Stop this goddamned game! Hire her! Right now! I approve!'

'Me too!' Sam Rogers insisted.

But Warrener persisted. 'Gloria who?' he repeated.

'Gloria Simms,' the young actress said, but she realized the director was toying with her.

'Good,' Warrener said. 'We have a number of girls yet to see. But we'll let Miss Simms know by the end of tomorrow.'

The young actress handed the script to the stage manager. She turned back to face the three men who were only shadows to her. She smiled and said sweetly, 'Gentlemen, tomorrow will be too late. I already have the offer of another good part in a very good play.'

With the bearing of a young queen Kit Lawrence walked proudly and confidently off the stage.

Rogers leaped up from his seat, shouting at Warrener, 'You arrogant bastard, you blew it!'

Because he himself feared that he had, Warrener talked to the stage manager. 'Charlie, go after her.'

While they waited, Sam Rogers paced the carpeted aisle muttering to himself. 'You wait your whole life to discover an actress like that and this young bastard lets her get away!'

'Take it easy, Sam. She'll be back,' Warrener predicted confidently.

'A young Katharine Hepburn and he lets her slip through his fingers. Gold! Sheer gold!' Sam lamented.

Warrener chuckled, as if his favorite sport were tormenting producers. But he turned quite serious when the stage manager returned alone.

'Couldn't you catch up with her?'

'Yes.'

'And?'

'She said she needed time.'

'What do you mean, "time"?' Warrener shouted, outraged.

'Time to think it over.'

'Think *what* over?' Warrener demanded, furious.

'She said she wasn't sure she wanted to work for you.'

Rogers turned on Warrener, 'Now, you sonofabitch, you see what you've done! Lost the best actress I've seen in years. Years!'

'Sam, don't worry. It'll work out.'

Rogers turned to the stage manager. 'You get on that phone! Tell Gloria Simms I want to start negotiating for that girl today! Right now!'

'Sam, if Gloria knows you're that anxious she'll make you pay that girl twice what any young actress is worth,' Warrener warned.

'I'll be glad to pay her twice!' Rogers declared, prodigal in his anxiety.

The stage manager returned to report, 'Gloria said she's not in a position to negotiate for the girl.'

'But she's her agent,' Rogers shouted back.

'Gloria said she's a most unusual girl. She insists on doing things her own way.'

'Sam, if she's going to be a problem we might as well find it out now,' Warrener said. 'An actor is only as good as his insecurity. The trouble with that girl, she is not insecure!'

Out in the wings, young actresses were waiting to read. Their readings only served to underscore how right Kit Lawrence was for the part. By the end of the day, Sam Rogers said, 'Boys, we all know who the girl is. What are we going to do about it?'

Warrener found it most difficult to concede, 'Okay, I'll call Gloria as soon as we get back to the office. We'll work it out. You'll have the girl, Sam.'

Warrener insisted on making the call alone, in Rogers' private office. If any apologizing or groveling had to be done, the other two would not witness his humiliation. When Jeff Warrener came out of that room, his face was pale, and his right cheek twitched. An involuntary response he exhibited only in times of great anxiety.

When Rogers demanded word, all Warrener would say was 'We'll have to wait and see.'

'I've done business with Gloria for twenty-five years,' Rogers said. 'I'll talk to her myself!'

'It won't do any good,' Warrener warned. 'Gloria said we have to wait. That's a very strange girl.'

'That's a very talented girl,' Rogers corrected.

Steve Brooks was to discover she was both.

# *Five*

Steve Brooks had left Sam's office dispirited and furious. He could already see the play, on which he had labored for more than a year, going down the drain because of Warrener's sheer perversity. Kit Lawrence embodied everything he had envisioned in the role. Having glimpsed that promise, he would never be satisfied with less.

If Warrener's pride was the obstacle, it might be possible to protect his pride and still not lose the girl. He turned off Broadway and headed toward Rockefeller Center. He burst into Gloria Simms' office saying, 'I've got to have that girl!'

Gloria laughed. He felt foolish for a moment; then he laughed too.

'Gloria, I need that Lawrence girl for my play. So does Warrener. But as you know, he's a stubborn bastard. What do I have to do to get her?'

Gloria said simply, 'Tell her.'

'What do you mean, tell her?'

'Tell her what you just told me. That you need her.'

'Okay. Where will I find her?'

Gloria gave him the address of The Dorm, an old building between Ninth and Tenth Avenues which had belonged to Sam Rogers. When the building lost its last commercial tenant, Sam had converted it into a dormitory for aspiring actresses to make it possible for them to survive in New York until success enabled them to afford other living quarters. The girls called it The Nunnery. They joked about its stringent rules. But it enabled many of them to survive and find careers in that most precarious profession known as acting.

When Kit Lawrence stepped out of the elevator to greet Steve Brooks, she appeared even younger than she had in the dim light of the empty stage. Her face was even more beautiful. Her hair was golden. She carried herself with a sense of importance as she deigned to hold out her hand.

'Mr Brooks?' she asked graciously.

'Steve. Miss Lawrence?'

'Kit,' she said. 'When you get to know me better you may call me Katherine.' They both laughed. He loved her laugh – light, yet not trivial, as if each moment had meaning for her. 'My grandfather always called me Katherine. He made me sound so important.'

'Can we go some place and talk?' he asked. 'Coffee? Or a drink?'

'I don't drink,' she said, studying him through frank blue eyes that seemed to be judging him.

'Dinner? Or is it too early?'

She considered it, then suggested, 'We've got a little reception room. The girls call it The Men's Room. It's where they have to wait. No man is allowed above the first floor here. But the number of pregnancies would surprise you.'

She led the way. He followed, admiring the grace with which she walked, noticing that her legs were nicely proportioned.

The Men's Room was empty. They were able to talk freely. He asked her about herself. She had come to New York from a small town in Southern California, which accounted for the fact that she had no regional accent. She had deliberately avoided Hollywood. She wanted to succeed on the stage first, become a star only later, after she had really earned it.

Brooks laughed. 'What if you get to be a star in your very first role?'

'That would be a disaster.'

He assumed she was joking. He realized she was quite serious.

'Mr Brooks . . .'

'Steve,' he corrected again.

'For what I have to say I'd better call you Mr Brooks. Mr Brooks, you are a very fine writer. And you like women. I don't mean in the sexual sense. You actually like them. You are willing to grant women a place on this earth. You provide room for their feelings, thoughts and desires. That's why I like your play. But the part is so good it's almost too good. I must be honest with you. I don't know if I'm ready.'

'Do you think you can do the part?'

'Oh, I'm ready to do the part. I can play the hell out of it. The question is, am I ready to be a star?'

Steve Brooks laughed. 'Believe me, when it happens it doesn't take much getting ready.'

She paused thoughtfully, as if still undecided.

'Do it!' he urged. 'Do it if only to show that bastard Warrener. And because the part's so right for you. In this business you never know when the next right part will come along. But mainly, do it because *I* need you to do it!'

Kit searched his eyes to see if she would find sincerity there or only glibness.

'You really need me?'

'As soon as I heard you read that scene I knew no other girl could please me in the part. For *my* sake, do it.'

She did not respond.

'I'll protect you from Warrener, and so will Rogers. He wants you too. Even Warrener does. But he's too stubborn to admit it. So all three of us need you. Very much.'

'You really need me . . .' Her words trailed off.

'Say you'll do it. We can settle everything this afternoon if you say yes.'

She finally nodded. He felt a strong desire to kiss her young, full red mouth. He contented himself with kissing her hand.

'If you need me . . .' she said thoughtfully, 'if you want me, then yes.' Then she added softly, 'That was the first time.'

'What?'

'The first time a man has kissed my hand that way. Most

of them go for my mouth. Or my breasts. Being kissed on the hand was very touching. I'll never forget that.'

He was unable to answer. Fortunately, she gave him no opportunity, for she began to laugh. It was not a malicious laugh, but tantalizing, one of delicious secret enjoyment.

'I must be a very good actress.'

'You are.'

'Even better than you think.' There was a smile on her lovely face, a look of victory in her blue eyes. 'I'll tell you a secret, if you promise never to tell Warrener.'

'Promise!'

'I was scared to death today when I came to read for you,' she admitted.

'You seemed so secure. Too secure. That's what Warrener resented about you.'

She smiled, obviously a bit skeptical.

'Honest. He said, "The trouble with that girl is she is not insecure." '

'I'd heard about your play,' Kit confessed. 'All the girls here know about it. Some have been to read for you. They're all crazy to do the part. Every young actress in New York is. Did you know that?'

'No,' Steve admitted.

'Well, they are! So when I heard about it, even though I hadn't been called, I stole a script from one of the other girls. I read it four times. I memorized the big scene in the first act. And that scene in the opening of the second act.'

'Even though no girl had been asked to read the second scene?' Steve said, doubtingly.

'Of course,' she said, quite firmly. 'I knew I would be so good in that first scene that the director would ask me to read the second one. So I sure as hell was going to be ready!'

'Then it wasn't all as impromptu as you made it seem?' Steve realized.

She laughed. 'You don't understand. You don't understand at all.'

'Then tell me,' he insisted, charmed by her laugh and her frankness.

'The real performance, the one that I did just for me, was pretending that I had never seen that second act before. And you believed it – you all believed it.' She laughed lustily now. 'Tell me that wasn't acting. Go on, tell me!'

'You mean, setting the stage, working without the stage manager, the whole bit?'

'The whole bit,' she conceded proudly. 'So I was really giving two performances. One of your play. And one of mine. I was going to play a Kit Lawrence you would all fall in love with, all need, all want. Terrified as I was, I had decided to walk out on you before I ever came to the theater. I was going to make you feel that you had lost the most marvelous young actress in this town!'

'You sure did that,' Steve agreed, admiring both her ingenuity and her skill.

'Yes, I did!' she said with a sense of triumph. 'And if you ever tell a word of this to Jeff Warrener, I'll kill you.'

She appeared most earnest when she said it, but lest her threat seem empty, she added, 'Where I come from, near the Southern California desert, we shoot rattlesnakes. I shot four of them before I was twelve years old. My grandfather taught me how.'

Brooks, never having even seen a live rattler, was inclined to think the girl exaggerated for effect. But from the determined look on her pretty face, he decided she was telling the truth.

'Kit ...'

She looked up into his eyes.

'Kit, did it ever occur to you that you didn't have to act the role of a young, beautiful, perfectly marvelous actress? Because you *are*. If you were just yourself, as you are right now, we would have been just as captivated.'

'If I hadn't walked out, would you have come after me?' she asked frankly.

Brooks had a choice between lying to make his point and being truthful and making hers. He decided to be truthful.

'No, I wouldn't have come after you.'

'That's what I mean,' she said.

Suddenly he asked, '*Were* you offered another role in another play?'

'Of course not,' she admitted freely, and laughed again, an infectious laugh that made him join in her joke.

'Then we must never tell Jeff Warrener,' he warned.

She escorted him to the front door. They stood staring into each other's eyes. If there had been no other girls in the lobby he would have kissed her. On her mouth. It was so inviting, so provocative. He contented himself with taking her hand.

'I'm going to love working with you.'

Her attitude changed suddenly. She became wistful, sad, as she said, 'You will, you will.'

Her sudden change made him probe. 'Kit, what is it you really want? What are you searching for?'

'Searching?' she repeated. His question took her by surprise.

'Your first big part. One that could make you a star. Most girls would be ecstatic. But I get the feeling you're disappointed somehow. It's everything any young actress could want. And yet . . .' He did not complete his question.

'What do I really want?' she considered. 'To act.'

'Why?' he persisted, very curious now.

'Why do you write?' she countered defensively, as if he were invading her private feelings.

'I guess to express the feelings of people who can't write,' he said.

'That's why I want to act. To express the feelings of all the hurt, silent people of this world. If I do that well, they will know it and they will love me for it,' she said quite passionately.

'You *will* be a star,' he was convinced.

'No, no,' she protested. 'First, I want to be good. Then great. And only then, finally, a star! I don't want to just flash across the sky and be gone.

'Because what that really means is that *I'll* still be there. But the *audience* will be gone. I couldn't bear that. I want always to matter. Always to count. To everyone. Oh, I'll work hard. Harder than anyone you know. But in the end I want them to love me. Is that asking too much?'

Her blue eyes, which earlier had been sparkling and joyous, stared up at him, and now he saw innocence there. And pain. And a lostness that was demanding to be found.

'No, Kit,' he said very gently, 'that's not asking too much. And you'll have it, you'll have it all. I promise you.'

More than ever he felt tempted to kiss her – not for himself, but because he felt she needed it. But he refrained.

He left The Dorm, walked swiftly east, hoping to reach Gloria's office before it closed. He was exhilarated in a way he had not been in many months. He had the actress he wanted for the part he wrote which, while he wrote it, he had told himself would be a bitch of a role to cast right. Now it was cast, not only right, but brilliantly.

Without knowing it, he had also fallen in love with a girl of whose existence he had not even been aware twenty-four hours before.

From the start of rehearsals, Steve Brooks and young Kit Lawrence had joined in an unspoken conspiracy. Without exchanging a word, they gave each other hints and signs about the way the work was going. The moments when she disagreed with Warrener, Brooks supported her. Not that she needed support. Her determination was as strong as her dramatic instincts were sound.

What little time Kit had away from rehearsals and her classes with Max Kronheim at the Actors' Lab, she and Steve Brooks spent together. They ate together. They walked the noisy streets together. They held hands like the lovers they were not. For intuition had warned Steve Brooks it would be dangerous to involve this tantalizing girl in a love affair now.

He was also aware of the dangerous hostility their affair might provoke in Jeff Warrener. A man of enormous jealousy, Warrener might find some way to use it to his advantage. For Kit's sake, Steve Brooks was determined not to make love to her.

They had opened in New Haven and received encouraging reviews. Special mention was made of the new young actress Kit Lawrence, whom the critics on the New Haven papers described as 'promising,' 'talented,' 'vibrant.'

Steve knocked on her door early that morning to read her the reviews. She had been asleep and came to the door not wearing her robe but holding it in front of her. She opened the door slightly, peered out, saw his face and said only, 'Tell me.'

Standing outside the door, he read her some of the critics' comments. She did not smile. Nor did she appear gratified. Only thoughtful.

'They're terrific!' he said, hoping to kindle her enthusiasm.

'No,' she said, still thoughtful, with sleep in her eyes. 'Good, but not terrific.'

'You couldn't ask for better than those on a very first performance.' He had so wanted her to be ecstatic.

'Come in.'

He entered, carrying the open newspapers with him. He turned to stare at her as she slipped into her robe. For an instant, he glimpsed her body through her transparent nightgown. The sight of her young breasts and the merest hint of her pubic hair aroused him. For an instant she stared back as if expecting him to make advances. But he did not. He could not tell if she was relieved or disappointed.

He ordered breakfast for them. She made him sit at the foot of her bed and read the reviews all the way through while she sat up, leaning against the headboard and staring out toward the old brown sandstone buildings that were Yale.

'I expected more,' she said, but softly, modestly.

'For the first reviews they're very promising.'

'Promising is not enough. It has to *happen.* There isn't much time.'

'Twenty, and not much time?' Steve Brooks asked, half joking.

He knew she did not dare to explain because she banished him from the room, saying, 'I have to catch up on my sleep. Jeff wants us for a noon rehearsal.'

'Of course.'

He kissed her lightly, then held her close until she sensed he was about to become more passionate. She freed herself gently from his arms. But for that moment he had held her almost naked body against him. And it was like embracing fire.

The memory of that moment had stayed with him forever.

What he should have known then, and remembered, was that even in her first moment of success, she had a premonition of disaster.

# Six

Boston had been a triumph. For the first time the word 'brilliant' found its way into Kit's notices. Edwin Mortimer, Boston's most esteemed critic, had used it in his review. A feeling of elation was beginning to inspire the whole company.

The trip to New York was a premature celebration. Everyone was high. Everyone except Kit. With each increasingly good review she had become more thoughtful and introspective. Success seemed to frighten and depress her.

Sam Rogers was disturbed. 'I've produced a lot of shows. But it's never been like this. Why can't she get a little joy out of it?'

'She's saving herself for the big opening,' Warrener diagnosed. 'That's good. I like a newcomer to go on nervous. It transmits itself to the audience and the critics. They like to help her out. If she's too cocky they resent it.'

Steve Brooks said nothing, only worried and watched. When they arrived at LaGuardia he collected her luggage, found a skycap, who got them to a cab. She gave the address of The Dorm, but Steve said, 'Let's go by the theater. I want to see how they dressed the outside of the house. If you got the right billing.'

'No!' she replied, so tense it made him abandon the idea at once.

He dropped her at The Dorm, tried to kiss her, but she was out of the cab too quickly. He had to follow with her luggage. She stood on the top step, looked down at him, like a child tempted to leap but terribly afraid. She desperately wished to say something, but could only whisper, 'Oh, Steve!' She turned and fled.

He stood there even after she had disappeared into the building. He wanted to pursue her, enfold her, comfort her, love her. Say to her, You are so magnificent, and so young. Enjoy your talent, your success, your youth.

He tried to assure himself that all that would begin to happen after the opening and her reviews.

Yet he came away feeling, She is like a terrified child who cannot enjoy childhood.

He made the driver proceed slowly past the theater. The house had been dressed. There were production photos of the cast. His title was in electric lights. On each side of the doors, posters announced the title, the cast, but most important, '*And introducing Kit Lawrence.*' She had to like that.

He returned to his apartment overlooking Central Park. He felt terribly dejected. He not only missed Kit, he missed them all. After weeks of communal living on the road, returning to an empty apartment was the loneliest of feelings. Even a mourner returning from a funeral was never so alone.

He decided he had been living alone too long. Till now he had never met a woman he felt driven to marry. He had had affairs. Girls had come to live here, some for weeks, some for months, but none permanently. Always he knew it, they knew it. But this one girl he had to have for his own, for all time. Soon, very soon, he would ask her.

The opening was an old-style black-tie event. The feeling of a hit was in the air even before the first curtain went up. Backstage there was excitement but no panic. The cast exchanged gifts. Steve Brooks had sent flowers to each of the actresses. In Kit's flowers he had enclosed a modest gold pin with tiny diamonds. He was in her dressing room when she discovered it.

Tears surged into her eyes and he was afraid they would spoil her makeup. He enfolded her. She let him kiss her lightly on the side of her made-up cheek.

'Nobody's ever given me such a gift before. Nobody. Not even my grandfather.'

'It's only a little pin, very inexpensive,' he apologized.

But she kept repeating, 'Nobody . . . nobody . . .' and she trembled in his arms.

Once the stage manager announced, 'Places, please!' she slipped out of the room without a glance toward him. She seemed to be quite alone within her stage character. No one else existed.

The first act went off with a few minor mistakes, which neither critics nor audience suspected. In the lobby, word of mouth was very good. At the end of the second act the word was even better.

In the third act, her triumph of deliverance from domination by the men in her life, Kit was magnificent. Strong, yet sympathetic, she throbbed with a passion that was physical as well as emotional. She had truly started her performance as a girl and was ending it as a woman.

She received an ovation, which she accepted with such modesty that some in the audience felt she was still acting. She received flowers onstage, from Sam Rogers, from Jeff Warrener, from Steve Brooks and from the cast.

Backstage was crowded with well-wishers, proudest of whom were Sam and his wife, Bertha. For Sam it was a double triumph, since Kit had lived her three years in New York at The Dorm, thus fulfilling Sam's purpose in establishing it.

'Well,' Sam beamed. 'I expect you'll be moving out tomorrow morning.'

They all laughed. Except Kit. She seemed tired, alone and somewhat afraid.

The party at Sardi's was almost an anticlimax. The reviews were extravagant, as anticipated. Great for the play, for the direction, the cast. Superb for Kit Lawrence. One critic hailed her as the finest of a new generation of great actresses in the American theater.

The party was still in full swing; people were getting drunk after the good reviews. But Steve Brooks found Kit sitting off in a corner of the upper floor of Sardi's looking like a little girl who had had too much Christmas. The fun had gone out of it.

'Take me away from here,' she pleaded.

'Sure. Anywhere. Even back to The Dorm,' he agreed. 'Though if you come to my place, I promise I won't ... won't touch you,' he found himself saying, and feeling quite awkward about not being able to phrase it more adroitly.

'Why won't you touch me?' she asked, her blue eyes staring up at him.

'You're exhausted; you look so tired.'

'Take me to your place.'

She entered Steve's apartment with the curiosity of a child. She went from room to room examining it all with an ingenuous air of discovery, loving everything she saw. Tired and bored as she had seemed at Sardi's, she was bright and excited as she wandered about these new surroundings. The kitchen intrigued her most of all. He had had it redone in the past year. It was all stainless steel and Formica.

'I'll make breakfast for you!' she announced, laughing.

'I have a Japanese houseman who comes in and does that.'

'Fire him!' she laughed, making an imperial gesture. 'From now on I'll make all your breakfasts!'

He laughed too. He embraced her. She pressed her face against his cheek. He held her so tightly she was barely able to whisper. 'Steve ... Steve ... *touch* me ... *touch* me ...'

In his huge bed, on fresh cool sheets, in a dark and quiet room, he made love to her for the first time. With all other girls there had always been that first awkward time when neither of them knew how it would go. With her there was no awkwardness. They made love to each other as if they had been doing so forever.

In the moments before they fell asleep, he whispered to

her, 'I love you. More than any woman I've ever known. Or ever will know.'

'Love me,' she whispered back. 'Love me. But don't fall in love with me. Don't? Please?'

He woke to find her leaning on her side looking down at him.

'Don't you ever sleep?'

'No, not much,' she said, smiling.

'You should, darling,' he urged.

'Don't call me that,' she corrected. 'Don't call me *darling* or *dear* or *honey* or *angel* or any of those trite expressions all men use on their women. Call me Katherine. And I'll know what it means.'

'Katherine?' he asked, puzzled.

'What my grandfather used to call me. He was the only one who ever really loved me,' she said sadly.

'Not your father, not your mother?'

'I never knew my father. My mother came back home pregnant by six months. As soon as she gave birth, she left again. Seventeen, a mother, and she left home seeking a new life. Without giving a damn about the new life she left behind her,' Kit Lawrence said, hatred obvious in her voice.

'Did you ever see her?'

'Never. And a good thing. I would have killed her. For what she did to me,' she said with unnatural ferocity. 'But my grandfather, there was a man. He brought me up. He was mother and father. What he didn't know, he asked neighbor ladies about. One way or another he fed me, dressed me, raised me, sent me off to school when it was time, had my lunch ready every day when I came back. Tired as he was, old as he was, he did it all.

'He even found out about what happens to girls when they get to be twelve or thirteen and explained it to me. And always he kept encouraging me. To do the best. To be the best. Always the best. I guess he thought that if I were the best I would never need a mother and father.

'And I was the best. The brightest. The prettiest. With the blondest hair and the bluest eyes. There wasn't a girl in my graduating class in high school who wasn't jealous of me. Even those with much prettier graduation dresses and whose fathers and mothers drove up to the school that night in the big Cadillacs.'

Because she stared past him, Steve Brooks was able to study her face as she spoke.

It's not vanity makes her boast, he thought, but need. She's fighting too hard. But with her sad past, she has to.

'My grandfather and I walked,' she said quite proudly, needing to make a virtue of their poverty. 'It was a balmy California night in May. The best kind of night God makes anywhere. A person would have to be foolish or just plain lazy to ride cooped up in a big air-conditioned car on a night like that.

'I won three prizes. English. History. And Dramatics. Three prizes worth all of sixty-five dollars. It was the most money I had ever had of my own. My grandfather made me put it away. For my trip to New York. He added to it all he had been able to save.

'When he gave me the four hundred and twenty-five dollars I wept at his generosity. Because he was a man who barely managed to get along. Wept because I was leaving him. Wept because I was afraid. But afraid or not, I was being pushed out into the world. By a loving old man who kept saying, "This is no town for a girl to spend her life in." '

'Is that when you came to New York?' Steve asked.

She nodded. 'And worked as a waitress for two years, studying with Kronheim, learning to act, then doing small parts, walk-ons, till now.'

'Wouldn't it have been great to have your grandfather here tonight?'

'He died not long after I left.'

'I'm sorry,' Steve said, not merely polite.

'He wasn't.'

'How do you know?'

'I think he only intended to live long enough to bring me up. So he could die without a guilty conscience. He felt responsible for what *she* did to me.'

She was silent for a time. 'When he died I cried. For two whole days. The only person in my life, and he had left me. I went to Saint Patrick's every day for a week and lit a candle for him.'

'I didn't know you were Catholic.'

'I'm not. But I had to go somewhere,' she said simply.

She started weeping silently. He brushed aside her tears with his forefinger. He held her to comfort her. She was in his arms, her naked body close to his. Soon they were making love.

They woke to the sound of a gentle knock on the door. Steve came to with a start, realized it was his houseman and whispered to her. 'That's Gichi.'

'Tell him to go away,' she whispered. 'I'll make breakfast for you, just as I used to for Grandpa.'

She wore his silk foulard robe while she prepared his breakfast. She never stopped talking. Her conversation was one long excited happy monologue, punctuated by laughter and anecdotes about her experiences since she had come to New York.

She became so involved in talking, making toast, scrambling eggs, crisping bacon that she permitted the eggs to scorch. After profuse apologies she started over again. By the time the eggs were done the bacon was too dry and the toast was cold. Steve thought it was cute and laughed. She began to weep.

He took her in his arms. 'You're too excited. It's been quite a night. How many women become stars and lovers on the same night?' he asked tenderly.

Lying awake now, twelve years later, in a cold New England

inn, in the dead of a winter night, on a most discouraging mission, Steve Brooks recalled what Ross had said earlier in the evening. How desperately Kit strove to be average, to do the things that average women do.

And how completely, if charmingly, she had failed.

Brilliant as she was on a stage, the most difficult and challenging role she had ever had to play was being Kit Lawrence. And she had not mastered it.

Now Ross was hinting that she never would.

For Steve Brooks it made a cold night even colder.

If you only knew, he argued silently with Ross, how warm, selfless and loving she could be. How sensitive to the problems of others, how thoughtful. How giving.

All that most theater people remembered about Kit now was what had become of her. These days when people in the business talked of her they only recalled those times when she had failed to show up for a performance. Or showed up drunk. They could name all the shows which she had signed to do and for which she had failed to appear.

They did not remember, or had never known, the other Kit. His Kit.

He could remember back years ago, when for days after her first hit, she seemed so terribly occupied away from the theater every afternoon. She could scarcely find time for all the interviews and photographing sessions that are the due and duty of a newly arrived success.

Nor would he have discovered what she did in her private time, if she had not needed his help one day.

She had been shopping, days on end, in toy shops and department stores. Buying dolls. All sorts of dolls. No two alike. Small cloth ones. Dolls whose eyes opened and closed. Dolls who talked. Dolls who wet themselves so their diapers could be changed. Dolls with wardrobes for changes of outfits. And one great big, very costly doll in a white dress trimmed with lace, and with golden nylon hair.

When she had assembled them all, and wrapped each one as a gift, she drafted Steve to help her take them to their intended destination.

They had barely been able to get all the colorfully wrapped gifts into one cab. The boxes filled the trunk, overflowed the back seat and piled up alongside the driver till they obstructed his side vision. It seemed like Christmas, a month early.

Then she ordered, 'Children's Hospital, please.'

On the way she said no more except to ask Steve once, and most gravely, 'Did you know that more children die of cancer than of any other disease?'

He did not answer, hardly knowing what to say.

When they arrived, he was surprised that the receptionist in the lobby knew Kit so well. On the floor of the children's Oncology Ward, the staff doctors and the nurses greeted her most warmly and familiarly. Steve trailed behind, loaded down with what seemed a hundred packages, small and large.

He followed her up the aisle of the ward. She greeted every child by name and handed each a box containing one of the dolls. Every child tried to embrace both her and the box at the same time. She kissed each child. And he heard them call her their 'golden lady.'

She gave the largest box to the small black girl, no more than eight, who lay in the last bed near the window.

When all the boxes had been distributed, opened, the dolls taken out to be admired, exclaimed over, kissed and embraced, Kit said only, 'Now, children . . .'

As if on cue, they nestled down in their beds, embraced their dolls, grew silent, their eyes glowing in anticipation.

Kit sat in the chair a nurse placed in the center of the aisle. The nurse left, closing the door quietly behind her. Kit drew a book out of her handbag. She began to read aloud.

She read from *Winnie the Pooh*. Not from the start, but

well into the middle. Steve realized that she had been coming here a long time.

She read with as much brilliance as she displayed in her most magnificent stage performances. She acted each part, changed voices from being the narrator to becoming each character in turn, using a different and distinct voice for each.

The children listened, entranced. They hugged their dolls. But they stared at Kit. Their golden lady. To Steve she had never seemed more beautiful. Some of the children fell asleep smiling. Others listened through to the end and begged for more when she had finished.

She passed down the aisle again, kissing each child and promising to return next week to read them the next chapter. She made each of them promise to be here to greet her next time.

She seemed not to have any favorite, yet she treated them all as favorites.

Some children embraced her so intensely she had to gently remove their locked arms from around her neck. Others were content to touch her, to run their fingers over her lovely features, or feel her hair and call her 'golden lady' again.

She paused longest at the last bed where the little black girl was.

Kit was bright and smiling until she left the ward. Once outside the door, she gripped Steve's arm and held it desperately. The tears she had fought and held back escaped her. She raced from his side to the visitors' ladies' room, so no one would see her cry.

As he waited in the corridor, one of the floor nurses came by. He asked, 'Would you go in and make sure she's all right?'

'She's all right,' the nurse assured him. 'She reacts that way every time. Some days I wonder why she continues to come. It takes so much out of her.'

Suddenly the nurse asked, 'Has she ever been very ill? Confined to a hospital for a long time?'

'Not that I know of,' Steve said.

'I wondered,' the nurse said. 'She seems to have such an affinity for unfortunate children. As if she knew how they felt. And she strings out her stories as long as she can. So they wait for her each week. It gives them something to go on for.

'Of course, in the end, most of them die. Nothing she can do to prevent that. Yet every time she comes back and asks for one of them that's gone, it's as if she'd lost a child of her own.'

On the way home Kit had been silent again.

Until she said, 'This time she wasn't there.'

'Who?'

'Denise,' as if she expected Steve to know. 'She wasn't there.'

Kit began weep openly now. In the privacy of the cab it seemed permissible.

'Such a beautiful child. Blue-eyed. And so blond. I think if I ever have a child, she'll look like that. But she's gone. Gone.'

'Maybe she was up on another floor being treated, or operated on,' Steve suggested, seeking to reassure her.

'Her bed was filled. The little black girl. The one who got the biggest, blondest doll. She was in Denise's bed. That doll was for Denise. But I was too late again. Too late.'

She kept brushing back tears, while staring out the cab window to avoid him.

'Kit?'

She would only say, 'Every child, before she dies, should have at least one big doll. One big blond doll . . . in a dress trimmed with lace . . . every child . . .'

For days she had wept over Denise. Sam and Jeff became greatly concerned. Though it did not affect the performance.

She went onstage each matinee, each night, giving all of herself to the role and the play.

But later, at night, in Steve's arms, she wept uncontrollably.

She had never told anyone of her work at Children's Hospital. Nor had Steve. It remained their secret.

This had been her own private way of giving to other unfortunate children the comfort and delight that she had obviously never enjoyed in childhood.

Dolls held a strange, unexplained fascination for her. Yet one Christmas, when, as an inexpensive fun present, Steve had given her a blond doll with a lace-trimmed dress, she became furious with him. But would never explain why.

On this cold winter night in Connecticut, Steve Brooks wondered if Kit had ever told Dr Ross about her secret work on the Oncology Ward. About her children. And how much they loved their Golden Lady.

Or did she tell him of the many other secret acts of kindness she had done without Steve or anyone finding out, except by inadvertence?

Such as the time nine years ago during their third play together. They had been approaching the end of the first week of rehearsals. The period when Jeff always devoted his attention to those cast members who were questionable in his mind. Always Jeff picked on at least one.

That time it had been Joseph Levenger, a character actor who in his career had played with the Lunts and Katharine Cornell. But in recent years he had worked little. Parts for old character men were few.

Nevertheless, Levenger had been a man of great pride. No one knew how he could afford it, but he always presented himself for readings and rehearsals neatly dressed in a well-pressed dark suit, a fresh white shirt and an old but still unfrayed tie.

He comported himself as if he were a distinguished lawyer

or doctor, not an overage actor who once every few seasons was fortunate enough to get a small part at a few dollars over Equity minimum.

Even then, his agent, who functioned for him out of loyalty, not profit, could manage to get him five or ten dollars above minimum only by asking reproachfully, 'You mean you want a man of Joseph Levenger's standing to work for scale?'

No one wished to be guilty of inflicting such an indignity upon a veteran actor who had given his life to the theater.

Jeff Warrener had nothing to do with setting the terms of Levenger's employment. But he was solely in charge of Levenger's fate once rehearsals were under way. From the second week on, Jeff insisted that all cast members with small roles start working without their scripts. Levenger began to have trouble. He did not have very many lines to learn. But since he played Kit's nosy next-door neighbor, his role called for him to keep watch over her. So frequently he had to barge into her flat uninvited. Each time he did so, he could be sure to get a laugh, provided he delivered his lines correctly and without faltering.

But since he had such repetitive actions – entering, speaking a few words, then exiting – the sameness of his role confused him, and he often came on with the wrong line or one he invented.

On the tenth day of rehearsal, after Levenger had again failed to deliver the proper line on his entrance, Jeff Warrener whispered to Steve and Sam, 'He's got to go! He's destroying the pace of every one of Kit's scenes.'

Sam counseled softly, 'He's an old man. He's having a little trouble learning his lines. Give him a chance.'

Jeff did not respond. Which meant that Sam's plea had made no impression. When rehearsal was over for the day, Jeff instructed his stage manager, 'Tomorrow at the lunch break, I want every old man who first read for Levenger's part back here.'

Kit learned of the impending change that evening at one of her now infrequent dinners with Steve Brooks. Whenever she was in the throes of creating a new role, she would not live with him, but stayed alone in her small apartment. She lived alone, slept alone, totally absorbed in the new character she was trying to become. An occasional dinner was all she would grant even to Steve. Until she had mastered the role; then she would move back in with him.

They were at one of those infrequent dinners. She had not talked of themselves, but only about the play. How she was progressing in the role. The moments of the play to which she looked forward. The moments she dreaded because they were still acting problems for her. The ways in which she intended to solve them.

She had talked on in an unbroken torrent, replete with thoughts, insights and critiques of her role, the play and its various scenes.

Steve listened intently, thinking, With her keen analytical sense of drama she could one day become a fine director. However timid or unsure she might be in her private life, once in the world of theater she became self-assured, brilliant and so right.

Many times when a scene had baffled Jeff, or even Steve himself, though he had written it, somehow, by instinct, Kit sensed precisely what was needed to make it work. So, when she discussed his plays, Steve always listened intently.

She had been talking quite seriously until she laughed suddenly and said, 'The moments I really look forward to are when Joseph comes on. I never know what he's going to say. Sometimes I think he does it on purpose, to see if he can send me up. He's such a dear man. I love him. I think I love him almost as much as I loved my grandfather.'

Knowing how distressed she would be by the impending cast change, and especially without warning, Steve felt it necessary to inform her. As simply as he could, he told her of Jeff's decision.

'Oh, no, he can't! I won't let him!' Kit protested.

'Joseph does slow down your scenes,' Steve said, preparing her to accept the inevitable, since Jeff was stubborn and likely to be more so if anyone dared disagree with him.

'Joseph's old,' she pleaded, 'so he hasn't got his lines yet. But he will. He will!'

'We open in Philadelphia two weeks from tomorrow,' Steve warned, sharing her compassion but not letting on.

'I'm going to call Jeff! Right now!'

She leaped up from her chair on her way to the phone in the rear of the restaurant. She returned minutes later, silent, pained. She sat down, pushed back her plate and like a child who has been severely reprimanded, said, 'He's going to do it. He's going to replace Joseph.'

She ate no more. Steve ordered dessert and coffee for her. She refused to touch them. She remained silent until she said, 'That old man, he brings such dignity to being an actor. He makes you feel it's a noble calling. A true profession. Not a grubby business to be done in dusty theaters by mean people. He carries himself like a prince, not an underpaid character man.'

Suddenly she determined, 'I won't let him . . . I won't . . .'

She insisted on going home. Alone.

One night, weeks later, after they had opened so successfully in New York, Steve Brooks had an after-performance sandwich and some coffee with Joseph Levenger. The old man confided in him.

'An angel. That Kit is an angel. A brilliant actress, of course. But I have worked with brilliant actresses before. Fontanne. Cornell. I have worked with the best. Fine human beings, too. But none like her. Do you know what she did?

'The middle of the second week of rehearsals I was still floundering with my lines. Believe me, there were times I wanted to quit. Times I said to myself, "Joseph, you've had it. You can't do it anymore. Pack it in. Forget it. Take your old scrapbooks, your glowing notices from Atkinson and John Mason Brown and Watts and Burns Mantle and sneak off to the old actors' home in New Jersey and live with your memories." That's how defeated I felt.

'I felt guilty, too. I was destroying her scenes. And that would be a crime. Because from her fingertips to her toes, that girl is pure talent. Before she's done, she will rank with the greatest. The greatest!' he said, carried away with admiration.

Then Levenger tried to recall what he had started out to tell Steve. 'Oh, yes. The second week of rehearsal. One night she calls me.

' "Joseph," she said. She never calls me less than Joseph. She has great love, but also respect. Always respect. Like ... like a loving granddaughter.

' "Joseph," she said, "I wonder if you could help me out. I'm having trouble with certain of my moments. Those interruptions which your character has, they seem to throw me. I know that my serious scenes need comic relief. So if we work on them a little, maybe I could get the dramatic values in my scenes and still play the comedy with you the way I should. So if you don't mind, could you come over to my place and work on them with me?"

'Well, I got dressed again and went over. It was almost half past ten when I got to her place. We worked until four in the morning. Eleven entrances, eleven exits – we worked on all of them. She read me into every one as many times as it took until I was letter perfect.

'Then, at four in the morning, she made me fresh coffee and a toasted English muffin and wouldn't let me leave till I finished. At the door she kissed me. And she said, "Thanks, Joseph, you've been a tremendous help to me." '

Steve had watched the old man's face as it lit up in a gentle smile of remembrance. 'That girl. What she didn't know was that *I* knew. Because earlier that evening an old actor friend of mine had phoned. He had got a call from his agent saying Jeff wanted him to come back the next day and read for my part.

'But Kit wouldn't let on. She pretended *I* was helping *her*. After that, no more trouble with Jeff Warrener. Now they're talking about me being nominated for a Tony for best supporting actor. If it hadn't been for that girl, today I'd be in the old actors' home in New Jersey.

'Or dead. If an actor has nothing to do at eight o'clock at night he might as well be dead.'

Levenger had been silent for a moment; then: 'A marvelous human being. Thoughtful. Gracious. Sensitive. An angel. An angel,' he repeated.

Days afterward, when Steve had hinted to her of his discovery of what she had done, Kit pretended she was puzzled and completely unaware.

On this cold winter night in Connecticut, nine years later, Steve Brooks recalled that shortly after Joseph Levenger did receive his Tony Award, he died. Successful at the end, and spared the ignominy and the heartbreak of ending his days in a home for old, defeated actors.

Why was it, Steve pondered sadly in the night, that the many secret saving kindnesses Kit Lawrence had done so magnanimously and magnificently for others she could not do for herself?

## *Seven*

Jeff Warrener had always been an instant sleeper. He could catch catnaps between setups on a sound stage. So when he sank into his bed in that quaint New England inn, he had fallen asleep almost immediately. The challenge Dr Ross had presented to them in the afternoon disturbed him greatly. But he knew that like most other problems, it would still be there in the morning and, refreshed, he would be better able to cope with it.

But he woke suddenly at twenty past three. It was no casual awakening. He came to with a start, to find himself in a strange bed, in a strange room. It took some moments to realize where he was, and why. Once he did, Jeff Warrener could not drift off to sleep again.

He groped on the night table for a cigarette and lit up. He blew smoke toward the ceiling, not lazily but aggressively.

His immediate reaction was one of anger. He was in a place he did not want to be. On a mission for which he had no time. His film was being cut and he should be on the Coast. This film was crucial to his career. If it proved a smash it could make him 'bankable.'

That was the magic word in Hollywood. Streisand, that homely girl, with contempt for her audience, was bankable. Redford was bankable. Newman was bankable. And a dozen other stars. But very few directors were. And in these times in the picture business, unless a man was bankable he could be unemployed day after tomorrow.

To be bankable was to be secure. This film could do it for him. He had no right to jeopardize it. Especially since what Ross was suggesting could turn into a prolonged involvement. Jeff Warrener had an overpowering impulse to leap out of bed, dress in a hurry, find some means of transportation and get the hell out of here to avoid facing Steve Brooks in the morning.

He convinced himself he owed Kit Lawrence nothing. He had made her a star. He had directed her first three plays, all hits, and thus solidified her career. That she had messed up her life was her own fault. Jeff reserved his special resentment for Dr Ross, who admitted he had bungled her case. The sonofabitch should not be allowed to practice psychoanalysis if he had no control over his own emotions. Jeff's resentment kept mounting – against Ross, against Kit and finally, against Steve Brooks.

Brooks was not blameless. He had done more than a little to mess up that girl's life. Kit's trouble twelve years ago would never have happened if Brooks had not gone off to Hollywood after their first play was a hit. True, the studios were flashing lots of money at him. And his agents advised that Steve go out to confer in person. There was a chance that if he made the right impression he could wind up not only writing the screenplay but as coproducer of the film as well.

Warrener could well remember now dropping by Kit's dressing room the evening Brooks had told her he was leaving. Though Brooks had promised he would be gone only a few days, Warrener could see the look of fear in Kit's eyes.

Brooks had laughed and reassured her: 'It's not as if I'm going by covered wagon. I'll fly out tomorrow and stay a few days. I could be back by the end of the week.'

He had taken her in his arms and kissed her. But Warrener's most vivid memory of that moment was Kit's face, pressed against Brooks's cheek. She was more than unhappy. She was terrified, as she said, 'I don't like being left. I can't stand being left.'

Brooks had smothered her protest with a kiss intended to be reassuring.

Now, twelve years later, as Jeff Warrener lay on his back, watching his cigarette smoke billow upward toward the ceiling, he could not recall precisely how it had happened between him and Kit.

He had always preferred to believe that when he dropped into her dressing room two nights after Brooks left, he had no ulterior intent. He convinced himself that he had done so only to comfort her. For he had detected signs of tension that exceeded her usual dramatic tension before going onstage. It was an inner turmoil that threatened dangerous consequences. She had difficulty making up. Difficulty doing her hair. Several times when she tried to draw the brush through her long blond hair, she dropped it. That night, the brush seemed to have a will of its own.

'Darling, what is it?'

'I don't know,' Kit said, tensely. 'I'm just jittery tonight.'

He did not pursue it, but made sure to come back the next night. And the next. On the following night she broke into tears just before going on. He took her in his arms to comfort her.

'Kit, honey, there's nothing to be uptight about. They'll love you tonight as they do every night. And you'll be great, as you've always been.'

She had permitted his embrace because she needed someone to hold her, to whisper reassuring things.

Warrener had convinced himself that holding her that way was merely a generous impulse on his part. But the way she returned his embrace, that was her doing. For during that closeness she had aroused in him a sexual hunger he knew he would have to satisfy.

He went back after the performance. She was besieged by autograph seekers. She was polite and gracious, but Warrener could detect the strain they imposed on her. A bit rudely, he cleared the dressing room. He closed the door firmly.

'Why did you shut them out?' she asked.

'They were overdoing it.'

'But they loved me,' she said plaintively.

'That doesn't give them the right to abuse you,' he said firmly.

'But they weren't—'

'Get dressed,' he said. 'We have a date.'

'They loved me,' she said sadly, and started to unbutton her costume.

Without being consciously aware of the effect on him, she slowly undid all the buttons and slipped out of the top part of her dress, revealing her young breasts. Only when she caught a glimpse of his eyes reflected in her dressing-table mirror did she seek refuge behind the screen. She had stepped out of her dress, naked except for her half-slip, when she felt him behind her. Gently he slid his arms around her; his hands cupped her breasts, causing her nipples to rise to his touch.

Her first impulse was to escape him. But for reasons she would not be able to explain to herself or to analysts later, she covered his hands and pressed them tight against her. He turned her about. He kissed her on the mouth, then on the breasts while she enfolded his head with fierce intensity.

All the while she whispered, 'We shouldn't ... we shouldn't ...' She broke free of him. But it was only a brief avoidance. Warrener knew it. In some way she must have known it too.

When they entered his apartment, she evidenced none of the usual nervousness a young girl might exhibit if she were expecting a man's advances and had decided to reject them.

They talked little over the final drink, which she insisted on finishing before letting him lead her to his bed. When he was poised over her, naked and admiring her breasts, she smiled up at him. In the darkness he could see her blue eyes, half closed and seductive. She reached up and drew him into her. He made love to her for hours, time and again, marveling at his own ability to respond to her insatiable need.

They were spent, moist, exhausted, breathing in short gasps when she whispered, 'He shouldn't have left me . . . I begged him, Don't leave me – I can't stand being left . . . I can't . . .'

They spent the next night together. After that, it was every night. After many days he had obliterated his guilt about Steve Brooks. It was himself and Kit. And only Kit. Or Katherine, as she had asked to be called after their first lovemaking. She had become more a part of his life than he had ever allowed any woman to be.

One night after they had made love and he had fallen asleep, he woke suddenly and reached in the darkness. She was gone. He leaped from the bed calling, 'Katherine!' A light from his study reassured him, but only for a moment. For she was not there. He raced through the apartment and finally found her, in his robe, standing at the kitchen counter pouring herself a drink of straight vodka. A large drink.

'You scared the hell out of me,' he said, taking her in his arms while trying to remove the glass from her hand. But she held it tightly. She permitted him to embrace her, but he could not dislodge that glass. Standing there that way, he did the one thing he had always avoided.

'Katherine . . . darling . . . you have to marry me,' he said suddenly. 'When I woke and found you gone, I knew it. I need you. Not just to make love to. But all the time. We'll be great together. We'll work together. Live together. Make love together. It'll be *us*. For all time.'

He tried to kiss her. She avoided his lips. He settled for pressing his face against hers. Behind his back she raised her glass and took a gulp of straight vodka. Only when the glass was empty would she surrender it to him.

He led her back to bed. Instead of making love to her he lay in the dark fantasizing. 'It'll be a quiet wedding. Then we'll send out announcements. "Katherine Lawrence and Jefferson Warrener . . ." '

'Not Katherine,' she objected strongly. 'Katherine is special.'

Without being aware of the significance, he agreed at once. 'Okay, "Kit Lawrence and Jeff Warrener are pleased to announce their marriage. They will be at home at One West Seventy-second Street, New York City." ' He laughed. 'Do you include ZIP Codes in wedding announcements?'

'Not Katherine,' she replied subbornly.

'I said okay. Besides, my name isn't really Jeff. It's Julie. How would that sound in *The New York Times*? Kit Lawrence of New York City and California has been married to Julie Warshafsky of the Bronx and P.S. Fifty-one.' He laughed uproariously. He turned to make love to her. She did not resist.

When it was over, he fell asleep saying softly, 'It's going to be great . . . great . . .' without realizing that she had never agreed.

When he awoke the next morning, she had gone, leaving no note, no trace, except for the empty vodka bottle in the kitchen. He called her apartment. She was not there. He waited impatiently for Kit to call him. Surely after the events of last night she must call. She did not.

He arrived at the theater early that evening wondering if she would show up. He was in her dressing room when she arrived, on time, ready to make up, dress and go on as if nothing had happened.

'You scared the hell out of me!' he greeted.

She went about applying her eye makeup.

'Where did you go? Why? What got into you?' he demanded. When she didn't answer he said, 'Okay, we'll talk about it after the show.'

'I won't be here.'

'I'll call you at home.'

'I won't be home.'

'Then where will you be?' he demanded. She didn't answer.

He waited for her after the performance. When she refused to go with him, he followed her furtively, feeling like a ridiculous lovesick juvenile. He followed her to Steve Brooks's apartment.

The next morning Steve Brooks had returned from the Coast on the red-eye special, arriving at Kennedy Airport at six forty-five in a foggy dawn. He spent the long cab ride into New York inventing ways to tell Kit his surprise.

As soon as he unlocked his door he knew she was there. Her special fragrance was in the air. He slipped into the bedroom quietly, found her curled up on his side of the bed. Her blond hair was spread wildly across the pillow.

She turned from her right side to her left, and in so doing opened her eyes just long enough to realize he was standing at the foot of the bed staring at her.

She woke, startled.

'Go on,' he said, beaming. 'I love to watch you sleep.'

'Steve,' she said in a pathetic voice. 'Oh, Steve.' She began to weep.

He took her in his arms. 'Don't cry. I was away much longer than I expected. But it was worth it. I got what I wanted. I'm going to produce the picture. And guess who's going to star in it?'

She did not venture any guess, only clung to him.

'That's what took so long. I said I wouldn't make the picture unless you starred in it. They gave me all kinds of arguments. You were a name only on Broadway. No one knew what you could do in front of a camera. But in the end I convinced them. Yesterday, five twenty-five p.m. Pacific Coast time, your career as a movie star began! They said yes!'

He ended with a burst of prideful enthusiasm. But she did not respond. He stared into her blue eyes.

'Katherine?'

She avoided his stare. 'You're not to call me that anymore.'

He tightened his grip on her arms. 'Kit?'

She shook her head, tried to free herself. He held her more firmly.

'What is it? What's wrong?'

'I'm . . . I'm pregnant . . .' she said in a hushed voice.

He burst into laughter. 'Pregnant! And I was trying to figure out some unusual way to ask you to marry me. Now you *have* to marry me!' She leaned against him, tears streaming down her pale, angelic face. He continued to enthuse. 'When did you find out? You should have called me out there. Did the doctor say how long you'd be able to run in the play before it shows?'

'There isn't any doctor.'

'You have to go to a doctor. It's important right from the outset. To find out what sort of diet. What sleep habits, what exercise.'

She interrupted to say tensely, 'You shouldn't have left me . . . you shouldn't . . .'

'But I'm back. We've got the picture. You've got our baby and . . .' He began to kiss her. Though she did not respond as usual, soon he was making love to her.

It was over. They lay side by side in his bed, covered only by the light sheet. He slipped his arm under her head.

'Everything,' he said. 'Everything I ever wanted.'

He felt her tears on his shoulder. He lifted her face so he could look into her eyes.

'Nothing to cry about. We can schedule the picture around the baby. You'll need at least four months between the time you leave the play and the time we start shooting.' He stopped. 'Katherine?'

'I told you not to call me that anymore!'

'What is it? What's wrong?'

'I have to have an abortion!'

'Oh no!' he countered. 'We'll get married. You'll have the baby. You can still have your career.'

'I'll have to have an abortion,' she insisted quietly.

'I have something to say about that,' he protested. 'After all, it's my baby too.'

Once he said it, there was a breathless quiet in the room that, for the first time, forced him to put the pieces together.

'Kit!' he demanded in a voice suddenly hoarse.

'You shouldn't have left me . . .'

Weeping, she told him what had happened. Every detail, as if in the telling she were pleading guilty and punishing herself.

At the end, she lay on the edge of the bed, staring down at the floor, her face stained with tears, her hair wild and disheveled.

He had remained silent throughout. Hurt as he was, he pitied her. His enormous hatred was directed at Jeff Warrener. That destructive, jealous egomaniac had abused this fragile girl as he had all the other women in his life.

'Get me a drink,' she pleaded.

He made her a large vodka on ice. He watched from the foot of the bed as she drank it down in several large gulps. He could not forget that minutes before, he had stood there loving the way she slept. No matter what she had done, he loved her. He would always love her.

'Katherine,' he said with sudden decision.

'I told you not to call me—'

He interrupted. 'We are going to be married,' he said firmly. 'And you will not have an abortion.'

'But—' she started to protest.

'You will have the baby. And we will consider it ours!'

He took the frosty glass from her hand, set it down on the floor and embraced her. While her head rested against his shoulder he told her precisely the order in which things would proceed. They would be married at once to avoid any later suspicions about the child's origin. Once it was time for her to leave the show, they would live quietly for four months before and after she gave birth. That would give him enough time to convert his play into a shooting script. They would embark for Hollywood, the three of them: Mr and Mrs Steven Brooks – she Kit Lawrence, star of the New York stage – and their child.

Kit did not protest, only rested in his arms, saying, 'You shouldn't have left me. I can't stand to be left . . . can't stand . . .'

'You don't have to explain. We will both forget what happened. And why.'

Two days later, as soon as Jeff Warrener learned Steve had returned to New York, he phoned.

'I have to see you!'

'If it's about the picture, the Studio wants Wyler to do it. Since it's a woman's story,' Steve Brooks said, deriving some satisfaction from turning down Warrener.

'I want to talk to you about something else.'

'I don't think we have anything else to talk about.'

'I think we do,' Warrener insisted. 'And it better not be in a public place. I could come up to your apartment.'

With Kit there, Brooks suggested, 'No, I'll come to your place. What time?'

'Name it,' Warrener said urgently.

'Four o'clock.'

'You got it.'

Before Warrener could open the discussion, Brooks said, 'I know what you want to tell me. Kit's already done that.'

Warrener was obviously taken aback. But only for an instant. 'Did she also tell you that I want to marry her?'

It was Brooks's turn to be surprised.

'I thought so,' Warrener continued. 'I want you to know that no matter how it started out, it turned out to be more serious. Much more serious.'

He waited for Brooks's response. There was none. The director exploded. 'Damn it, Brooks, I love that girl! I'm sick with love for her. I've never felt this way about any woman before.'

It was a self-conscious confession, as if to Warrener loving were a weakness of which he was ashamed.

Steve said, 'Kit and I, we're going to be married. Just as soon as the required tests are done and we get a license.'

'You sonofabitch!' Warrener shouted, then asked softly, 'Getting married – was that your idea or hers?'

'*Ours*,' Brooks emphasized.

Warrener shook his head regretfully. 'I could have done so much for her. You can't. Authors can't deal with real life. With you, it's all on paper. As soon as it gets up off the paper, you're lost. That's where we come in. She needs me. You'll never be able to make it work. Never!'

The director began to pace, paying little attention to Brooks now, driven by an incessant need to explain to himself.

'She needs a total life as a woman. She needs a husband. A home. A family. Children.'

'She'll have children,' Brooks said.

As if he hadn't heard, Warrener continued, 'The first thing she has to learn, life isn't all acting. The richness of life, the very thing an actress needs to draw on, isn't learned on the stage. It's learned doing the simple earthy things that all people do. She needs a home. And a family. Yes, a family.'

He turned to stare at Brooks suddenly, as if accusing him of being a meddling eavesdropper. For Warrener had revealed all the fantasies he had been composing about the girl. And which had now come to nothing. Still unable to accept it, he asked again, 'She actually said she would marry you?'

'Yes.'

'Why you and not me?' Suddenly he decided. 'I know: it's because I'm a Jew.'

'I think it's simpler than that.'

'Then why?' Warrener demanded.

'I think it's because you're you,' Brooks said, and left.

# *Eight*

Steve Brooks had left Warrener's apartment and walked north back to his own place high up in the tower of a building that looked out on Central Park to the east and the Hudson River far to the west. He walked slowly, trying to absorb the impact of his confrontation with Warrener. In retrospect, what seemed most remarkable to him was that neither of them had accused Kit. She was not to blame for what had happened to her. She was hardly a participant, only a victim. With any other woman there would probably have been vulgar slurs. The two men might even have joined in her condemnation, thereby serving their own vanity. But not with Kit. Kit was different. Always different.

As for the child, Steve devoutly resolved that to the world, and to him, it would be their child, as he had promised Kit.

By the time he reached his apartment, he had decided against telling her of his talk with Warrener. They must both consider that unfortunate episode ended. He rang. There was no answer. Gichi should be there. But if he had not come in, Kit should be there. Unless she had gone back to her place to pick up some clothes until he arranged to move her.

He unlocked the door, called out, 'Anybody home? Kit? Kit?' There was no answer. There were no lights on. So the last person who left must have left in daylight. He went to his study, snapped on the desk lamp, dialed Kit's number and heard it ring and ring. On the eighth ring he hung up. He tried to think where he might find her. He could call Gloria – but Kit never kept in touch with her unless there was business to discuss.

He was pondering his next step when he became aware of

a sound, a slight and distant gasp. Someone was in the apartment. The bed was still unmade. Evidently Gichi had not been in. He heard the sound again. It drew him to the bathroom. The door was closed. He tried it and discovered it was locked from inside. He pressed his ear against it and listened. He heard a sound, a moan, Kit's moan. He called out to her, then hurled himself against the door. It refused to yield. He stood off several paces and thrust himself against it. He heard the door mirror crash to the bathroom floor and shatter.

'Kit! Kit! Open up! Do you hear me? Open up!'

On his fifth attempt the door finally burst open.

He found her lying on the white-tiled floor, surrounded by her own blood. Bits of shattered mirror gleamed about her, creating an eerie effect which he would never forget. He dropped beside her, seizing both her arms to examine her wrists. But they were intact. Another glance told him the source of her blood. He lifted her carefully, placed her on the unmade bed and fetched a handful of thick towels. He hesitated for only a single instant, decided to hell with the consequences, and called for an emergency ambulance from Roosevelt Hospital.

Sam Rogers had rushed into Roosevelt Hospital Receiving to find Steve Brooks waiting for the doctor's verdict. Minutes later they had been joined by Jeff Warrener. They waited, Brooks and Warrener silent, their eyes accusing each other. Rogers sat alone on a small hardwood bench and mumbled, 'Why would she do such a thing? She had everything to live for! Everything! A girl with such a success to take her own life. Why? Why?'

Steve Brooks did not feel free to tell Sam Rogers what had really happened. He would surely not tell Jeff Warrener.

Two hours later, the resident came out of the admitting room.

'Which one of you is the patient's next of kin?'

'None of us,' Sam Rogers volunteered. 'But she's dear to all of us.'

'Well,' the young doctor hesitated, 'one of you must be closer to her than the other two.'

'What do you mean?' Warrener demanded.

'Don't any of you know?' the doctor asked.

'Know what?' Warrener seized the doctor by the lapels of his lab coat.

'There are better ways than using a sharp instrument. Someday they're going to legalize abortion.'

'She tried to abort herself?' Warrener asked. Before the doctor answered, Warrener turned to glare at Steve Brooks, asking the question which Brooks refused to answer.

'Doctor, how is she now? The truth!' Sam Rogers asked.

'She's lost a lot of blood. We're giving her transfusions. The main question is, will there be an infection?'

'How long before we know?' Steve Brooks asked.

'Three or four days.'

'Doctor,' Sam asked, 'will there be any other ... complications?'

'I have to make out a hospital report.'

'Of course,' Sam acknowledged. 'But will it go any further than that?'

'The law?'

'The law,' Sam admitted his concern.

'That wouldn't do anybody any good, would it?'

'Thanks, Doctor. And if there's anything at all I can do for you ...' Sam offered.

'There is one thing.'

'Name it!' Sam said eagerly.

'Don't try to bribe me. Because that I would report.' He turned and started down the hall.

Jeff Warrener turned on Steve Brooks. 'You sonofabitch! That was *my* baby! Wasn't it?'

'It isn't anybody's baby anymore,' Steve said grimly.

'This is your fault!' Warrener accused, seizing Brooks by

the collar and twisting it so hard it became difficult to breathe.

'My fault? Or yours?' Brooks demanded, struggling to break free.

'You should have told me! I wanted to marry her even without knowing. But you kept it from me. You're responsible for this!'

Warrener struck out, his powerful fist catching Brooks on the side of the face and knocking him to the floor. Steve rose to strike back, but Sam Rogers stepped between them. Like an irate patriarch he commanded, 'Stop it! Both of you!'

Warrener seethed but backed off. Brooks dropped his arms, straightened his clothes and felt the side of his bruised cheek. Sam stood between them.

'I am not interested in which of you is responsible. I am only interested in one thing. That girl.'

'Of course,' Warrener interjected sarcastically.

Rogers turned on him. 'I know. You think I'm only worried about the show. Well, let me tell you, Mr Big Director, with the advance and the momentum we have now I can run this show for two years with Sadie Glutz in the part! If you want to know the real truth, I don't need this show. My income from real estate alone, after tax deductions and depreciation, is enough to put me in the ninety-percent bracket. I do this because I love it! Because it is more exciting than building a new shopping center, or a high-rise office building. Buildings exist. But they don't live and breathe. Theater lives, breathes. It comes alive with each performance. And so do the people who make it.

'That girl. She is a precious, fragile bit of humanity. She is magic. When I watch her I think, This is as close as Sam Rogers is ever going to come to immortality. If I am remembered for anything, it won't be for building some fancy structure but for being the first producer to bring Kit Lawrence to Broadway.

'So how do you think I feel now? When they find my little

girl in a pool of blood, after she tried to do such a terrible thing to herself? And how do you think I feel when you two argue about which one is to blame. You're both to blame! But even that doesn't matter now. Only one thing matters. Save that girl. And I don't give a damn whether she comes back into the show or not. Save her!'

Rogers started down the hall, then half turned back to say, 'Tell them to send all the hospital bills to me.'

An hour later, a nurse wheeled Kit Lawrence out of the admitting room on a gurney stretcher. Both men tried to accompany her. But the nurse said they would have to wait until Kit was comfortably in her bed in her own room.

They waited outside. The nurse came out and asked which one was Steve. The patient wanted to see him. But the other man was to go away. Warrener glared at Brooks, then started down the long, quiet hospital corridor, empty now that regular visiting hours were over.

Steve Brooks entered as quietly as he could.

Kit lay in bed, the sheets taut around her slender body. An intravenous hung on the pole by her side, dripping a life-saving infection-preventing solution into her arm. Her face was very pale, accentuating her delicate features. The nurse must have brushed her hair, for it was neat and glistening in the dim light. Her eyes were closed. But she heard him.

'Steve?'

'Yes, it's me,' he said. 'Don't talk. It's too much of a strain.'

'They won't be able to hear me in the mezzanine,' she tried to joke bravely: 'not the way I am tonight.'

'Let me do the talking.'

'Hold my hand?' she pleaded.

Her hand felt cold, very cold. He wondered if they had given her enough blood. He pressed it gently, massaged it, hoping to impart some of its warmth to her.

'Katherine,' he began, 'I want you to listen to me.

Everything that's happened, it's all past. You're going to be fine. The doctor said so.' He stretched the truth a little. 'And you don't have to go back into the show if you don't want to. Okay?'

She did not answer. He could tell from her breathing that she was asleep again. He sat by her bedside until eleven, when the night nurse insisted he had to leave.

When he reached his apartment his phone was ringing. He raced to it, fearing it might be the hospital.

'Hello?' he shouted, breathless.

'Brooks?' It was Jeff Warrener. 'Well?'

'She was okay when I left.'

'Look, what I said still goes. Child or not, I want to marry her.'

'Aren't you proposing to the wrong person?'

'If I could see her, I could convince her,' Warrener insisted.

'I don't think so,' Brooks said, seeking to terminate the conversation.

'You know, Brooks,' Warrener confessed sadly, 'I don't think I'll ever get over her. She leaves a mark.'

# *Nine*

Two days later, Steve Brooks waited outside Kit Lawrence's room while the resident examined her. When he came out, he reported, 'She'll be free to go home in a few days. She ought to be on a special diet to make up for the loss of blood. And I don't think she should go back into the show for another two weeks.'

'Anything else?' Steve asked.

'You mean resuming her sex life? As soon as she feels the urge.'

'I mean, will it affect her ability to have children?'

'She'll never have children,' the resident said simply.

'Does she know?'

'There's no reason to tell her yet.'

She was sitting up in bed, tying red ribbons in her blond braids while studying herself in the mirror she balanced on her thighs. She looked up at him, smiled. 'Hi, darlin',' she called out. Her voice had its old huskiness; her tone was quite cheerful.

Too cheerful, Steve cautioned himself. She was playing a part again, the recovered patient, bright, gay, as if the terrible episode of the last seventy-two hours had been neither serious nor near fatal. She was avoiding reality by acting instead of feeling. He excused her, on the ground that she had come too close to death to face the fact of it.

'How do you feel?' he asked.

'As you Hollywood fellows say, fantastic,' she jibed at him. 'Now that you're a big picture producer I have to learn your language.'

He took the mirror from her, sat on the edge of the bed,

kissed her. He held her, cheek against cheek, so that he could whisper into her ear.

'The doctor said you can leave here in a few days. Sam says you don't have to go back into the show until you want to. So we'll go down to one of the islands and have a long, lazy honeymoon. You won't have to worry about eight-o'clock half-hours, eight-thirty curtains, is it Wednesday or Saturday and do you have a matinee. It'll be a whole different life.

'We'll be beachcombers. We'll roam the white sand. We'll feel the warm ocean wash over our naked feet. We'll swim in the surf . . .'

He stopped, and suddenly remembered: 'You know, I never thought to ask. Can you swim?'

'Uh-huh,' she whispered.

'Good! We'll have days, weeks, months if you want, of swimming, sun, good food, balmy nights and . . . and love. Lots of love. Kit?'

When she didn't answer, he leaned back to stare at her pale and lovely face.

'We can't get married. Not after what I did to you,' she said.

'I forgive you. Understand? *I forgive you.* It never happened. There is no Jeff Warrener! There never was! It's just you and me. You and me!'

'You can forgive, you can forget,' she said, 'because you didn't do anything wrong. But I did. I did. I did.' She would have repeated it endlessly, if he had not interrupted.

'Stop saying that!'

'But I did,' she said in one last whisper, as a rebellious child might after an adult has left the room. She slipped down to her pillow, lay on her side, her arm trailing over the edge of the bed. She stared down at the floor to hide from him.

'I hate her. I have always hated her. I thought, What a slut. To do what she did, to go off, get herself pregnant, then dump her child on her poor father and disappear. When I was little and went to other kids' homes, poor as they were, there was always the sweet smells of baking and cooking, the sound of laughter, even the sound of voices raised in anger.

'I used to envy them so. My grandfather tried to make up for it. But he wasn't a cook, or a baker. And he was never angry with me. Times I did things to provoke him, deliberately. He would start to punish me, then couldn't. He'd say, "Child, you've been punished enough already." So I never even had that.

'I promised myself no child of mine would have to live the way I did. That's what I was saying when I plunged that thing into me. He's not going to suffer like I did.'

Her voice had trailed off into nothingness. Steve Brooks stood at her bedside and watched her slender body heave involuntarily as she sobbed.

'My whole life I promised myself, I'll show her. No matter where she is now, or what she is now, somehow she'll know I'm better than she was. But now . . .' She never finished the thought.

He knelt beside the bed, took her hand. 'Don't think about it now. Don't even think about getting married. Just get better. We've all the time in the world. All the time.'

He kissed her hand and held it.

Dry-eyed at last, she said, 'I kept thinking, at least I've no one to go back to. Because I could never have gone back home and said, "Grandpa, look what I've done." He would have hated me. And I couldn't stand that. He loved me. The only one who really loved me,' she recalled.

'*I* love you, Katherine.'

As if she had not heard, she repeated, 'The only one who really loved me.'

She came out of the hospital, but she would not move back in with Steve Brooks. She went back into the play. The day of the first brush-up rehearsal, they were all there. Steve

Brooks, Jeff Warrener, Sam Rogers and his wife, Bertha. The cast walked through the scenes to allow Kit to refresh herself on the physical moves. Then, though Warrener had cautioned them not to play at performance level, Kit began to do so. Soon the entire cast was under her spell. To an empty house they gave one of the finest performances Steve's play had ever received.

Sam sat in the dark house during the third act whispering to Bertha, 'Gold. That girl and her talent, pure gold. It makes you want to kiss her feet.'

Steve was greatly reassured. She was the same Kit. The same shining young talent, the same beauty, the same strength. No longer the little girl who had made her sad confession in that hospital bed. She was Kit Lawrence. Star. She had carried the whole cast along with her. They could not resist; they could only follow and obey.

Since this was a rehearsal, when the play was finished, the curtain remained up. The entire cast applauded her.

From out in the house, Sam Rogers called, 'Bravo! Bravo! We ought to sell tickets to our rehearsals,' he joked exuberantly.

The night Kit played her first return performance, the major critics all attended to re-review the show. This time their praise was even more extravagant than before. Evidently her bout with pneumonia (which was the official story) had endowed her with a maturity she had not possessed before. Her close brush with death had somehow infused even more life into her performance, one critic wrote.

She resumed her affair with Steve. She moved back in with him. But she would not marry him. She preferred their life as it was. He began to write a new play for her, to follow their film. After reading the first act, Sam Rogers agreed to produce it. He persuaded Brooks to allow Warrener to direct it.

'After all,' Rogers pleaded, 'why break up a winning team?'

Possibly because Brooks felt a gnawing guilt toward Warrener for not having told him who was the father of Kit's child, he acceded to Rogers' request.

In California, Kit insisted her relationship with Steve Brooks be the same as it was in New York. They lived together in a bungalow at the Beverly Hills Hotel. Still she would not marry him.

Once shooting on the film began, Steve noticed a change in her. Even when they were making love. She was no less ardent and artful, but she kept talking about the film, about her performance, about how empty it was. Despite the fact that the men in the front office, with the big cigars, were beaming at the prospects for the film.

She came onto the set each morning knowing her lines perfectly. She remained secluded in her dressing room between takes. She spoke little to anyone in the cast. When she did, she was modest and respectful, as though she were an apprentice and they the stars.

Her only moments of difficulty with the director came after takes when he raved about her performance but she pleaded to do just one more. Most times he was able to talk her out of it. But not in the crucial scenes.

Against his better judgment, he began to permit extra takes. She would do them and end up facing the camera and holding that pose for a long moment. Then she seemed to collapse, as if all breath went out of her. Everyone on the set respected those long silences, though each of them wondered. Perhaps, they explained to one another, it was one of the idiosyncrasies of her unique talent.

Steve Brooks noticed that as shooting drew to a close, she became more tense. Her hands were constantly cold. She made love as if it were an afterthought. She continually badgered him with questions about her performance. No matter how he tried to reassure her, her doubts grew. The talk around the Studio was that it would be their top film for the year. They doubled their advertising budget. They laid out a lavish promotional campaign to secure her an Academy Award. But she felt her work was empty. Her scenes were flat. No one could convince her otherwise.

When Steve felt that the rough cut was in proper shape, he insisted she see it. She would consent only when she was assured she could witness it by herself in a closed projection room. She would not even allow him to be present.

After the film had run, she sat in the dark saying to herself, 'I knew it, I knew it. It's no good. *I* am no good.'

Despite the fact that the studio wanted to sign her to a four-picture contract, she insisted on hurrying back to New York. She would lose herself in Steve's new play.

Steve agreed, thinking, Films will never satisfy her. There is no audience to respond. Those long silent moments at the end of takes, when she stared into the camera, those were her pleas for applause. For love. That never came.

In the fall they went into rehearsal with the new play. Despite the fact that she worked much harder than before the camera, she enjoyed it far more. She was first to arrive at the theater, last to leave. With her as an example, the rest of the cast outdid themselves. Sam would sit back in the house watching rehearsals and whisper to Steve, 'Do you know what it means to *kvell*?'

'What, Sam?'

'Why, to *shep naches*, of course.' Then, chuckling at his own joke, Sam would explain, '*Shep naches* means to derive great joy. As a proud father from the accomplishment of a daughter. And *kvell*? That's obvious. It means *kvell.* That's the way I feel about her. Such a girl! Marry her, Steve, Marry her! Before she gets away.'

Steve would nod. But never tell Sam how many times he had proposed, how many times Kit had seemed to accept, and how many times they had never got married. Nor did he tell Sam how many times Kit had moved in with him. And then moved out. The times she was there were marvelous. When she was gone it was torment. When she left for the fourth time he resolved never to take her back. But he did. In her arms he could forgive her anything. And when he watched her on stage, he knew he was in the presence of greatness.

The following year, when she did Steve's third play, which was their third hit, he determined that either she would marry him or he would end their affair. He could no longer live the erratic, transitory relationship she demanded. But when it came to ending it, he was powerless. He fantasized himself clutching desperately to the wrists of a woman who hung suspended outside a fiftieth-story window. He could not pull her up; neither did he dare to let go.

# Ten

The fourth Steven Brooks play in five seasons went into production as planned. Jeff Warrener was directing. And, of course, Kit Lawrence was starred. Sam Rogers rounded out the quadrumvirate.

As always, Kit approached the new play with fierce enthusiasm. She worked hard, demanding more of herself than other actors did. She made suggestions for lines she wanted changed, scenes she wanted rewritten. Steve was quick to agree. He wished her instincts about her own life were as sound. He was determined that this time he would insist, and this time she would marry him.

The last run-through before they left for New Haven took place on a snowy night, in an empty theater on Forty-fifth Street. Sam and Bertha were there with Emil Friedman, the publicity man Sam used on all his shows. And a reporter and photographer who had come down to do advance publicity for a New Haven paper.

At Kit's insistence, Sam had invited Max Kronheim, her dramatic coach and dean of the Actors' Lab. A middle-aged man with a professorial look, Kronheim sat off by himself. He spoke to no one between acts. He would reserve his comments for his prize pupil.

The run-through went off flawlessly. At the end, in an old superstition of the theater, Kit did not speak her curtain line but ad-libbed a nonsense line. The actual curtain line was always reserved for the very first performance.

Sam and Bertha came up on stage, delighted. They both embraced Kit and kissed her. Bertha insisted that Kit, Steve and Kronheim join them for a late supper at the Oak Room in the Plaza. But Kit begged off – she had last-minute packing to do. When Steve offered to take her home, with the implicit intention of making love to her, she put him off.

'Go with Bertha and Sam. They're such nice people; you shouldn't hurt their feelings.'

'And you?' Steve asked.

'I'm fine, fine!' she insisted, flashing her bright blue eyes with the special brilliance she reserved for the stage and for lovers.

He kissed her, whispering, 'You're magnificent. Always. But tonight more so than ever. Marry me?'

'Soon,' she promised.

Suspecting it was another evasion, he insisted, 'This time, darling, this time after we open, we are going to be married.' He said it in a whisper so determined that she stared up into his eyes and seemed almost afraid. Then she smiled and nodded.

Max Kronheim took Kit off to a corner of the dimly lit stage and talked to her intently for some minutes. At the end, he kissed her tenderly and held her hand before he would let her go.

New Haven was a smashing success.

Boston was even better. She received five solo calls, from an audience that stood and cheered. She came off breathless with excitement, rushed into Steve's arms, holding on to him to keep from trembling. Her body seemed consumed by an orgasmic elation.

He recalled how different it was from the time, a few years ago, when she had worked in Hollywood. The tension was obvious. A camera was an instrument that recorded but did not respond. She needed the response, warmth, affection of an audience.

Their two weeks in Boston were a good time. After glowing reviews, audiences packed the house. There was little rewriting to do. Steve and Kit had time for delightful intimate suppers in the small late-hours restaurant on the mezzanine of the Ritz. Or they availed themselves of the hotel's all-night room service. He would insist on champagne and gray caviar. Or rich, creamy oyster stews – always ordering far more food than they could possibly consume. He wanted to lavish things on her, but she always refused his expensive gifts.

Later, when the rest of the world was asleep, they made love. She was in constant ecstasy.

'When we marry, it will be this way all the time,' he would say to her. 'The day after we open in New York we'll get the license,' he insisted.

'The day after we open,' she would agree. Then she would laugh and tease and kiss him.

In her dressing room she flirted with him as she sat before her mirror making up. He watched as she brushed her long golden hair, knowing she did it to arouse him and he had no defense against it. At the call of 'Places, please!' when she stood up to go, he would hold her.

'Someday,' he once whispered to her, 'I am going to make that whole audience wait while I attack you right here in your dressing room.'

She laughed, kissed him back, open-mouthed, to arouse him even more.

They closed in Boston on their second Saturday night, struck the set, loaded out and were on their way to New York. To face the critics who really mattered.

Sam Rogers and Jeff Warrener sat next to each other on the plane. Sam was beaming.

'What a feeling!' he enthused. 'To come into New York with confidence! To know what the critics will say before they say it.'

'I hope you're right, Sam,' Jeff Warrener said soberly.

'Don't be so goddamned superstitious. You think I'm giving it a *kaneh hovra*? I tell you, we're in like Flynn!' Sam said, signaling the stewardess for another round of drinks. 'The play's great. She's fantastic. We have a tremendous advance. Cheer up! Don't be so Jewish!' Sam said, and laughed.

They were halfway through their third drinks when Jeff Warrener said, 'Sam, there is such a thing as being *too* good, *too* perfect.'

'What the hell does that mean?' Sam asked, annoyed now.

'I have a feeling she's too high. Something is wrong, Sam.'

'What?' Sam demanded, exasperated.

'I wish I knew' was all Warrener could say.

The night of the opening, after the applause, the backstage congratulations, kisses and embraces, they all went over to Sardi's for the inevitable party. Kit waited until the reviews were in. The critics all agreed. They called Kit Lawrence's performance brilliant. Kerr called it the most memorable performance by an actress that he could remember.

After she read that, Kit smiled, said she was tired and asked Steve to take her home. Her own home.

Because she pleaded exhaustion, he left her at her door. But first he kissed her and whispered. 'It's all arranged.'

'What?'

'Tomorrow afternoon we go downtown and get the license! Finally,' he said, and kissed her again.

She kissed him back – a long, lingering kiss – and sent him away.

No one dared disturb Kit the next morning. She had more than earned her sleep. When Emil Friedman had word that *Life* wanted her for its cover, Sam Rogers said they had to wait. That girl was not to be annoyed or driven.

By midafternoon when no one had heard from her, Steve Brooks became concerned. He called her home. Her line was busy. He called again. Still busy. After his fourth call he asked the operator to verify it. The report came back: her line was out of order.

For an instant he was relieved. But only for an instant.

Then he raced out of Sam's office, hopped a cab up to East 66th Street. He rang her doorbell, pounded on her door, called out to her. He insisted the superintendent open it for him. Reluctantly, the man complied. He unlocked the door, but they found the guard chain in place. Steve hurled himself against the door, ripping the chain bolts out of the framework. He raced down the hall to her bedroom. The door was closed. He threw it open. He found her.

Sprawled across the bed, she was breathing in an unnaturally labored manner. The phone was off the hook. He shouted, 'Kit! Kit!' She did not respond. He dialed the operator and ordered, 'I need a doctor and an ambulance!' and gave the address.

He lifted Kit from the bed. Light as she was, her legs would not sustain her. She was completely inert, barely breathing. He held her, dragging her around the room, walking her, talking to her, trying to make contact with her.

Some time later a white-coated ambulance doctor appeared accompanied by two attendants with a stretcher. They covered her with a blanket and carried her out. When Steve sought to follow, the doctor said, 'You'd only be in the way.'

Steve Brooks was left alone in a room in which he had made love to Kit Lawrence many times. He noticed on the floor an envelope that he had dislodged from the phone when he grabbed for it. He ripped it open.

*Steve, darling, forgive me. I begged you once, love me, but don't fall in love with me.*

*But you wouldn't listen.*

*Say good-bye to my children at the hospital. Don't tell them what I did. Just say I went away. Went away.*

He sank down on the bed, reached for the phone, dialed Sam Rogers' office.

'Sam ...' he started to say, and could not continue. For

the first time since he had been eleven years old, Steve Brooks wept.

'Steve . . . kid, what is it?' Sam called frantically. 'Where are you? What's wrong?'

In a visitors' room in Mount Sinai Hospital's private pavilion, three men had waited grimly. Sam Rogers, Jeff Warrener, Steve Brooks. Despite their frequent inquiries, the word had not changed. The doctors had pumped her stomach, were bringing to bear all available life-support systems. As yet she was not responding.

It could take many hours. Perhaps even two or three days. And then if she did respond? There was always the possibility of permanent brain damage in such cases, one doctor informed them quite frankly.

Sam kept reassuring Steve Brooks: 'I've seen worse and they come out of it. She'll be okay. Okay!' he repeated, to bolster his own weak conviction.

'I told you,' Jeff said morosely to Sam. 'She was too high. The whole thing was too good to be true.'

Out of respect for Steve's torment, Sam said, 'For God's sake, Jeff, please!'

'I sensed it all along,' Warrener persisted. 'It's a madness. The very thing that makes her so fascinating on the stage, that charmed us so, is what made her do this.'

'Shut up!' Steve commanded.

Determined to have his way, Warrener continued: 'Sure, you hate me because of what happened between Kit and me that time. Instead, you ought to thank me. I did you a big favor. I saved you from a lifetime of waiting nervously like this in hospital corridors.'

Steve seized him by the throat, shouting, 'Damn you! Shut up!'

A nurse appeared from a doorway to reprimand them in an officious whisper. 'This is a hospital! And it's late. You'll wake the patients!'

Steve Brooks relaxed his grip on Jeff Warrener, who had made no effort to defend himself.

The doctor came out of Kit's room.

'Doctor?' Sam asked anxiously.

'Her signs are beginning to stabilize.'

'Can you tell anything yet?' Steve asked.

'About damage? Not yet.'

The next morning Kit awoke to find herself alive, in a hospital, Steve Brooks standing at her bedside.

Within four days they had determined that she had sustained no neurological damage. All her systems functioned well. But the psychiatrist who had been called in on consultation advised that she not try to go back into the show. Instead, she must go into treatment at once. It might even be desirable that she move out of New York, away from the stresses the city imposed on her. A retreat of some kind, a rest home, of which there were several good ones close by.

It was the first time that she had been sent to a sanitarium. But it would not be the last.

In the months that followed, Steve Brooks had gone to visit her regularly. Eventually the doctor said that he had better not come. His visits always rekindled her guilt. Steve resigned himself to sending her gifts and an occasional letter. Sam Rogers took care of all her bills. When Steve offered to share the burden, Sam said, 'If I had a daughter in this kind of trouble, would I hesitate to pay her bills?'

Steve Brooks and Jeff Warrener never worked together again. A year later, Warrener went to Hollywood to escape the boom-or-bust hazards of the theater. Steve Brooks gradually deserted Broadway. He found himself writing an occasional screenplay, interspersed with a novel whenever he had an idea worthy of all that effort.

The quadrumvirate of Kit Lawrence, Steve Brooks, Jeff Warrener and Sam Rogers, which everyone had expected would reign on Broadway for a generation, had disbanded.

What promised to become an era had turned out to be a brief span of years that ended tragically.

Eventually, a year later, when she felt up to it, Kit Lawrence began to do television work on the advice of her doctor. The parts were not so long or the rehearsals so intense. She tried several plays after that, but there were no successes.

Audiences came to see her, hoping to experience the fire that had once been there. They were rewarded only with sparks. She began to miss performances. She resorted to all sorts of excuses. Pains with no pathological origin. Difficulties with her vocal cords, which she had never suffered before. Gradually her box-office appeal dropped off, since people were never sure she would appear.

She tried desperately to describe her symptoms to doctors. When she correctly suspected they did not believe her, she would insist, tearfully, 'But it does hurt. Please, believe me. The pain is unbearable. Do something!'

They prescribed pills, most of them placebos. One orthopedist prescribed a thick foam whiplash collar for the psychosomatic pains in her neck. She wore it like a martyr, almost proudly, as if it justified her lack of professional discipline.

She explained to producers and directors, 'I want to go on. I really want to. But I can't. The pain is too intense. I can't. I can't.'

The only duty for which she was always on time and which she never forsook was her readings at the hospital. Once a week, no matter how bad the pain, she took off her foam whiplash collar and went to see her children. She was bright and happy for them. But when she came home, the pain was unbearable again and she took many pills to fight it.

Along with the pills, her drinking had increased. Some nights when she did appear on stage, her condition became obvious to the audience. Steve Brooks had seen her on one of those nights. He was so disheartened he did not dare go back to her dressing room.

Jeff Warrener had tried to get her several supporting roles in pictures he was directing. Each time her agent had said she did not wish to appear in films.

There were two more suicide attempts. Two more rescues. Both times the doctors said she had no real desire to die. Her attempts were classified as cries for help.

But nothing seemed to help.

After several years, Steve Brooks had married Melinda. She was a tall girl, blond, with blue eyes. She worked in the agency that represented Steve. She had sold one of his books to a large publishing house for a sizable advance. The book had a good sale, in no small measure due to Melinda's continual prodding of the publisher's sales and promotional departments. He began to see her, socially more than professionally. Though she was nine years younger than Steve, they seemed compatible. He enjoyed her company, liked her directness, her ability to organize his time. He greatly admired her efficiency.

They had understood between them that there would be no children for a while. She wanted to develop her career before she was willing to take long periods of time out for pregnancy, childbearing and child rearing.

That was the reason she resorted to whenever the subject of having children arose. She had another reason, more persuasive and quite secret. She was keenly aware of Steve's previous deep attachment to Kit Lawrence.

Melinda had spent a good part of one rainy Sunday afternoon alone, staring into a mirror, making comparisons with a photograph of young Kit Lawrence. Both blond, blue-eyed, similar in features. If it was not apparent to Steve, it was quite clear to Melinda. He fancied himself in love with her because he was still seeking a Kit Lawrence with whom he could make his life.

The same sensible qualities that made Melinda such an effective agent warned her of the dangers of marrying Steve Brooks. But she loved him enough to chance it. However, she did not wish to expose her unborn children to risks they had no choice in taking.

Three years later, despite Steve's protestations of love, Melinda asked for a divorce. She explained she could no longer stand by and watch him make love to Kit Lawrence. He had flared into a fury of denial. He had not seen Kit in years. Years!

'That isn't what I mean,' Melinda explained. 'When you make love to me, I feel like a voyeur. I'm watching you make love to her. At first I thought I'd win you over. But after three years, it's the same. I want out. While I'm still young enough to make a solid marriage and have children of my own.'

He could not dispute her.

Gently she said, 'It's not that I don't love you, Steve. You don't love me. Don't you see that?'

They had agreed to be intelligent about it. She would continue to represent his novels. He would do a year as Author-in-Residence at a Midwestern university. If during the year she changed her mind, he would come back. They corresponded. They spoke on the phone whenever she had business to discuss. But she never indicated any lessening of her desire for a divorce.

Gradually, during the last few months, Steve Brooks had come to realize that Melinda was probably right. Dear Melinda, lovely Melinda, intelligent, efficient, conscientious Melinda was usually right. For when he was crossing the campus on a sunny fall afternoon, with the gold and red leaves being blown across the yellowing fields, and he saw the wind whip back some coed's long blond hair, the stab of recognition in him was not of Melinda but of Kit.

Kit had become a chronic disease, transmitted by intimate contact, and threatening to defy any cure.

Steve had been more relieved than resentful at having to accept Dr Ross's request to come to Connecticut because of Kit's condition. Perhaps he could finally end the torment this time. And if he did, there might yet be a chance for him and Melinda.

# Part 3

# *Eleven*

'Because Ross asks the impossible, doesn't mean I have to break my back to accomplish it!' Jeff Warrener exploded.

The few early-morning skiers in the inn's coffee shop turned to stare at them.

'What are you going to tell him?' Steve responded in a voice much lower but no less urgent.

'That I am going back to the Coast and cut my film!' Warrener declared with finality. 'If we had just a glimmer of an idea . . . but we don't.'

He fell silent for a moment, then asked grudgingly, 'Tell me one thing, honestly. Is there ever a day goes by that you don't think of her?'

'No,' Brooks admitted. 'Unfortunately, my wife knows it even better than I do.'

'That the reason you're getting a divorce?'

Brooks avoided answering. 'Melinda's a terrific girl. I'm just not the right man for her.'

Warrener confessed, 'Every actress I cast I keep looking for Kit. I'll never find her. But that doesn't stop me from searching. Still, Ross is right about one thing. Borderline cases like Kit can manipulate people. The question is, do we want to be manipulated? Well, *not me*!'

'Then I'd better call Ross,' Brooks said.

Ross interrupted an early session with a patient to take Brooks's call.

'Doctor, we want to help. Desperately,' Brooks said. Across the room, Warrener was nodding his head vigorously. 'But desperation is not a solution. Not in our business. Otherwise, every play would become perfect in Boston.'

'I never expected you'd find a solution overnight,' Ross said. 'That doesn't mean you won't find one tomorrow. Or the day after. I'm sure if you realized the danger of the situation . . .'

'We do, Doctor. And we'll keep trying. But just sitting here in this little hotel isn't going to do it. The right idea might come tomorrow, or next week, or next month.'

'Or never,' Jeff Warrener warned in a grim whisper.

'We can't promise anything,' Brooks continued, 'except that we'll try. I give you my word, we'll try.'

'Please do!' Ross said, using the precatory phrase as an order. 'Because prolonged failure now might push her over the brink from borderline to hopeless. Then it'll never end. Never end.'

With the roads in icy condition, making Hartford by plane time was not easy. Their cab raced along, slipping into and out of deep frozen ruts with such precipitous jerkiness that they expected at any moment they would be thrown into a skid that might catapult them against the guardrails or off into a ditch.

Nevertheless, Jeff Warrener leaned forward, urging the driver, 'We haven't got much time. And it's the last plane out this morning.'

Steve Brooks hunched in a corner of the cab, feeling not haste but guilt. One phrase nagged at him. What Ross had said: *It'll never end. Never end.* At first Steve used it to exonerate and console himself. If a psychoanalyst as experienced as Ross was willing to concede such a hopeless prognosis, why did it become the burden of a playwright to reverse it? If doctors could not help her, surely he could not. So he had no need to feel guilty.

But the longer he dwelled on Ross's phrase, the more it accused him. It also sounded familiar. As if it had a history going back long before Ross used it.

They were edging forward in the slow-moving check-in

line at the airport when Steve suddenly said, 'We've got to get back!'

'We'd have been on our way last night if you'd listened to me,' Jeff said angrily.

'I mean back to Silvermine!'

'Are you out of your mind?' Warrener demanded impatiently.

'There *is* an idea. One idea that might work. But Ross has got to approve. So we're going back!'

'Call him!' Warrener ordered. 'If there's time before take-off.'

'We're dealing with Kit's life! I'm not going to risk it on a phone call. We're going back. We're going to see Ross!'

'I can't,' Jeff protested. 'I've got reservations out of New York. I've got to make my connection. They're waiting for me out there. I could be in breach of contract if I don't show.'

'Damn it, we can't leave without knowing that at least we tried!' Brooks insisted.

As soon as they arrived in Ross's office Steve began: 'Doctor, what you said earlier, the specific words you used. *It'll never end. Never end.* Were those *your* words?'

'Yes,' Ross admitted, puzzled by Steve's question.

'I mean, have you ever heard *Kit* use the words?'

'I may have. They're not so unusual. Other patients have used them.'

'Maybe so,' Steve conceded. 'But as they relate to Kit they may have particular significance. I've heard her use them. Especially once, in a way I never forgot.'

'When? Under what conditions?' Ross asked, far more curious now.

'It was early one morning. Three, maybe four, o'clock. We had made love. We lay on our backs, staring up at the ceiling. She was smoking a cigarette. Each time she took a puff the glow lit up her profile. She always looked her loveliest in that special fleeting light. I thought to myself, What if she had all the talent she has, but weren't so beautiful? Would she be as fine an actress if she were plain or homely?

'So, trying to be playful about it, I asked, "Katherine—" '

Ross interrupted, 'You call her Katherine?'

'Didn't she tell you? She's only permitted two men to call her Katherine. Her grandfather, and me,' Steve said.

'And me,' Jeff corrected.

'And me,' Ross added. 'And probably every man she ever made love with. Now, what about that night and what she said?'

'I asked her what she would have done if she had been born homely but with her great talent for acting. She said, "Then I would have acted myself beautiful." Somehow my question started her talking. She rambled on. Touching on many memories from her childhood.

'I will never forget it. Because it was the closest I have ever come to the real Kit Lawrence. It was as if she were a child again, speaking as a child, feeling as a child. As nearly as I can recall, this is what she said:

' "Grandpa loved me very much. He used to knock himself out trying to play with me, but he was an old man. Times I used to catch him breathing hard when he thought I wasn't looking. So I'd ease up and not play as hard anymore. Other kids had daddies who ran slow to let their little ones catch them. I had to run slow to let him catch up with me. He tried so hard to be everything to me. But he never was able to fool me. I could tell he was only an old man trying hard.

' "I never got to play with other kids much. It wasn't only that we lived so poor. It was not having a mother and father. It told them what I was. So most other kids weren't allowed to play with me. Some of them said pretty terrible things. I didn't mind that so much. It was being alone all the time that was bad.

' "I lived alone. Played alone. Being alone, I began to make up plays in my head. I would act them out. In them my dreams became real. I was rich, and beautiful, and desired. People invited me everywhere. Other children came to visit me, and they envied me.

' "Then in school we actually had a play. We all tried out for it. I was chosen. Because I was very good. The night of the play, when I took my bow they all applauded. One man even whistled. I smiled, and they handed me roses.

' "Later I found out it was Grandpa who bought them. That night I was so excited I couldn't sleep. I sat by the window and watched the moon, which was huge and orange colored, a real desert moon. I said to myself, They loved me; people really love me when I act. So I decided to be an actress. That's the way it started.

' "Sometimes, though, I get this strange feeling that one day, after a performance, when the applause is done, the autographs are all signed and I'm back in my dressing room alone, removing my makeup, there's a knock on the door. I say, 'Come in.'

' "The door opens and there's a woman. A plain woman, looking tired from a difficult life. But I can tell she was very pretty once. She wants me to sign her program. So I do. As I hand it back to her, she looks at me and says, 'Don't you know me?'

' "I stare at her. At her face, her blue eyes. Suddenly it's as if I'm looking into a mirror. Even before she says it, I know. She's my mother. She embraces me and kisses me. But I do not kiss her back. I just stand there, like stone, unyielding.

' "She tries to explain what made her do what she did to me. How frightened she was, having a baby and alone, deserted. She says she left me for my sake. She knew I'd be safe and well taken care of by Grandpa. But I do not let myself be moved. I just stand and listen, as if it's a scene I'm playing and I have no lines. When she's done, I say nothing. Nothing at all. I just stare at her.

' "She can see in my eyes the hatred I have for her. The contempt. She breaks down, begins to cry. I do not relent. I tell her of all the pain she made me suffer. The loneliness. The times I cried every night, for weeks on end. The hurtful things people said about me. The way they shut me out. Then I order her out. She goes, and I feel good, I feel free! I feel . . . I don't know what I feel, only I know that it's better than it was.

' "That's what I imagine. Except, of course, no woman has ever come to me like that after a performance. But I keep waiting, expecting." '

Steve Brooks paused in his recounting, before he said, 'This is the significant thing, Doctor. Right after that was when Kit said those words: "It'll never end, I guess. Never end." '

Jeff shook his head sadly. 'Poor kid. Christ, no wonder.'

Dr Alvin Ross stared thoughtfully out the window at the snow-covered countryside. 'During the analysis she has reported a similar fantasy about her mother. What's your point, Brooks?'

'That her fantasy might serve as the basis of the play you want for her.'

Ross swung around to demand, 'Do you have any idea how she comes to be here?'

'*Variety* said she withdrew suddenly from a play that was out of town.'

'*Variety* didn't say it all, then,' Ross informed him. 'She happens to be here because she broke down during a tryout. And when I say *during* a tryout, I mean that. Literally. In the middle of a performance.'

'Onstage?' Jeff asked, incredulous.

'She came down to the apron of the stage. Dropped to her knees. Sat there playing with her hair, like a little girl. She began to talk directly to the audience. She asked if anyone out there was her mother. And if she was, would she stand up so Kit could see her. Of course, no one stood up. So she began to revile her, calling her coward, whore, bitch. At first the audience thought it was part of the performance.

'They realized it was her sickness only when she started to berate them. "How dare you sit out there and judge me? I'm as good as any of you. Better! I wouldn't even come to your house if you invited me! I don't need you. I don't need anyone".' She ended up sitting there, childlike, weeping pathetically.

'They brought her here the next morning. That was fourteen months ago.'

'Doctor, Kit has spent her life searching for a mother she never knew,' Brooks said.

'True,' Ross conceded.

'What if she finally met her?' Steve asked pointedly.

Ross stared at him. 'Exactly what do you have in mind?'

'A play about a woman's search for a mother who deserted her when she was an infant. In the third act she does find her mother. And we have a powerful confrontation. Daughter facing mother. The hostility of a lifetime pitted against the guilt of a lifetime.'

'No matter how it comes out,' Jeff said, 'it would make one hell of a third act.'

'How *would* you end it, Brooks?' Ross asked thoughtfully.

'I don't know that yet. First, do you think Kit could handle it?'

'It would be an enormous risk. You might call it an unusual form of shock therapy.'

'Would it be worth that risk?' Steve persisted.

'If she responds to the idea, it would at least point her toward wanting to leave here to resume the only life she's ever found rewarding.'

'And if it failed?' Jeff asked.

'It could shatter her completely,' Ross admitted softly. 'I'll have to consider this very carefully.'

'How long would you need?' Jeff asked. 'I have to get back to the Coast.'

'Overnight,' Ross said. He mused for a moment, then said, 'Come to the house for dinner tomorrow evening. Seven.

Meantime, work on it. Flesh it out. Consider how you would present it to her. Because if I do decide that we take the risk, you had both better be ready.'

The next evening Lisa Ross answered the doorbell. She was surprisingly pretty, dark-haired, trimly built, with a certain sinuous sexuality. She was most pleasant and warm as she announced, 'Alvin is on the phone. An emergency. But do come in and make yourself comfortable.'

She showed them into the living room.

'Drink?' she invited, indicating the bar. 'Please help yourselves. I'm not good at mixing drinks. I usually make them too weak. A hangover, you might say, from taking care of too many alcoholics.'

In view of what Ross had confided in them about his affair with Kit, it was difficult to make casual conversation. She tried to put them at ease by asking questions about Hollywood and the theater. Steve and Jeff found themselves giving the routine answers, as if this were the usual radio or TV interview.

Finally, Mrs Ross smiled and said, 'Let's relax. It's futile to pretend. The only thing in common we three have to talk about is Kit. And we can't very well talk about her, can we?'

Steve had to admire her ability to introduce the subject with so little apparent resentment.

'I can understand why men feel that way about her. She's fascinating.'

'Then you've met her?' Steve asked.

'Psychiatric nurses, good ones, are hard to come by. Even though I retired when I married Alvin, I help out whenever they're shorthanded. So, yes, I've seen her. Several times. And she knows me. I always have the feeling she wants to talk to me. To explain. To apologize. She just follows me with those big blue eyes. I'm so sorry for her that I'm tempted to say, "All right, let's talk about it. It will make you feel better." It's really rather sad. She'd like to flaunt what she considers her triumph. But instead of victory, she feels only guilt.'

Dinner was delicious and ample. Conversation was an exercise in avoiding conversation. It was a relief to Steve and Jeff when Lisa excused the men, saying, 'Coffee is waiting in the den.'

Ross opened the meeting with a simple frank statement. 'Before I give you my decision, you should know something of the psychiatric pathology of actors as a group. Any person who chooses acting as a career does so out of certain emotional needs. Every actress, like every child, has strong exhibitionistic drives.

'The direct narcissistic need for applause. The indirect satisfaction of wielding a magical power over the audience. Further, acting is much like sexual intercourse. There are forepleasure and endpleasure. Rehearsals, painful and difficult as they are, are made pleasurable by the anticipatory tension of endpleasure, the release of opening night. The ultimate orgasm being the experiencing of the applause and love of the audience.

'That is also why actors and actresses generally resist permanent personal one-to-one relationships.'

He looked sharply to Steve Brooks. 'Your insistence on marrying her precipitated her first suicide attempt. Actresses resist being pinned down to a single mate. They prefer the audience. Because audiences are like casual lovers. Audiences don't make demands after the affair is over. The curtain comes down. They just go home. Leaving the actress free for the next lover, the next audience.

'Equally important, acting is a means of getting rid of anxieties. So that acting can have a therapeutic effect. In a play, life takes on a precise, defined course. The actress knows at the outset what will happen, with whom it will happen and how it will be resolved. Where else can one have such total control over one's life?

'Why do you think Kit was so immutably driven to the theater as a career?' Ross asked.

He turned to Steve once more. 'How else is she ever going to meet her mother, rid herself of all the hatred she has nurtured all these years? Live out her childhood fantasy of confronting her?

'So, yes, I think your idea might possibly not only prove attractive to her, but it could have an even greater therapeutic effect than any other idea.'

'Then you approve?'

'Not without stressing the dangers. If a role comes too close to painful emotions in an actress's unconscious, she may no longer be able to cope with it.'

'We would be approaching that here,' Steve admitted.

'The thing that finally convinced me is that we are not dealing with her *unconscious* feelings. Her hatred for her mother is openly expressed. So I think this might well prove to be a valuable cathartic experience for her, and most constructive in the long run.'

Jeff said, 'Good! Because I can see now how she would play that third act. She could be magnificent. It could very well be like the old times again!'

'Let me warn you now,' Ross intervened sharply, 'it had better *not* be like the old times. The one thing we cannot risk, and the most likely risk, is the one I precipitated. It would be fatal for either of you to become emotionally, sexually involved with her again. It could doom the entire experiment, and it's risky enough to begin with.'

'You don't have to worry about that,' Jeff assured him.

'Warrener, in my profession we are most suspicious of those assurances which are given too quickly.'

'How do we go about this?' Steve asked.

'When Kit comes for her usual hour tomorrow, I will tell

her I've heard from you. I informed you I feel she might wish to resume her career, if she finds your play to her liking. So you are both here.'

'And if she says *she* doesn't feel she's ready?' Steve asked.

'That's exactly what she'll say,' Ross predicted.

'Then what?'

'She'll ask me what I think. We'll discuss it for the rest of the hour. At the end, she'll say, "If you think I'm ready, then *I* think I'm ready." '

Ross nodded slightly, thoughtfully. 'She'll want to do it for me. To show me how strong she's becoming. Thinking I'll love her more, will resume our affair.

'Her real conflict will arise when it's time for her to finally leave here. But in the end, if all goes well, she will leave. Which would be the best thing for her. Continued dependence on me could be most damaging. It could become a lifelong addiction; in a sense, a terminal illness.'

'When can we see her?' Jeff asked, anxious to get on with it.

'As soon as you both feel ready to discuss the story with her. And I must warn you, she may be sick, but she has all the insight and cunning of a highly intelligent neurotic. If there are weaknesses in your story line, she'll find them. And if she does, that could be the end of this, even before it gets under way. So be alert and careful.'

'We will be,' Steve promised.

Ross was not easily reassured.

'I must warn you, most emphatically, confronted by such a challenge, she may rise to it. But she may also go completely to pieces. So be persuasive, but not overpowering.

'An adverse reaction at this time might trigger highly dangerous consequences. If she didn't have such a deep attachment to you both, I would never chance it.'

Lisa Ross was upstairs, in bed, leafing through a pile of the latest psychiatric journals, selecting those papers which were important for her husband to read.

Ross undressed silently, until the rustling of the glossy pages tormented him beyond enduring. Suddenly he turned on her.

'It would help, it would help one hell of a lot, if you weren't so goddamned stoic and "understanding!" '

'Under the circumstances, what do you want me to do?'

'Scream! Curse! Accuse me! Call me vile names! Beat on my chest. Scratch my face. Make me bleed! Anything! Just give vent to your feelings! I could cope with that. But not with all this silence.'

'That would be your release. I'll have to find my own,' his wife said quietly.

He continued to undress in silence.

'If she agrees,' Lisa asked, 'will you be sorry to see her go?'

'No.'

'Be honest with me, Alvin.'

'No, *and* yes,' he admitted.

'I thought so. You've been trying very hard to be so professional about this. To remain the analyst, when you're really part of the problem.'

'Just once, let me hear you say it!' he demanded fiercely. 'Not in sterilized words like I am "part of the problem." I was her lover. I took her to bed. Had sex with her. Many times. Well, say it! Then hate me for a time. But get over it, so we can take up our lives again. If that's possible.'

Lisa Ross did not answer.

He had slipped into his pajamas and was sitting on the edge of their bed when he asked, 'Do you think you'll ever be able to forgive me? Lisa?'

'Only if you save her.'

He turned to stare at her, suspicious.

'Otherwise, you won't ever forget her,' she said gently. 'This has to work as much for your sake as for hers. Because you could never accept such a failure, Alvin.'

'Are you going to keep calling me "Alvin," as if we were merely acquaintances?'

'For the time being, I guess that's what we are,' she said sadly.

# *Twelve*

The receptionist at Administration was expecting Brooks and Warrener. She directed them to Carlisle Cottage, where they were greeted by a middle-aged woman who, though dressed in the style of a suburban matron, was actually a psychiatric nurse. She ushered them into a small sitting room, decorated in tasteful Colonial style. A welcoming fire blazed in the fireplace.

'Miss Lawrence will be right down.' She withdrew, closing the door.

After some moments of nervous waiting, Jeff asked softly, 'What's your guess?'

'The last time I saw her she looked pretty bad,' Steve admitted. 'Bloated. Red-eyed. She'd just come off a binge. I was shocked.'

'I meant, how do you think she'll react to the story? To seeing us? To the whole idea?'

'I don't know. But I'm going to do my damnedest.'

'Right. If I see her losing interest, I'll take a hand.'

They continued staring at the door, waiting silently. Ten minutes had passed. Jeff Warrener shot up from his chair, as he said in a low, angry whisper, 'One thing hasn't changed! She likes to keep people waiting!'

'She was prompt at rehearsals,' Steve reminded him.

'Only in the early years,' Jeff agreed. 'Later on, I understand sometimes she didn't show at all.'

Steve nodded solemnly, reminded of all the stories he had heard about her.

Suddenly, Jeff concluded, 'She won't come down. She doesn't want to face us. Let's get out of here while we still have our own sanity.'

Though Jeff had expressed the same fears that were plaguing Steve, he insisted, 'We'll wait. Of course she's reluctant to face us. She knows she doesn't look as young or as beautiful as we remember. No matter how she looks, don't let on!'

'Of course not.'

To distract Warrener from his impatience, Steve Brooks asked, 'Should we have called Sam Rogers?'

'What could we tell him, before we know how she'll react?'

'It might help persuade her if Sam was willing to produce. It would give her the feeling of a reunion of the old team. We should at least have called him.'

'I don't think so,' Jeff confided. 'I heard a rumor that Bertha is dying of cancer. The slow, lingering kind. And Sam is going out of his mind trying to find help for her. Even resorting to quack doctors.'

'Oh, God. Bertha. Such a nice lady. No, we shouldn't bother Sam unless it becomes absolutely essential,' Steve agreed.

'Damn it, where is she?' Jeff exploded impatiently. 'I'll tell you one thing. If she starts out playing the star with me, I'm leaving. I don't owe her anything. She was not the first woman to become pregnant. Nor the first to have an abortion. So I don't want that held over me!'

Steve Brooks did not respond. There was no need. Jeff himself realized that, more than a protest, his was a confession of guilt. He turned away to watch the fire. For a time its crackling was the only sound in the room.

'It's been almost half an hour,' Jeff warned impatiently.

'She'll be down,' Steve insisted, trying to convince himself as much as Warrener. For he recalled Ross's warning about what the mere suggestion of acting again might do to her.

'Christ! I've got a picture to edit!' Jeff protested.

At that instant there was a knock at the door. It was crisp and commanding. Both men turned expectantly. In the instant before the door opened, they glanced at each other, their doubts and questions reflected in their eyes.

The door seemed to burst open. Kit Lawrence stood before them, smiling warmly, her blue eyes clear, bright. Her hair was long, loose as it used to be. And just as golden as they remembered. This was not the bloated, faded woman they had expected. She was almost as slender as she had been the very first time they had seen her. Now, maturity served to make her body even more sensuous. She wore a trim gray flannel skirt and a light blue cashmere sweater that both complemented her eyes and enhanced her breasts.

The two men were tremendously relieved.

The first words she said were, 'Steve! Oh, Steve, how wonderful to see you again.' Her voice had the same quality – vibrant, and a bit husky.

She swept into the room toward him. Instead of offering her cheek to be kissed, she kissed him. For an instant she clung to him. She leaned back and stared up at him.

'Steve, you look so – well, so ... so distinguished.' She was a queen dispensing decorations. 'And how is your wife?'

'Melinda? Fine.'

'Good! I'm so happy for you. Any children?'

'No. Just one divorce. In the works.'

'Oh, I'm sorry, terribly sorry.'

He suspected there might be a flicker of satisfaction in her disarming blue eyes. But he realized she was truly compassionate about the failure of his marriage. She turned her attention to Warrener, as if she had just become aware of his presence.

'Jeff?' she exclaimed. She held out her cheek as in the old days when she had come to rehearsals and he always kissed her. He performed that ceremony, but at the same time reached for her hand.

He pressed it – usually a gesture of warmth and friendship. This time it had added purpose. Always suspicious, Jeff knew she was actress enough to have staged her impressive entrance. To have dressed, made up, arranged her hair in just the way she had, for just the reason she had, to remind them of the old days. To prove to them, I am the Kit Lawrence you remember, the girl you both loved.

If this was a performance, her hand should be cold. Countless times he had stood in the wings with her to make sure she went on. And always her hands had been cold. Icy cold.

Not this time. Kit's hand was warm to his touch. She was not merely playing the serene, prepossessing lady. Jeff not only felt tremendously reassured, he felt a stab of his old love for her.

'I saw your last film, Jeff,' she enthused.

Then she laughed. 'Isn't that the cruelest *faux pas.* Yet people are always saying that, "your *last* film, your *last* play." As if you had just died. I meant, darling, your *latest* film. They played it here in town. Magnificent!'

Now she took his hand, as she continued. 'I sat there admiring it and saying to myself, I wonder if his star knows how much Jeff's done for her with his use of the camera. Very skillful, darling. No, better than skillful. Sensitive. Tasteful. Powerful. Stunning, actually. I was inside her mind every moment. I could read her thoughts. Even the thoughts she wanted to hide from us. I said to myself, Jeff's talent has grown. He's better than ever.'

Now she kissed him fondly on the cheek. 'I left the theater feeling proud that I'd known you, proud that I'd worked with you.'

'Believe me, Kit, I yearn for those old days too. When you, Steve and I could work together on a bare stage and create magic. Magic!' he said in fervent honesty.

'Don't you like doing pictures?'

'Yes. But it's so big. So corporate. So cumbersome. The old days were better. Believe me. Far, far better.'

He kissed the palm of her hand, and stared into her frank blue eyes.

She turned back to Steve. 'And your novels. I've read them all. Loved them all. Especially the one about your boyhood in Indiana. I kept saying, My Steve, my Steve, as though I owned part of you. Selfish, I know, but I like to feel that our years together helped make you the writer you are. I felt such satisfaction. As Sam Rogers used to say, I had *naches.* Dear Sam. I think of him so often. And Bertha.'

For an instant Jeff seemed tempted to tell Kit about Bertha, but Steve's eyes forbade it.

'Tell me, Steve, did it help your writing? Not just me. But working with actors. Or did you turn to novels because you were fed up with actors?'

She laughed, stimulated by a fresh thought. 'What a relief it must be, not to have actors ruining your beautiful dialogue. I'll bet no heroine in a book ever said to you, "What a terrible line. I want it rewritten!" '

'No. Now editors do that,' Steve joked back, delighted with her cheerful attitude.

All three of them laughed. Until Kit turned quite serious.

'Ross tells me you wanted to see me about a new play.'

'I don't know how much Dr Ross told you—'

Kit interrupted pleasantly, 'Only that. I thought you'd send me a script first. You know how I like to worry over a script for days before I decide. There's nothing worse for a star than finding herself trapped in a play she doesn't really like. There's that terrible conflict of loyalties. All those people in the cast depending on you, and you hating what you have to do night after night.'

She had grown quite serious now. 'Once the show opens, the author is free to leave. The director only drops back every few weeks to make sure it's playing well. But the star must go on, every performance. Whether she believes in what she's doing or not. She is exposed every night. As if she were appearing naked before all those people.

'I know you've heard rumors about me. How I failed to appear. Or refused to go on. That was why. I was trapped in plays I did not believe. In parts I could not respect. I was a prisoner of other people's ideas and feelings. I can't work that way. I won't work that way again. I'd rather not work at all!

'So these days, unless I see a script and have a long time to ponder over it, I say, No, thank you. Yes, you should have sent me a script,' she rebuked them.

Jeff looked to Steve, who took the initiative.

'Kit, darling, there isn't any script,' he admitted.

'No script?' she repeated, offended. 'But Ross said ... I don't understand.'

Studying the effect on her, Steve spoke cautiously: 'There's only an idea. And if you don't like it, there won't *be* any script.'

'Oh?' she said, obviously surprised.

'This play is for *you*, or else I won't even attempt to write it.'

'I see ...' she said, touched, and yet quite thoughtful. 'I wonder if that's fair.'

'Fair?'

'Asking me to decide whether you should write an entire play. Suppose I say no, and there was a very good play in it for some other star. I would feel terribly guilty having stopped you.'

'On the other hand,' Jeff intervened, 'what if you like it, and a perfectly wonderful play comes out of it? Wouldn't that be satisfying? To have a hand in helping to create it from the outset?'

Kit thought seriously for a moment; then her face lit up in a smile that led to laughter. 'Ah, now I understand. You two remember damn well how I used to insist on changes in the script. So you figure you might as well make my changes from the beginning. Okay! I'm game!' She turned to Steve. 'Let me hear your idea.'

She sat back in her regal pose, waiting.

'The working title of this play is *Reunion,*' Steve began.

Kit smiled at both of them. 'That seems appropriate, considering the three of us are together after so long.'

'The way it feels to me now,' Steve continued, 'this is a three-act play. Because I can sense three very strong curtains. Act One ends with our heroine deciding to search for something traumatic in her past. Act Two concerns her search for that past, ending with the question: does she dare confront that? Act Three–'

Kit interrupted, 'Of course she decides to face it. So naturally Act Three deals with her coming face to face with a situation she has been avoiding all her life.'

'Exactly,' Steve agreed, glancing toward Jeff to see if he agreed that they had passed the first hurdle successfully.

But before he could continue, Kit asked, 'Exactly what is that confrontation all about?'

Unwilling to jeopardize their effort at the outset. Steve evaded, 'It's going to be a surprise for the audience and for the character herself until the end of Act One. Let's treat it that way for the moment.'

The quizzical look on Kit's face was the first hint Steve had that she might reject the idea. He pressed on quickly before her resistance could congeal.

'Act One! The way I see your character, Kit, darling, she is successful, bright, admired and well loved by men. She is beautiful and self-assured. The audience assumes she possesses everything any woman could desire.'

'She's got to be vulnerable if they're to sympathize with her,' Kit warned.

'Of course. But that emerges later. In your first scene, I am going to have you do an act of great kindness for a person of no importance. But in doing this totally generous act you discover something distressing about yourself. Something that starts to torment you. And the exact nature of which neither the audience nor you discovers until the curtain of Act One.'

'Something in my past that disturbs me,' Kit considered.

'Right!' Steve agreed, relieved that she had begun to speak about her character in the first person. That had always been a good barometer of her involvement in any new play.

'And so I decide to search for it,' Kit said thoughtfully. She was up from her chair suddenly. She began pacing, flexing her fingers as she used to when she was impatient with herself or others in the course of creating scenes that would not come easily.

'The girl . . .' she said unexpectedly. She turned on Steve, annoyed at his slowness to respond, 'The girl for whom I do that kind and unselfish thing in the first scene . . .'

Steve and Jeff were both surprised and delighted. For Steve had not mentioned it would be a girl, but Kit had anticipated them. They both thought, This is the old Kit. She has the instinct, the drive. She is emotionally involved in the idea. In the old days, if that had happened, all other problems in a play could be solved. Once her creative ideas began to flow, she was tireless as well as highly inventive. She was no longer discussing a play; she had become part of it.

'Yes, of course, the girl,' Steve agreed.

'The young girl is my . . . my assistant . . . my protégée . . .' Kit improvised.

'Good! So she has a reason for being within your orbit.'

'Aha!' Kit enthused suddenly. 'If in the play I were an actress, a star, she could be an ingenue. Better still, just a walk-on. That would make her more sympathetic. And thus make me more sympathetic when I help her.'

'Right!' Jeff agreed. 'And she would be scared to death, working with a star for the first time.'

Suddenly Kit interrupted her pacing to turn on Steve

'How do I discover she has a problem and needs help?'

Steve had anticipated her. 'It's got to be simple. But it could be effective. Since she's a walk-on, the script could call for her to do some perfectly ordinary piece of business. Say, bring you a sweater from your dressing room. But she can't quite manage to present it to you gracefully.'

Kit picked up the thought. 'And the director' – minx-like, she turned to Jeff – 'a most intolerant bastard, shouts at her. She breaks down and starts to cry. So the director blows his top completely and terrifies her even more.'

'Right,' Steve agreed. Then, darling, what does your instinct tell you to do?'

'The only thing I can do,' she replied. 'I order that bastard director to clear stage. So it comes down to just me and the girl, onstage, in only a work light. I take her aside, put my arm around her, treat her like my own daughter . . .' Suddenly she looked to Steve. 'Do I have a daughter in the play?'

'No.'

'Good!' Kit said, very professionally. 'I make the audience sense that. I have maternal instincts, but no daughter. For the moment, this frightened girl becomes my daughter. And I coax out of her what's wrong.'

'She's pregnant,' Steve supplied.

'Of course,' Kit murmured, not permitting his interruption to intrude on her mood. 'Pregnant and terribly scared. So I promise to arrange that she'll have an abortion. Safely. Secretly. And at my expense, naturally.'

She considered the scene for a moment, then nodded, saying only, 'Good.' Then she smiled flirtatiously at them. 'Of course, the Catholics in the audience won't like that.'

'Only those Catholics in the audience who haven't had abortions,' Jeff joked back, delighted with her co-operative attitude.

Fearful lest they be trapped in disruptive diversions, Steve pressed on. 'Now, the important thing in Act One—'

But Kit interrupted. 'Steven, please, please, whatever you do in the scene with the girl, don't give me any long speeches. It would be wrong. Totally wrong. Let my emotions do it all. Give me a chance to act. Please?'

'Okay,' Steve agreed. Then after a moment of thought, he asked, 'What if after the girl has told you what the trouble is, you go to the phone and dial a number? The girl watches you, afraid to speak. And all you say is "I'm calling a doctor I know".'

'Terrific!' Kit enthused. 'Half a dozen simple words says it all. I've made the girl's problem my problem. I'm going to arrange for the abortion. And I am going to pay for it. No sordid details, no moralizing, no arguments. Understated. In excellent taste. I love it! And the audience is going to love me for helping that poor girl without any long lectures.'

'Right. But that scene has to do more,' Steve warned. 'Don't forget, the curtain of Act One is your decision to look for your past. So something in that scene with the girl has to catch your inner self, the way a thorn might prick your finger when you reach for a lovely rose. That unselfish action must leave you feeling uneasy, disturbed, in a way you can't explain, not even to yourself.'

'Perhaps,' Kit ventured thoughtfully, 'it has to do with an abortion I had as a young girl.'

The sudden memory of an earlier time was so uncomfortable for her she had to resort to joking about it. 'She had been raped by this ferocious director and become pregnant.' She tried to laugh at Jeff's discomfort, but could not quite carry it off.

To extricate her before her own sad history overcame her, Steve suggested, 'Kit, darling, don't you think that's too pat? The star had an abortion, so she sees to it the girl has an abortion. Too on the nose. It should be more subtle.'

'Of course,' Kit agreed at once. 'Subtlety would add suspense. And it would provide a surprise for the audience when it's finally revealed.'

She suddenly turned to confront them and raised both her hands, forefingers pointing upward. It was a gesture familiar to both men. It was her way of commanding silence during rehearsals when she had an important suggestion to make.

'What I think . . . what it feels like,' she said thoughtfully as she assembled all the elements in her mind, 'the thorn you mentioned before, it disturbs me. I let the audience know that by my attitude. But then I brush it off. Until late in Act One, in a scene with my lover, he too notices a change. He asks, "What's different about you today?" Of course, I deny it. I insist I love him as much today as ever. But he has reinforced my own doubt about myself. Now I *am* concerned.'

'Terrific!' Jeff enthused. 'I like it, Steve, I like it.'

But his enthusiasm was punctured by Kit's sudden question, 'Exactly what is it that troubles me? You haven't told me that yet, Steve.' Her blue eyes were penetratingly demanding.

Steve responded slowly, making his suggestion sound tentative. Because this was the moment he had feared, when it would be necessary to divulge to her the crux of the story. It was the moment Ross had warned them about. If she reacted negatively, Steve would have to withdraw the suggestion and improvise a different ending. So he proceeded cautiously.

'Well, as I first envisioned it, the connection between the girl and you is not an abortion. But the *opposite*.'

'You mean,' Kit asked, 'that the star faced that same problem early in her life and chose to have the child?'

Steve and Jeff exchanged swift, worried glances. For they both noticed that Kit no longer referred to her role in the first person. She had erected a wall between herself and the character. Before Steve could intrude, she continued.

'If she didn't have an abortion, there would have been a child,' she said gravely. 'What did she do with the infant? Give it away for adoption? Is that her problem? Or did she kill it? There have been shocking stories in the papers recently. A nun who killed her infant in a convent. And that girl in some private school. It happens. It happens,' Kit said sadly. 'No, she couldn't have killed it. Even if the audience loved me, I would hate myself. No, I couldn't play that. Besides, Steve, you did say there would be that great confrontation in the third act. If the child is dead, how could that be?'

She did not give him a chance to respond.

'No, she *had* the child,' Kit insisted, 'and gave it up for adoption. Then, later, guilt makes her decide she is going to find her little girl and make amends. Of course! It fits. My feeling about the girl in Scene One, when I treat her like a daughter.'

'That's one possibility,' Steve conceded.

Before he could suggest the other, Kit resumed command. 'Yes, it would be a terrific third act. There's only one trouble.'

'Yes?' Steve asked.

'It wouldn't work. That child would never forgive me! Never! I couldn't play that scene! Couldn't!'

She turned to them, with a finality that indicated she was bringing the meeting to a close. 'Sorry, Steve. But I have to say no.'

Her lips quivered ever so slightly. The light reflected off them, for they were red and moist, accenting her trembling.

'Tell her the other possibility!' Jeff insisted impulsively. 'It's the star herself who was deserted!' He had blurted it out to prevent her from reaching any irrevocable decision.

Both men waited, breathless. Steve would rather Jeff had introduced that dangerous suggestion more delicately. Now they could only wait for her reaction.

'If she were the one ...' Kit contemplated aloud. 'If she were the one who was deserted ...' She turned away from them, facing out toward the winter day and the snow-covered New England landscape.

Steve glared at Jeff Warrener, whose stolid face rejected any criticism.

'If she were the one who had been deserted . . .' Kit whispered again.

Steve moved to her, taking her hand, speaking softly, intensely: 'Kit, darling, listen to me, hear me out before you make up your mind.'

She did not respond. But neither did she withdraw her hand.

'Think of it this way. Our star had gone through her whole life feeling she would not have suffered such rejection if her own mother had had an abortion. So what she does in Act One is not alone for the young girl; it's also for that unborn child. To protect it from a lifetime of feeling deserted, deprived and unloved.'

Kit remained distant and unyielding.

'Now, out of that comes a determination which has always been latent, to find the mother who deserted her. So Act Two is concerned with her search. Just before the curtain of Act Two, she finally finds out where her mother is. Her problem then becomes, does she dare risk seeing her mother?'

'And I decide that I *will* see her . . .' Kit concluded slowly, unconsciously resuming in the first person, to Steve's great relief.

'Exactly! Now the audience is still on the edge of their seats waiting for Act Three. For that climactic confrontation . . .'

'. . . when I am waiting for my mother to walk onstage,' Kit upsurped his thought in a steely voice.

'It could be one hell of a scene,' Jeff encouraged.

'Yes,' Kit agreed calculatingly, 'one hell of a scene.'

'Now, in that scene,' Steve began.

But Kit broke away from him and commenced pacing again, nervously flexing her fingers, and refusing to look at them.

'Don't tell me! That scene can only play one way! I have

to let that woman know how much I have despised her ever since I can remember. I must destroy her. Steve, I want the damnedest speech, the most vitriolic attack, the most ... when that scene is done, that woman must be destroyed! Totally destroyed! I could play that scene. Yes, I could play the hell out of that!'

'Fantastic!' Jeff enthused, sincerely. 'Terrific structure, too. Act One sets the premise and you decide to find your mother. Act Two, you actually find her. Act Three, your confrontation and the resolution. Boy, is the audience going to want to see you settle that score finally.'

'They will. The way I play it, they will,' Kit said with fierce determination.

'Kit, if you agree,' Steve said, 'I can start writing at once. We could go into rehearsal in August.'

'August would fit my schedule fine!' Jeff agreed. 'What do you say, Kit? Darling?'

She did not respond at once. After a brief silence, she said, 'I'll have to think about it.'

She nodded – a slight imperious nod of her head: still the queen, the star, in complete control, promising nothing but her consideration.

'Kit,' Steve asked, 'can we come see you again tomorrow?'

'You'll have to ask Ross.'

'If he says it's all right?'

She nodded, and smiled. 'I'll be here. Where else would I be?'

Moments later, Steve Brooks and Jeff Warrener were walking down the path that led back from Carlisle Cottage to Administration.

'Well, what do you think?' Steve asked.

'You want my honest opinion?' Jeff responded. 'I think Ross is the one who's crazy. She never looked better. Never sounded better. Her mind never worked better. She was with it all the way. Her ideas and instincts were as sound as ever.

Frankly, I think Ross has panicked. He's projecting his difficulties onto her.

'If she does say yes, it would be like old times. We ought to call Sam now,' he urged.

'Let's wait till tomorrow and see what she decides,' Steve said.

Kit Lawrence stood in the window of Carlisle Cottage and watched her two former lovers walk down the path toward Administration. She was smiling. With great excitement she said to herself, I convinced them! One of the best scenes I've ever played! I wasn't too eager. I didn't say yes right away. Yet I didn't discourage them. They want me. They want me!

She brushed aside her long blond hair with the back of her hand, her palm extended outward. She laughed aloud. So loudly that the nurse came rushing into the room. Kit Lawrence's laughter terminated at once, as if her enjoyment were a secret not to be shared with anyone. She went back up to her room, repeating over and over, They want me, they want me, they want me again.

Once in her room, she tried to see the two men from her small window. She could not. Frustrated, she slipped down to her bed, sat staring at the wall. Gradually she began to tremble. Eventually, her trembling became uncontrollable.

Her elation of moments ago had turned to utter despair. Too often and too painfully she knew such times. When moments of ecstasy suddenly gave way to total terrifying panic.

What if they don't really want me, she began to fear. Maybe they didn't like me? They seemed to like me. Yet what if they were acting, just as I was acting?

What if they went away saying, She's old, she's sick, she's no longer beautiful? What if they don't love me anymore?

Trembling led to weeping. Weeping led to prayer.

She had never been religious. In childhood when people

spoke of God, she had silently hated Him for permitting all those terrible things to happen to her. Yet in more recent times, in her most depressed states, she had begun to pray. To a God she had never known.

'Dear God,' she prayed now, 'make them want me. Make them give me this one last chance. I promise to behave. I won't drink. I will show up for rehearsals. I'll be on time at every half-hour. No matter how much pain I have, I'll go on at every performance. And I will be great. Great! Just give me this one last chance.

'Because if I fail this time . . . if I fail this time . . .'

Desperate though her prayer was, she hesitated before admitting, 'If I fail this time, I will become a demented, unkempt, gray-haired old woman who nightly wanders the empty halls of some institution, crying aloud and no one to answer. Don't let that happen to me, dear God! Don't let it happen! Please!

'Please?

'Give me back their laughter, their applause, their love.

'No matter what I did before, just give me this one chance. And I swear to You, this time I will be good. This time with Steve, with Jeff, it will be different. With them it will be like the old days. For them I will be bright and shining. And I'll work so hard, so hard.

'So make them want me, dear God, make them want me.

'Do this for me this one time and I promise never to ask for anything again as long as I live . . . as long as I live . . .'

Still weeping, she went to her bare dressing table. She stared at her face in the metal mirror. She pressed the puffy areas that had begun to work under her red wet eyes. She must keep looking well for them. So they would not suspect. So they would want her for their play. So . . .

Her terror at the thought of not being wanted collided suddenly with another equally frightening thought. Her sudden realization that to do a play would mean leaving here.

More specifically, would mean leaving Ross.

In her fantasies she always called him Ross. Not by his first name, or any endearing diminutive. Just Ross. Ross might be angry with her if she decided to leave. He might accuse her of being disloyal. He might not love her anymore. And she wanted him to love her. Otherwise, to whom could she turn? Who would take her in if Ross turned her out? She must secure his permission to leave, but in such a way as to make him keep loving her.

She reached for the fragrant plastic bottle in the drawer. She was no longer permitted perfume in glass bottles. Not since her last attempt, which had involved shattering glass and trying to slash herself. She dabbed perfume on her earlobes and in the graceful crevice between her breasts. Ross had loved to kiss her there.

She would seduce him again, secure his permission to leave, and he would continue to love her. Or perhaps he would love her so much that he could not bear to let her go and would insist she remain. Perhaps that was what she would desire most of all. Never to be let go. Never.

A panic of indecision overwhelmed her. Her trembling seized her again, followed by more tears.

Always these sieges ended the same way. Within herself she would cry out, 'Someone, somewhere, love me?'

But there was never any answer.

# *Thirteen*

'How did it go?' Ross asked, when Brooks and Warrener reported to him.

'Terrific!' Steve said. 'Better than I hoped!'

'Did she exhibit any marked signs of uneasiness when you got into the guts of the story?'

'Yes, but she welcomed that climactic scene. She said, "I could play that. I could play the hell out of that." From her, that's a strong expression for the first time around. My feeling is, she'll say yes. Equally important, I now feel I can develop this into quite a play. It's got all the elements.'

'And the critics are waiting for her,' Jeff enthused. 'She's been away too long. And there's never been anyone to replace her. I think we could have a hit!'

Ross listened patiently, secretly amused that without knowing it, in a small way they shared some of the elements of Kit's sickness. All creative people did. The undue enthusiasm at the outset. The almost overpowering discouragement when difficulties arose. The abject distress at failure. Theirs was a profession that fluctuated between unjustified optimism and utter despair.

'I hope you realize that getting her to come out and do this play is not an end, only a beginning. The emotional drain of rehearsing that third act day after day might do unexpected things to her. We have no way of knowing what this is going to dredge up from her past. And of course, there is that inevitable moment. The night she has to face an audience again . . . critics again.'

'Critics have always loved her,' Jeff assured him quickly.

'Men too have always loved her,' Ross countered. 'But she

still feels the need to keep seducing them for fear they won't.'

'Doctor, it's possible we're a little naive about these things,' Steve said, 'but to us she looks terrific. Alert. Interested. Inventive. She gets the feel of a scene and builds on it. All her instincts are as sharp as they ever were. So . . .'

'So?' Ross asked, prodding Brooks to continue.

'So we can't help feeling that maybe you've been involved in her case so long that you've lost *your* objectivity.'

The look on Ross's face was one of undisguised anger.

'One thing analysts resent is laymen who try to make diagnoses without a knowledge of the techniques! But more important, without a basic knowledge of the patient involved.'

'I love her too!' Steve shot back. 'She's no stranger to me!'

'That girl is a stranger to herself. So how could you expect to know so much about her?' Ross countered.

Jeff came to Steve's defense. 'There's no better way to know someone than to work as closely with them as we do in the theater. We're like a family. One moment close, intimate, loyal. The next, enemies, hostile, venomous, with a rage to destroy. All the facets of any human being will be revealed in the course of the production of a play. So we know her. In fact, in some ways we know her better than any doctor could.'

Instead of healing the breach, or defending Steve Brooks, Jeff had only opened another front in the same conflict.

'Break one basic rule, and you must inevitably break others,' Ross said regretfully. 'I am about to, knowingly and intentionally, violate the secrecy of the analytic process. I excuse this to myself by saying that once you agreed to help me, in a sense we became colleagues.

'I caution you never to reveal what I tell you. Especially not to Kit. Because if the time ever comes when I have to treat her again, as it may, I would not want her confidence in me destroyed.'

They both nodded grimly.

'You told me that during your story conference she suggested that the actress in your play had been raped?'

'She was only joking,' Steve said.

'Did she ever tell you that *she* was raped?'

'No,' Steve said, startled.

'She was. At the age of twelve. By her grandfather.'

'That's impossible!' Jeff declared vehemently. 'She loved that old man!'

'What makes you think that love and rape are mutually inimical?'

Neither man responded.

'Or that rape cannot be invited?' Ross continued. 'That touching story she tells about running slowly so that her old grandfather could catch her? A fable. What we call a screen.

'Think about it and you will realize that her "old" grandfather really wasn't that old. When she was twelve, her mother was twenty-nine. And her grandfather only fifty-three. A man of fifty-three has not lost his sexual desires, nor his potency. A man of fifty-three certainly can run fast enough to catch a girl of twelve. So if she slowed down, it must have been for another reason. To make *sure* she was caught.

'She is a natural temptress. She does it with men. With audiences. With critics. She did it with that "old man" of a grandfather. I am not saying she wanted to be raped. But she did want to be loved. And if it meant being raped, she was willing to undergo that, just to have someone want her, love her.'

'But she always spoke so lovingly about him,' Steve protested.

'She had to,' Ross agreed. 'A screen defense. To repress her unhappy childhood.

'This hunger to invent screen defenses is a prevalent disorder in your world. It is indigenous to writers, musicians and actors.' Ross smiled ruefully, admitting, 'It is also common among psychiatrists, I must confess.

'Tell me,' he asked, 'did she ever mention to you that on the night of her school play she received flowers onstage?'

'Yes,' Steve admitted, 'from her grandfather. Don't tell me that's not true.'

'Oh, it's true,' Ross agreed, 'as far as it goes. He did send her flowers. Because she decided she wanted flowers presented to her onstage, as she had seen them do in films, where the great star always receives flowers at the end of her performance. She forced him to send them by threatening to tell the whole world that he had raped her. More than once.'

'Christ,' Jeff said softly.

'What about his giving her the last of his money to come to New York?' Steve asked.

'The same,' Ross said. 'She blackmailed him. Then, once she had what she wanted, she had to invent this loving grandfather to cover up her own deceit.

'The significant fact is not that she resorted to blackmail. But that she felt so unloved, so undeserving, that she didn't think she could get anything without blackmail.

'Take the name "Katherine," ' Ross continued. 'Her grandfather never called her Katherine. She wanted him to, but he never would. Each time they had an argument, each time she disobeyed one of his orders, he called her what he considered her to be, "You little bastard!" And she would fight back, insisting, "My name is Katherine! Call me Katherine!" But he never would. Now she insists that all her lovers call her Katherine.

'I tell you this to give you a realistic view of our problem,' Ross said. 'It won't be easy. The gains she makes one day may evaporate the next. You must be prepared for surprises. Good ones. And bad ones.

'The point is, you must not react to her attitudes. You must never be too hopeful. Or too discouraged. But, most of all, you must never be *sympathetic.* Never cross the line from empathy to sympathy. There is a vast difference. Empathy means sharing the feelings of the patient, seeing things from the patient's point of view. But sympathy involves condolence, agreement or pity. For an analyst to pity the patient or agree with her is to surrender his independent professional judgment.

'That,' he confessed sadly, 'is what I did. I found myself observing her, her beauty, her intelligence, her talent, her sensitivity, yet all blighted by her tragic background. I gave up judging her and began to justify her. I fell in love with what she could have been, not with what she is. She finally ended up manipulating me as she did audiences, and all the men who have ever loved her.

'That's what I mean to say. Don't let her manipulate you. Be tough, be realistic. It's the only way you can help her regain the one thing she can do well, function on the stage.'

It had grown dark. Ross snapped on his desk lamp.

'What's the next step?' Steve asked.

'Kit and I will have to discuss this,' Ross said. 'It will take more than one session. But we have to work it out before she is ready to give you a final answer.'

The next morning, promptly at ten twenty, Kit Lawrence arrived at Dr Ross's office for her usual hour. He knew at once that she was in one of her seductive moods. She wore tight jeans and a dark blue cotton shirt, which clung to her body. Her golden hair hung free.

She moved gracefully to the couch, assuming a pose Ross could only describe to himself as languid.

She stared up at the ceiling, toying with her hair, smiling. He noticed that she was breathing in a way deliberately intended to make him conscious of her breasts. He could also detect that she had used a heavy dose of perfume, undoubtedly applied generously to that delightful crevice between her breasts. She was obviously planning to seduce him.

She was silent for some minutes.

'Well? Did you see them?' Ross asked.

'Yes, I saw them,' she said in her provocative naughty-little-girl attitude, waiting to be coaxed. He refused to play her game. After more minutes of silence she volunteered, 'They want me to come out and do a play for them. It isn't even written yet. Because if I don't agree, Steve won't even write it.'

She half-turned on the couch to look back at him. 'You see there *are* men who still love me.'

'There will always be men who will love you, Kit,' he agreed.

'Katherine,' she corrected.

'Katherine,' Ross complied, not wishing to be diverted by that argument at the moment. He decided it was time to be firm, to make her face the problem. 'Is that why they came here, to tell you that they loved you?'

'I told you,' she snapped back, annoyed that he was frustrating her game. 'They want me to do a play for them.'

'And?' Ross urged, feeling that she would waste the hour meandering unless he held her to account.

'Aren't you interested in what kind of play? Ross?'

'Should I be?'

'I would be, if I were the doctor and a patient of mine wanted to leave me and go do a play,' she reprimanded.

'Why did you say "leave me" instead of "leave here"?'

'What's the difference? If I leave here I'll be leaving you. You're only trying to be difficult today, Ross. You're trying to make believe we don't love each other. But we do. Don't we, Ross? Don't we?'

'We've been through that,' he said firmly. 'From now on I will only be your doctor. Unless you'd rather have someone else. There are three other doctors here. All three very good. Dr Prendergast is an excellent man.'

'Not Prendergast,' she toyed. 'Kendall. He's young. Nice-looking. He smiles at me every time we pass. He'd love to get his hands on me,' she teased. 'I'll bet you told him about me. Is that what you're doing, Ross? Passing me around? To the other doctors? Because you're tired of me? Is it? Well, maybe I'd like that. I'm getting a little tired of you!'

She twisted about, turning to stare up at him, her blue eyes taunting him.

'Are you?' he asked.

'Yes. And tired of your wife, too. I can tell that she knows about us. And she hates me. She'd like nothing better than to see me leave here.'

'You think she's jealous of you?' Ross asked.

'She ought to be. That mousy little dark-haired woman. She could never be me. Or make love like I do!' she asserted, desperately needing to feel superior.

But her insecurity forced her to resort to a softer, indecisive tone as she begged for reassurance. 'Does she, Ross? Does she make love like I do? Does she put perfume between her breasts? And are they as lovely as mine? Are they?' she begged, seeking reassurance.

Ross deliberately refrained from answering. She had been writhing on the couch in imitation of her movements during sex, as if she were again experiencing their love-making. Finally she came to rest. After a silence of some minutes, she said, 'You want me to go! You don't care if I ever get well. You don't even want to screw me anymore. You don't care if any other man does. Or all other men do. You wouldn't be jealous. I could screw the whole world and you wouldn't be jealous! Would you! Would you?'

She suddenly leaped up from the couch and turned to defy him. 'I am going to that door and if you don't stop me I'll keep walking. You'll never see me again! Never. Until they bring you in to identify my body. Then you'll be sorry. But it'll be too late. So I'm going!'

When he refused to respond, she started for the door. Her

first steps were brisk and aggressive. But as she approached the door, she faltered, taking smaller, slower strides.

'I'm going,' she threatened, like a willful child hoping to be called back.

She was at the door. She grasped the knob. Without looking back she said, 'It's your last chance to call me back!' Then softly, entreating, 'Call me back? Please? Ross? Call me . . .' She did not finish, for she was in tears and unable to speak.

She stood at the door, facing away from him. Finally he said softly, 'Kit.'

'Yes?' she managed.

'Would you like to come back?'

She nodded, turned back, hiding her eyes. She went to the couch and lay down. She buried her face in her hands and wept for a time. She reached backward. He passed the box of tissues to her. She blew her nose, dried her eyes, gasped to recover. 'I must be a mess.'

'Do you feel like a mess?'

'Uh-huh.'

'Why?'

'You want to be rid of me, so I want to be a mess.'

'No one can make you go. You have to come to that conclusion by yourself. But if I thought it wasn't right I would have advised against it. So that must mean I think you can do it,' Ross said sincerely.

'I could be magnificent in that part,' she said with fervor.

'What kind of part?' he asked, to bring her face to face with the reality she would be dealing with if she undertook the play.

She started describing it as if recounting a play she had just seen. But as she progressed, she became deeply involved, improvising details and moments that she, Steve and Jeff had never discussed. The entire character and situation came alive in her mind. She had begun to live it.

Ross watched her as she lay on the couch, active, animated, using her hands, her eyes, her entire body in her performance. Once she was separated from herself and her past, once she became someone else, she was an incomparable woman.

Only when she approached the final scene, the climactic confrontation with the mother, did her memory become hazy and her ingenuity begin to flag. She ended by saying, 'Steve has the end in mind. We didn't talk about it much.'

Ross was keenly aware of her evasion but did not press the point.

'It does sound very interesting.'

'Interesting!' Kit scoffed, with her taunting laugh. 'When I play it, it'll be fascinating! I'll be magnificent! I can be when I want to. And this time I want to!'

She turned again to face him, now all beaming and happy. 'Will you come to see me?'

'Kit, this can't be something you do to please me. It must be something you do because you want to do it. *Do* you?'

She became pensive, sliding down onto the couch again.

'Kit?'

'Come to see me,' she pleaded. 'I'll be so good. So good, just for you.'

'Be good for Kit,' he urged. 'Good for Kit is all you ever have to be.'

The hour had been over for some time. Divorcing himself from his personal involvement as much as possible, Ross had assessed the risks, Kit's expectations, the possible crises and disappointments. He felt sure now that her only possible salvation lay in the play.

He would meet with Brooks and Warrener and tell them to proceed.

# *Fourteen*

Steve Brooks had written a rough draft and sent it on to both Kit and Jeff Warrener. It had passed back and forth among them numerous times for rewrites in accord with her suggestions. At the end of five months it was completed to all their satisfactions.

Jeff had proved right. The original structure was sound, solid. Act One set up the premise and the heroine's desire to search for her past. Act Two carried forward with the search, and led dramatically and inexorably to the climactic confrontation of deserted daughter versus penitent mother in Act Three.

Kit was eminently pleased with the speeches Steve had written for her in the final scene, in which she devastated her despised mother.

When the script was done, Sam Rogers received a copy and called Steve that very night.

'I'll do it! I'll do it!' he exclaimed to Steve in a strange whisper. Steve had no way of knowing that Sam was calling from Bertha's bedside in the hospital.

Now it was two months later. Steve, Sam and Jeff were seated in the rear of Sam Rogers' Cadillac limousine as the car sped north toward Silvermine along the Merritt Parkway past the lush green of a summer in which rain had been plentiful. Sam sat between them, thoughtful and silent. Both Steve and Jeff correctly assumed Sam was thinking of Bertha, whom he had recently buried after a long and ravaging battle with cancer. Self-conscious about his sad introspection, Sam forced himself to assume a more cheerful attitude. 'Jeff, I hear your picture is cleaning up at the box office.'

'A smash! Not exactly a classic in artistic terms, but a box-office hit. And these days, that's all anybody is asking,' Jeff said, trying to maintain an air of modesty.

'Never apologize for making money, *boychik*.' Sam had a tendency to resort to Yiddishisms out of respect for the humble surroundings from which he had risen. 'If it wasn't for the money we've all made, who could afford this journey we're taking now?'

It suddenly occurred to Steve, 'Sam, you're not going to finance this whole production myself?'

'When I tell Kit *I* want to produce her play, I want to mean it! Down to the last dollar.'

'Even with a unit set, it'll cost two hundred thousand minimum,' Steve warned. 'And if we run into trouble, a hell of a lot more.'

'So it'll cost more,' Sam said, disposing of the possibility lightly. 'I'll tell you one thing I would like. If you two boys don't mind.'

If they all lived until Jeff was sixty-seven and Steve sixty-five, Sam Rogers would still call them 'boys.'

'I don't know if it's ever been done before. But I would like on a single page in the playbill a simple note reading that "This play is dedicated to Bertha Rogers." Would you mind, Steve?'

'No, of course not.'

'Believe me, you all owe it to her. Many was the time I didn't want to go into a show and it was Bertha who insisted, "Do it, Sam. So you'll lose a few hundred thousand more. So I'll have one less sable coat." I would say, "But the play needs work." Bertha would say, "Then give it work." I would ask, "Why this play?" And she would say, more times than I can count, "I like that young writer. He's good. He's honest. Give him his chance." She once said that about you, Steve.

Other times she would say, "I saw a girl in a little Off Broadway piece. She has marvelous potential. She deserves to be seen. Give her the chance."

'I have the reputation for taking more chances with new talent than any other producer on Broadway. But it was always Bertha. She was the one who nudged me, forced me, many times against my own judgment.'

He reached into his inner pocket for a cigar, bit off the end, but did not light it.

'The last thing Bertha ever read was your finished draft of this play, Steve. Actually, I had to read it to her. She lay there, eyes closed, and listened. When I was done, she said, "Do it, Sam. Do it. It's beautiful." Then she went to sleep. They give them so damn much dope in those hospitals.'

He exhaled wearily before saying, 'So for Bertha's sake too, I want to finance this whole production myself.'

They had turned off the Merritt Parkway and were on the last leg toward Hartford.

Jeff said, 'Sam, I ran into Ben Block of the Shubert office right after I got in yesterday.'

'Oh? How is Ben?'

'Looked fine,' Jeff said. 'He said he'd read Steve's script. And loved it.'

'Oh?' Sam Rogers said. 'That's nice.'

'But he said the Shuberts wouldn't put a dollar in any show that starred Kit Lawrence,' Jeff said pointedly. 'He said no one on the street would risk a nickel, not with her reputation for signing to do a show, then not showing up.'

'Ben said that?' Sam asked casually, trying to minimize the import of it.

'He said you were crazy to put up all the money.'

'I've been crazy before.' Sam chuckled.

'Is it true, Sam?' Steve asked. 'Nobody wants to put a nickel into this production?'

'What difference does it make?' Sam scoffed, irritated that his strategy had become so transparent. '*I* want to see Kit

Lawrence on Broadway. And I am willing to pay for the privilege! So who's going to stop me?'

Eventually he admitted self-consciously, 'Steve, what I said about Bertha loving your play, believe me, that part is true. I'm sorry she won't be there to see Kit. Bertha, Bertha . . .' He shook his head sadly. It was as if she died anew each time he mentioned her name.

They stopped for gas up before reaching Silvermine. Sam excused himself and went to the rest room. While he was gone, Jeff said hastily to Steve, 'Ben Block also said something else yesterday. Real estate in New York has gone to hell. The constant threat of the city going bankrupt did tremendous damage. Sam has taken some big losses lately. That new building up on Seventh Avenue and Fifty-third Street, across from the Americana. That was Sam's. The banks took it over a few months ago.'

'You mean he really can't afford to risk a quarter of a million,' Steve said.

'Exactly!'

'Then maybe we ought to quit now,' Steve said, but immediately abandoned the idea. 'We can't. There's Kit. We have to think of Kit.'

Jeff added sadly, 'And Sam. We have to consider his pride.'

'God, Jeff, what the hell are we into?'

'That's what I've been asking myself ever since yesterday,' Jeff said.

At the same time that Sam Rogers' limousine was pulling out of the gas station and heading for Silvermine, Kit Lawrence was having her last session with Dr Alvin Ross. She had come to his office attired differently than on other days. Today no simple skirt and sweater, no slacks and shirt. Today a dress. A bright print of reds and yellows, to complement her blond hair, which she had labored over since early morning. In place of her usual makeup, she had done a meticulous job – face, lips, eyes. She was radiant.

Ross received her as he always did, with a pleasant 'Good morning, Kit.'

She eyed him saucily, inviting him to comment on her appearance, or daring him to. When he did not, she mimicked, 'Significant! Highly significant.' She laughed at her own joke. 'Yes, Ross, it is significant that the patient appears looking so different today but the doctor does not remark on it. Why? Today you lie down, and I will sit in that damn chair.'

'If you'd rather not lie down and wrinkle your new dress, you may sit.'

Now as serious as he, she asked, 'Today, may I look at you?'

'Whatever makes you feel most comfortable.'

She sat in a chair across from him. The teasing minxlike quality had gone out of her eyes. She did not smile. She seemed to shudder slightly before she said, 'It's the last time, isn't it? The last time we'll be seeing each other.'

'It doesn't have to be. The fact that I was your doctor doesn't mean we have to part as strangers or enemies. Or do you still resent my letting you go? I thought we'd worked that out, didn't you?'

'Yes,' she said, becoming plaintive. 'Until last night.'

'What happened last night?'

'I . . . I . . .' she began, but faltered. She had to regroup her thoughts before admitting, 'Last night, lying in bed, I began to panic. I broke into a sweat. I started to tremble. Suddenly I didn't want to leave. I wanted to remain here with you. Even if you won't make love to me, I need you.'

She began to weep. Her eye makeup started to run.

He extended the box of tissues. But she brushed away her tears with the back of her hand.

'And then?' Ross asked gently.

'I tried to fall asleep. Eventually I did. In the morning I

looked at myself in the mirror. At my eyes. And I knew I needed to do something to them. So I made them up. Now I've ruined them all over again. Oh, Ross, Ross, what's going to happen to me? What am I going to do?'

'Make up your eyes again to greet them when they come to pick you up.'

'I mean what am I going to do if I get an anxiety attack during rehearsal? Or when I have to go on, for the first time?'

'You won't be alone. There's Steve Brooks. Jeff Warrener. And Mr Rogers. And, if necessary, there's always me. The fact that you're no longer here doesn't mean I've deserted you. Feel free to call. Any hour of day or night. Remember that.'

She nodded, still making the gesture of brushing back tears, though her eyes were dry now.

'I made up some things to say to you this morning. Last night, before the panic set in, I was rehearsing them.'

'What sort of things?'

'I was going to apologize to you. For when I accused you of letting me leave because you wanted to get rid of me.'

'That's a perfectly understandable reaction. I don't blame you.'

'I wish you would,' she suddenly insisted.

'Why?'

'Because then I'd know you cared. This way, you make it sound trivial. You make *me* sound trivial. And I want to be important to you. Am I?'

'Every patient is important,' Ross said.

'But I want to be your most important patient,' she insisted. 'I want to know that of all your patients you'll remember me. Always. Tell me that.'

'I'll always remember you, Kit. You know that.' And he knew the truth of it even more than she.

'I had to hear you say it.' She seemed content for the moment. Then she asked, 'You'll come to see me in the play?'

'Of course.'

'When?' She tried to pin him down.

'Either Boston or New York,' he promised. 'It will depend on how crowded my schedule is.'

'New York!' she said fervently. 'Come to New York! For my opening! Promise!'

'I can't promise, Kit. If I have an emergency, I couldn't leave the patient.'

'Not even for me?' she asked, threatening tears again.

'Not any more than I'd leave you if you needed me,' Ross corrected.

'Then at least say you'll *try* to come to my opening,' she pleaded.

'I promise you, if it is humanly possible, I will be there.'

She sighed in relief. Then asked, 'Is my time up?'

'You still have a few minutes.'

'What shall we talk about?'

'Whatever you wish.'

'Last night I had so many things to say. Now I can't think of any of them,' she said, with a laugh that was intended to be light and amused, but sounded pathetic. 'I ought to go. There's nothing worse than an untidy exit.'

'Kit, is there something you want to say but are afraid to?' Ross asked.

She hesitated; her lip quivered. She had to forcibly gain control of it before she was able to say, 'I'm sorry I'm not healthy and strong so you could love me, really love me. Then I would be safe and happy for the rest of my life! I could have been so good for you, Ross, if I were healthy. So good.'

She turned away, self-conscious.

'Kit, I'm touched. Very touched. It took a great deal of courage to say it. That's good. A sign that you're much better. I have every confidence you'll see this play through. And you'll be excellent.'

She turned back to face him, daring to smile.

'Now your time *is* up,' he said gently.

'Would you do one thing for me?' she asked.

'What?'

'Kiss me?'

'You know that's not advisable.'

'Don't make me beg you. Just kiss me. Is it too much to ask?'

He contemplated that for a moment, then kissed her on the cheek. She clung to him briefly but desperately, finally relinquishing him, unwillingly. But of her own accord.

'Remember what I said: if ever you need me, call.'

She nodded. She raised her face to him; tears were threatening again. He cautioned, 'They'll be here any moment. Look good for them. Look your very best!'

She smiled through her tears and nodded.

At that moment the big black Cadillac limousine approached the gates of Silvermine. It pulled up at the Administration Building. Rogers looked around the grounds and murmured, 'Nice place. Good acreage. Turn this into a development, it could be worth a few million.'

They filed into the building, asked to see Dr Ross and were told to wait. They had just been seated when they heard a bright, slightly husky voice call out, 'Sam! You old bastard!'

It was Kit. She came racing down the hall, threw her arms around Sam Rogers and kissed him full on the lips.

'Sam, Sam, Sam,' she kept saying with enormous delight, in great contrast to the pathetic waif she had been only minutes before in Ross's office.

Sam held her by the arms so he could look into her face. No tears there now. Her eye makeup had been repaired, her lips shiny and so red, her skin smooth and glowing.

'Darling, you look marvelous!' Sam enthused. 'Better than ever!' He stood aside to display her to Steve and Jeff. 'How do you like my girl? Bertha used to be jealous of you,' he lied. 'She used to say to me, "Sam, if you leave me for that girl I'll sue you for every cent you have." '

Sam laughed heartily for the first time since Bertha had died.

Steve Brooks and Jeff Warrener watched, exchanging glances that asked, Which of them is giving the better performance?

In the moments that he held her in his fatherly embrace, Sam Rogers had sensed the difference in her. Her body was slender enough, lithe enough, to be the young Kit Lawrence. She embraced him with the same warmth and eagerness. Her face against his was soft. She was even wearing the same scent. In almost all ways she was the Kit Lawrence he had gloried in.

Yet in some indefinable way she was quite different. In a flush of solicitude he excused her, saying to himself, Of course she is different; she should be after all she has gone through: alcoholism, obesity, several attempts at self-destruction. Even her treatment, for which he had paid–even that must have left scars.

Then was a sudden stab of doubt in Sam Rogers' mind. Did he dare risk it with this girl? It was no longer the old days, when a quarter of a million was merely a tax write-off. Now there was no income to write it off against. He was living on capital. Limited capital. The limousine, to which he had become so accustomed that it seemed an appurtenance to his own body, even that would have to go one day soon. The proud license plate SIR, for Samuel Irving Rogers, would have to be retired forever.

He banished all such discouraging thoughts by resolving, To save a life you take any risk you have to. This is not another production, this is a venture in salvation. Besides, Bertha would have insisted.

On their way back to New York they talked in a jumble of overlapping conversation, as if fearful that even a single moment of silence might precipitate a crisis. They talked about the play in brief, disconnected snatches.

Kit's costumes. Who were the best candidates for the role of her mother. There had been a nibble from the Coast on the screen rights. The set, who should design it. The pre-production tour. Actors for the male lead. The right Broadway house. Emil Bernstein would handle publicity.

The only thing not permitted was a moment of silence. The three men had become manic in their uneasiness at being alone with her in the first hour after her release.

Kit remained aware and sensitive throughout. She pitied their frantic efforts.

Poor Steve; poor Jeff; poor, poor Sam, she thought – knocking themselves out to keep a crazy lady interested, involved, amused, as if a brief silence might cause her to go berserk.

The harder they tried, the more obvious it became. Until she reproached herself, Why am I such a burden to everyone? Why are they so worried about me?

And instead of being pleased that they care, why do I feel so guilty?

After an hour of frantic conversation, as if winded by their efforts, the men fell into an awkward silence.

Sympathetic as she had been to their attempts, once she was no longer the center of conversation, she felt driven to regain their concern.

So, very softly, yet provocatively, she announced, 'I know where I'm going to live in New York.'

Sam asked, 'How could you? It was supposed to be a surprise. Which one of you told her?' he demanded, pretending anger.

'No one told me,' she teased. 'Because no one knows.'

'*I* know,' Sam insisted. 'You are moving into Suite Fourteen oh Four at the Plaza. I selected it myself. I know the manager.'

'No, Sam,' Kit said quite self-assuredly, 'I'm going to stay at The Dorm.'

'The Dorm?' Sam asked, aghast. 'That's for beginners, not stars!'

'The Dorm,' Kit persisted, smiling.

Steve tried to glance across her at Sam, but could not manage it without betraying himself.

Sam had had it all worked out so neatly. The Plaza. Where, in shifts, they could be with her when she ran into those periods of stress that were bound to occur in the course of rehearsals.

They had each scheduled their time so that her evenings would be completely taken up with them and with the play. Sam had even arranged for the assistant stage manager, a girl, to cue her so that she could learn her lines. They had such meticulous plans, all of which would be defeated if she lived at The Dorm, where she would be free from their surveillance. She was more likely to slip out at any time of night and find a liquor store if she wished. There would be no hotel staff to check up on her. She might spend the night away with some man, any man, and fall into old patterns.

She must not be allowed to live at The Dorm.

They were silent the rest of the way. Kit sat smug and smiling. She had created exactly the tense concern she intended. She was not going to surrender herself to three guardians. She would be free and on her own.

'It's going to be very embarrassing,' Sam Rogers lamented, 'after the way I insisted to the manager that I would not accept any suite except Fourteen oh Four. Right on the corner, facing both the plaza and the Park, looking north with the biggest garden in the world spread before you. Yes, very embarrassing.'

'You know, New York's changed,' Jeff picked it up. 'You can't walk around safely at night. When I walk up Eighth Avenue I keep looking back. And where The Dorm is located, west of Eighth, on that dark street, Kit – you really ought to reconsider!'

Steve Brooks glanced at her. She had that small satisfied smile on her face that showed she enjoyed being the subject of everyone's deep concern. She had bent them to her willful perverse design. Had she changed very much, after all? Or was she determined to follow old patterns, old ruses, old stratagems? Was that the Kit on whom they had all decided to risk so much?

The limousine was speeding down the West Side Highway when Sam pleaded, 'At least take a look at the place. You might like it. Kit? Darling?'

She smiled. 'Well,' she acquiesced, teasing, 'there's no harm in taking a look.'

The manager greeted them extravagantly as they entered the Central Park side of the Plaza. He escorted them to the elevator, at the same time dispatching a bellman to fetch Miss Lawrence's luggage. He snapped his fingers in the direction of the registration desk. A young woman came racing to his side with the key.

He unlocked the door of 1404, threw it open and invited them into the sunlit suite. The draperies had been pulled back, presenting a magnificent view of Central Park in full early-fall green. With a gracious flourish he invited Kit in. She entered, made a wide and graceful circle, holding out her arms and calling out, 'It's magnificent! So bright. So cheerful. It must be a federal crime to be depressed in a place like this.' She laughed – a gay, uninhibited laugh that sounded genuine and was.

Sam, Steve and Jeff stared at each other, greatly relieved. Sam's relief lasted only a moment. For he spotted the usual VIP arrangement on one table. A vase of red roses. A large bowl of fresh, oversized fruit. And the inevitable three bottles: Scotch, bourbon, vodka. Someone had ignored his express instruction 'No liquor!'

'Don't you want to see your room, darling?' Sam asked, 'Show her the bedroom, Steve!' he commanded, gently shoving Steve toward her like an anxious father trying to encourage a match.

Steve took her hand and led her to the bedroom while in an angry whisper Sam ordered, 'Get that liquor out of here!' The manager started to move, but Sam countermanded, 'Not now. While we're down to lunch!'

'Of course. Sorry, Mr Rogers, terribly sorry.'

They came out of the bedroom, Kit and Steve, she flushed as a young bride.

'Well?' Rogers asked.

'I like it, Sam. I love it.'

'Then you'll stay?'

'I don't deserve it, but I'll stay,' she said, crossing to kiss him.

'*Wunderbar!*' He beamed. 'Now where do you want to have lunch? Twenty-one? The Edwardian Room? The Oak Room? You know they permit ladies in the Oak Room for lunch now.'

Smiling, Kit said, 'Equality may be all right for Women's Libbers. I won't settle for anything less than superiority.'

'So where? Sardi's?' Sam suggested.

'Not Sardi's. Not till rehearsals start. But I know exactly where!'

'Name it and it's yours,' Sam promised extravagantly.

'There's a place right across the street,' she teased.

'The Pierre?' Sam asked.

'A little place. In the park. One of those hot dog carts with a big yellow umbrella. For months I've been dreaming of getting one of those hot dogs loaded with mustard, sauerkraut and onions.'

'*And* onions?' Jeff asked, smiling.

'*And* onions,' she repeated, laughing. 'Please? For me?'

She was so excited none of them could say no to her, about

anything. So glad were they to see sparks of the young Kit Lawrence again.

Sam personally supervised the preparation of her hot dog. He insisted on just the right amount of mustard, sauerkraut and onions. He wrapped it tenderly in a napkin, as if he were handling caviar. He presented it to her with a flourish, as he chuckled to Steve and Jeff, 'You bastards, get your own.'

They found a green wooden bench under a large maple tree. Three of them devoured hot dogs; only Sam did not. The travails of the last year had given him a stomach condition which prohibited all spicy food. So he busied himself tending Kit. Like a mother he hovered over her, concerned when the drippings from the hot dog threatened to stain her colorful dress. He brought her a can of sugar-free cola to wash down the spicy repast. And he sat on the end of the bench and beamed as she ate.

They walked through the zoo. Some people recognized her and sent children over to ask for her autograph. She signed slips of paper, even napkins. One boy brought over a Polaroid shot of her taken a minute before. She liked it and signed it for him.

They leaned against the rail of the seal pond, watching those sleek, shiny-coated mammals dive into the water, disappear, only to reappear moments later on their backs, playing to the crowd much as actors do.

Sam fetched them ice cream cones from the kiosk nearby. He bought one for himself, too. Bland vanilla ice cream was good for him, his gastroenterologist said. Bad for him, his cardiologist said. The gastroenterologist won. Today, he was too busy to worry about his cholesterol count.

When they returned to 1404, the room had been slightly rearranged. The flowers were on an end table near the Fifth Avenue window. The bowl of fruit was centered on the table before the Park window. The three bottles of liquor were gone.

# Part 4

# *Fifteen*

First rehearsals are always a time of great beginnings, great hopes, great love.

The first rehearsal of *Reunion* was different in only one respect. There was an even greater feeling of excitement, since it marked the first time in years that Kit Lawrence was to star in a Broadway play.

So the cast arrived earlier than the appointed ten o'clock. There were greetings, handshakes, embraces and much kissing.

Sam Rogers had thoughtfully provided a huge tray of Danish pastry and a large urn of freshly brewed coffee. Jeff Warrener went from actor to actor assuring each of them how delighted he was to have them in the company. Steve Brooks chatted with one of the older actors who had been in his first play. They were catching up on old times, filling one another in on the intervening years.

First rehearsals are not only nostalgic times, but in themselves provide the food for future nostalgia. Actors, authors, producers, directors have indelible memories of those singular and crucial days.

This one was to prove more memorable.

For Kit Lawrence did not arrive at ten o'clock. Nor by quarter after.

To avoid creating any panic among the cast, neither Jeff nor Steve drew attention to it. They tried to maintain an air of unconcerned calm, continuing to recount stories of other first rehearsals, other openings. But each in his turn slipped away from the cast and met with an intensely concerned Sam Rogers, offstage and up the dark aisle.

'Christ, Sam! Why didn't you pick her up in your car?' Jeff demanded in a hoarse whisper.

'I offered, I insisted,' Sam explained. 'But she said no, she wanted to come on her own. I thought it would be a good way to restore her confidence. Let her make an entrance on her own. It would be good for her and everyone!'

'Then send the car now! We can't wait, not without demoralizing the rest of the cast!'

Sam stared at Jeff, his eyes not only betraying concern, but misting up in a way that suggested that he was on the verge of tears.

'Sam?' Jeff demanded, gripping the older man's arms.

Sam confessed, 'My chauffeur just came back. She's not there. She left the hotel early. Very early. That's all they know.'

'Then we've got to go out and look for her!' Jeff insisted.

'Look? Where?' Sam pleaded.

Steve joined them and received the news. He was stunned. 'She was coming along so well. She was great all through the casting. I thought she was getting stronger every day. Damn it, I'm going to find her!'

'Where?' Sam demanded. 'How?'

'I'll find her!' Steve said, racing up the aisle toward the front doors.

Steve Brooks ran from the theater and never stopped running. He ran across to Sardi's, where they were just preparing to open for the day. He did not want to ask, so he stared in the window at the bar. She was not there. Even the bartender was not there yet.

He raced down the block to Eighth Avenue to Downey's. He found one man at the bar, an alcoholic who needed that first drink to get him started in the morning. But no sign of Kit. He raced up Eighth, turned the corner and headed for Joe Allen's, the next most likely place she might be. But Allen's had not even opened yet. He stared through the window into the dark cellar club. No sign of life.

There was another place in this part of town. The Dorm. Perhaps in a moment of terror she had reverted to an old haunt, where she felt more secure. He raced toward the old converted building. He leaped up the few steps and into the lobby. Breathless, he demanded of the receptionist. 'Is she here? Have you seen her?'

'Who?'

'Kit Lawrence, of course!' he exploded impatiently.

He stood on the steps of The Dorm, wondering where to search next.

He could feel his damp shirt sticking to his back. The chill fall air reminded him that he had not even paused to put on his jacket. But he did not dare go back for it. That would demand explanations which he could not give.

He tried to reason calmly for a moment: if Kit had left the Plaza and started for the theater, where could she have gone – what bar could have diverted her on the way?

He raced toward Seventh Avenue, turned north along that street, which had become a realm of topless bars in recent years. They seemed to be open twenty-four hours a day. Knowing her as he did, the sickening thought occurred to him that she might have wandered into such a bar. And if she did, she might not only have had several drinks; she might have gotten up on the bar and danced topless, or even totally nude. He raced from one bar to the next, bursting in, searching, brushing aside bouncers, finding no sign of Kit.

He had reached Fifty-fifth and Seventh, breathing hard and sweating profusely. There was one place yet to look. He set out in a determined run for the Plaza.

He asked at the desk. No one had seen her in the last hour. He went up to her suite, listened at her door, as he had done on previous stressful occasions. He heard nothing. He prevailed on the cleaning woman to open the door. There were no signs of disarray. No empty bottles. All Kit's things were there. Her robe was still fragrant from freshly used bath oil. Her bed was rumpled and slept in. It had neither the odor nor the look of any sexual activity. Everything was in order.

Only Kit was missing.

Perhaps, he thought, unable to finally face the challenge of a new play and a new production, especially one in which the story was so close to her own life, she had, at the last moment, been unable to go through with it and taken a train to Connecticut, back to Silvermine.

He slumped down on the edge of her fragrant bed, picked up the phone and gave the operator Ross's number. He insisted on talking to the doctor though he was in a session with a patient.

Steve could sense the turmoil in Ross's voice even though he was trying to maintain an air of professional calm in the presence of a patient.

'Yes, what is it, Brooks?' Ross asked, trying to sound perfunctory and crisp.

Steve explained.

A whispered, tormented 'Oh, God!' escaped Ross. 'You searched everywhere?'

'Everywhere I could think of,' Steve said. 'She hasn't been in touch with you, has she?'

'Not in days,' Ross said.

'Then I don't know, I just don't know,' Steve said hopelessly.

'Look, Brooks, report to me as soon as you find out anything. If she needs me I'll come down at once!' Ross assured him. Then, fearing he might have alarmed his present patient, he concluded by saying, 'I'm quite sure she is fine. Fine!' But his attempt at achieving an appearance of calm did not mislead Steve Brooks.

It was almost eleven when Steve Brooks returned to the theater. He was considering how best to phrase his failure so as not to alarm the cast. And, emotionally, he cherished the one last hope, that she had arrived at the theater while he was gone. That had happened in the past; times when she seemed to be missing, he would go out searching for her only to discover that she had returned to the apartment during his absence and the reason she had seemed to be missing at all was as harmless as that she had stopped off at the Museum of Modern Art to see some new exhibit which had escaped his attention.

He tried to assure himself it would be like that now when he entered the theater. She would be there. Bright, and lovely, and effervescent as she used to be at first readings in the early days.

But he could tell when he came through the wings onto the dimly lit stage that Kit had not arrived. For the excitement and anticipation that had brightened the cast before ten o'clock was gone now. Cold coffee had reduced the plastic cups to soggy messes. Half-eaten Danish had been tossed into the waste can. The hopes, the sense of great beginnings had slowly been reduced to fear and foreboding.

As Steve came onstage, he almost collided with Jeff and an actor who had taken the director aside to consult him in confidence.

'So you see, Jeff, there's still a chance I can get that part in the other production. Just give me the word, release me and I'll call my agent. It might not be too late,' the actor pleaded. 'You know how it is in New York these days, Jeff. Jobs are scarce. And that's a good part.'

'Give me another hour,' Jeff pleaded.

'Jeff, who are we kidding?' the actor asked. 'She's done it before. Too many times. Let me call my agent. Please? Jeff, I've got a pregnant wife! I need the work!' the young man pleaded intensely, yet trying to keep his voice down all the while.

Jeff saw Steve enter. Jeff's eyes asked the questions. Steve's answered.

Jeff said, 'Okay, make your call.'

'Thanks, Jeff, thanks,' the actor said, racing offstage to the pay phone at the stage door.

Jeff asked, 'No sign?'

'Nothing,' Steve said. 'Where's Sam?'

'Sitting in the back of the house. Crying.'

'Oh, no,' Steve said, knowing exactly how Sam felt and almost reduced to tears himself. Poor Sam, Steve thought. This is all he needs now. Losing Bertha, now losing Kit, who was to him his only child, and his only tie with the past.

Steve came down the steps into the house and started up the aisle to console Sam when he was arrested by a lilting, slightly husky voice that called from the wings, 'Well, good morning, everybody!'

Steve turned and stared. There she was. Bright, fresh, sober, smiling, radiant, her blond hair tied back in crimson ribbons. Far from what he had feared, she looked almost as young and fresh as the girl she was supposed to befriend in that first scene.

With no sign of guilt at being late, no attempt to apologize, Kit Lawrence opened her large carryall, took out her script, then proceeded to produce one after another a succession of small packages, colorfully wrapped in gay gift paper and ribbons.

She went from one member of the cast to another and handed each a box. She kissed them, male and female. She saved her last gift for Maria Patrick, the character woman whom Jeff had carefully selected to play Kit's mother in the crucial climactic scene. Jeff had chosen her not only for her physical rightness for the part and her quality, but most especially for her long theatrical experience. No matter what unexpected emergency Kit might precipitate onstage during a performance, Maria had the ability to cope with it.

When Kit reached Maria, she greeted her playfully, 'Oh, Ma*ma*! How nice to see you, after all these years.'

The entire company joined her in laughter, for it played off the scene in the third act between Kit and Maria. Kit handed Maria a gift that was larger than the others and kissed her on the cheek, embracing her warmly. Then Kit turned to explain to the company at large.

'Actors are always exchanging gifts on opening night, by which time they've all grown to hate each other.' She laughed. 'Well, I wanted to do it while we all still love each other.'

Whatever fears or secret accusations everyone in the cast had entertained about her, all were dispelled by her gracious and thoughtful gesture.

She turned to Jeff and Steve. 'Sorry I'm a bit late, but I had to pick these up and see they were properly wrapped. Then I walked down.'

Relieved at her bright and loving attitude, Jeff and Steve were quite willing to overlook her flagrant breach of discipline. Sam Rogers came up on stage, kissed her and said with great warmth and relief, 'Welcome, darling, to what is going to be a big, big hit!'

'Sam, darling!' she responded; then she kissed him and held him close as she said, 'I hope I didn't upset you by being late.'

'As long as you're here,' Sam said. 'That's all that matters. All that matters!' His eyes shone in teary relief. He pressed Kit's hand against his cheek and repeated, 'All that matters.'

Steve Brooks held her for an instant when she bestowed her morning kiss on him.

'You scared the hell out of me,' he confided.

'I had to,' she whispered back.

'Why?'

'Because,' she confessed, 'I knew what they would be saying about me today. Even if I showed up on time. They'd be watching me, judging me. Trying to discover if I'm still the crazy lady. So I said, I'll put an end to all the rumors and the gossip.'

All Steve's anger, fear and frustration dissolved at once, as he realized that with her unerring sense of the theatrical, she had very correctly analyzed her fellow actors, dealt with their fears and criticisms and instilled in them, instead of suspicion, a love and respect for her that was so essential from the start of this particular production.

Steve slipped out to the manager's office to call Ross and report.

Ross was tremendously relieved, and made a comment that stayed with Steve a long time: 'Amazing instincts, that girl. She would have made an excellent analyst. If she weren't such a complex patient.'

All their fears having been put to rest, Jeff brought his cast to the rehearsal table. 'Let's get going! First read-through. No stopping for any reason. I want to get a sense of how it plays and how it times.'

He read the scene-setting description and the action that took place once the curtain went up, leading the cast into their lines in the first scene.

They had reached the moment for Kit's entrance. Everyone at the table turned to her. But Kit did not speak her lines. Puzzled, they all waited, breathless and concerned. Still, no line from Kit.

Then, as if emerging from a trance, Kit seemed to become aware of them. Still she did not speak, but tilted her head slightly as if listening thoughtfully to some distant voice. Jeff glanced nervously to his assistant – an order to stop her timing watch. Sam leaned forward in his chair, anxious. Steve did not dare to move.

Would it all suddenly end here? All their plans, all their work, all their hopes?

Finally Kit smiled, and without glancing at her script, spoke her first line. So she continued through the entire act, never once referring to her script. Jeff and Steve exchanged surprised and delighted looks. She had come to a first rehearsal knowing all her lines. She was full of surprises that girl, some of them fascinating and most encouraging.

During the break at the end of Act One, Jeff asked Kit why that long pause before her first line.

'Applause, Jeff, darling. When I come on there's going to be applause!'

She laughed and moved from Jeff's side to Steve.

'Did I disappoint you, darling?' she asked.

'You were fantastic! Is that what you were doing all those nights, learning your lines?' Steve kissed her on the cheek. She held him close for a moment and patted his face.

'It was a surprise just for you. Because you've written such a beautiful play,' she whispered. 'I could play your material forever,' she promised.

She was as sure and effective in the second act as she had been in the first. Her air of security seemed to light up the empty theater. The entire cast gained confidence from her. She was indeed proving herself to be the star they all remembered.

'Third act!' Jeff announced after a brief break. 'Let's get into the third act!'

To Steve, this was the crucial act. This first time Kit Lawrence would face the actress who played her mother. If Kit could play this scene, the entire play would work. Ross's therapy, unconventional as it was, would work.

The act started well. Kit knew all her lines. She had even begun to try bits of performance which proved that she had formulated approaches to various key moments in the act. Her theatrical inventiveness had already begun to manifest itself, even at this early stage of rehearsal. A most encouraging sign.

Still, Steve awaited the moment when she had to play against Maria and confront the basic conflict and the ultimate climax of his play.

As that scene approached, Kit's pace suddenly began to lag. Rather than building toward the climactic scene, she had lost her energy and her sense of involvement.

Soon both Steve and Jeff realized that though Maria was playing to Kit, Kit had become strangely aloof and withdrawn, as if she were rejecting not only her mother, but the entire play. The scene had slowed depressingly. Maria, who had started securely and confidently, became halting, adopting Kit's slow, aimless pace.

Instead of the conflict and the dramatic peaks Steve had envisioned when he wrote the scene, it had become a mere exchange of words between two women who had little or no personal relationship, dramatic conflict or antagonism. The act and the play ended on a soft, turgid note. Hardly a curtain that would inspire an audience to applause, or a critic to a rave review.

All the fears that usually assaulted Steve Brooks on the first reading of any new play had become a reality this time. The thought of his own failure did not depress him; he had had failures before and surmounted them. But if *Reunion* were a disaster, Kit Lawrence would return to Silvermine. Perhaps for the last time.

Sam and Jeff realized the same dread possibility, too. So at the end of the reading, with forced enthusiasm, Jeff announced, 'Great! For a first reading, terrific! We'll break for lunch. Everybody back promptly at two fifteen!'

The three men huddled in a dark corner at the rear of the house, protected from stage view by the draperies which separated the last row from the lobby noises during a performance.

'Well, boys, what do you think?' Sam asked.

'I think . . .' Jeff began, but went no further.

'Steve?' Sam asked.

'I don't know,' the disturbed author replied, but his tone betrayed him.

At that moment, unseen by any of them, Kit Lawrence slyly and silently moved up the aisle to eavesdrop on their furtive but frank discussion. The first words she heard were Sam's.

'One of the best playwrights in the American theater "doesn't know." One of the best directors in Hollywood can only "think" without telling us what he is thinking. Well, let an old real estate man tell you what *he* thinks.

'I think,' Sam continued grimly, 'that we have ourselves a very treacherous situation. The last scene does not play. The question is, Why?' He addressed himself to Jeff: 'Tell me honestly, in Steve's presence, do you think it's the script?'

'The script is fine. Maria is fine,' Jeff said. 'The scene does not play because Kit refuses to play it. Or can't play it.'

'That's what I wanted to know,' Sam said. 'So what do we do? What's our next move?'

'Frankly, if this were a film I'd be tempted to shut down right now and recast,' Jeff said.

'You can't do that to Kit!' Steve warned.

'That's my only concern,' Sam said grimly. 'How do we harm that girl least? By stopping now? Or by going on and maybe having the critics stop us in Boston? Which could destroy her. Steve, can you rewrite the scene so it works for her? Jeff, can you direct her so she can do it? Answer those two questions and I'll answer all the rest for myself. What do we do?'

Jeff betrayed the depth of his concern by saying, 'Do? We should call Ross. That's what we should do. After all, this was his idea! He should know what to do!'

At those words, Kit Lawrence, stunned, turned and slipped down the aisle. Unaware, the three men concluded their discussion.

Steve said, 'Ross has never directed a play, or written one. He doesn't know what it takes. We do. We have to decide.'

'So what do we decide?' Sam pressed.

'Let's see what happens on the second reading,' Jeff equivocated.

The second reading went no better.

At the end, Jeff covered his concern with a routine and clichéd director's speech. 'Tomorrow we'll start blocking the first act. But I want all of you to know now that I will expect you to know your lines and get the books out of your hands by the end of the week.'

The cast departed. Except for Kit. She remained seated in her place at the table. Her very presence created an issue which had to be faced.

Steve, Jeff and Sam exchanged glances, determining who would begin. It devolved upon Jeff as director.

'Kit? Darling?' he asked softly, pretending he was intruding on her thoughts.

She tossed her head in a gesture she often used onstage to indicate impatience. Then, though her hair was securely held in place by the red ribbon, she made a pretense of brushing it back with her open hand, palm outward. To Steve it was the first clue of the illness taking command of the actress.

'She will have to go,' Kit said flatly. 'I simply cannot play that scene with her.'

'Maria?' Jeff asked.

'That woman.'

'Give it a chance, Kit,' Jeff suggested. 'It's only the first day. If it doesn't work, we have plenty of time to change her.'

'You directors always say that!' she exploded. 'Then you hang on and hang on until it's too late to change, and I'll have to come to Broadway playing my big scene against a woman I can't stand. Can't stand!'

Sam intervened. 'Kit, sweetheart, I promise you, if it doesn't work, she goes. After all, she has only one scene. It won't be difficult to replace her. Give it a chance.'

Kit stared out into the dark house, avoiding their entreating looks. 'She'll come off well. *I'll* be blamed for it. They'll say, In the end it was too much for Kit Lawrence. She let the play down. Ruined it. A very good play and she ruined it.'

'They won't say any such—' Sam began to say.

She overruled him. 'They will! You know they will. You even said it yourself!' she accused.

'Who said?' Sam demanded.

'The three of you! Standing back there like the witches from *Macbeth*. "What's wrong?" "Nothing wrong with the script." "Nothing wrong with the cast." "Nothing wrong with the director." "Nothing wrong with anything except Kit Lawrence!" '

For the first time all three men realized that she had managed to eavesdrop on their whispered meeting.

One frightening thought occurred to Steve before it struck the other two. Had she heard their entire conversation?

The answer was not long in coming, for Kit leaped up from the table violently and in so doing overturned it, scattering scripts, pencils, coffee cups and notes across the bare stage. She cried out, 'I heard you! I heard you say it.' She directed her tirade at Jeff Warrener, ' "*We should call Ross. After all, this was his idea!*" '

She strode about the stage in bold sweeping moves reminiscent of the best performances she had ever given. Except that now she was no longer Kit Lawrence, actress, star, but Kit Lawrence, patient – pathetic, disillusioned patient.

'What's wrong with Kit Lawrence?' she cried out to the empty theater. 'Send the word up and down Broadway! Kit Lawrence is screwing up the play! Destroying it! Send for Ross! Send for the police! Send for the National Guard! Keep her from going berserk. Rewrite the script? No. It's perfect.

'Change Maria? No. She is fine. We have only one problem. Kit Lawrence! She has done it again! Destroyed herself! Destroyed everyone around her!'

When her outburst reached a crescendo, she turned and ran into the wings and out the stage door. Steve raced after her. He caught up with her just before she reached the iron gate leading from the alley to the street. He seized her. But she grappled so violently, she broke loose. As she reached the gate, he overtook her again. She clung to the iron bars with a grip so fierce he could not dislodge her.

'Kit! Kit, no! Don't let them see you this way!' he pleaded.

But it was too late. A small crowd had already begun to gather. Someone recognized her. The crowd grew larger. He interposed his body between her and the staring onlookers. He enfolded her in his arms, and though she struggled with all her power, he did not release her. Finally she ceased to struggle. She became quiescent, then limp in his arms. He picked her up and carried her back into the alley.

There, in the dim light, he set her down, wiped her tears away, straightened her hair. He held her tenderly while she leaned against him. She pressed her damp face against his shoulder and whispered into his ear, 'I didn't mean to do that. I don't know what happened to me. I don't know.'

'It's over, now. Relax. Forget it,' he urged her.

She was silent for a moment. She sniffled, then regained breath sufficient to ask in a small, pathetic voice, 'Is it true?'

'What?'

'*Was* this Ross's idea?' she dared to ask.

Because he felt it would do no good to compound the situation with dishonesty, Steve Brooks admitted simply, 'Yes, it was Ross's idea.'

'From the beginning?'

'He felt it was the best way to help you.'

'He did want to get rid of me,' she decided, deeply rejected.

'He wanted to help you, cure you.'

'He wanted to get rid of me,' she was repeating, when Sam and Jeff came out into the alley to join them.

'Kit,' Steve commanded severely, pulling back from her so that she could look into his eyes when he said it, 'Ross did it because he felt this was best for *you.* But you don't have to go through with it. Sam will end it here. Right now. If that's what you want.'

She turned away to hide from them.

'Kit?' Steve persisted.

'Ross wanted to get rid of me' was all she said.

'And us,' Steve demanded, 'what about us? Did Jeff come three thousand miles from the Coast to get rid of you? Did I leave my half-finished novel to get rid of you? Did Sam put up his last quarter of a million to get rid of you?'

Sam edged forward, shaking his head, pleading with Steve, Don't tell her. I don't know how you found out, but don't tell her. But the anguished look on his face acknowledged that it had already been told.

Kit turned to Sam. 'Did you, Sam?'

'I've made fortunes before; I'll make them again . . .'

'Oh, Sam . . . Sam . . .' She kissed him. 'I'll do it for you. For all your sakes I'll do it.'

'Terrific!' Jeff enthused. 'You are my star. You always were. If you say you'll do it, then you'll do it.'

'Come, Kit,' Steve said, 'I'll take you back to the hotel.'

Sam and Jeff watched them start toward the street. Once they were out of earshot, Sam asked, 'What do you think, Jeff?'

'It's one thing for a girl in her condition to *say*, I'll do it. And quite another to *do* it. But I am going to make sure of one thing tomorrow.'

'What?' Sam asked anxiously.

'You'll see' was all Jeff would say.

Kit and Steve walked hand in hand up Broadway to Central Park and along the park toward the Plaza. She had been silent all the way, until the moment of parting came. Nor had he pressed her to speak. It would be better, he thought, to allow her feelings to recede.

But when they stood across from the hotel, she said

in a soft pleading voice, 'You wouldn't do it, would you?'

'What, Kit?'

'Send me back?' she asked, finally disclosing the real source of her anxiety.

'Back?'

'To Ross. That's the first thing I thought when Jeff said to call Ross. I thought, They're going to send me back to him and he doesn't want me. Doesn't want me.'

He was afraid she might begin to weep again on the crowded street. He gripped her hand, drew her close, spoke intensely to her: 'We are not going to send you back. I promise you. Kit, I've never lied to you before, have I?'

'No,' she admitted.

'Then believe me now. I won't let them send you back.'

She nodded as she accepted his promise.

'I wanted today to be so different. I learned all my lines. Wore this dress . . . Brought those gifts. This was going to be the best first rehearsal day of my entire life. Now look at me.'

She held up her face to him, ran her fingers under her tear-reddened eyes. Tears were starting to well up again.

'Don't,' Steve pleaded.

'I won't. As long as I know you won't send me back.' Her chin quivered and he thought she might cry after all, until she forced a smile. 'It's so strange. One moment I was so deeply hurt that Ross wanted to get rid of me. The next moment I was afraid you'd send me back to him.'

She shook her head, smiling. 'I am a crazy lady: I must be.'

# Sixteen

On a stage bare except for a few pieces of makeshift furniture, and with masking tape on the floor defining the geographical confines and the doors of the set, Jeff Warrener began to block the actors' moves in *Reunion*. He invented action that would keep the play from becoming static. He sought moves that intensified moments of conflict. He searched out opportunities to make Kit Lawrence the focus of audience attention.

A first blocking day was always exhausting. Jeff seized on that as an excuse to dismiss the cast an hour early. Kit departed with the others. Jeff, Steve and Sam did not.

Fifteen minutes later Maria Patrick returned with Janet Vail, Kit's understudy.

'Maria. Janet. Open your scripts to page three-nine,' Jeff said. 'Read that scene for us. Right to the final curtain. We just want to hear it.'

On their feet, but making no specific attempt to invent moves to suit the dialogue, Maria Patrick played the mother who had been summoned to face her abandoned daughter. Janet Vail played Kit's role. This was her triumph, her supreme moment of revenge.

All the mother's attempts to explain were savagely demolished by the angry star, in the scathing speeches Kit had wanted and Steve had written. When her mother pleaded for understanding, the star remained unmoved. Without even looking at her mother, she dismissed her as if she were a common whore.

Her rage prevailed until the defeated mother exited. Then, at the sound of the door closing, the star slowly turned upstage, facing away from the audience. Jeff had deliberately planned the scene that way. It would be too obvious to let the audience see her tears. Far better to imagine them, and have their imaginations confirmed when the actress reached out to pick up her handkerchief from the nearby table and bring it to her eyes. That simple gesture, with her back to the audience, that bit of lace handled with the skill of Kit Lawrence, could have far more impact than obvious tears.

So the curtain would come down on Kit Lawrence alone onstage, and in tears, despite her retribution.

The reading conveyed the potential power of the scene. It was a silent, magical moment of theater.

'It works,' Jeff whispered. 'The scene works. I had to be absolutely sure.'

Sam agreed. 'Steve, it's one of the most powerful and poignant scenes you've ever written.'

'Then why doesn't it work for Kit?' Steve asked.

Rehearsal had been called for ten o'clock as usual. The cast assembled early, sat around drinking coffee, exchanging gossip.

Jeff Warrener was not onstage. He was waiting outside the stage door. He stared anxiously down the block toward Seventh Avenue. He kept consulting his watch. It was almost ten. What he feared most could happen in the next few minutes. Kit Lawrence and Maria Patrick might arrive at the same moment. That would completely destroy his strategy.

Just as he feared it was doomed, Maria rounded the corner, coming not from Seventh Avenue, as he had anticipated, but from Eighth. He ran swiftly down the street to intercept her. He kissed her hastily while ushering her across the street toward the hotel lobby.

'What's wrong, Jeff?'

'I don't want us to be seen.'

Once safely inside, he asked, 'Where were you? I tried to call you last night.'

'I was out,' Maria said, resentful that her privacy was being invaded.

'All night?' Jeff asked, irritated.

'Yes, all night,' she answered defiantly.

'Sorry, darling. I didn't mean that the way it sounded,' Jeff apologized. 'But I was trying to reach you.'

'Why?' she asked.

'I don't want you to show up for rehearsal today.'

'You've got other women coming in to read for my part,' she concluded painfully.

'You don't understand. It's because we *don't* want to replace you that I'm doing this.'

'Doing what?' Maria Patrick asked, her strong-featured face set against the fear that she might break down. She needed this job desperately.

'Today I want to do the third act with your understudy.'

'You don't like what I'm doing,' she concluded. 'Be honest with me, Jeff. The least I've earned after years in this rotten business is a little decency!'

Jeff felt compelled to be frank.

'Maria, darling, I didn't come back from Hollywood just to do a play. I'm here for the same reason Steve is. And Sam is. Because this play has got to work. For Kit's sake.'

'And you think I keep it from working,' Maria anticipated.

'Listen to me! I don't have much time! Sam, Steve and I think you're perfect for the role. We not only want you, we need you. Desperately. But we do have a problem.'

He hesitated before confessing, 'Kit thinks she doesn't like *you.* We want to direct her hostility where it belongs, toward your character. To do that I have to work with your understudy until we can straighten out Kit's confusion. Maria, she's a complicated girl. Because she's a very sick girl. And if you tell anyone what I just told you, I swear I'll see you never work again!' he threatened desperately.

He apologized at once. 'I'm sorry. I know you won't say anything. And if it will make you feel more secure, I'll have Sam give you a run-of-the-play contract.'

'I don't need a run-of-the-play,' she said pridefully. 'I'll do what I can.'

'Thanks, Maria. You were always understanding and cooperative.'

She laughed – a small, sardonic laugh. 'You know what understanding and cooperation will get you in the theater.'

Jeff kissed her. He whispered, I'm sorry about asking where you were all night. I had no right.'

'Oh, that. Lou Lattimer.'

'You and Lattimer? I thought that was over years ago.'

'It was. But he's sick. And he won't go to a hospital.'

'But if he needs medical help . . .'

'He's terminal.'

'Oh, I'm sorry. Goddammit, I am sorry,' Jeff said, reaching out to pat her cheek. 'Maria, can I tell you something?'

'Of course.'

'You won't think I'm foolish. Or lying. And you won't tell anyone?'

'If you're not lying I'll know it,' Maria said simply. 'The rest goes without saying.'

'When I was a kid, just coming up in the theater, I used to sit in the balcony and look down at the stage at Maria Patrick. With her finely cut features. Her magnificent hair wound in that luxurious braid around her head, a glistening frame for a beautifully made face. I was love-struck. I would think, By God, if only time would stand still for her so I could catch up. I would make her love me. She is not only beautiful, and talented, but good. Just plain shining good through all the artifice of acting. That's how I felt about you. Today, I still do. You're a terrific lady, Maria Patrick. I am depending on you.'

'Kids, we've got a bit of a problem today,' Jeff said as he opened the rehearsal: 'that's the reason I'm late. I had a call from Maria. She's got a stomach virus. She should be okay in a day or two. So we'll have to work Act Three with her understudy.'

April Calvin came forward. A bit younger than Maria Patrick and not so stately, she was nevertheless a competent actress.

'Kit, darling?' Jeff invited. 'Let's start from the top of Act Three.'

Jeff, Steve and Sam sat out in the dark house. Before Kit would signal that she was ready, she stood alone in the wings. After what seemed an overly long time, she came back onstage, smiling. But it was not a smile that put the three men at ease. It was forced. Brittle.

Yet she started the act confidently and with a brisk pace, which the other actors adopted. The whole scene seemed to coalesce for the first time. Kit gained momentum and confidence as she continued, as if she were determined the act would play better without Maria.

Until the moment came when the actor playing the doorman entered to announce that her mother was waiting. Suddenly Kit's verve, pace and brightness seemed to fade. She was motionless until she made a slow turn in the direction of the door. Her turn seemed an eternity.

To Steve Brooks her move was both exciting and terrifying. If it was an intentional theatrical move, it was magnificent. If it was involuntary, Kit's personal reaction, it was frightening. He whispered to Jeff, 'Christ, what do you think?'

'Shhh' was all Jeff said.

Sam said nothing, only edged forward to rest his chin on the back of the seat in front of him.

Kit Lawrence and April Calvin, deserted daughter and deserting mother, were facing each other. Kit had the first line, a simple line. 'So it's you. Finally.' But she took an inordinately long time before she could say it.

Thinking she had gone dry, the stage manager called the line to her. Kit turned on him in a rage, 'Damn you! When I want a line I'll ask for it!'

She took a long time to recapture the mood. She finally spoke the line as if surmounting a hurdle. Once past the opening dialogue, the two women went through the scene with a minimum of effort. Now came the final moment. Her mother had been expelled. Alone in her dressing room, the star faced away from the door until she heard it close. Then she turned upstage, reached for her handkerchief, brought it to her eyes, as the stage manager softly said, 'Curtain.'

They had played the scene, but there was no impact, no magic.

'Let's take five,' Jeff called out, sounding quite casual. But he sank down in his seat, whispering, 'We've got trouble. Big trouble.'

'She breezed through it,' Sam protested, considerably relieved.

'Sam, this is not a scene she should breeze through. She just doesn't care,' Jeff said.

He ran the scene twice more with no better effect. Finally, he called an early lunch break.

Alone with Steve, Jeff confessed, 'She's not giving me anything. So much as I hate the bastard, I've been thinking of calling Max Kronheim. Maybe he could help.'

'If Ross felt Kronheim was the man to help her, would he have asked us?'

Steve Brooks tried Ross four times before he could reach him. Briefly, he informed the doctor of their problem.

'Kronheim?' Ross interrupted. 'Did Kit suggest consulting him?'

'It was Jeff's idea.'

'Before you contact Kronheim, you and I should meet. Can you come up? Tonight?'

'Yes, sure. I'll skip the afternoon rehearsal.'

'Meet me here at the office. I'd rather not discuss this at home.'

'I understand,' Steve said.

'I don't think you do,' Ross replied curtly.

# *Seventeen*

'Frankly, Brooks, the situation does not appear as bad as you try to make it,' Ross said once they had settled down in his office. 'Kit is appearing at rehearsal every day. You yourself said she came knowing all her lines. She seems quite professional. Works hard. She doesn't ask to be excused early. Doesn't drink. I would say it's gone quite well. Personally, I am relieved and delighted.'

'I guess you could say it's gone well,' Steve agreed. 'Till now!'

'Till now,' Ross conceded. 'When at the first sign of trouble, panic sets in. In the patient? No. But in those who are trying to help her.'

Ross chuckled. 'I ofttimes think it would be more constructive to treat the patient's relatives and friends than the patient. What you and your director are going through is not unusual. You're so concerned with what the right thing to do is, that you abdicate your own common sense. Let it ride, go along with it. I'm sure things will straighten themselves out. After all, she's only been in rehearsal for a week.'

'Dr Ross, you know your business, but we know ours!' Steve said angrily. 'When an actress is having trouble with a scene, it could be the scene. But we've tested that. The scene works. It plays. It has power. The trouble is, she simply won't play it. So by our standards and experience, things have *not* gone "quite well." '

'So your first thought is run for help. To Kronheim.'

'You have to understand that relationship,' Steve explained. 'Even when Kit and I were living together, the one thing she would never do for me was give up a single class with Kronheim. Times, though I wanted her very much, she left our bed to go keep her session with him. After a while I realized I would have to accommodate my desires to his strict schedule. I agree with Jeff: if anyone can get her to do the scene, Kronheim can.'

Ross nodded as he carefully considered his next words. Steve Brooks suspected it was a decision of great consequence.

'I don't resort to narcosynthesis with patients,' Ross began, 'except when it is the only possible way to achieve a breakthrough. At such times I record the patient's recital of the painful memory. Otherwise, afterward the patient tends to deny her revelations and feel it was something the doctor invented.

'I was forced to this extreme with Kit because she steadfastly refused to discuss Kronheim. She mentioned him often. But each time she became very tense and evasive. The more I prodded, the more she avoided, often becoming quite hostile. Twice she walked out in the middle of her hour, saying I was trying to treat Kronheim, not her. After the second time, I determined to use pentothal. I will play that tape for you now. But you are never to discuss it with anyone!'

Ross placed a cassette in the machine which was discreetly disguised in the bookshelves across from his desk. The tape began with Ross's voice:

'Kit, starting with ten, count backward slowly.'

Steve heard Kit's voice, slightly less confident than usual, drone, 'Ten, nine, eight, seven, six, five, four . . .' Her voice drifted off into silence as the pentothal took effect.

Ross's first questions on the tape were general, about acting, what it meant to her, how she prepared to play a role.

She responded slowly in a voice that sounded distant and very young, as if she had assumed the role of a novice. 'Kronheim says it is not enough to know who you *are* as a character, but also who you *were*. Like the rings of a tree, you must contain your entire character life within you. It is not necessary that the audience see all the rings. But the rings must be there. And *you* must know them.

'Kronheim also says you must come on conveying to the audience all the realities of the immediate life around you. You must acquaint them with place, time, weather, atmosphere, all by what you do and the way you do it.'

She went silent for a moment, until Ross's voice prodded. 'And how does one achieve that?'

'Exercises.'

'What kind of exercises?'

Kit's voice changed from girl novice to stern taskmaster, as she became Kronheim.

'Now, my dear, you will stand erect. Erect but at ease! Tension is the enemy of creativity. So you will stand there now, experiencing no tension. *Ah, ah!*' the voice suddenly rebuked, 'I can see tension exhibiting itself in your left hand. Relax! At ease! Stand at ease! I said, *at ease*!'

Her novice voice pleaded. 'I can't be at ease and stand erect; I can't.'

'You can and you will!' her Kronheim voice commanded. 'You will stand there until I am satisfied that you are relaxed. Even if it takes the whole hour. Don't move. Don't sway! No! I can detect it in your left leg. It is trembling. Stop trembling! Control it! Did you hear me, Kit? Stop trembling!'

'I can't,' her novice voice pleaded.

'You will retain that position until you do! So stand there! Relax! Relax! Relax! But in total control of yourself.'

There was a silence on the tape. Steve Brooks was about to ask a question. Ross stopped him with a gesture.

The novice voice came at them, this time tenser than before, 'Please, I can't . . . I can't . . .'

She interrupted herself in the commanding voice of Kronheim: 'You can! And you will! Suffering is part of acting. Without it there can be no true emotion. Even comedy has an underlying base of suffering. So I do not ever, mind you, not ever, wish to hear the words "I can't." Is that clear?'

'Yes, yes,' Kit's girl voice admitted, defeated. There was silence, until she was heard to weep softly.

The Kronheim voice became lower but no less dictatorial: 'I do not like to see involuntary tears from an actress. Tears for effect, yes. But tears like yours only mean surrender to petty emotions. Kit, you will stop crying! Because we have our other exercises yet to accomplish. Stop it! Do you hear me!'

'I can't . . . I can't . . .'

Now when she imitated Kronheim's voice it was softer, more intimate, less strident.

'Child, do you think I like to do this to you? But these are the things you must learn to put to use your talents. Which are great. Rough, unrefined, but enormous in their potential. There is within you a reservoir of feeling, from a life which has been harsh, brutal, but upon which we can build. What psychoanalysis does for others, acting does for us. You must invest your acting with your total life experience. My exercises will enable you to do that. It is not easy. And if you fail to achieve perfect relaxation and freedom from tension one day, we will find it the next. So for today, enough.'

'Thank you,' Kit's novice voice said, exhaling in great relief.

'Now we will begin our earth exercises. I want to see on your face that you are standing in a hot sun. Beastly hot. It is New York on the worst sultry summer day. Your eyes cannot withstand the bright sun, so they close. Good. But I want to see you feel that hot sun on your face. What do people do when they are hot?'

'They sweat.'

'Exactly!' Kronheim commanded. 'I want to see you sweat.'

'I can't . . .'

'You can. Will yourself to do it and you can. It is hot. You are standing in the sun. A sun so bright and strong you can't open your eyes. Therefore, you must be sweating. Sweat!'

'I can't . . .'

'Sweat!' he commanded.

Another long silence; then, when she imitated Kronheim's voice, it was softer and victorious. 'That's better, much better. Very good, my child. Here, my handkerchief, wipe your face dry.'

The voice became more intimate as he said, 'You may have overdone it a bit. Rest. Open your blouse. Let the cool air get at your skin. That's right; here, I'll help you unbutton it. Better, isn't it?'

'Yes,' the novice voice said. But now there was a change from young actress to young girl, aware that she was in the presence of a man with desire in his eyes.

The tape was silent until Ross's voice asked, 'Were there other exercises, Kit?'

'Yes.'

'What kind?' Ross's voice asked.

'Feel cold. Feel rain. By that time I knew how. I could look up and actually feel the rivulets running down my face. Once . . .' She giggled like a proud child. 'Once Kronheim said I made him hear the thunder. I liked that.'

'Did you like *him*?'

There was a pause; then, 'Yes . . . yes, I liked him.'

'Even when he criticized you?'

'Yes,' she responded staunchly. 'Even in class, before all the others.'

Her voice took on the stern attitude of Kronheim in one of his most vitriolic attacks. 'Well, Kit, I have sat back watching your acting exercise. Personally I would not have chosen that scene for you. That was your first mistake.

'However, we will work on what you did choose. I must say I am disappointed. You forget every rule I ever laid down for you. You allowed the part to dominate you, not you the part. Remember always, it is *your* experience, *your* feelings, the expression of what is within *you* that makes a role come alive. The more we reveal what is in your guts, the more electric the performance. Nothing else counts. But what did you do in your paltry effort? You read your lines like a ten-year-old in a grade-school performance of a Nativity play! You were atrocious!

'You want to know what I saw? Not a sexily avaricious young woman lusting for her impotent husband, but a little girl in pigtails. Not a woman who has experienced sex herself. But a child who only heard it gossiped about. For God's sake, where the hell were *you*? Not the role. Not the actress. But *you*! Have you never been had by a real man? Have you never rolled on a hot moist bed after some man has screwed you to the ecstasy of orgasm? Answer me! Have you?'

The girl voice responded, shyly and apologetically, 'Yes, I have.'

'Well, then, I want to see memories of your ecstasy in that scene. Do you understand me?'

'Yes, yes, I understand. I'm sorry,' Kit's voice said.

'Now, you will go away and rethink the scene. When you return and do it again, I want to see the twitching in your pubic area when you let us know how hot and hungry you are for that husband of yours.'

'I'll work on it,' she promised meekly.

Another silence on the tape.

Steve Brooks observed, 'He's destroyed more than one young actress.'

'There's more,' Ross warned.

'Kit?' Ross's taped voice prodded. There was no response. '*Did* you rethink the scene, Kit? *Did* you go back and do it again?'

'Yes,' her voice responded shyly.

'What happened?'

'He . . . he didn't like it . . .'

'What happened, Kit?'

'Before the whole class he humiliated me. He said I was

not capable of an honest sexual emotion. That I played the scene like a whore who was being paid for sex, not a woman who really wanted it. He said all kinds of things . . . all kinds.'

'Such as?' Ross's voice coaxed.

'Hopeless. He said I was hopeless as an actress. I became afraid.'

'Afraid of what?' Ross's voice probed.

'That he would kick me out of his class.'

'Did it mean that much to you?'

'It meant everything. Without him I was nothing. Nothing,' she confessed, weeping again.

Steve Brooks interrupted furiously, 'She would have been a great actress if she'd never met him!'

Ross silenced him with an impatient gesture. The tape continued.

'Kit, *did* he kick you out?'

'No.'

'*Why* didn't he turn you out?'

'Because I . . . I went to his home. I pleaded. I said I would do the scene again and again. Until it pleased him. And he said, "You can't do it right, because you have never experienced the feeling. You must know it to act it." And I said, "I do know it. I've had men. Many men." And he said, "Prove it." So I did.'

'How?' Ross's voice asked.

'I opened my blouse to him. I drew him to my breasts, made him kiss me there. In a while he was kissing me everywhere. Then he made love to me.'

'Did you enjoy it?'

'I pleased him,' she evaded.

'I asked did *you* enjoy it, Kit?'

She laughed, the laugh of a mischievous little girl.

'Kit?'

'I made him believe I did.' She laughed again. 'He never knew. He thought it was real. He never knew I was acting. That was the greatest praise of all.'

'Was that the only time it happened with him?'

Her laughter was gone suddenly. 'It happened again ... again ... again ...'

'Always that way. He deriving pleasure, you acting as if you did?'

'I hated him. All the while it was going on I hated him. But I needed him.'

'The same way you needed your grandfather?' Ross's voice asked.

'I needed him to love me,' she said simply. 'I needed him to approve of me.'

Neither Steve Brooks nor Dr Ross said anything until the tape ran out and the machine shut itself off.

'No, I would not call on Max Kronheim to help her,' Ross said.

'Then what would you suggest?'

'Continue.'

'And if she can't make it?'

'One of the first things we learn as analysts is that we must not blame ourselves for the patient's illness. The patient comes to us sick. We do what we can. But some patients are beyond helping.'

'That's pretty callous,' Steve Brooks accused.

'Is a pathologist who arrives at a diagnosis of a malignancy callous?' Ross asked.

'If we need you, will you come?'

'I'd go anywhere for that girl. You know that.'

'Sorry,' Steve Brooks said.

'I'm no different from you,' Ross confessed sadly. 'I too dream of what it could have been like with her if she were healthy. I watch that waste of beauty, talent, charm, warmth, and I am powerless. My best was not enough. Let's see if yours is.'

# *Eighteen*

It was the end of the third week of rehearsal. Jeff Warrener insisted on the first of what would be daily runthroughs. He wanted his cast to grow used to the rhythm of playing the entire play. A first run-through is an event of crucial consequence in the life of a play. It is the occasion when all the pieces should fall into place.

Some producers like to invite a few selected friends who are bound to have a fresh and dispassionate view and will be sensitive to flaws and incongruities to which, by now, the playwright, the director and the actors have become immune.

Sam had invited another producer and a woman of considerable wealth who was an inveterate investor in theatrical ventures. Jeff invited two friends.

Steve Brooks invited no one. Melinda had inquired. He had promised to let her know. But when the day came, he pretended to forget. This first time, he wanted to view the complete run-through of his play by himself. He climbed up to the second balcony, dropped into an aisle seat in the front row.

Quiet had settled over the theater. The stage manager announced, 'Places, please!'

One of the critical moments in the life of Steve's play was at hand. He leaned forward against the rail, stared down at the stage.

Jeff sat in the middle of the eighth row in the orchestra. His assistant sat alongside, with pad, lighted clipboard and pencil ready. Jeff was a ruthless note-giver during run-throughs.

Sam Rogers and his guests sat several rows behind Jeff, not wishing to disturb him.

'Curtain!' the stage manager announced crisply.

The opening moments played with brisk efficiency. The play really became alive and vibrant when Kit Lawrence made her entrance. In her first scene with the pregnant young girl, she projected such warmth that Steve felt, My God, everything she ever had she has now, plus a maturity that becomes her like a crown. She is magnificent.

The confidence the cast gained from her during the first act reflected itself in their sureness in the second act. The taste of a hit was in the air. Everyone sensed it.

Down in the orchestra, Sam was being congratulated in enthusiastic whispers by his two guests. The wealthy woman insisted on being allowed to invest. The only thing that quieted her was the stage manager announcing Act Three.

Optimism, which had soared so high in the first two acts, was totally shattered in Act Three.

When Steve came down from the balcony, he found Sam and his wealthy lady standing at the head of the aisle. He only caught the last of the conversation.

'Sam,' she was saying, 'just get that third act straightened out and you're home free.'

A casual kiss on Sam's cheek and she was gone.

'An hour ago she was insisting on putting in a hundred thousand. And was insulted when I refused,' Sam said.

Steve nodded, commiserating.

Jeff came up the aisle, wearily, as if climbing a steep mountain. 'Well?'

'Do we have to ask questions, and give each other answers?' Sam replied. 'We know. We all know. I only hope word doesn't get started on the street.'

'My people won't talk. I made them promise,' Jeff assured him.

'Nobody ever talks. But somehow, if the word is bad, it gets around,' Sam lamented. 'We could be dead before we get to New Haven.'

'Somebody better say something to Kit. She's waiting,' Steve suggested.

'You go,' Sam said. 'I couldn't carry it off. Much as I love her, I just couldn't,' Sam said sadly.

Steve and Kit were sitting in Sardi's, at a table in the most remote corner. Jimmy, the maître d', knew how Kit hated the front celebrity tables.

Though it was late afternoon and Steve would have welcomed a drink, he suggested, 'Tea? A sandwich? You must be hungry.'

Instead of answering, she asked, 'What did you think?'

'For a first run-though it was terrific.'

'Was it?'

'It showed us the potential. That's what a first run-through is for. We don't have to recast any role. We're close to playing time. And the play works. That's the most important thing. It works!'

'Even the third act?'

Fortunately, the waiter arrived with a menu so Steve did not have to answer. But once the waiter left, Kit insisted, 'Even the third act?'

'The third act could have been better,' he conceded, trying to treat it as a trivial matter. 'I'll examine it again. Maybe we can strengthen it.'

'The third act is fine,' she said angrily. 'It's me. I can't play it. *I* stink! I never should have tried, never!'

'Don't say that!'

'It was a mistake, a terrible mistake! Let me out, Steve,' she pleaded suddenly. 'Let me out. Before it's too late.'

Her voice had risen in panic. He seized her hand and whispered forcefully, 'Not here. Not now. Kit? Please?'

She was tense, painfully tense. Her hand told him so. He knew he must get her out. Without making a scene, if possible.

'Let's go. We'll walk. You've been cooped up all day in that damned theater. You need some fresh air.'

She breathed rhythmically and deeply for a time, as if doing an exercise before making a stage entrance. She nodded. She was ready. They started the long walk toward the front door. The waiters were setting tables for the dinner hour. some did not notice her pass by. Those who did reacted with delight: 'Ah, Miss Lawrence.'

At the door, Steve whispered to Jimmy, 'Sign for me. And put on a fat tip.'

'Of course, Mr Brooks.' Jimmy replied. He understood perfectly and was sympathetic.

They headed west on Forty-fourth Street. She reached for his hand. They walked like the young lovers they used to be. As if her illness had never interrupted their lives.

They reached Ninth Avenue, where small Italian bakeries displayed an endless variety of honest breads and lusty pastries, where vegetable stores boasted extensive street displays of luscious produce.

At the Hudson River they ventured out onto a deserted pier and stood admiring the sun, which was setting behind the new high-rise buildings that had grown up to disfigure the Jersey shore.

To break their long silence, she said, 'Pretty soon there won't be any sky left. Only buildings. We'll have to tell our children how it used to be.'

She laughed. 'But then we won't have any children, so we won't have to tell them. Will we?'

'No, we won't,' he said.

'When I first came to New York I used to walk down here. Used to stand on piers like this and look across the river and think, That's where I came from. The West. And I am never going back. I am going to stay. And become a star. Be admired. Envied. Loved. Mostly loved. All my life I wanted to be loved. But once I was, I discovered their love isn't what I thought it would be. Their applause isn't what I thought it would be.'

'Kit?'

She laughed suddenly – a deliberate tactic to avoid revealing herself any further. 'Applause is like Chinese food. An hour later you're hungry again.'

He took her by the arms, made her face him. 'Kit?'

'The opening of your play, the big hit, the applause, the flowers, the reviews, my first big night. Star! I was a star! That night it all came apart.'

'That night?' he asked surprised. 'You spent that night at my place. The first time we made love. It was one of the great nights of my life.'

'I cried that night.'

'You did?'

'I waited until you fell asleep. I didn't want to spoil it for you.'

'What spoiled it for you? Kit? Was it me?'

'In a way.'

'Something I did? What?' he demanded, ready to make amends.

'I kept asking myself, What happens tomorrow? He loves me tonight. But tomorrow? Tonight they love me. But tomorrow? Each performance would be a test. Would I please them? Would they love me? Each time you made love to me was a test. Would I please him? Would he love me?'

'I've always loved you, Kit.'

'You don't understand,' she kept protesting.

'Tell me so that I will.'

'You'll hate me.'

'I've never hated you. Have I?'

'I'm a liar. A fraud. All those times you made love to me and I pretended to love you back, it was a fraud.'

'Kit?' He tried to find her eyes, but she avoided him.

'I don't know how to love. I only want to *be* loved. I want men to desire me, love me, want me more and more. Each day is a fresh day. Yesterday's love doesn't mean anything. Who will love me today? And once they do, the question is who will love me tomorrow! I have to know I'll be loved tomorrow.

'The best times, Steve, were with you. Not during. But after. When you would cradle me in your arms and hold me so close that we were one warm body. I could feel your breathing. I knew that I had satisfied you. And you loved me. But then . . .

'Then when your breathing changed and I knew you'd fallen asleep, the fear returned. Will he love me when he wakes? It was the same with every man. Even Ross.'

She was suddenly direct and straightforward as she asked, 'What did he say about me?'

'What do you mean?'

'The other afternoon, when you weren't at rehearsal, that's where you went, wasn't it?'

He had to be truthful with her. 'Yes.'

'Did you ask him about the third act?'

'Yes.'

'And?'

'He feels you can do it.'

'Can? Or should?'

'Both!' he said firmly.

'Then why can't I?' she asked plaintively.

'If you really want us to recast Maria, we will. Anything!' he promised in desperation.

'I need her. I need someone to hate in that scene.'

'Then hate her! But play it! For God's sake, Kit, play it!'

'I try,' she said weakly, 'I try.'

It was evening. And becoming cool. She wore only a thin knit shirt to protect her.

'Come, I'll find a cab.'

'Let's walk,' she pleaded.

They passed vegetable markets, butcher shops, bakeries.

Suddenly Kit said, 'Let's buy some food. I'll cook dinner for you!'

He tried to smile as he said, 'I don't have a kitchen at the Algonquin.'

'Oh, yes, that's right,' she remembered sadly.

They walked on.

'It would have been fun. Like in the old days. Remember those terrific meals I used to cook for you?'

He glanced at her. She believed what she had just said.

Fortunately, the word along the street after the first run-through proved not to be as damaging as Sam had feared. At Sardi's, Joe Allen's and Downey's, professional gossip had it that the first two acts were strong. The kind which Kit Lawrence played so brilliantly. The third act had a problem, which three experienced theater men like Steve Brooks, Jeff Warrener and Sam Rogers should certainly be able to solve.

The only three men on Broadway who were not so confident were Steve Brooks, Jeff Warrener and Sam Rogers.

But, as theater people do when in trouble, they placed their faith in the audience. They encouraged one another by saying, and almost believing, an audience can do miraculous things for an actress. Remember what Ross had said, how much she needed the approval and love of an audience? In New Haven she would begin to enjoy that. Yes, they had to believe, all troubles would be cured once Kit was in front of an audience.

Steve did not confide in the others, but he nurtured the fear that while New Haven could produce a miracle, it might also prove a disaster.

He called Ross, to prevail on him to come to New Haven. Ross declined.

'It's only a short run from Hartford,' Steve argued.

'That isn't the point,' Ross replied. 'Who does she feel thrust her into this situation? Who said it was okay to do a play? In her mind, who shoved her out the door and said, Make it on your own? I did.'

'All the more reason for you to be here,' Steve insisted, 'to show her that you still care for her.'

'If she knows I'm there for her first performance, she may say, "You turned me out. Well, I am going to show you how wrong you were. I am going to fail. Miserably!" And she would. Miserably,' Ross said grimly.

'What can we do?' Steve asked.

'Let events take their course. And call me.'

'What do I do in the meantime? Take two aspirins?' Steve exploded, and hung up before Ross could answer.

# *Nineteen*

At the end of the first preview in New Haven, Steve and Sam waited in the lobby to catch the comments of the audience as it departed hastily.

'Boy, it was great till that third act,' one man said.

'Terrific for two acts, then it just died. This'll never make it on Broadway,' a woman declared.

'It's a shame to make a talent like Kit Lawrence play such a lousy third act,' a Yale student said.

The blame they heaped on his play did not offend Steve. Audiences were no more discerning than critics. Whatever was wrong with a production was always the author's fault. Whatever was right was always the actor's doing. It was the only inflexible rule in the theater.

Sam had arranged for two tables at Kaysey's, the only good restaurant in New Haven open after a performance. The cast sat at one table. Star, producer, director and author at another. He had selected tables discreetly far enough apart to allow for privacy.

'I'd like a drink,' Kit said immediately.

'Darling, let's forgo the drinks for now,' Sam suggested in a most paternal way. 'We've a lot to talk about.'

'I'd like a drink,' Kit insisted, evidencing more than a hint of displeasure.

To avoid a scene, Sam relented, signaled their waitress.

'What'll it be, honey?' the aging waitress asked.

'Double vodka on the rocks,' Kit said sweetly.

'And you gentlemen?' the waitress asked.

'Nothing,' Sam said.

'Nothing, thanks,' Jeff said.

Reading the look in Kit's eyes at this rebuke, Steve ordered, 'Scotch and water. With a twist.' That seemed to placate her.

Sam opened the meeting. 'Well, they sure liked the first two acts. So we've got a solid base to work from.' He had tried to sound optimistic. He failed.

Jeff picked it up. 'I think I staged Maria's entrance wrong. I'll restage it so we can try it tomorrow night before we open.'

Steve was relieved that the drinks arrived, since there was nothing he could say to avoid the real issue. While Kit sipped her drink, Sam consulted the menu, trying to tempt her with all the foods he knew she liked. She ordered another drink.

She had four. Doubles. The conversation continued. Sam and Jeff struggling to talk while avoiding the issue, the only issue. Through the discussion, Kit had sat imperiously silent, sipping iced vodka. She withdrew deeper and deeper within herself. Eventually her silence discouraged all talk. Sam signaled for the check.

It was a windy night. Kit shuddered and leaned close to Steve. He put his arm around her and walked her down the block and around the corner toward the hotel.

Sam and Jeff dropped behind. Deliberately.

'Jeff, Jeff, what are we going to do?' Sam entreated desperately.

'If I had any brains, I'd get on the first plane for the Coast and make a deal on a new film before this failure hurts my chances.'

'Can't be saved?' Sam asked.

'Sorry, Sam,' was Jeff's brusque professional prognosis. 'Sorry as hell I let you put your last dollars into it.'

'No regrets,' Sam said. 'When you've been through one terminal illness, you learn the libretto. You know everything you do is futile. The patient will die. But you have to live on. And you can't face asking yourself, Did I do everything I could for her? And then have to give yourself the wrong answer. For Kit, I would do it all over again.'

'You taking the show to Boston?' Jeff asked.

'Are you?'

'Whatever you say,' Jeff answered. 'After all, I don't want to give myself any wrong answers either.'

On the ninth floor of the hotel, Steve assisted Kit Lawrence out of the elevator. She maintained an air of dignity, walking with that determination alcoholics assume when they know they are drunk and under observation. She fumbled with her key. Steve had to open her door for her.

'Thank you, Steven,' she said, trying to maintain the aloof attitude of a star.

He held out the key to her. Instead, she grasped his hand desperately. 'Don't leave me, Steve. Don't leave me tonight. No matter what I did to your play.'

'You were great in the first two acts.'

Without relinquishing her grip, she pleaded, 'Steve, be smart! Get yourself another actress.'

'No, Kit!'

'Stay with me tonight?'

'That's no good – you know that.'

'I promise I won't seduce you. Just stay with me. Hold me? Hold me?' she pleaded. 'I need someone tonight.'

He undressed her. He put her to bed. He held her in his arms until she drifted off. He watched as she slept. The torment had gone out of her face. It was now innocent, lovely, untroubled. If the vodka helped her sleep, it had served a good purpose. But he dared not leave her alone for fear she might wake and, by one means or another, come into possession of a whole bottle.

He woke at dawn. She was in his arms, still sleeping. He had to gently disentangle himself to get back to his own room so he could call Ross.

He stood beside her bed taking one last look at her in

repose. He could not resist admiring her beauty. Her right arm raised and lying back on the pillow exposed her naked right breast. It was as perfect and enticing as it had ever been. He drew the blanket up to cover it.

Ross was waiting for his call.

'How did she take last night?'

'She had a few drinks.'

'A few?'

'Four. Doubles.'

'Uh-huh,' Ross observed, obviously distressed. 'She say anything?'

'She said, "Steve, be smart, get yourself another actress." '

'In a way that's good.'

'What's good about it?' Steve demanded. 'If we let her quit, she's right back to you. And this time, forever.'

'It's good that she's facing up to reality.'

'Tomorrow night after we open and she reads those notices, that'll be reality and also the end.'

'What would you rather do?' Ross asked. 'Close the show right now?'

'I don't know,' Steve confessed. 'I thought you would suggest something.'

'Brooks, there are no miracles in psychiatry. Despite what you authors keep writing,' Ross said sternly. 'This started as a desperate gamble. It still is. We have to proceed. But don't expect any miracles!'

'I picked the wrong story line.'

'If it does any good to assign blame, *we* picked the wrong story line,' Ross corrected, then decided, 'If I promised to come to the Boston opening, I'm quite sure that would sustain her.'

'Then do that, please?'

'Call me after the New Haven reviews are in.'

Following a very first performance, it was incumbent on the

director to discuss with the cast his own reactions and those of the audience.

'Well, kids, as *Time* magazine would say, "Last night, as it must to all theatrical companies, the first public performance came to the cast of *Reunion.*" How did it go? I am not going to tell you any fairy tales.

'We did well. And we did badly. I have a million little notes on Acts One and Two. Things we have to clean up. Sloppy entrances and exits. Crosses that are awkward. And more fluffs than I like to hear even on a first performance. I want everyone letter perfect for tonight's preview! If anyone, I said anyone, fluffs tonight, there's going to be hell to pay!'

Steve and Sam both felt Jeff was being too harsh. But as Jeff continued, his strategy became clear to them.

'I also found a million things wrong with my own direction. So I don't want anyone to be sensitive about criticism. Maria!'

'Yes?' Maria Patrick responded, sitting up alertly, prepared for a rebuke.

Instead, Jeff said humbly, 'I owe you a great big apology, darling.'

'Oh?' She relaxed somewhat.

'The way I staged your entrance. The attitude I gave you in the first few exchanges. Wrong. We'll have to work on it today. In fact,' Jeff said, making it appear a sudden inspiration, 'Charlie, tell you what! You take the cast down to the greenroom and run them through their lines. I'm going to work with Maria and Kit on the final scene.'

The cast cleared stage. Only the two women were left. Jeff Warrener leaped from the stage down into the house. He started up the aisle, calling out, 'Okay! From the top of the scene! Kit, you've dismissed everyone from your dressing room. Maria, you're outside the door waiting to be admitted. Let's go!'

In the front row, Sam and Steve were greatly relieved at

the skillful manner in which Jeff had focused on the chief weakness of the performance without once aiming any unsettling criticism at Kit.

They watched patiently as Jeff proceeded to redirect the entire scene, moment by moment. He did not alter the dialogue. But he changed the action completely.

At the start of rehearsals he had had Kit play the scene with a minimum of movement, to present the image of a fortress, solid, impregnable against the attacks, approaches, entreaties of her contrite mother. Maria was the one who should move, circle, trying to find a soft spot in Kit's armor. In the end Maria would fail and depart. Only then was Kit to reveal her soft inner self.

Now Jeff proceeded to reverse the entire choreography. Maria became the object of Kit's scrutiny and contempt, a defendant pinned in the witness chair. While Kit became the prosecutor, circling the guilty defendant.

Jeff's strategy was now clear to Steve. Force Kit into playing the scene by making her physically active.

Long experienced in the stratagems and wiles of stage directors, Maria Patrick sensed what Jeff was trying to accomplish. She cooperated eagerly.

From time to time she volunteered, 'Of course. I should have sensed that myself. I've been too aggressive in the scene.' 'Yes, Jeff, I see what you mean. I'm the guilty one. I'm the defendant, not prosecutor. Of course.'

Often she would murmur, 'Good. I love it, Jeff. Love it.'

Slowly, in the course of one long, difficult afternoon, Jeff Warrener had changed the entire aspect of the climactic scene. Kit cooperated to the extent that she did not resist, but dutifully did as she was told.

Steve and Sam watched, making no comment, though one thing disturbed them both. It was not like Kit Lawrence to accept change without contributing inventive and creative suggestions of her own. Today she made none. Eventually, her submissiveness became unnerving.

Steve was relieved when the woman from the box office came down the aisle to whisper, 'Call for you, Mr Brooks.'

'Brooks here.'

'Brooks here, too,' a woman's voice replied, joking.

'Melinda? What's up?' he asked, trying to sound casual and relaxed.

'Two things,' Melinda said, now very businesslike. 'First, your publisher insists on a firm delivery date. They're going to press with their catolog and they have to know.'

'I told you, I can't get back on the novel until after the New York opening.'

'And are the dates for your opening still firm?'

'Of course,' he replied defensively. 'What makes you ask?'

'The second thing,' Melinda said. 'The Shuberts had a man up at your preview last night.'

'How do you know?' he asked resentfully.

'In the theater only one thing travels faster than good gossip. Bad gossip.'

'Such as?'

'Kit Lawrence trouble.'

'That's a lie!' Steve denied vehemently.

Too vehemently, as it turned out. For Melinda did not reply, making his overreaction even more obvious.

'It'll get straightened out,' he said, in a less aggressive voice. 'They're working on it right now.'

'Mind if I come up and take a look?'

'Have I ever been able to stop you from doing anything?'

'Okay. Arrange a ticket for me for tonight.'

'It's only a preview,' he said, trying to stall.

'It'll be the same play tomorrow night, won't it?' she persisted.

'They'll be shaky tonight. We're putting in a lot of new staging.' He realized he was pleading with her not to come.

'What about the opening tomorrow night?'

'Openings are murder.' He offered a compromise, 'Come

Friday,' for he remembered that Sam had said there would be a fairly good house Friday night.

'Okay. Friday. Can we have dinner before the show?'

'Of course. We're only divorcing, we're not enemies.'

He went back into the auditorium. Kit and Maria were about to run through the entire scene with the new staging. Jeff had given them a five-minute break to look over the new moves they had noted in their scripts.

As Steve came down the aisle, Sam whispered, 'Anything important?'

'The Shuberts had a man here last night.'

'Oh, Christ!' Jeff said.

'Too bad,' Sam said, wondering, Would they have the nerve to deny him the New York theater, even though his deposit was already in? It would be a breach of contract. But the Shuberts were capable of anything. He must call New York his first free moment.

They ran through the scene. But Kit Lawrence gave no more of herself than she had given the night before. Resigned, Jeff hoped her new moves would at least beguile the audience into believing she was more involved. He had fooled audiences before. Perhaps he could fool them one more time.

Tonight they would see.

# *Twenty*

At seven thirty Kit Lawrence showed up at the theater, signed the attendance roster as every actor, star or bit player had to do under Equity rules. She went to her dressing room, slipped out of her clothes and into the worn dressing gown she relied on as a good-luck charm. She sat before the mirror, staring at her eyes as she worked on them. They flicked upward as a face in the doorway appeared in her mirror.

'Steve?'

'Yes, Kit.'

'Come in,' she invited casually.

'Not if you want to be alone.'

She had times when she hated the thought of anyone in her dressing room. Even during the height of their affair there had been times when she excluded him.

'Don't be afraid. I won't rape you.' She laughed.

He tried to sound enthusiastic. 'I think the work Jeff did this afternoon was terrific. He had you pinned down before. Now you can really let loose. It gives you a chance to really play it.'

She let him talk on until he finally realized it was futile. She had not responded to anything he said. He was relieved when the assistant stage manager called through the closed door, 'Five minutes, Miss Lawrence.'

She rose from her dressing table, slipped off her dressing gown, was completely naked and totally unselfconscious as she slid into her half-slip and her costume. As she turned to leave, she suddenly kissed Steve on the cheek.

'I know you're doing your best, Steve. And I do love you.'

What she did not say, but what was more apparent, was

that she had no confidence the scene would work. Worse, she seemed to have no will to succeed. No will to survive. She was walking through life as if she were walking through a technical rehearsal. Giving nothing. Partaking of nothing. Steve Brooks tried to believe that that would change when Ross called and told her he would come to the Boston opening.

The new staging did not help Kit or the scene. The reaction of the second-night preview audience was no better.

With the indomitable optimism and self-delusion it takes to survive in the theater, Sam declared, 'Look, she always came up for openings. I'm sure tomorrow night she'll be better. A whole lot better.'

Very early the morning after the opening, Steve Brooks dressed hastily and rushed down to the newsstand in the lobby to buy the morning papers. Sam and Jeff had already preceded him. Each held one newspaper open and a batch under the arm. They read hastily, but their faces told Steve all he had to know.

'Polite. They are killing us with politeness,' Sam moaned, passing one paper to him. Jeff gave him another. He read the first headline: '*New Play at Shubert Promising.*' To a hardened theater person, 'promising' was the courteous *coup de grâce.*

The second headline was less courteous. '*REUNION? Not Quite.*' The critic went on to counterpose the play's title against the reunion of Sam Rogers, Steve Brooks, Jeff Warrener and Kit Lawrence. He felt that the power and professionalism which had marked their earlier successes were sadly missing. He was especially harsh with Kit, saying she had been away too long and her technique had become rusty.

They sat in the coffee shop, over cold cups, pondering how to present the reviews to Kit.

Sam volunteered. 'She looks on me as a father; maybe it would hurt less if I did it.'

Jeff said, 'As director I should do it. That would make it more professional, less personal and painful.'

'I'll do it,' Steve insisted.

He went up to his room, studied all the reviews, hoping to extract some affirmative phrases with which to encourage her. He found none.

He called Ross. Ross was contemplative and silent, until he offered, 'I think now it's time for me to call and tell her I'll be at the Boston opening.'

'Are you going to say anything about these reviews?'

'I'll have to mention the Hartford reviews. She knows we get the *Courant*.'

'That one picks on her specifically.'

'With a patient as alert as Kit, my failure to mention it would be even worse.'

All the newspapers under his arm, Steve Brooks went to the door of Kit's room and listened. He heard music. She must be up. He knocked gently.

'Yes?' she called out.

'It's me.'

She was wide awake and must have been for a time, since her hair was brushed and she was in her light blue dressing gown. She smiled and offered her cheek to be kissed.

She noticed the papers under his arm. She settled back on the chaise and said, 'Read!'

With radio music as the background, Steve Brooks started. By the time he reached the last review, Kit was staring grimly out the wide window toward the ancient buildings of Yale. In reading the last review, he carefully edited out the specific criticsm of her.

'Not very good,' she said after a long silence.

'Promising – they said it was promising,' Steve tried to encourage.

'I haven't been called promising since my first play,' she said sadly.

She went off to the bathroom. He desperately hoped Ross would call.

He had waited for what seemed an unduly long time. Fear overcame him. He went to the door, pressed his ear against it, heard the sound of rushing water. It was not spasmodic, as when one is washing, but a continuous torrent. It alarmed him.

'Kit!' he called out. 'Kit! Are you all right? Kit!'

She did not answer. He pounded on the door. 'Kit! Open up! Do you hear me? Open up!'

Soon the sound of water ceased. She unlocked the door and peered out, smiling. 'God, can't a lady go to the john without creating a scene?' she stepped out and stared at him. 'What did you think, Steve?'

He did not answer.

'Go on, tell me,' she teased, smiling. 'What did you think? That I'd gone in there to slash my wrists? Or take some pills? Tell me!' she insisted, no longer smiling but angry now.

'Of course not,' he said, hoping he made it convincing.

'I wouldn't do anything so stupid,' she said, 'though it's nice to know you care.'

Deeply pained by the reviews and unwilling to let on, she had needed to make sure he was still worried about her.

She patted his face lovingly. 'Dear Steve, dear, dear, Steve, I told you, get yourself another actress. Now they've told you, so you must know.'

Before he could answer, her phone rang. 'Do you want to talk to anyone?' he asked.

'No.'

He picked up the phone. 'Yes?'

He put his hand over the mouthpiece. 'It's Ross.'

She hesitated, then took the phone. As if she had stepped into a character she was playing, she teased him. 'Oh, Ross! How nice of you to remember!'

He must have said something flattering, for she smiled and

responded. 'I bet you say that to all your patients. Or is it only the ones you have affairs with?' She overrode his protest. 'Now, Ross, don't be so sensitive. To me, it was the best part of the treatment. If you want a testimonial, I'd be delighted. "Psychoanalysts make the best lovers." Or should I write, "*Jewish* psychoanalysts make the best lovers"? Be honest with me: if I'd been Jewish, would you have divorced your wife and married me? You can tell me now that you're safe.'

His reply made her stop laughing and apologize: I'm sorry, Ross. I was only teasing. You know I hate myself when I say things like that. I just can't help it. Can't.'

She listened a long time, smiling, toying with her long blond hair. But as the subject changed, her attitude changed.

'The *Hartford Courant*?' she asked, soberly. 'What did it say? I see.' She glared at Steve, covered the phone. 'You didn't read me that part. About my being away from the theater too long.'

Something Ross said surprised and delighted her. 'You will? Wonderful!' She paused before she asked, 'Will you bring your wife?' He had obviously said no, for she was satisfied with his answer.

She hung up, her hand resting on the phone as if reluctant to break off contact. 'He's coming to Boston,' she said, with great satisfaction.

'Terrific! You can't accuse him of not caring.'

'No,' she said provocatively, enjoying a secret of her own.

To make the most of the moment, Steve urged, 'You'll have to be great for him. Show him what you can really do.'

'Oh, I will,' she promised.

Steve was not reassured. Something going on in her tormented mind gave him reason for enormous concern.

# *Twenty-one*

They had rehearsed all Friday afternoon. Steve walked Kit back to the hotel. He made every pretense at being cheerful and optimistic. She remained silent and thoughtful. In the lobby, she permitted him a casual kiss on the cheek and ran to the nearest elevator. He went to the desk for his messages. There was only one.

*'I'm in Room 1819.'*

At first he was puzzled. Then he remembered. Melinda! And he had forgotten to reserve a seat for her. He called the box office at once. He freshened up before he dialed 1819.

'Mel?'

'Yes, Steve, it's me.'

'Ready for a drink?'

'We have things to discuss before we start drinking.'

'Okay.' Then he laughed. 'My place, or yours?'

'That's not funny,' she said curtly. 'I'll be right down.'

'It's room fifteen—' He was interrupted.

'I know. Fifteen eighteen.'

That was Melinda. She always knew everything a little before she was supposed to. Efficient, practical Melinda had never needed special legislation or a constitutional amendment to secure her rights.

He was surprised to see that instead of one of her usual well-tailored expensive suits she wore a black semiformal theater dress with the distinctive look of a designer original. He noticed, too, that her neckline was cut quite low. Not too obvious, though. Melinda would never be obvious. Just suggestive enough to let him know how good a body she possessed.

She submitted to his dutiful kiss.

'Shall I order up some drinks?'

'We'd better talk first. We can go out later,' she said.

'Shoot.'

She slipped into an easy chair, crossed her long, graceful legs and leaned back, as much in control as she was in her own office.

'First, your publisher is furious. Because they like what you've done so far.'

' "Like"?' Steve interrupted, pointing up her breach of professional etiquette. An agent talking to a client never said someone "liked" his work. They always "loved" it.

Melinda took an almost imperceptible pause, then continued: 'You have a contract. With a delivery date. They're furious because you're past that already. We're in a flush time for paperback auctions. Prices have never been higher. And everyone feels the bottom may drop out sometime soon. So it would have been helpful to have the whole manuscript by this time.'

'Sorry,' he said sincerely, 'but I had to do this.'

'*This* is another thing I want to talk about,' she continued without pause. 'If "this" goes down the drain, as I have every reason to believe, it will affect your price. In books. Films. Even television.'

'I'm into it. What can I do?'

'I'll bet you're *into* it!' Melinda said acidly. 'It's started all over again. Kit. That's who you're into.'

'That's not true!'

'If you didn't find her irresistible, you wouldn't have got involved in this mess. Now, there's one way that might reduce the damaging effects of a disaster.'

'And that is?' he asked belligerently. Melinda had a way about her. She was dictatorial. Smotheringly motherly. And damn near always right. If only she were wrong once in a while, he lamented silently.

'Close the show. Here. In New Haven. There's a certain dignity in a smart playwright, a good director and an able producer admitting they made a mistake. "We goofed. Sorry. We are bowing out gracefully." '

'You know I can't do that, Mel.'

'Of course. What happens to lovely, lovable, alcoholic, psychotic, darling Kit?' She no longer made any attempt to conceal her hostility.

'We've given each other our word, we are going to save that girl . . .'

'Or die trying?' Melinda asked in controlled anger.

'Let's go get that drink.'

'I've never seen a drink that solved anything,' Melinda persisted. 'Face the facts. You have lost a half-year of time, plus the chance at a paperback sale under most favorable conditions. You have a nasty disagreement with your publisher. And it's not worth it. Everyone in the theater knows it won't work. I've checked around. The smart money says forget it.'

He did not answer.

'I know. You can't forget *her* so you can't forget *it*. Yes, let's get that drink. It won't solve anything. But it might make me feel better!'

They drank at Kaysey's, making small talk, meaningless talk. He left her at the front door of the theater and went backstage to make his usual encouraging visits to the dressing rooms. Whatever qualms or fears a playwright nurtured, he never let on to his cast.

During the intermissions he avoided Melinda. He waited tensely for the climactic third-act scene. And as usual, he was distressed and frustrated.

He could no longer avoid Melinda. He waited in the lobby. He asked the inevitable 'Well?'

'That is a very good play,' Melinda said in the unemotional voice of a doctor rendering a diagnosis. 'Another actress in that part could make a hit out of it.'

'We can't replace her,' Steve said. 'That's it. Final.'

'May I go back and see her?'

'Don't say anything to upset her,' Steve warned.

He knocked on Kit's door.

'Who is it?'

'Me.'

'Come in, Steve.'

He opened the door briskly. Kit was naked except for her half-slip. He tried to back out. But Melinda was too close behind him. He knew she would not fail to mark his familiarity with Kit, who thought nothing of welcoming him half nude. Worse, Kit made no effort to cover herself until she saw Melinda. Only then did she seize her robe from the back of her chair and cover her naked breasts.

'Sorry. I was only expecting Steve,' she apologized, the slightest trace of feline vindictiveness in her voice. She retreated behind the screen and continued dressing.

'I enjoyed your performance,' Melinda said, deliberately sounding insincere.

'Did you? The critics didn't. And I don't think the audience cares for it much either. I keep telling Steve to replace me, but he won't.'

Melinda glanced toward Steve. The look on his face, embarrassed and pained, made no denial.

'You're his agent. You tell him. "Now, Steve, I insist you replace that girl." Is that the way agents talk? Or is it different if the agent is also the wife?' Kit laughed.

She emerged from behind the screen, not in the slacks and shirt she usually wore going to and from the theater, but in a bright figured dress. She began to brush her long golden hair, speaking to Melinda by glancing at her in the mirror.

'Why can't you talk some sense into that man of yours?' Kit asked. But she kept brushing her hair until the very act assumed a pointedly obvious sensuality of which Melinda became noticeably aware. Christ, Steve said to himself, she's trying to seduce me while Melinda watches.

Kit tied no ribbon about her hair but let it fall loosely over her shoulders. She looked like a young girl. With meticulous care, she proceeded to apply street makeup. She worked slowly, seductively. Her lips became red and voluptuous. Her bright blue eyes appeared even more luminous than on the stage.

Melinda kept glancing at Steve Brooks, who grew more and more uncomfortable with every bit of self-adornment Kit applied. Finally, Kit turned from the mirror and presented herself to them.

'Kit,' Steve said, 'if you have a date and we're keeping you . . .'

'You know I have no date,' she said blithely.

'Then . . . then why not come out with us and have some supper?' he was forced to ask.

'Oh, I'd feel I was intruding.'

'Please do!' Melinda insisted, smiling as convincingly as she could manage.

'I wouldn't dream of it,' Kit said, smiling back graciously.

Steve stared at Kit. Then at Melinda. He was astounded at the resemblance. Both blond; both tall, slim figures, good breasts, which they were now both showing off to advantage. There was so little difference between them that he felt he should as easily love Melinda as Kit. Yet there was an indefinable difference between them that made *all* the difference.

Once more Melinda insisted, 'Please, come out with us.'

'No, really, I'd feel uncomfortable. You two must have lots to talk about.' Then Kit added, 'Besides, I've had so much of Steve these last two months, I feel guilty. I ought to share him.'

At Kaysey's they ordered drinks, talked a little, ordered seconds.

Melinda said, 'I can see what it is. She's fascinating. A

woman all the way. Everything she says, everything she does is aimed at the man. And she is so good at it.'

Steve did not dispute her words; it would have been foolish to try.

Melinda said, 'She can't have done what she just did and be as sick as you say.'

'She is.'

'Winging that whole scene, from the moment we caught her bare-breasted. Covering up only when she saw me. Making up so beautifully just to walk back to the hotel and go to bed alone. If that's sick, I'd like to be sick.'

'The whole thing is an act,' he protested. 'She always has to make sure some man loves her. When her competition came on the scene, she went to war.'

'She fights a damn good war,' Melinda said enviously. Adding as an afterthought, 'And *do* you?'

'What?'

'Still love her? I don't mean from before, I mean from now. From the time rehearsals started. Steve?'

'What are you talking about?' he evaded.

'You were the one who said, "She has to make sure some man loves her." Does he?'

'Look, let's order.'

They studied their menus. In silence. Until, from behind the protection of his menu, Steve said, 'I give you my word, nothing's happened. Not even once.'

When they stepped into the hotel elevator, Steve pushed the button marked 18. She stared at him.

'I'll walk you home. It's the least I can do.'

At her door, she handed him the key. He unlocked the door, pushed it slightly open. He kissed her on the cheek – a casual good-night kiss. Then, whether out of need or from familiarity, he embraced her. She slipped into his arms and they clung together. He could feel her breasts against him, and her long, graceful thighs. He pressed against her cheek and whispered, 'Melinda?'

'Uh-huh,' she breathed, acquiescing.

It had been a long time for them – months. Yet throughout the passionate act he could not separate in his mind Melinda from Kit, or Kit from Melinda. Finally they were one woman.

He lay on his back staring up at the darkness. Her head rested in the crook of his arm. They said nothing. To speak would only destroy their satisfaction.

Steve thought, Damn it, why can't I love her as she deserves? She's bright and good and affirmative. While Kit . . . It did no good for him to dwell on the dangers Kit presented.

Melinda thought, He doesn't love, he performs. He doesn't conquer, he seeks refuge. He needs someone to take his mind off Kit. Which only means that he's more involved with Kit than he can ever be with any other woman. Give him up. Forget him. Tell him to change agents. Only get him out of your life. Otherwise, you'll be as sick about him as he is about Kit, who is so sick she will endanger us all. Let him go. *Make* him go. But in the morning. Not now. Not while he's here and we're lying this way together.

She turned on her side to kiss him on the lips with an open mouth. He made love to her again.

Melinda woke first, slipped into the bathroom, dressed quickly. She paused only long enough to write a note.

*Steve, dear, had to rush. Taking early train back to NY. The room is paid for. Love, Mel.*

The sound of the stubborn ball-point pen scratching on cheap hotel stationery roused him.

'Mel?'

'Sorry. I didn't mean to wake you. Go back to sleep.'

Instead he turned on the bedside lamp. 'What's that?'

'I was leaving you a note.'

He held out his hand. She surrendered it. He glanced at it and smiled.

'What's funny?'

' "The room is paid for." Typical Melinda. Takes care of all the details. Don't leave any loose ends.'

'Don't, Steve,' she pleaded, suddenly visibly distressed.

'Mel?' he asked solicitously.

'I wanted to avoid this. That's why I tried to leave early. I'm not as good at it as she is. I don't know how to improvise a scene. And if I did, I wouldn't know how to play it. So I was trying to get off gracefully without an exit line. But it didn't work.

'Or I didn't *want* it to work. Maybe I wrote that note just to wake you. So now you're up and I have to say my piece before I go.'

'If it's going to make you uncomfortable . . .'

'No, that wouldn't be Melinda. You said it yourself. Take care of the details. Don't leave any loose ends. Okay. Let's get one last loose end out of the way!' she said with determination.

'I used to feel that you were making love to her all the while you were in me. Last night was even worse. She deliberately seduced you, aroused you and left you panting. You didn't make love to me. You just used me to get over the passion you have for her.'

'Mel, no . . .' he tried to protest.

'It's true!'

'I didn't want you to come up. You insisted. Remember that, you insisted!'

'Oh, I remember,' she agreed in a most argumentative way. 'Yes, I "insisted." That's one way to put it. The man who is still my husband is endangering his career and the rest of his life to save a woman who is beyond saving. The woman who destroyed our marriage. Who might destroy him. And I'm supposed to stay in New York and go about my business, taking care of details and loose ends.'

She exploded in a burst of anger as she demanded, 'Well, what the hell do you think I am?'

'Mel, Mel,' he said, as he tried to take her in his arms. She rejected his embrace.

'I came this far to have my say and I am going to have it!'

'Okay, Mel,' he said, trying to soothe her, 'say it. Please.'

His gentleness disarmed her. The enormous protest she had been harboring emerged more softly.

'Steve . . . Steve . . .' she began. 'I had to come up to see for myself. Partly about the show. Mostly about us. I've done a lot of thinking in the months you were out at the University. I said to myself, God, I have so much to give him. Looks, and brains, and most of all I have love to give him. I can do for him all the things he hates to do. Take care of all the loose ends. I can free him to do the best and most mature work of his career. I can give him all that if he'll only accept it.

'But he won't. Why? I asked myself. Why does he continue to love her, and not me? I could find only one answer. She's in trouble, in danger, always has been. She needs him. But Melinda, Melinda is so good with loose ends. Melinda is self-sufficient. Melinda doesn't need anyone.

'Well, Stevie, boy, the tragedy is, Melinda is *not* so self-sufficient. She only *seems* to be. She does need someone. But it's so hard to convince him. So hard.'

'Mel, when this production is over, we'll talk about it,' he promised.

'By the time this production is over there won't be anything left to talk about.'

'Mel, I had to do this. I owe it to her.'

'What?' Melinda asked with surgical incisiveness. 'Exactly what do you owe her? I'd like to know. She lived with you for a time. You wanted to marry her; she never wanted to marry you. She must be great in bed. She would have to be, to have had so many men—'

'Mel,' he tried to interrupt.

She would not be stopped. 'So many men. You, Jeff, Dr Ross and how many hundred others? Deny it. Tell me it isn't so. She needs men. She devours them. She has no devotion. No loyalties. Yet all of you feel such loyalty to her. I want to know, Steve, exactly what is it you owe her? Your career? Your life? What is it that makes all of you so indebted to her that she has you dancing to her insane tune? Tell me! I'm curious. I am very curious!' Her bitterness was only to camouflage her hurt. Her lips began to quiver. She turned away.

'Mel?' His voice was asking her to face him. 'Mel, there's nothing wrong in weeping. Nothing wrong in being vulnerable.'

She turned back, eyes moist. 'I didn't want you to see that. I was determined to be solid, strong Melinda, as usual. I was not going to say nasty things about her. I was going to be cool and professional. I was going to be your agent, not your wife. Maybe I shouldn't have let you make love to me last night. Or maybe I shouldn't have made love to you. Because I did. God knows, I tried. I thought, I love him more than she ever could. I'll prove it to him. But I didn't figure on the only thing that counts. You love her more than you could ever love me.'

'That isn't true,' he protested. 'I couldn't live with myself if for the rest of my life I had to think that she was rotting in some institution, or had killed herself because of something I failed to do.'

'And when you get to Boston?'

'The reviews?'

'Yes, the reviews. You can precipitate exactly what you're trying to guard against.'

'We may,' he conceded.

'Then will you go on blaming yourself forever?'

'At least I'll have done my part.'

'No, Steve, it won't be that easy for you. The very thing that makes you such a good writer, conscience, won't let go of you. For the rest of your life you'll be asking, What did I do wrong? What didn't I do right? What more could I have done that would have saved her?'

He did not dispute her words.

'Don't you see, Steve, she not only has an incurable disease, but she's a carrier. She infects everyone who has contact with her. To love her is to catch the disease. And evidently there's no cure. No cure.'

'Believe me, Mel, when this is over, and I finish my work, we'll talk about us. Seriously. We will,' he promised.

'Without her present it would still be a *ménage à trois.* No, thanks. As your agent I'm content with ten percent. But as your wife I want all of you: not just what she left over.'

She dried her eyes, repaired the damage and was gone. He picked up her note. He stared at it. 'The room is paid for'. It said more than that. It summed up the total difference between the two women. Kit would never have had a thought for anything so practical. Melinda would never have thought of anything less.

Damn it, why can't a man love the woman who's best for him?

Kit was sitting at her dressing table, making up for the Saturday matinee, when Steve opened her door.

'Kit? How's everything?'

'Oh, fine,' she said cheerfully.

'Good house this afternoon,' he lied. The box office had just told him it would be a poor house, in view of the unfavorable reviews.

'Are you going to stand in that hallway all afternoon?' she asked, flirting through the mirror. Her blue eyes were sparkling and mischievous. He knew the look. But he came in nevertheless.

The etiquette of the theater made its demands. He kissed her lightly. She held his face close to hers while she said with a pathetic pout, 'Steve, I tried to reach you.'

'When?' he asked, trying to lean back from her, but her hold was too firm.

'Early this morning. I was up most of the night, thinking about that scene in the third act. I wanted to ask you something. I called your room. You weren't there.'

'No, no, I wasn't,' he admitted, wondering that she could make him feel guilty about having spent the night with his own wife.

'Do you still love her, Steve?'

'I'm trying to figure that out.'

'I wouldn't blame you,' Kit said. 'She's pretty. And young. Younger than I am. And she isn't sick. Is she, Steve?'

'Please, Kit.' He tried to terminate the conversation.

'Does *she* love *you*?' Kit persisted.

'Yes.'

'Not as much as I do,' she said, pressing his face to hers. She had to move only slightly for their lips to meet. She kissed him, with a moist open mouth. After a long moment, she drew back slightly and whispered, 'Steve, you'll see. In Boston, I will be great. Just for you. I'll make your play a hit in Boston. We won't have any third-act trouble there,' she promised.

He used that opportunity to change the subject. 'Kit, what did you want to ask me about the third act?'

'Ask?' she echoed, puzzled. Her face betrayed that she had no memory of having just said that.

'You tried to call me because you wanted to ask something about the third act,' he reminded her.

'Oh, that. It was nothing. Nothing, Steve.' She kissed him again. 'Now, you're going to make me late for "Places, please!" ' she said, disengaging herself to continue making up.

He stared at her in the mirror until she looked up and caught him. She smiled.

'Boston, Steve. You'll see,' she said, making a seductive promise.

Steve Brooks and Jeff Warrener watched the crew begin to strike the set. Outside the loading doors, two huge trucks waited to receive it in sections so that they could start up to Boston by four in the morning.

Long after midnight, Jeff said. 'Let's get some sleep.'

He knew, and Steve Brooks knew, that neither of them would get much sleep between now and morning, when they had to emplane for Boston.

At the hotel there was a note in Steve's box. 'Call me' was all it said. No name. No room number.

'Kit?'

'Yes, Steve?'

'You sound sleepy. I wake you?'

'No. I've been watching a prehistoric Brando film on TV. *The Young Lions.* God, he was pompous. Even in those days.' She laughed.

'You've got to be up early,' he warned. 'We all do.'

'I've already turned it off. Boring. Though maybe it was Monty Clift. I got chills when I saw his new face. It's spooky. He was so handsome before his accident. Now it's a mask.'

'Kit, you call me?'

'Yes.'

'What about?'

'Melissa . . . I mean Melinda: what's her address?'

'Why?'

'I want to write her a note.'

Steve became wary. 'Why, Kit?'

'To apologize.'

'What for?' he asked, with curiosity and concern.

'I'm a bitch. A rude, thoughtless, destructive, jealous bitch.' Her voice was calm. She sounded completely sincere and contrite.

'What do you mean?'

'Last night. I did that deliberately. Standing there half naked, making up, dressing up. It's as if I wanted to say to her, "He's mine if I want him." That was wrong. Bitchy. I had no right. No right, Steve.'

He heard her voice break. If she was acting, it was superb. Before she could begin to weep, he said, 'There's no need, Kit. I'm sure she understands.'

'I don't want to be "understood"! Or have allowances made for me! I don't want people saying, She's a crazy lady, don't blame her for what she does. When I'm wrong, I should be told so. And I should have a chance to set things straight. So I want to write to her. What her address?'

He hesitated. There was no predicting what Kit might write.

'Steve?' she insisted.

'Eight eighty-nine Madison.'

'Is that where you lived, when you were together?'

'Yes.'

'And made love?'

'Kit, two people, when they're married, they generally make love. Do we have to talk about it?'

'I just . . . just wondered, that's all,' she said, still contrite. 'I'll write her. Tonight.'

'Let it wait. Get some sleep,' he urged.

'No, I'll write to her tonight!' Kit insisted.

She went to the desk, opened the drawer and found the usual meager supply of hotel stationery, the usual dry pen. She wasted one sheet of paper trying to get it to write. Once she did, she began to compose a letter.

*Dear Melinda, I want to tell you how sorry I am . . .*

She crossed that out and began anew. *Dear Melinda, I owe you an apology. For my conduct of last night. I deliberately tried to give you the impression that Steve and I . . .* She crossed out *Steve* and made it *Steven . . . that Steven and I have something going. That's not true. We just work together. I admire him. But I don't love him. And he does not love me . . .*

She crumpled that sheet of paper and began again. *Dear Melinda, That was pretty terrible what I did to Steve last night. I mean, putting him on the spot that way. Trying to make you believe that we're getting it on together.* She crossed out *getting it on together* and changed it to *that we're having an affair.* She did not like it, crumpled that sheet and started a fresh one.

By the end of an hour she had used up all the stationery. She could not avoid the mirror that confronted her across the writing desk. Devoid of any makeup, eyes puffy from lack of sleep, she stared at herself. She began to weep. She asked herself in a bitter whisper, 'Why can't I ever do anything right? Why?'

She flattened out one of the crumpled sheets and on the clean side she wrote, *Dear Melinda, I am a bitch. I always have been. Forgive me. Somebody, please, somewhere, forgive me.* She tried to sign it but could not.

She lowered her head to the writing table and wept, asking in a childish whisper, "Why? Why?'

# Part 5

## *Twenty-two*

With previous shows, Steve Brooks had always looked forward to returning to the Ritz in Boston. It was a place of fond memories, of past successes, a place that offered perfumed elevators and always held the promise of good things.

This time the fragrance in the hallways and the air of luxury mocked him. He knew he would leave here sadder and less successful than at any time in the past. The bellman had carried his bags and his portable typewriter to a large room that looked out over the Boston Common. On such a windy fall day, with the dry leaves being tumbled and driven across the great open park, the Common was a pleasing sight. But nothing could please him today.

As he was tipping the bellman, the phone rang.

'Yes?'

'Steven Brooks?' a modest New England voice inquired.

Familiar, yet he could not identify it immediately, so he admitted cautiously, 'Yes.'

'Edwin Mortimer,' said Boston's most esteemed drama critic.

'Oh, Edwin, sorry. I should have recognized you at once.'

Mortimer said drily. 'I don't know why. Since you've deserted us for writing novels. How many years since you've been up here with a new play?'

'Five?'

'Six,' Mortimer corrected. 'Free for lunch?'

'Unless some emergency crops up.'

'Locke-Ober's?'

'Okay. One o'clock.'

They were seated in a quiet corner of the ancient restaurant,

Mortimer toying with a glass of white wine, Steve nursing a bourbon and water. They had disposed of all the clichéd conversation critics and playwrights make together. Why good playwrights drift away from the theater to write novels or screenplays. The depressing mortality statistics inherent in Broadway plays. The outlandish costs. But it was all passing talk, interesting but inconsequential.

It was over coffee that Mortimer observed, in his dry and modest way, 'You're going to preview tomorrow and Tuesday.'

'Yes.'

'Good idea.'

Steve glanced across the table at Mortimer. He was a white-haired man with a ruddy complexion, a lean face, his sunken cheeks giving evidence of his advancing years. But his eyes still remained steel-blue and sharp – not the teary eyes of age. For a moment the men stared at each other.

'Then you heard?' Steve asked.

'I heard,' Mortimer admitted.

'Did you see the New Haven reviews?'

'No, but I know.'

'Of course.'

'I would like to come to your preview tomorrow,' Mortimer said. 'I've never done that before. But this time I want to see a preview.'

With any other critic, in New York or Philadelphia, Steve Brooks would have been suspicious and evasive. But Edwin Mortimer was truly a friend of the theater. Fair, though quite negative when he felt justified, he was never vicious or ruthless. Nor did his contact with a play end with his review. Playwrights, directors and producers always felt free to consult him for advice or suggestions.

'However,' Mortimer was saying, 'I won't come unless you say it's okay.'

'It's okay.'

'Can we talk after the show?' Mortimer asked.

'Where?'

'Is Kit staying at the Ritz?'

'Yes.'

'Then we better not make it the Ritz bar.'

'She's not drinking, if that's what you're worried about,' Steve said defensively.

'It isn't that. But I wouldn't want to meet her. Not yet. She'd ask me what I thought.'

'And you'd tell her.' Steve knew.

'I may lose friends that way. But I sleep better at night.'

'Where, then?'

Mortimer named a small restaurant just off the Common.

'May I bring Jeff Warrener and Sam Rogers?'

Mortimer paused to sip his coffee, then said, 'Might as well.'

Mortimer was waiting for them at the restaurant. Sam thanked him for the nice note he had sent when Bertha died. Mortimer complimented Jeff on his last two films and invited him to address the Dramatic Arts class he taught at Boston University.

Then Mortimer added, '*If* you can find the time, of course.' It was a more than subtle hint that Mortimer felt there was considerably more work to do on the production.

'All right, Edwin, let's have it,' Sam said.

'It's a pretty solid play. And I like most of it. However . . .' Mortimer paused.

'There's always a however,' Sam said sadly.

'Her third act made me wish the rest of the play wasn't so good.'

'How can there be such a thing as too good?' Sam demanded.

'Because,' Mortimer continued unhappily, 'you know the old biblical saying, "To whom much is given, from him much shall be required." Well, with audiences, and critics, "To whom much is given, by them much more is expected."

Her third act does not fulfill the promise of her first two.'

Sam nodded sadly.

'I had heard rumors. So I was afraid of what I might have to do in my review. That's why I wanted to see a preview. After all, I have an obligation to my readers.

'But I also have an obligation to the theater. And to those who work in it. I have an obligation to Kit. In a way,' he recalled modestly, 'I helped to make her a star. Her first big review was the one I gave her. I feel I own part of her legend. I've always felt sorry for her. There's something there, some secret sorrow, that like the grain of sand in the oyster finally created the pearl. Till now, that element has made her performances electric. But this time, for some reason I can't explain, it's destroying her performance.'

None of the three felt able to dispute what he had said.

'She's been away a long time,' Mortimer observed.

'This is her first play in years,' Steve said.

'I meant,' Mortimer corrected, 'she's been in an *institution* a long time.'

Steve nodded. Mortimer's steel-blue eyes reflected his discomfort at what he had to say now.

'Sam, can you close this play? Before it opens here?' Mortimer asked.

'I can't do that to her.'

'If you don't, it will be worse,' Mortimer warned regretfully. 'I can't give her a good review. I will let her down as gently as I can. But my colleague on the other paper is sadistic. Totally ruthless. I know what he'll do to her.'

'Damn it,' Jeff exploded, 'the least she's entitled to is respect! Whatever problem she may have, she has been a great lady in the theater!'

'Respect,' Mortimer echoed, smiling bitterly. 'That bastard doesn't know what the word means.'

Sam suggested, 'Couldn't you talk to him? I don't mean to tell him what we just told you. But somehow, in some way

. . .' He apologized at once. 'Sorry, Edwin. That was an insulting thing to propose.'

'It would only infuriate him,' Mortimer explained. 'He's one of those journalists who believes that vindictiveness is the main function of a free press.'

A sincerely troubled man, Mortimer left.

'Don't be so depressed, Sam,' Steve said. 'We still have one chance.'

'What chance?'

'Ross'll be here for the opening. She knows that. I have a hunch that for the first time you're going to see that scene play the way it's supposed to.'

Jeff nodded skeptically. Sam picked up the check and said, 'Let's go, boys.'

Because he was far less optimistic than he pretended, Steve Brooks placed a late-night call to Dr Ross.

'If you're calling to make sure,' Ross anticipated, 'I said I'll be at the opening and I will.'

Steve reported Edwin Mortimer's prediction.

'I see,' Ross replied, grim now. 'Believe me, Brooks, I've been giving this a lot of thought. That's why I'm anxious to be there tomorrow. To see if I'm right.'

'About what?'

'My theory as to why she's having such difficulty with that final scene.'

'Isn't it a little late to be having "theories"?' Steve responded angrily. Then relented. 'Okay, what's your theory?'

'The reason Kit is having such difficulty with the scene is guilt. Guilt about her mother.'

'She never did anything against her mother. Her mother is the one who should experience the guilt,' Steve protested.

'But Kit *did* do something. Has *always* done it.'

'Done what?'

'Hated her,' Ross responded, 'still hates her. And that hatred is so enormous that she feels guilty for harboring it, feels even more guilty about expressing it openly. Feels that she will be punished for expressing it. I'll watch very carefully for that tomorrow night.'

'And if you're right? Where does that leave us?'

'Then you'd better start thinking about some way around it in your script,' Ross suggested.

'Like what?' Steve demanded, with the aggressive defensiveness of playwrights when their work is being challenged or impugned.

'See you tomorrow night' was all Ross said before he hung up.

There was a pretense at a gala opening. Old-line Back Bay society mingled with young professionals from the suburbs and college students from Cambridge, who were a mainstay of Boston theater. Mortimer, his colleague and two dozen press representatives from local papers and radio and television stations were there.

Ten minutes before 'Places, please,' Steve went backstage. He found Kit in her dressing room, finishing her makeup. She looked radiant. Before he could say anything, she asked, 'Is he out there? Did you see him?'

'Ross? Yes.'

'He came. He came,' she said with tremendous excitement.

'I spoke to him. He's looking forward to your performance.'

She seemed exhilarated by the challenge.

'Is he leaving tonight?' she asked, trying to make it seem a casual question.

'I don't know. I didn't ask.'

'He'll stay,' she decided confidently.

She turned from her mirror and presented herself. 'There! How do I look?'

'Fantastic,' he said truthfully.

Her natural beauty seemed to have been illuminated by

her expectation of seeing her cherished Ross again. Her eyes beamed. Her skin seemed to glow.

She rose to find her first-act costume, and as she did she let her robe slip open. He caught sight of her naked body. He felt guilty until he glanced up and caught her staring at him, a superior little smile on her face. She was in a seductive mood tonight. Though it was Ross she was obviously intent on seducing, Steve felt no jealousy. Only a surge of optimism. She would go onstage and do it for Ross tonight.

Steve waited in back of the house. The light broke across the apron of the stage. The curtain went up with a whisper. There was a polite reception for the set. The play was on.

On her entrance, Kit received a star's applause. She waited indulgently until it was dying down before she spoke her opening line. Her first act went very well.

In a hasty conference in the lobby, Sam spoke to Steve. 'It's different. Better. It *is* better, isn't it, Steve?'

'Yes, Sam.'

Across the lobby Edwin Mortimer stood alone, making notes on the small pad he always carried to first nights. He glanced at Sam and Steve, giving them a slight encouraging nod. Word of mouth in the lobby was excellent.

The second act went even better. Kit was brilliant. She slowed her pace in some places to let the audience savor her best moments. She made up for it with certain of the lines, which she delivered with the same brilliant pizzicato effect that Heifetz could extract from a violin. The applause at the end of the second act was enthusiastic and prolonged. She had brought them up to a height of expectation that sent them out into the lobby enthralled.

Sam was so excited he was trembling. Steve said, 'I told you. What she wouldn't do for us she's doing for Ross.'

Edwin Mortimer, across the lobby, appeared quietly delighted as he made his notes.

'We're home free,' Sam said. 'Even that other critic has to admit she's brilliant. Brilliant!'

Jeff Warrener made his way out of the house against the tide of the returning audience. 'I was just back to see her,' he enthused. 'She's the old Kit. I mean the young Kit. She is the young Kit again!'

The audience waited anxiously to participate in the third act Kit had promised them by her brilliance in the first two. She came on bright, fresh, eager. It was only just before the entrance of Maria Patrick that a line of dialogue seemed to elude her. She improvised one of similar import.

The audience would never have noticed, except that a moment later Kit recalled the correct line and used it, leaving the other characters onstage momentarily hung up and having to ad-lib their way back to the continuity of the scene.

The confidence of the audience began to dissipate. Steve could sense that silent but alarming uneasiness which infects an audience when a play begins to come apart. Edwin Mortimer slumped slightly in his seat, as if the air had gone out of him. The other critic leaned forward, skeptically. Dr Ross sat immobile, staring diagnostically.

At the moment of Maria Patrick's entrance, Kit Lawrence went dry, completely dry – and she remained so. Maria was forced to ad-lib virtually the entire scene. The act staggered to a conclusion, leaving Kit alone onstage as Maria exited.

When Maria had gone, Kit did not turn upstage and make the subtle final gesture Jeff had devised. Instead, she slumped to the floor and like a mute, withdrawn child began sketching invisible patterns on the carpeting.

The curtain came down. There was a hush in the house. Someone started to applaud. The rest of the audience joined in. But the applause was grudging – obligatory.

Edwin Mortimer passed them as he left the theater. He gave no sign, no farewell. They listened to the reactions of the audience as they filed out. One long-haired young college girl in jeans summed it up: 'Weird! That's the flakiest thing I've ever seen.'

Backstage, Kit had locked herself in her dressing room. She would admit no one. Steve knocked on her door, gently at first, then more insistently. She would not answer. Ross came down the corridor, followed by Sam and Jeff.

'What about your theory now?' Steve challenged.

Ross admitted, 'I never expected what happened tonight.'

He gestured Steve back from the door.

Leaning close so that he could speak in a low and comforting tone, he said, 'Kit, Ross is here. Open up. Please?'

There was a long silence before her door was unlocked. He signaled Steve and Sam to stand back. He opened the door slowly. Steve lingered long enough to glimpse Kit sitting on the floor, a lost and wistful child, drawing with her finger on the carpet.

'Kit?' Ross said gently.

She looked up, her face wet with tears. 'Ross! Oh, Ross!'

'Kit, stand up.'

She refused to budge, applying herself with even more diligence to the figures she was sketching on the carpet.

Ross held out his hand to her. 'Kit?' She looked up at him. 'Kit!' he persisted, extending his hand farther. She seized it, and though he tried to dissuade her, she started to kiss it slavishly. He lifted her to her feet.

'Kiss me, Ross? Just once, kiss me,' she begged.

He kissed her gently on the cheek. 'Now get dressed and we'll get out of here.'

Steve was in the box office. He dismissed the staff, demanding to be alone. He dialed a number. He asked for the Drama Desk.

'Edwin, Steve. I have to know what you are going to say.'

'I'll be gentle with her. I'll take it out on the play. I hope you understand?'

'Of course. What about your friend?'

'I didn't see him. He left the theater before I did.'

'What if I called him?'

'He's an arrogant sonofabitch. Psychotic, if you want my honest opinion. So make up your own mind.'

'Thanks, Edwin,' Steve said sincerely.

'Take care of that girl,' Edwin Mortimer warned.

Steve debated for several minutes, trying to anticipate the reaction of a man he had never met and about whom he had heard only the most forbidding reports. He decided that even if the worst was true, it could do no further harm to call.

'McManus!' a brusque, angry voice answered. 'Make it quick. I'm working!'

'Mr McManus, this is Steve Brooks.'

'Oh? Brooks. What can I do for you?' Though the critic's words were phrased as a request, his tone indicated that he was not amenable to any suggestion.

'Mr McManus, I've never contacted a critic before he reviewed a play of mine. But this is a very special circumstance.'

'Every play is always a special circumstance to every playwright,' McManus responded impatiently. 'Look, I have to get my review over to the desk. I only have twenty minutes.'

'I'll make it brief. Kill the play, if you have to. But don't kill her. There are reasons that I can't go into. But don't take it out on her,' Steve pleaded.

'What if I happen to think it's a good play and she destroyed it?'

'Say it's a lousy play and she went down trying to save it. Please?'

'Brooks, I only know what I see on the stage.'

'This one time,' Steve tried to impress on him.

'You want some good advice? If you don't want to get hit by a truck, stay off the highway. You should have thought of this before you opened. And one other thing. Stick by your own rule. Never try to influence a critic again. Not this critic!'

McManus hung up. Steve Brooks knew now they would have to expect the worst.

## *Twenty-three*

Dr Ross had taken Kit Lawrence back to her suite at the Ritz. He gave her two five-milligram tablets of Valium and ordered a light supper.

Steve called, and Ross said, 'Please, we would rather be alone!' He discouraged Jeff and Sam with similar curt rejections.

The waiter came with their supper. Ross took the cart, refusing to admit him to the room. He locked the door. He waited while Kit wept until the sedation took effect. Finally she gasped her way to a quiet state.

'Now, Kit, we'll have something to eat. Then we will talk,' Ross said warmly.

'I'm not hungry.'

'You will eat,' Ross said firmly, 'because I said so.'

She welcomed being bossed by him. She came to the table. To provoke him, she toyed with her food. He ignored her and began to eat with obvious enjoyment. Eventually she was eating too. Once she started, she ate ravenously. Conscious that he was watching her, she said impishly, 'I'm not hungry. I'm only eating to please you.'

'You were brilliant tonight.'

'I was?' she asked, quite pleased.

She smiled, contented. 'Do you love me again?'

'And then,' Ross said, not taking the bait, 'then you had to spoil it. You made yourself pathetic, inept, forgetful, amateurish. You embarrassed yourself before all those people. Do you know why?'

She refused to answer, withdrawing within herself again.

'Kit?' He was calling her to account. She turned away.

'Kit, we've talked about this before. You know what I mean. Don't you?'

She shook her head, perversely disagreeing.

'Kit?'

She stubbornly refused to face him. He waited. After a long silence she began, slowly, petulantly, 'I didn't do it intentionally. I started out promising, Tonight I am going to be spectacular. For him! I am going to give the best performance of my life! For Ross! All for Ross! Then ... I don't know what happened ... it just ... came apart ... the whole world just came apart,' she ended sadly.

'Kit,' he said gently, 'what were you drawing on the carpet?'

'Carpet?' she echoed, confused.

'You were sitting on the carpet onstage, drawing figures with your fingers.'

'Was I?'

'Yes.

'What figures? Do you remember?'

She shook her head.

'Perhaps if you sat on the floor now and tried to draw, you'd remember. Kit? Try?'

She turned to face him, uncertainly.

'Try,' he urged gently.

She slipped from her chair and gracefully settled on the floor. Her legs folded under her, she sat like a child at play. Her hand ventured out. Her forefinger tested the nap of the plush carpet. She rubbed her finger across it, enjoying the prickling sensation. Her action took on more defined intent. She began to draw in long strokes – two long, close, parallel strokes. Then, many inches away, two more close strokes, parallel to the first pair. She went back and retraced all four a number of times, intent on making a permanent imprint on the stubborn carpet. She began to sketch a connecting archway between the sets of parallel lines.

Ross watched as she kept repeating the design. She did it

with the intense concentration a child of five might apply to an early drawing or the learning of letters and numbers. The look on her face was ingenuous, engaging and most appealing.

He stared at the figures.

'Is that what you were drawing on the stage?'

'I think so.' Her thoughts were far off.

'What is it?'

Without looking down at it, she answered, 'I don't know.'

'Look at it,' Ross suggested. She refused. He insisted, 'Look at it, Kit!'

She stared down.

'What do you see?'

'Lines.'

'Just lines? Or does it remind you of anything?'

She stared down at the figure she had sketched. It was beginning to disappear as the fibers regained their resilience.

'Kit?'

'It . . . it could be an archway.'

'A familiar archway?' Ross asked gently.

'The . . . the archway at Silvermine,' she admitted.

'Are there any words on your archway, any letters?'

'No!' she said impatiently, evidencing signs of resistance again.

'But there are letters on the gateway to Silvermine. You know that. Letters that say "*Silvermine.*" '

'Yes . . .' she granted.

'But only on the *outside*,' Ross pointed out. 'Yet your gateway has no letters. You said so yourself.'

'No letters . . .' she repeated.

'The way the gate looks from the *inside*? From your window in Carlisle Cottage?' Ross asked.

She did not answer.

'Is that what you want, Kit? To be back at Silvermine? To be *inside*? Is that why you broke down in the third act?

So I would say, "Poor girl, she's so sick I must take her back with me"?'

When she refused to look up, he called her to account. 'Kit?'

'I *am* sick. I'm no good! I can't act! Without you I'm nothing. I was always nothing. That's why my mother left me! I kept telling you that. But you wouldn't believe me. Well, tonight you saw it. I'm sick!'

'You were magnificent as long as you wanted to be. Just as you can be well, *if* you want to.'

'If I got well, would you divorce your wife and marry me?' she blurted out.

'Of course not. You know that,' Ross said gently.

'Then I'll stay sick!' she said fiercely.

He made no attempt to dissuade her, but waited until she was ready to proceed on her own.

'I could be so good, so great if only you would love me again. I could be brilliant. All the time. Brilliant!' she said, trying to buy his complicity.

'Tonight you saw just a hint of what I could be,' she said, then confessed, 'During the performance I looked for you. I found you. Third row, first seat in from the aisle. Right?'

'Right.'

'I kept watching you watching me. I could read your face. I could see how much you admired me. And I kept asking myself, Then why doesn't he love me? He used to love making love to me. But no more. No more,' she ended softly.

'Kit, we've gone over that many times. My making love to you was a terrible injustice. All I want to accomplish now is see that you get better. I want to see you live the life and achieve the success you're entitled to.'

'So you can be rid of me!' she accused.

'That's your fantasy. So for the first part of the play you show me how brilliant you can be. Thinking, I'll admire you, love you. Then you become afraid that if you *are* brilliant, if you *are* well, I won't take you back. So you have to show me how terrible you can be. How sick. Does that remind you of anything?'

She turned away, legs tucked under her, her back to him.

'Something you told me in the past?' Ross suggested.

'I know what you're getting at, and it's a lie,' she said petulantly.

'What is a lie?'

'You think I'm treating you like my grandfather. He wouldn't do anything for me, wouldn't love me, wouldn't give me anything until I was bad. I could beg and plead and the old bastard wouldn't buy me a dress or a pair of tight jeans or even a bobby pin. But once, once I had something to threaten him with . . .'

'Once you had seduced him . . .' Ross corrected.

'*He* did it. I never wanted to; he made me!' she insisted. 'Once he did, I could get anything I wanted out of him. Anything.'

'So you thought, It'll be the same with Ross. Once I get Ross to make love to me, he'll have to do anything I want to keep it from coming out. I'll have something to threaten him with. Just like the old bastard. But it didn't work, did it, Kit? So you said, I'll be sick. If I'm sick, he'll have to take me back.'

'You will!' she insisted.

'Even if you did come back, I couldn't take care of you.'

'You'd have to! Professional ethics. You can't turn a patient away!' she declared angrily. Then she softened. 'Can you? Can you, Ross?'

'I would have to.'

'Then I'll do something desperate. I'll kill myself. That's what I'll do. Kill myself!' She half-turned, staring at him angrily over her shoulder.

'Is that what you were trying to do on the stage tonight – destroy yourself?'

She turned away.

'Were you saying to me, "Ross, I will destroy myself unless you love me"?'

'I will, I will,' she persisted like a stubborn child.

'Did that ever happen?'

'What?'

'Before you came to New York, before your suicide attempt there, did you ever do that? Back home?' Ross asked, for it had always puzzled him.

'No,' she said, sounding quite frank.

'Never threatened your grandfather that way?'

'Threatened . . .' she equivocated. 'Well, maybe I did threaten. But I never did anything. Never tried.'

Ross waited. In a moment, she giggled. 'I didn't have to.'

'Why not?'

'Because once . . . once I did threaten and he didn't believe me. So I . . . I made up this dummy. Two pillows and some of my own clothes. And I hung it in my window. It cast a hanging shadow on the wall he would see when he opened my door. Then I hid in the closet. I heard him call me. I didn't answer. I just waited in that dark closet. I could hear him growing more and more angry. "Kit, Kit, where the hell are you?" I could hear him come close to my door. I didn't let on. I heard the door open. I could tell he'd seen the shadow, because he was in the middle of saying my name and he stopped. He gasped. Then he let out a cry, "Katherine!" And he began to cry.

'It was the first time anyone ever cried for me,' she confessed sadly.

'Did you let him make love to you then?'

'I felt so sorry for him,' she explained. 'So I let him . . . let him . . .' Her voice drifted off. 'I use that memory sometimes, in acting. When I have to feel intense emotion, regret, sorrow, sympathy. I recall that feeling and use it.'

'Only in acting?' Ross asked pointedly.

She glanced at him, as if to deny she understood.

' "I will frighten Ross. I will let him think that I have

destroyed myself. On the stage. In full sight of all those people. He will feel so guilty, he will break down and cry for me. Then I will let him make love to me." Is that what you thought tonight, Kit? Deep down? Was that it? "I will let Ross make love to me and he will take me back to Silvermine forever." '

She turned to look up and stare at him. She held out her hand to him to draw him down beside her. He did not move. Her eyes welled up with tears, but she controlled them.

'Love me, Ross. Make love to me. Just once more. Just once?' she entreated softly.

'You know that can't ever happen again, Kit,' he said gently.

'Never right,' she said. 'Nothing I do is ever right. When I make love I have to spoil it. When I get pregnant it's with the wrong man. Now, even when I go out on the stage, I can't do anything right. Can't!'

'You were brilliant for two acts,' Ross reminded her.

'And I spoiled that too,' she lamented. In one final plea she begged, 'Ross! At least hold me? Hold me? Is that too much to ask?'

He had no need to answer. She answered for him. 'I know. Not allowed. Not permitted.' Sadly she said, 'Katherine . . . oh, Katherine . . . And I had looked forward so to this night.'

She extended her hand to him. Again he avoided taking it. She smiled sadly. 'Not even to help me up from the floor?'

He lifted her to her feet. They were eye to eye for a fleeting moment. He asked simply, 'Kit, what is it about the end of that third act that disturbs you so?'

'Time. It'll take time.'

'What?'

'For me to summon up the hate I need to play it. The hate is all inside. It takes time to externalize it.' She smiled indulgently. 'A term we actors use. You see, we have our own mumbo jumbo, just like you analysts.' She laughed.

'Is it only time, Kit?'

She glanced at him, her look a mixture of guilt and resentment, as though he had intruded on a part of herself private even from him.

But he continued, 'Or is it that you're *afraid* to play it?'

'I'm not afraid to play anything. I never have been! Daring parts that other actresses shied away from. Who played the first overt lesbian on the New York stage? Who would have dared, except me? No, I am not afraid!' she disputed angrily.

Ross was not put off. 'I meant, could it be that your hostility toward your mother is *so* strong that you're afraid if you give vent to it on the stage you will be punished?'

'Punished how?' she countered.

'It's *your* fantasy. How?' When she did not respond, he suggested, 'Perhaps audiences won't love you because you hate your own mother so. Or perhaps God will punish you. We all labor under those old biblical admonitions about loving and honoring our parents. You're not exempt. Is it fear? Kit, tell me. Please. It's important. Is it fear?'

She shook her head slowly, pensively.

'Then what?' Ross insisted.

'I told you. Time. It takes time to conquer a scene like that. Then one day, during a rehearsal or a performance, suddenly it happens. It just happens, and you have that scene forever. It just takes time.'

He gave her ten more milligrams of Valium and insisted she got to bed. He waited till she was asleep. He left, taking the bottle of Valium with him, as well as the medications he found in her bathroom cabinet.

In the morning, Dr Ross met Steve Brooks and Jeff Warrener before taking off for Silvermine. The reviews were out. Mortimer had written:

> After being positively brilliant and soaring in the first two acts of *Reunion*, Kit Lawrence was earthbound by a

third act that ground to a halt rather than rising to the shattering climax we were led to expect.

But McManus had written:

> It may be the style these days for stars, mainly female, to show utter contempt for their audiences. As far as this critic is concerned, that indulgence reached its peak last night when Kit Lawrence insulted an audience that was willing to heap praise and applause on her and received only stones and ashes in return. Whatever values there are in 'Reunion,' and there are many, were destroyed by the most careless and ill-prepared performance we have seen in Boston this season.

Sam joined them in the coffee shop of the Ritz. They sat in the corner at a table looking out on the Common. Though it was only mid-October, it was a gray day, warning of rain, possibly even snow. Sam had all the open newspapers under his arm. He was silent while Ross gave them his prognosis. He felt that Kit's salvation depended on her ability to continue. To let her quit, to let her come back to Silvermine in defeat, or retreat to some other institution, was a retrogression that would be final.

She must be made to go on was his advice.

Steve and Sam said nothing. Jeff exploded in a harsh and angry whisper, 'Why you sonofabitch! You precipitate this crisis! Get her into this condition! Bring her to the edge of a total, final breakdown! Then you leave us holding her like a hand grenade with the pin pulled!'

Though he spoke in a whisper, people at surrounding tables looked up from their morning newspapers to stare. Jeff glared back at them, forcing them to retreat behind their papers.

' "She must be made to go on," ' Jeff mocked. 'By whom? The Svengali legend is just that, a legend, my dear doctor.

Directors do not have supernatural powers. We do not hypnotize actresses and say, "Go onstage and be magnificent," and the actress obeys, in a trance, under a spell. I have tried everything I can to make her do that third act. And I have failed.'

'She says she feels it, she just can't externalize it yet,' Ross explained.

' "*Yet*"?' Jeff mocked. '*Yet*? We have had three and a half weeks of rehearsal. Ten days in New Haven. Three performances here in Boston. And she hasn't been able to do it, "*yet*"? My dear Dr Ross, this is not psychoanalysis. We don't have years. We don't have months. We have weeks. *Had* weeks,' he corrected. 'We are now down to days. Did you hear me? Days!

'Exactly eleven days from now we will be in New York. We will be playing our first preview. What happens that night will get around town in twenty-four hours. It will predispose the critics. Our fate will be sealed before we ever open.

'So I don't want to hear words like "yet"!'

Jeff had raised his voice so loud that the maître d' approached their table and respectfully said, 'Please, gentlemen.'

Jeff recovered sufficiently to whisper a courteous 'Sorry'.

Ross spoke softly but urgently: 'If there were anything I could do, I would stay on. But there are crises that patients have to face alone. However, if you notice any signs that she is becoming suicidal, let me know. Instantly.'

Steve asked, 'You think she might?'

'I've taken all her dangerous medications. But there's no telling what she might prevail on some strange doctor to prescribe for her. Be alert.'

Ross had left. While Steve and Jeff sat grimly rereading the reviews, seeking any quote that might be salvaged for an ad, Sam stared, pensive and troubled.

Finally he said, 'That bastard McManus killed us. We

won't do any business up here.' He estimated glumly, 'We'll lose twenty-five thousand dollars a week, at least.'

Jeff interrupted composing an ad to ask, 'Sam?'

Steve put down Mortimer's review.

'Any other show,' Sam said, 'I could hit the investors for the overcall. But I'm the only investor.'

'You mean you don't have the money,' Jeff concluded.

'I mean,' Sam confessed, 'the only building I still owned outright, I had to mortgage to get the money to produce the show. But we lost thirty-seven thousand dollars our ten days in New Haven. We stand to lose another fifty or sixty thousand here. It isn't in the budget, boys. Just isn't.'

'When it's ten o'clock Coast time,' Jeff volunteered, 'I'll call my agent on the Coast. Maybe we can get a picture company or a TV network to buy in.'

'I could scrape up some cash,' Steve volunteered.

'Has your wife got a good lawyer?' Sam asked.

'Yes. Why?'

'Then he's probably got your assets tied up until your divorce settlement is agreed on.'

'Then what can we do?'

'What we can do,' Sam figured aloud, 'is call New York and see if some bank will put a second mortgage on that building.'

'And if they won't?'

'There's always money around, if you look hard enough,' Sam said.

At one o'clock Boston time, Jeff called his Coast agent. He received the promise of best efforts and a return call. Within two hours the agent called back. Every picture company had covered the Boston opening. The word was out. The production was foundering. Kit Lawrence was up to her old tricks. No company would risk a dime.

By three o'clock Sam Rogers had made several frantic calls to New York. Finally the money was promised. But he would have to fly down at once to sign second-mortgage papers.

Steve insisted on taxiing to Logan Airport with him.

'Sam, what if you can't pay off?'

'So they'll take the building.' Sam made it sound simple and logical.

'But if that only covers the first mortgage?'

'That's their worry,' Sam replied, evasive and trying to sound untroubled.

As Sam was passing through the boarding gate, Steve seized him by the arm and insisted, 'Sam! I want to know! Are you dealing with the Mob?'

Sam's first reaction was to deny it vehemently, until his eyes turned less defiant. 'Bloodsuckers! Bastards! To get a second mortgage of fifty thousand, I had to promise them a bonus of another fifty. But where else could I go?'

'Sam, if you can't pay, you know what they'll do . . .'

Sam interrupted, 'They're boarding my flight!' He pulled free of Steve's tight grip and lost himself among the passengers who crowded toward the plane.

In silent protest, Steve could only lament, Sam, Sam, no!

# *Twenty-four*

There was no use trying to prevent Kit seeing those reviews. Instead of waiting until she arrived at the theater, Steve called her at the hotel in midmorning.

He could hear the depression in her voice.

'Ross is gone. When I needed him most, he left me. He never loved me. Never.'

Steve knew his mission would be even tougher than he had anticipated.

Despite her forlorn attitude on the phone, when he arrived she was made up, and her hair had been brushed and hung loose so that when she moved her head suddenly it achieved a seductive flow. She wore her light blue silk peignoir, which opened gracefully to reveal the tops of her breasts.

Ross had rejected her. She did not intend to be rejected now. Steve knew all the signs.

'I saw Ross before he left,' Steve began. 'He wants you to go on with the show.'

'Of course,' she scoffed. 'That lets him off the hook. He doesn't have to be responsible for me.'

'That's not true. He's tremendously concerned about your welfare.'

'He is?' she asked, momentarily seizing on that. Then she said sulkily, 'He didn't act like it.'

'Kit, he was here as your doctor.'

She turned her head quickly, causing her blond hair to move in a graceful swirl. 'Why do they leave me? Why do they always leave me?' she asked, seeking his solicitude.

He refused to become involved. He read her Mortimer's review. Then he had no choice but to read her McManus' damning critique. He read it with as little emphasis as possible. But still the words were cold and brutal.

'It's Ross's fault! Two acts I was brilliant for him. Then I watched his face at the end of Act Two. He didn't love me,' she said wistfully. 'Then he wouldn't take me back with him. I begged him. But he wouldn't.' She was on the verge of tears. She turned to him. 'Steve, oh, Steve . . .'

He knew that plea. It was a need to be made love to. He changed the subject and the mood. 'Kit, we're going on to New York. Sam is down there arranging it. We have eleven days here in Boston to fix that third act. If we do, we have a shot. If not, what these reviews say is what the New York critics will say. Or maybe worse.'

She did not respond.

'Did you hear me?'

She nodded, almost imperceptibly.

'If there's anything you want me to try in the third act, or you want Jeff to try, now is the time to say it.'

'I haven't found it yet,' she said impatiently. 'So stop bugging me! I'm tired! Overrehearsed! I need time off. Last night was an opening. I need to get over the strain. Over the reviews.'

He knew it would do no good to persist.

'Okay. You're right. We'll take the afternoon off. What would you like to do? Go for a walk? Browse in the shops? I know: I have a friend who teaches a course in The Novel at Harvard. Would you like to go over and have lunch?'

'I want to be left alone,' she said perversely. 'I don't want to be indulged! Or watched over! I don't need a keeper! If you're all afraid that I'll make another suicide attempt, you're wrong!' Her voice was rising to tense and dangerous levels.

'I know what Ross told you!' she accused. 'Watch over her, day and night. Don't leave her alone. Isn't that what he said? Of course, you'll deny it. After all, nobody ever tells a patient the truth. In all the time I was at Silvermine he never told me the truth. He lied to me. Always. Even when he said he loved me. He did say that. But it turned out to be a lie. He never loved me!'

Steve knew it was futile to disagree. In her present rage she would believe no one. After a brief silence she said, pouting, 'He took all my pills. He *is* afraid of what I'll do.' She seemed to derive some satisfaction from that.

She stared out at the Common. Then quite calmly, and as if there had been no explosion only moments before, she said, 'If you don't want to make love to me we might as well go for a walk. Or over to Harvard. Yes, let's go over to Harvard!' she said in a sudden burst of enthusiasm.

The ate in one of the faculty clubs. As morose, petulant and erratic as Kit had been before, she was charming, bright and flirtatious with Steve's friend. She asked highly intelligent questions about academic life, about the novel as distinguished from the play, about his choice of careers, about his private life. When she discovered he had a wife, she became increasingly flirtatious. Before they left she insisted Steve invite them to see the play.

In the cab on the way back, she pressed her head against Steve's shoulder and talked softly.

'He's a nice man. What's his wife like?'

'I don't know. I've never met her.'

'She must be a little brown-haired, mousy type. Like Ross's wife. Have you ever seen her? She is the plainest woman I have ever seen. I don't know what Ross sees in her.'

When Steve returned to his room, he found a message slip on the doorknob. 'Ms Melinda Brooks called. Please call back.'

He started off by conceding, 'Okay. So you heard about the reviews.'

'Matter of fact, I didn't.'

'Then what made you call? My publisher?'

'No.' Then she asked with unusual concern, 'Steve, how is she?'

'She's fine,' he lied. 'Why do you ask?'

'Two days ago I received a note from her.'

'Oh? Well, pay no attention. She has moments when she's liable to say anything to anyone. Just forget it.'

'I can't, Steve.'

'Why?'

'It was written on a piece of hotel stationery. Sheraton stationery.'

'From New Haven,' he realized.

'But it had been used and badly crumpled. Then obviously straightened out. The letter itself was written on the back. In a handwriting that seems like a six-year-old's.'

'What did it say?'

' "Dear Melinda, I am a bitch. I always have been. Forgive me. Somebody, please, somewhere, forgive me." It isn't signed. But it's quite obviously her.'

'Yes,' he conceded sadly, 'that sounds like her.'

'What can I do, Steve?' Melinda asked. 'Should I write her, or call?'

Steve laughed bitterly. 'Oh, Mel, Mel, is she going to draft you into her army too?'

'If I could just let her know that I have no animosity toward her . . .' Melinda started to suggest. 'That wouldn't be true, though.'

'No, it wouldn't.'

Melinda confessed, 'I had the strangest reaction.'

'What?'

'I almost felt as if I should give my consent to you two to have an affair,' she admitted. 'If it would help her.'

'Once infidelity becomes therapy, then it's okay. Is that it?'

'I just feel so sorry for her.'

'The time to feel sorry is when we flop in New York,' he said gravely.

They walked to the theater together. Steve Brooks and Kit

Lawrence. It was a clear, brisk fall evening. The wind from across the Common was a bit stiffer than it had been. She clung to his arm with both hands, ostensibly to protect herself from the cold, actually to enjoy a sense of possession. He glanced down at her face. She was fair and beautiful as ever. In such moments, the old regret always overcame him. If only things had been different, even a little different.

'I like to walk against the wind like this, with you protecting me,' Kit said suddenly. 'Will you always protect me, Steve?'

'Sure,' he agreed too easily.

She stopped suddenly, stood on tiptoe, and kissed him on the lips. 'There! That's so all of Boston will know how I feel about you.' She laughed. It seemed a carefree lark of a laugh. She confessed, 'Those questions I asked you in the cab . . .'

'What questions?'

'About your friend, the professor,' she reminded. 'I wouldn't let him touch me. I only did that to make you jealous. Are you?'

'Yes. I'll go right out and challenge him to a duel,' Steve said.

They both laughed.

'Steve, you're insane.'

Somehow, once that word found its way into their conversation all the laughter ran out of it.

They were silent until they reached the Wilbur. She invited him into her dressing room. He begged off. As he turned away from the door, the stage manager signaled him.

'I wasn't to tell you in front of anyone,' he whispered. 'But Mr Warrener said to see him. He's out front. He says it's urgent.'

Steve went out into the house, raced up the aisle and found Jeff waiting at the front doors. Some early theatergoers were already beginning to congregate. Jeff gestured him to a corner of the lobby.

'What's wrong?'

'I was coming into the theater a while ago to reset some of the lighting in the second act, and the box-office man stops me.'

'No phone business?' Steve anticipated. 'It's those reviews.'

'He had just got a call for a ticket. A freebie. And he wanted to check it with me before he issued it.'

'It's going to be a thin house,' Steve said. 'Okay the ticket.'

'No matter who it's for?'

'Who? Tell me.'

'Max Kronheim!' Jeff said.

'Christ! Not Kronheim.'

'You still want me to okay it?'

'We can't keep the bastard out. In fact, it would be worse if we tried. He'd buy a ticket and then complain to Kit. Okay it,' Steve finally advised.

'And what happens after?' Jeff asked. 'There's no telling what he'll say to her.'

'Is there any way we can keep him from talking to her?' Steve asked.

'Kronheim? He has the ingenuity and persistence of a cockroach.'

'Then we mustn't leave them alone,' Steve warned.

# *Twenty-five*

Steve Brooks was standing at the back of the house when Max Kronheim entered, the last patron to be admitted. He evidently had waited to achieve that distinction. He noticed Steve but gave no sign. He strode regally down the aisle behind the plump usherette. The house lights were going down and the curtain warmers were shedding their soft light as Max Kronheim finally took his seat, prepared to judge Kit's performance.

From the back of the house Steve could see the shock of white hair that was Kronheim's trademark. He had been caricatured on a dozen occasions in *The New York Times*; always his wild white hair was the cartoonist's chief target.

Throughout the first two acts Kronheim seemed not to move. He did not applaud when Kit made her appearance. Nor when an act concluded. Throughout a discouraging third act he sat impassive.

The audience started up the aisle in haste, signifying its disappointment. The house was almost empty before Kronheim deigned to move. He went to the heavy fireproof door that separated the house from backstage. He rolled it open with an imperial gesture. Steve was right behind him.

'Mr Kronheim?'

Kronheim turned. With an air of condescension, he said, 'Ah, Brooks. Nice to see you.' He made no attempt to shake hands.

'What did you think?' Steve asked, to keep the older man involved.

'Interesting play.'

From Kronheim that was not an opinion, it was an evasion.

'Where is she? Where is my little girl?' he asked.

Steve had no choice. He led Kronheim back to Kit's dressing room. He knocked.

'Kit! It's me. With a visitor.'

'Just a moment.' Then she called, 'Okay.'

He opened the door to find Kit standing half naked, but with her robe held to her breasts in a pose of great modesty. She was smiling. Until she saw, behind Steve, the austere figure of Max Kronheim. Her face turned as fearful as that of a young recalcitrant child forced to face a stern father.

'Max?' she dared.

'My dear,' Kronheim said with special kindness. He came to her, kissed her on the lips. He held her for a moment, pressing her young body close. 'It's been a long time.'

'I . . . I have to get dressed,' she apologized tensely, retreating behind the screen.

Kronheim settled himself in the one comfortable chair in the room. Steve remained, determined not to leave them alone.

Kronheim began quite affably, 'I was saying to our friend Brooks, quite an interesting play you have here. Fascinating subject. Especially for you, my dear.'

'We chose it together,' Kit called from behind the screen.

'Oh? Really? I didn't know.' Kronheim was still affable. He drummed lightly on the arm of the easy chair before he asked, 'Your director, he agrees? I mean, does he like this play as much as you two do?'

Steve interceded, 'Yes!'

'Why do you ask?' Kit called.

'I get the feeling – and mind you, I think the audience gets the same feeling – that your director is fighting the play.'

Still in her dressing gown, Kit Lawrence came out from behind the screen to listen like a devout disciple. Steve realized that she had been so conditioned in earlier years that the mere presence of Kronheim had a mesmerizing effect on her.

'I sense,' Kronheim continued, 'that he resents the third act. Else how could he have directed it in such an anomalous manner? And how, my dear, could he have placed you in such an awkward position? It destroys your performance. Totally robs it of all truth, all honesty.

'The first two acts, quite acceptable. Some good moments. You do them very well. But that third act – atrocious. In all candor, and for your own good, I must say it – atrocious.'

Kronheim enunciated the word as if he were brandishing a weapon. Steve was tempted to intercede. But his only truthful rebuttal would unsettle Kit even more. Meanwhile, she had slipped into her chair, shaken and mute. She stared into the mirror at her own pained face as Kronheim continued.

'You are sleepwalking. Throughout the entire third act, sleepwalking! It is a very bad, very dangerous performance.'

Steve noticed that Kit's leg had begun to tremble. He had seen that sign before. It was a prelude to danger.

'Look,' he intervened. 'Kit is tired. She needs to rest. If you're staying over, perhaps we can discuss this tomorrow. Or perhaps it might be better if you discussed it with Jeff. After all, he's the director.'

Kronheim nodded – a gesture not of assent but of regret. 'Ah, yes, Jeff Warrener. Films corrupt a director. He begins to think in terms of images, composition, movement.

'He forgets the challenge, the sheer artistry of the living performance. The immediate impact on the audience. It is no wonder this production is as bad as it is. Never, never would I have selected a picture director to touch a play as sensitive as this, or a performance as powerful and yet delicate as Kit should be giving. The first thing we must do is get rid of Warrener,' Kronheim declared imperiously.

He turned to Kit. 'Don't you agree, my dear?'

She stared at him, fearful, incapable of contradicting him.

'My dear, I can see how far you have drifted from the actress that you were. The fundamentals you absorbed at the

Lab are lost. Your performance is tense. That transmits itself to the audience. What has happened to you? My dear child, what has happened?'

He reached out to touch her cheek with his forefinger. Though she was strongly tempted to draw back from him, she was unable to move.

'We will have to start from the beginning. How long since you've done your preparatory exercises?'

'A time,' she whispered evasively.

'It's so obvious. The Kit Lawrence I knew, the girl I trained from an eager, nervous young novice is gone. Gone,' he repeated sadly.

Steve could see the man's influence engulf Kit like an aura. She had no defense against it. Recalling her confession under pentothal, he had to intervene.

'Mr Kronheim, Kit's just given a performance. She's exhausted. She needs a bite to eat and some sleep, lots of sleep.'

'You call that a performance?' Kronheim scoffed. 'I call that a desecration! I would not even use the word acting, much less a performance.' He turned to Kit, 'My dear, I am trying to save you from disaster, from totally destroying your career. A few days, a few weeks, and I can lift you out of what you are doing and make this a truly memorable performance. But not if I am going to meet with resistance.' He turned on Steve Brooks with a resentful glare.

Tension was now painfully obvious on Kit's face. Steve suggested forcefully, 'I think you had better leave now!'

Max Kronheim did not move. He only smiled – a small, indulgent, pitying smile. He stared at Steve, but he spoke to Kit. 'My dear, this is your dressing room. Do *you* want me to leave?'

Her face flushed, her eyes averted from Steve, Kit managed to whisper, 'No. But I would like Mr Brooks to leave.'

Steve refused to move. Kronheim fixed Kit with his stare.

Her voice became tense. 'I want you to leave!'

Kronheim watched smugly as Steve turned and left the room. Steve heard the door lock behind him. He was tempted to linger and eavesdrop. He decided not to. But he would wait. She must not be allowed to spend a night alone after what Kronheim had done to undermine her already tenuous security.

Alone with Kit, Max Kronheim touched her lips gently as if to test their youthful softness. He kissed her tenderly, pressed against her as he whispered, 'What have they done to my little girl? What have they done?' He took her hand, led her to her chair, seated her. He lifted her hands and laid them in her lap, palms up, hands crossed. He stood back from her, staring. 'I have always wanted to have a painting of you posed just so.'

He sank to the couch opposite her. 'Now, tell me.'

'What?' she asked tensely.

'I want to know everything that has happened to you since I last saw you.'

'So much . . .' was all she could say.

'I heard. I told you, years ago, once you left me it would never be the same. You need me, Kit, my darling. You need my discipline. You need my training. As the athlete keeps the muscles supple and alive, so the actress must keep her technique and her emotions supple and alive. But don't fear. We will find it again. We'll have to start from the beginning. But we will find it.

'Stand up!' he ordered suddenly.

She rose, stood free of her chair, arms at her sides, hands rigid.

'Relax, my dear. I can see tension in both your hands. Relax. Gradually. Effortlessly. Easily. Let it start in here and gradually permeate your whole body. Let relaxation flow through you like your own blood. Arms, hands, toes, fingertips. Better, my dear. There! There, now you have it!'

She had indeed relaxed; her hands had become easy and

loose, resting gracefully at her sides. She lowered her head, letting her chin fall lightly on her chest.

'Before we even start discussing the role, we must do your earth exercises. Or have you forgotten, my dear?' he rebuked her gently. 'Ah, if only you had never left me. But that's past. We must deal with the present. We must keep you from this impending disaster.

'So let us begin. Feel the earth under your feet. Slip off your shoes. Let your naked feet feel the earth! Feel it . . .!'

She kicked off her shoes. She planted her bare feet on the dressing-room floor. She seemed to absorb a feeling through the soles of her feet like a tree drawing moisture from the soil. She breathed deeply. Her face reflected the feel of earth permeating her entire being.

'Good, good. Now, my dear, feel the rain on your face. Look up and feel the rain. Eyes closed! I want to see your face glisten. I want to see your eyelids as the drops fall there and run down your cheeks. I want to see you welcome the warm, soft rain. And I want to see you love it.'

She raised her face, gradually creating every sensation the old man had described. Until her face glowed in a smile.

'Excellent. And now the wind is beating against you. Against your face, your breasts, your entire body. Beating so hard you must lean against it. It is a harsh wind, a bitter wind. To walk against it you must exert yourself to the full. It makes breathing difficult. Every step is a battle. But you thrust your young strong body against it.'

Her face reflected the force of the wind, her breathing the energy she had to expend to press against it. Soon she was panting in painful gasps.

There was a knock on the door. Steve called out, 'Kit? Shouldn't we be getting back to the hotel?'

Kronheim spoke in a commanding whisper: 'Tell him you don't want to be disturbed! Tell him not to wait!'

'Kit?' Steve rattled the doorknob.

She called out, 'Go away. Please! I don't want to be disturbed!'

'You've got two shows tomorrow. You need your sleep,' Steve persisted.

'I said, *go away*!' she ordered fiercely. '*Go away!*'

Reluctantly, he decided to go back to the hotel and wait there.

Once sure they were alone and he was in complete control, Kronheim continued:

'I want to see you feel cold. Bitter cold. Freezing cold. I want to see it in how your body contracts. Your hands curl up trying to warm themselves. They press against your body, between your breasts, trying to find some warmth there. For unless you do, you will freeze and die. I want to feel it. I want the audience to feel it.'

Eyes closed, she generated the feeling within herself. He could see it attack her fair skin, which grew paler, and began to form little prickly bumps. She drew her hands close against her belly. Then to her breasts and finally between them, hoping to surround her hands with their warmth. Her nipples puckered from the cold. Soon she was trembling and begging permission to be released: 'Please? Please?'

Kronheim did not respond. He was concentrating hungrily on her erect nipples, which had aroused him almost to the point of pain. Finally, he relented. 'The wind has died down. The clouds have passed. The sun has come out. It is growing warmer. Much warmer.'

Kit began to relax. To feel at ease. Her hands slipped from between her breasts and were at ease at her sides once more.

'Remember in class, you used to tell me that feeling heat was not difficult for you because you had only to recall how it felt in your grandfather's old house? Well, feel that now. It is the afternoon of a day when the desert heat has reached a hundred and ten degrees. And you feel it. Your body begins to sweat until your shirt is wet through. It clings to your breasts until one can see your nipples, round and brown, erect and proud.

'You feel the sweat begin to trickle down. Down your neck. Between your breasts. Down your belly till it mingles with your pubic hair. I want to see all that, Katherine! I want to know not only how hot it is, but what the heat does to you.'

Step by step, in compliance with his suggestions, she was able to feel it so intensely that perspiration began to form rivulets on her face, her neck, her shoulders until it gathered as one river to flow down between her breasts and beyond. She began to breathe laboredly as if the heat of the day were too much for her.

The heaving of her breasts excited him. All the desire he had ever felt for her, every memory he had of making love to her returned now. Among the many pupils he had made love to, none had excited him as she had. Whether it was her madness or sheer abandon, she had made him feel younger and more vigorous than all the others.

He rose from the couch and moved to her. She stood still, eyes shut, breathing laboredly, damp and hot. Surprised by his touch, she recoiled.

'Don't be afraid,' he comforted. 'It will be like the old days. When we were teacher and pupil. And more.'

He wiped the perspiration from her face with a gentle forefinger. 'Sitting out there, watching you, I was afraid you had lost it. The magic. But I can see now, no matter what they have done to you, you have never lost it. We will work hard. We will find the ending of this play. You will be more magnificent than you ever were before. Greater. Much greater!

'When I see the others, see the acclaim they receive, I say to myself, Beside Kit Lawrence, they are pale. They are obvious. They are surfacy. They are only *acting*. But Kit, my Katherine, she didn't act. She *was*. She *felt*. She *lived* every moment on stage. We will make it possible for you to do that again. It *will* be like old times,' he promised.

Eyes still closed, Kit nodded, the compliant disciple seeking her master's approval.

He pretended to wipe away the glistening film of perspiration that glowed on her throat. His hands moved down gently, stopping first at the tops of her breasts, then coming to rest on them. She tensed and sought to draw back. But he held her tightly. One hand had slipped within her dressing gown, gently forcing it apart. He stared at her breasts and kissed her there.

His face pressed against them. 'I used to call them my icons. So beautiful and inspiring, they were meant to be worshiped.'

He kissed them hungrily and whispered, 'Come, my dear, my darling Katherine.'

He tried to lead her to the couch. She trembled in a moment of indecision. The old habit of obeying urged her to surrender; the rest of her resisted. Suddenly she cried out, terrified, 'No! No, I can't. I won't!'

'Katherine!' the old man ordered. When she did not relent, he pleaded, 'Kit?'

'Take your hands off me!'

'Kit?'

'I said, take your hands off!' She forcibly removed his one hand from around her waist and the other from her breast.

'What have they done to you, those doctors?' he demanded. 'What lies have they told you about me? That you don't need me anymore?'

'Nothing,' she said evasively.

'Be honest with me! I came up here only because you needed me. The word is all over New York. Kit Lawrence is in trouble. She has lost the spark. Her talent has rusted in the last six years. I couldn't believe it. My Kit, my Katherine, she had never had a part she couldn't play better than any actress in the world! I must go up, see what they have done to her. So I came. And discovered it was true. What I saw out there tonight was not acting.

'So I said, I will stay on. I will work with her. I will make her the old Kit! She will be what she was always intended to be. The finest American actress of our age!'

He paused, then said, 'Kit, without me you are nothing. You must know that now.'

She dared to say, 'Dr Ross doesn't think so.'

'You told him about us?' Kronheim said. 'What did you tell him? That I seduced you? Or did you tell him the truth? That you seduced me.'

'I never did . . .' she began to protest.

'Didn't you? There is something within you that reaches out to men. You are not even aware of it. But you do seduce them. As you did with me. As you do with all men. But I had something to give you that no other man had. I could mold you into a great actress, and I did. I can do it again, Kit. But it has to be my way. I cannot work without making love to you. We need each other, Kit. No matter what any doctor says.'

Whatever he had been to her before, however she had given herself to him then, she looked at him now and he was an old man, a lecherous old man with sexual greed in his eyes, using promises of greatness to buy her back.

She could not find the words. She could only shake her head in tiny, fearful, guarded movements which reflected her inner tension. She wanted to call out for Steve. For Jeff. For anyone. She knew there was no one to hear.

She dropped into her chair. She stared into her mirror, saw him standing behind her.

'Kit Lawrence,' he said, 'I want you to remember what I say now. Something I have never wanted to say to you before.

'What talent you had,' he continued scathingly, 'was not talent at all. But a sickness. A sickness within you so electric that people came to see you as they would a freak in a sideshow. Why do you think I kept making you relate every role to your own past experience? Because it served to bring out the sickness in you. That's what dazzled critics. What made people applaud you.'

'That's not true!' she declared, fighting back.

'Isn't it?' he demanded. 'Ask yourself. Six years away. All that treatment. Hiding in a sanitarium the past year and a half. Being treated by your Dr Ross. Revealing yourself. Unburdening yourself. Being "cured." And what has it done for you? Robbed you of the one thing you had. Your ability to use your sickness to act.

'You will *never* play that third act! Instead, you will go to New York. You will fail. In full sight of the audience that used to adore you. And when they reject you, what will be left? Steve Brooks! Dr Ross? What? You could never be satisfied with any one man. You need the world to adore you. But it won't. Not this time. Not ever again.

'I could have saved you from that. And all I asked in return was for you to share my love. But no. You, whom other men have treated like a common tramp, you're suddenly too good for me. Well, be what you are. A sick, demented whore! Seeking to find love somewhere. Anywhere. And never finding it.

'I can see now how it will end for you. An old and ugly woman, faded hair, unkempt, as you wander aimlessly down the corridors of some mental institution crying out for someone to believe you. You will tell them that you were once a great star. And they will laugh. You will cite famous actors to them, but they will no longer be familiar. They will brush you aside as what you have become – an old, demented woman destined to spend your life in empty corridors crying out to be recognized.'

'No!' she fought back. 'It won't happen!'

'Who can stop it if you fail this time? Steve Brooks? Jeff Warrener? Sam Rogers? You will have destroyed them too if you do in New York what I saw you do tonight.

'You were embarrassing. You were disgraceful. You made me cringe. You made me wish I had never come up here to see you.'

He strode to the door, paused, turned to glare at her in the mirror. 'Thank you, my dear. For preventing me from making a terrible mistake.'

He unlocked the door and left. The sound of the door banging shut echoed through the empty theater. The stage doorman went back, knocked cautiously and asked, 'Miss Lawrence? Anything I can do for you?' She did not answer.

'Everyone's gone,' he said. 'And I'll be locking up.'

'In a little while,' Kit called back breathily.

Kit Lawrence stared into her mirror. The lights that surrounded it were harsh and revealing. She studied her face. She could already see signs of the fate Kronheim had forecast for her. Her blond hair, loose and abundant, hung down in strands which now seemed not so golden. She shook her head to make her hair flow in those entrancing swirls that she knew captivated men. It did not respond. She could already visualize the old, unkempt woman who stalked the empty corridors. Staring into the mirror, she could admit to herself it was the fear she had always had but which she had dared to utter aloud only once. To Kronheim in one of those long, torturous acting sessions. He had never forgotten. Nor had she. For it was the image of herself she had had during her most tormented episodes, when she had tried to take her own life.

Ross had assured her many times that she never really intended to die. It was only a cry for help, he said. But she knew better. She had been seeking a way out of becoming the old, demented woman Kronheim talked of.

'The crazy lady' she used to call herself when joking with other actors. But inside she was not joking. Within herself she truly nurtured that fear. She could admit to herself now that once she had actually improvised that scene. Alone in Steve's apartment, she had played the whole scene, aloud, before a mirror. It had frightened her so badly that shortly thereafter she began her affair with Jeff. To avoid being alone. To avoid seeing herself in the mirror that way.

Suddenly she dug into her handbag and seized all the coins she could find. She went to the pay phone on the wall outside her dressing room. She deposited a dime, dialed the long-distance operator and gave her the number. On request, she deposited a stream of quarters and dimes. She waited. When there was an answer, she begged frantically, 'Dr Ross, please? Please?'

The Silvermine operator explained that Dr Ross could not be reached at his home. He had left word that he was out for the evening.

'Please? It's very important,' Kit insisted, trying in vain to keep from sounding desperate. 'Can't you reach him where he is?'

'I'll try,' the operator assured her. She was gone for some minutes. When she returned, she said, 'I'm sorry, but Dr Ross is in transit. If you leave a number, I'll have him call as soon as he returns.'

Kit hesitated then left her name with instructions that Ross was to call her at the hotel. The operator promised that he would.

Kit hung up the phone, went back, finished dressing without daring to look at herself in the mirror. After tipping the stage doorman five dollars, which he reluctantly accepted, she left.

# Part 6

# *Twenty-six*

It was twenty past twelve. Two hours since Steve had left Kit Lawrence in Max Kronheim's charge. He had called her room every fifteen minutes, but there was still no answer. He inquired at the front desk. No one had seen Miss Lawrence return. But it was possible she had slipped in the side door unobserved. And there were times when she perversely refused to answer her phone.

He went to her room, eavesdropped at her door, heard nothing. Four different times he did that. Surely if Kronheim were there there would have been some sound – a voice, laughter, tears.

Perhaps they had gone out to have a bite of supper. When it was past the time when they would have been eating, Steve became alarmed. Was it possible that Kronheim had persuaded her to go to his hotel? It was not impossible, especially when one knew their past relationship.

Steve called each of the hotels at which Kronheim might have registered. He found him at the third. Kronheim answered, sleepily.

'Is she there with you?' Steve demanded angrily.

'No, she is not!' Kronheim said vindictively.

'Then where is she?'

'I don't know and I don't give a damn!' Kronheim said, and hung up.

Steve raced to the theater. On the way, he passed through what had come to be known in Boston as the Combat Zone – a section of streets adjoining the theater to which the police had confined clip joints, prostitutes, porn shops, topless and bottomless bars, homosexual hangouts and all other businesses of whatever sexual orientation which other neighborhoods refused to tolerate.

Steve raced down the street beneath garish neon signs advertising explictly or by implication every form of sexual gratification. He raced past prostitutes, black and white. He was accosted by two girls, both black, in skirts only midway down their thighs, wearing boots that came up to their knees and short fur jackets that covered, but only slightly, the sleazy nylon blouses which exposed their breasts the way fruit merchants lay out their wares. They were both tall, but no more than seventeen years of age. Their hair was hennaed to a red that contradicted their complexions. They accosted him from both sides, closing in with a persistence that forced him to stop.

'Would you like a little fun?'

'Some other time, girls,' he said, attempting to move. They pressed in on him, closer, tighter. One of them reached for the zipper on his fly. The other reached for his pockets, frisking him skillfully to see where he kept his wallet. He pushed the one aside and turned to break loose from the second. The first one cried out, 'Give it to him!'

The second girl pulled a switchblade out of her ratty fur jacket. He heard it click open. He had not served his basic training without learning how to disarm an enemy in close combat. He seized her wrist, snapped it back so hard that she had either to drop her weapon or suffer a fracture. The knife clattered to the pavement.

'Blow!' the second girl called out. They raced down the block and disappeared.

A riot-helmeted policeman, his .38 exposed and ready, came to his aid.

'Everything okay?' the policeman asked.

'Yeah. Okay.'

'You got to watch it down here,' the policeman said, in a Boston accent that had its derivation in an Irish brogue. 'Fact, a man dressed like you don't belong down here at all.

Not at this hour. Take my advice, mister, go back to your hotel.'

'How do you know I live at a hotel?'

'No Bostonian who looks like you would be down here at this hour. You know, we lost a college kid here few months ago. Harvard football player. Knifed and left for dead. And later he did die. So take a little friendly advice. Move on.'

'Okay,' Steve said, proceeding toward the Wilbur. The theater was completely dark. He reached the alley that led to the stage door. The night watchman was just affixing the lock that chained the iron gates shut. He turned to confront Steve, raising his arms to protect himself as he would face a mugger.

'Oh, it's you, Mr Brooks.'

'Miss Lawrence gone?' Steve asked casually, not wishing to cause any alarm or inspire gossip that might leak to the press.

'Yeah, long time,' the old man informed him.

'The man – Mr Kronheim – did he leave with her?'

'I don't know his name, but if you mean the old man with all that white hair, he left before her. I'd say 'bout a good fifteen minutes before.'

'So Miss Lawrence left alone?'

'Yes, sir.'

'Did she say anything?'

' "Good night" was all.'

'You're sure that's all?' Steve asked, his anxiety no longer secret.

'She gave me five. I didn't want to take it. But she insisted.'

'I see,' Steve said solemnly, wondering what course to pursue next.

'Something wrong, Mr Brooks? Anything I can do?' the old man volunteered. 'She's a nice lady. I wouldn't want nothing to happen to her.'

'Nothing wrong,' Steve said. 'Thanks a lot. See you tomorrow night.'

He turned away from the iron gates. The cold fall air penetrating his jacket told him he had started to sweat profusely. He had memories of one other such night. Kit had been living with him at the time. They had argued about something. She had left the house, defiant, half drunk. Stubbornly he had refused to follow her at first. Within the hour, though, he was out searching Columbus Avenue for her. He had finally found her at a bar down near Sixty-seventh Street, drunk and offering to go with any man in the place and do anything. Only the bartender, fearing that his license might be jeopardized, had intervened to save her from two men who were anxious to take her up on her offer.

Steve was suffering the same fear now which he had experienced that night. He retraced his way along the neon-lighted street. Starting with the first bar, he entered, made his way down the long dark aisle, battered by blaring rock music. He went past elevated platforms lined with teen-age girls, bare-breasted, some totally nude. Their young bodies kept frantic but monotonous time to the rock beat. They tried to make their young breasts more enticing by making them gyrate in rhythm to the incessant blaring music. Men standing at the bar and others crowding around small tables nursed their cut drinks, leered hungrily at the young bodies.

Steve Brooks went the length of the bar, ignoring the girls, searching every dark corner and booth. He could not find Kit. He had started to leave when the bartender came out from behind his barricade to block his way and ask, 'Hey, mister, you the law?'

'No, I was looking for someone.'

'She's not here?' the bartender asked.

'I didn't say it was a woman.'

The bartender smiled. 'Only two kinds come in looking for someone. The law. Or some guy who's lost his wife. And if she was here, she wouldn't be here long.'

Steve decided he had better seek help. 'She's a blonde. About this tall. Very good-looking. Long hair down to her shoulders.'

The bartender thought a moment. 'Only the regulars've been in tonight so far. But if I see her, who shall I say was looking for her?'

'Just say Steve.'

He inspected two more topless bars. The din was the same. The young girls tried as frantically to be enticing. The men stared, as frustrated and lecherous. He made his inspection, going from one end of the place to the other, peering into every booth, every dark corner. Twice he came on girls engaged in sexual acts with men who sat on rickety bentwood chairs.

He came out of the fourth bar, feeling the cold night air even more. The temperature could not have changed that much. He was sweating more profusely. He questioned going into the fifth bar, but the lack of alternatives forced him. He was assaulted by the same blaring beat; the same faces it seemed; the same young girls, some no more than fifteen, flaunting their young breasts. He walked the length of the bar and into the back room. He searched every booth. He came to the darkest corner in the farthest reaches of the place.

Finally, he heard a voice that arrested him. He had found Kit.

She was standing before a man who was seated. She had exposed her breasts, and he was fondling one while tonguing the other. Steve could tell she was drunk from the way she kept urging him on. 'Go on, go on,' she said, holding her breast up to his mouth. 'Aren't they beautiful?'

With her other hand she had raised up her skirt to expose herself to him. The man was reaching for her when Steve Brooks called out fiercely, 'Kit!'

At the sound of Steve's voice, she turned on him, crying out, 'Get out of here, you!'

'Kit! Come on!' Steve insisted, reaching for her hand.

'Leave me alone!' she cried out in a loud drunken voice.

By now her partner was so sexually aroused and hungry for her that he held her in a painful embrace as he devoured her breast. Steve reached out to tear them apart. The stranger leaped up.

'You dirty sonofabitch! She's into me for six drinks! She's mine now!' And he swung out at Steve, viciously.

Steve evaded his first swing. But the second caught him high on the head. It opened a cut in his eyebrow and sent him staggering back against the wall.

'Hit him! Kill him!' Kit urged the stranger on.

Steve recovered and started to attack. They traded blows. Until Steve let go one wild swing that caught the stranger on the jaw, hurling him back into his chair. From there he slumped slowly to the floor.

The bartender came racing toward them, wielding an old bung starter as a weapon. When he realized the fight was over, he stared at Kit, then at Steve.

'Get this broad the hell out! We don't want the law in here!'

Steve seized her arm and tried to urge her down the aisle past the bar toward the front door. But she refused to go, calling out, 'I want another drink! Who'll buy me another drink?'

He picked her up and carried her toward the door while she shouted hoarsely, 'Put me down, you bastard! I don't want to go. I want another drink!'

She called back over his shoulder, 'This bastard is nobody to me. I want another drink! You take your hands off me! Somebody! Anybody! Buy me a drink and I'll go with you for the night.'

As she struggled with him she called out to the crowd, which had interrupted their drinking to stare, 'How many of you bastards have ever had a star! How many? Well, I am a star! Who wants to screw a star?'

The bartender came out from behind the bar to threaten, 'I said get her the hell out! I don't want trouble!'

Steve succeeded in carrying her outside. He held her in a tight grip while he searched for a cab. A helmeted policeman came to his side.

'Trouble, mister?'

'I need a cab.'

The policeman went out into the street, waving a flashlight until a cab came round the corner. With his help Steve managed to force her into the cab.

'Where to, mister?' The driver turned, not for instructions but to stare at Kit, who kept muttering fierce and obscene accusations at Steve.

He dared not bring her into the Ritz in such condition.

'Just drive around for a while.'

'Just drive around?' the cabbie asked suspiciously.

'I said just drive around!' Steve exploded.

The driver set out aimlessly, going wherever the oneway streets took him.

Kit's protests grew less belligerent but more garbled. All Steve could make of it before she dozed off was 'Called me a whore I'll show him. I'll *be* a whore.'

He was relieved when she fell asleep. He found a comb in her handbag. He worked on her long tangled hair, restoring it to some semblance of order. Her lipstick had been smeared. Who knew how many men had kissed her before the one he found her with? He used his handkerchief to wipe her face clean. He cradled her in his arms, while she slept off the alcohol. He became aware of a trickle of blood from his eyebrow. He mopped it away.

It had been almost two hours. She stirred.

'Kit?'

'H'mmm?' she responded vaguely.

'Kit, you awake?'

'Uh-huh,' she barely enunciated. She opened her eyes. She looked out at the dark night. 'Where are we?'

'In a cab.'

'Take me home?' she pleaded pathetically.

'Do you think you can make it?' he asked. 'Into the hotel and up in the elevator, Kit?'

'I . . . I think so. It's cold,' she said suddenly.

He rolled up the window and ordered the driver, 'The Ritz.'

Steve held her under the shower, letting the stinging water beat down on her. Gradually he could feel the tone returning to her body. He rubbed her dry with a huge towel. He dried her hair, trying to untangle it at the same time. When he ran the comb through it, she tried to twist out of his grasp every time he hit a knot. Finally he brushed the long golden strands until they glistened.

She was clean again. He carried her to the bed. She fell into a restful, easy pose, looking youthfully innocent, far different from the drunken woman who had been offering herself to strangers.

He lay down on the other bed, but was unable to sleep, though it was long past three and he was exhausted.

He drifted off. She woke him, calling softly, 'Steve . . . Steve . . .?'

He came to with a start, like an anxious parent guilty at having fallen asleep while tending a sick child. 'Yes, Kit?'

'I'm thirsty, very thirsty,' she whispered entreatingly.

'What would you like?'

'Juice. Lots of juice.'

He went to the door and pressed the waiter's button. Within moments there was a knock. He ordered through the door. 'Three large glasses of orange juice!'

He handed her the first frosty glass. 'Sip it slowly.'

She sat up in bed. Her clean blond hair, disheveled from sleep, fell over her naked shoulders. She modestly kept the sheet tucked around her breasts. She sipped slowly. Stopping to stare at him frequently, she reached out to touch the fresh wound in his eyebrow.

'Poor Steve . . . the things I've put you through. Why don't you just forget me? For your own sake.'

'Drink your juice. You're dehydrated. You need it,' he urged, trying to divert her from any serious discussion.

'Was it really bad last night?' she asked. 'I remember this man . . . and . . .' She did not pursue it any further until she said, 'It must have been terrible for you. I'm sorry, Steve. Sorry.'

She had finished the first glass and was halfway through the second when she said, 'The old bastard only wanted to take me to bed. When I wouldn't let him, he said cruel things, vicious things.'

'Kronheim?'

She related in detail what happened once Steve had left her dressing room.

'Never leave me like that again, Steve,' she pleaded. 'No matter what I say, never leave me.'

She realized how pathetic she sounded, for she embraced him suddenly, pressed against his chest and pleaded, 'Steve, help me? Help me!'

He held her, tried to comfort her, knowing all the while that comfort was the one thing he could not give her. She would find it herself or never find it at all.

She relaxed in his arms. Once her breathing assured him she was asleep, he laid her down gently and covered her well. He went to the window to peer between the draperies and discover the first red glow of a fall dawn reflecting off the golden dome of the Massachusetts State House.

It was a new day, with all the old challenges.

Jeff and Sam would surely ask about Kronheim and his opinion of Kit's performance. He had to tell them something. He decided it would serve no purpose to tell them everything.

Ross must know. This was an episode of enormous imporance to her prognosis.

It was past ten when she woke. She stretched and in so doing became aware of him.

'Steve?' she exclaimed, surprised to see him there. Then she remembered and said only, 'Oh.'

'Hungry? You must be. Shall I order us some breakfast?'

'Please,' she begged.

While he ordered a huge breakfast for them, she slipped out of bed, naked, and tiptoed to the bathroom. When she came out, her face had the bright glow of having been freshly washed in icy water. She was gathering her light blue robe about her. And she brought with her that fragrance that was distinctly Kit.

They sat across from each other over the breakfast table. She ate ravenously – scrambled eggs; Canadian bacon; croissants thick with butter, topped with rosy strawberry jam. She ate like an eager child, licking the jam from her fingers. Every so often she glanced at him, to see if he approved. She was eating for him.

She pushed back her plate and took her coffee cup in hand. She stared over it at him, not smiling now.

'I think,' she said soberly, 'it was because I was angry. I realized that he hadn't come up here from New York to help me. But because he wanted me again. Once I refused him, he said those vile things. So I said to myself, "I'll show him!" '

Her eyes filled up with tears. 'I wanted to show him that he couldn't have me. But any other man could . . . any other man . . . any bum off the street, but not him. Not him!'

Her cup hand began to tremble. She tried to steady it. But she could not prevent the coffee from spilling over, and staining her dressing gown. He came to her aid to mop away the stain with his napkin. She looked into his face and asked, 'Forgive me? Forgive a crazy lady?'

'Don't say that!' he commanded, still trying to mop up the coffee stains.

When he came back to his room he found a number of messages from Jeff and Sam. Before he responded, he called Ross and reported the events of the night before.

'I warned you, Kronheim is a dangerous man. You never should have left them alone. But I would say, based on what you report, her reaction was not unexpected.'

'That's all, "Doctor" – is that all you have to say? "Not unexpected." You should have been there!' Steve Brooks exploded.

'I have been,' Ross said sadly. 'Many times. I'd say, based on what you told me, we were lucky.'

'What do I do now?'

'Keep working.'

'And when we get to New York and get murdered by those reviews?'

'We'll deal with that when it happens,' Ross said with an enforced professional coldness that made Steve Brooks slam down the phone.

Ross himself set his phone down very slowly. It was not easy for him to remain professional while he was torn between guilt over her, on the one hand, and an unquenchable desire for her on the other. His training and his experience both told him that he had made the right professional decision. Some crises could not be avoided. One could not protect a patient from all the consequences of her own conduct. Not without permanent, highly restrictive confinement. To which, he had to admit, he might yet be forced to resort.

Steve did not explain to Jeff or Sam how he had spent the night. Anything they might suspect would not be as chilling as the truth. When they asked about Kronheim's reaction, he answered evasively.

'He didn't like the direction,' Steve said, 'but I think he only said that because he thought we might invite him in to polish the show. I told him where he could go and what he could do with himself when he got there. So he left.'

## *Twenty-seven*

It was past noon, and Emil Bernstein, who handled press relations, was being most insistent. Sam had forbidden him to talk to Kit about publicity without first clearing it with Jeff. She was never to be forced to do television talk shows. Her radio interviews were always to be taped, not live. Nor was she to be subjected to newspaper interviewers unless she consented in advance. Bernstein had adhered strictly to all that.

But today, Bernstein explained to Sam, 'How can anyone say no to *The New York Times*? They promised us a big front-page piece in the Sunday Arts and Leisure section right before we open. Hell, you can't buy that kind of publicity! Naturally, I said yes.'

Now the *Times* man was here, with a *Times* photographer waiting down in the lobby of the Ritz.

Jeff was ready to agree. But knowing Kit's condition on this, of all mornings, Steve refused. Bernstein appealed to the producer.

'Sam, the return of Kit Lawrence to Broadway is an event! That's the only reason the *Times* agreed. It could help at the box office. Maybe even stimulate some theater parties. Our advance is now so skimpy we've got to do it!'

Sam, too, was reluctant.

Bernstein pressured. 'With me, it isn't only this production. It's my reputation. If I cross the *Times* now, they'll never give me front-page space again! I can't say no. Don't you understand that, Sam?'

Finally, Steve agreed to ask Kit. He tried to ring her room, but Miss Lawrence had forbidden all calls.

He went up, pressed his ear against the door, heard nothing. He knocked. Softly, at first. Then loudly.

'Kit! Kit, it's me.' When she did not respond, he became alarmed. He prevailed on the elderly Irish maid to unlock the door for him.

The room was dark. The draperies were still closed as he had left them. He glanced past the bed he had slept in. There in the other bed Kit was curled up and uncovered. He was relieved when he detected that she was breathing at a normal rate and depth.

He bent over her. He had always loved the fragrance of her when she slept. Her perfume mingling with the aroma of her body was aphrodisiac. All traces of last night's vodka were gone. She slept in unencumbered innocence.

'Kit?' he whispered.

She stirred, turning to face away from him. He sat gingerly on the side of the bed, leaned over her and whispered into her ear, 'Kit . . . it's me . . . Steve.'

She turned back, slipped her arm around him and drew him down, enfolding him as if to make him join her in sleep. They had slept that way in those earliest days.

'Kit, darling, listen to me. The *New York Times* has sent a man up to interview you. With a photographer. You don't have to do it, unless you want to. But Sam would appreciate it. And it could help us in New York.'

'Do you want me to do it, Steve?' she asked, not yet fully awake.

'It would be a good thing. But only if you feel like it.'

She made a heroic effort to spring out of bed. But the moment she was on her feet she became dizzy and fell back. He caught her. He held her until she regained her equilibrium. She went to the bathroom. She tried to talk to him while furiously brushing her teeth. Her conversation was garbled, following no logical sequence.

When she returned, her face glistening, her eyes brighter, she wore her blue robe again.

'See,' she said, 'the coffee stains all came out.'

'Shall I call Bernstein and tell him you'll do it?'

'Of course,' she said with such enthusiasm that there seemed never to have been any doubt.

He started for the phone, but she intercepted him as she said, 'I did a terrible thing to you last night.'

'That's over, done. Forgotten,' he assured her glibly, trying to diminish something he would not forget for the rest of his life.

'No, Steve.' She sealed off his protest by pressing her fingers to his lips. 'I'll make it up to you. I will!' she insisted. 'Steve, tonight I am going to play that third act for you! Yes!'

He had heard too many promises from her in his lifetime, too many in these past days. He knew how extravagant she could be in her manic moments. Or when guilt pursued her. Nevertheless, there was something in him that responded hopefully each time. It did again.

He freed himself to reach the phone. 'Emil? Steve. The dining room. Say half an hour?'

She sat at the dressing table, brushing her hair, making up, talking incessantly.

'What shall I tell the *Times*, Steve?' Before he could answer, she continued, 'I know! I'll tell them this isn't just another play, another role. For me this is a way of bringing hope to so many people who, like me, have had to fight their way out of the darkness. How does that sound?'

'Are you sure you want to be quite so open about it, Kit?'

'Why not?' she asked, turning to him, hairbrush in hand, confident smile on her face. 'Think of all the people like me who can take courage from this. I'll tell them how I decided to come out and face the world again. How I decided to regain my career, after everyone said I couldn't. I'll tell them about you. And what you did for me. You'd like that, wouldn't you, Steve?' Detecting his reluctance, she added, 'I won't tell them about last night. I'll never tell anyone about last night. Will you?'

'Of course not.'

'Not even Melinda?'

'Never Melinda,' he promised.

'I don't know,' Kit said strangely. 'I think she might understand. Did you know she sent me a note?'

'Melinda?'

'Yes, and very sweet.' Kit was no longer manic and bubbling, but quite touched. 'I sent her a note. From New Haven. The other day I got an answer. It was in with a single red rose. She told me how much she admired me. How much she wished I'd have a success in New York. And when I did, we would have lunch together. And we wouldn't talk about you. That was very nice of her to do. Wasn't it, Steve?'

'Yes, yes, it was. She's really a very nice lady,' he said.

'What will I tell the *Times*?' she asked again suddenly, turning from her mirror, her makeup completed.

No one could have guessed how Steve had found her the night before.

In a corner of the formal mezzanine dining room Sam, Jeff and Emil Bernstein waited, making small talk with the young *Times* reporter. The photographer was plugging in his lights and setting them up, focused on the chair in the corner where Kit would sit. By the time Bernstein and Sam were becoming anxious, Kit Lawrence and Steve Brooks appeared.

The efficient maître d' greeted them profusely and loudly enough to alert all the other diners who watched as he led Kit to the corner table.

The introductions over, the photographer asked to take several shots of Kit standing. She posed alone. She posed with Steve. She posed with Steve and Jeff. She posed with Sam. Those shots out of the way, the photographer was content to lurk in the background taking candid shots all during the conversation.

The interviewer, young and irreverent, owned a reputation based on a number of scathing sketches and interviews he had done. From the outset it became apparent why.

'The first thing our readers will want to know is why you've been away so long,' he began. 'There've been all kinds of rumors.'

Steve detected a slight flush originating in Kit's neck and slowly rising into her face. Whatever had been her intention to talk freely before, once driven, she seemed to resist, especially after Steve's warning.

'What rumors?' she asked, pretending to be completely ingenuous.

'They say you don't handle straight vodka very well,' the young man said pointedly.

'I haven't had a drink in years,' she said with such self-righteousness it was utterly convincing.

'But it is true you've been in treatment the past five or six years?' the reporter persisted.

'God, who hasn't?' She laughed. 'Haven't you ever been in treatment – honestly, now?'

It was the young reporter's turn to blush slightly. He smiled and nodded.

'Well, then,' Kit said, 'we start out even. Ask me anything,' she invited with easy abandon.

'Then why *have* you been away so long?' he persisted.

Steve and Jeff both awaited her reply, wondering how much of herself she would expose.

'It isn't easy to describe. And I don't expect someone in your profession to understand too readily. Because in your work things happen every day that give you the substance of what you do for a living. Today you interview me; tomorrow it's George Scott or Laurence Olivier or some other personality your readers would like to know about.

'But not so with an actress,' Kit said. Steve noticed how,

almost imperceptibly, she was transposing herself from a human being named Kit Lawrence to a character named Kit Lawrence which she was now assuming.

'An actress invests a part of herself in every role she does. She must bring to it what *she* is, what *she* feels, what is deepest within her. She lays bare her inner feelings.

'Well, before an actress does that she must find a role worthy of such devotion. Of such self-revelation, such investment of self. Unfortunately no such roles have come along,' she said sadly. 'After all, there have to be other plays for women besides the tired old *Three Sisters.* Or *Anna Christie.*

'We need roles that give today's woman a chance to reflect today's view of life. So I waited, thinking, Someday soon some author will come along with such a role. Plays came to me, where I live in Connecticut—'

'Connecticut? Where?' the young reporter intruded.

Steve stared – a fixed stare. How would she handle that?

Pausing for an instant, then smiling sweetly, she said, 'I assumed you knew. I have a place right outside Hartford. A charming place. In the Connecticut countryside. Someday you must come up and visit.'

Having disposed of that, she resumed what she had been saying. 'Plays came to me, picture scripts, television specials. All trivial. All surfacy. So one day I decided to take the bull by the horns . . .'

She laughed charmingly, intending to beguile the young reporter and succeeding. 'Whenever you hear that phrase, don't you wonder? Just what would you do if you had a bull by the horns? Let go, I say. Let go and get the hell out of that pasture. Still, as a figure of speech it does nicely if you don't think about it. So I decided to do that. In this case it meant calling Steve Brooks and Jeff Warrener and saying, "Let's get together. Like in the old days."

'So Jeff came on from Hollywood. And Steve from the

university where he's Author-in-Residence. I sat them both down and said, "Let's do a play together. And we'll call it *Reunion*." And that's how our play got its title.'

She looked for support to Steve and Jeff, who were relieved to agree with her version.

She seemed aware that no one had ordered. She became the hostess. 'Surely you'd like a drink.' She snapped her fingers in the direction of the waiter who lurked at a respectful distance.

'What would you like?' Kit asked the young reporter.

'Whatever you'd like,' he said.

'Oh, I never drink.' It sounded like both a statement of fact and an expression of disapproval, after which the reporter did not dare order a drink.

Once they had selected lunch, Kit resumed, as if bursting to tell her story:

'Well, it wasn't as easy as it sounds. I mean, one doesn't just create a play out of thin air. Or out of an actress' whim. It takes hard work. I can't tell you how hard Steve worked before we had a rough draft. Then Jeff and I did our meagre bit. Mainly as sounding boards. We were Steve's audience. He acted. We reacted. I must confess I picked the right man. No playwright in the American theater can write for women the way Steve Brooks does.

'It has been the greatest theatrical experience of my life,' she said as fervently as if she believed it.

Once she had preempted most of the reporter's prepared questions, the interview proceeded along more conventional lines. By the time it was over he had been completely captivated. When he rose to permit her to leave the table, he asked, 'Miss Lawrence, I know this sounds gauche, but would you autograph my menu?'

'Of course, dear boy.' With a huge flourish, Kit inscribed the menu, *To dear dear Tony, as ever, Kit.*

She started out, Steve following after her closely. They stepped into the elevator. She still carried herself erectly, but he noticed she had begun to tremble. He guided her from the car and to her room.

Once inside, she leaned against the door for support as she said, 'That should hold that nasty little sonofabitch!'

'It certainly should.'

'Get me a drink!' she pleaded.

'No, Kit,' he pleaded.

'I need something. Something!' She could not control her trembling.

He took her in his arms. 'You were great. You handled him like a baby.'

He held her tightly until her chill seemed to have passed.

'I wasn't going to let him take my life and throw it away in one of his nasty sarcastic interviews. He's not going to climb to glory over my misfortunes.'

She laughed as she imitated, 'Miss Lawrence, I know this sounds gauche, but would you autograph my menu?'

The phone rang. Steve answered it: 'Yes? . . . Oh, Emil . . . She's fine. Fine . . . He loved it, did he? Good . . . You think he'll give us the front page along with a big shot of Kit? . . . Terrific! I'll tell her!' He hung up. 'Well, you heard. You can do it when you set your mind to it, darling. You can do anything.'

'I will do it. For you. Just watch your third act tonight. Just watch!'

Still unaware of the events of the night before, Sam and Jeff were both in high spirits when they arrived at the theater.

'That's a whole new girl!' Sam enthused. 'The way she ad-libbed that story of how the play came to be written. Fantastic!' He laughed uninhibitedly for the first time in weeks.

Jeff, too, was tremendously encouraged. 'She's coming out of it. Whatever's been bothering her, I think she came out of it today.' He took Steve aside and asked, 'Last night when we were trying to reach you, were you with her? Were you making love to her?'

Because it was a lesser crime, Steve pleaded guilty by nodding.

'I thought so,' Jeff said. 'Well, it worked. Maybe that's what she's been needing all along. Out on the Coast I find it works with actresses all the time. Keep it up!'

With renewed confidence and anticipation, the three men stood in the back of the house to watch as Kit played the first two acts almost flawlessly. But she had done that before.

She played the opening of the third act with more than her usual conviction. She approached the climactic scene with a greater sense of anticipation than she had ever exhibited. She did not shy away from it as she had done in the past. She played more fully to Maria Patrick, and Maria, delighted, responded. There were moments when Steve felt hopeful that Kit was about to realize the scene for the first time.

But his hopes did not deceive him. Hers was all surface effort. The inner dynamics of her performance, the true talent of Kit Lawrence were still missing.

The audience applauded with more enthusiasm than before. But Steve and Jeff both knew that such a performance would not fool an opening-night audience in New York. Nor the one critic on the *Times*, whose approval they needed if the show was to run.

Walking back to the hotel, past the same neon-lighted joints in which Steve had searched for her last night, she said, 'I tried, Steve. God knows, I tried.'

Steve arranged a light supper served in her room. She ate nothing, only stared at him across the table.

'What are you thinking?' she asked.

'How much better your performance was tonight.'

'No, Steve. More energy. More effort. More desire to make it work. But it didn't. It just didn't.'

'It will,' he said encouragingly.

'Steve, if I tell you something, you won't get upset? You won't call Ross? Or tell anyone? Promise!'

'I promise.'

'Tonight was the strangest experience I've ever had on a stage. I wasn't playing the part. I was pursuing it. And it kept eluding me. Like a dream I used to have as a child. There was a certain doll, a doll almost as big as I was. With golden hair and a beautiful white dress trimmed in lace, real lace. It was displayed in the window of the toy store in our little town.

'Every time I went by there I would insist on stopping to admire that doll. Till one day, right before Christmas, I went by and it was gone. Someone had bought my doll. I didn't want to own it. I just wanted to look at it. But someone had bought it away from me.

'I dreamed about it that night. And many nights after. Even now I still see that doll in my dreams. I pursue it. But it's always just a little ahead of me. No matter how fast I run, I never quite catch up to it. Never!

'Except once. Only once, in one dream I did catch up with it. When I found it, I picked it up. It had been dropped in some mud. I wiped it off. But when I wiped it clean I discovered her face was smashed. Someone had smashed my doll's face. Since then when I dream about it, I never want to find it.

'That's how it felt tonight. I was pursuing the part as I pursue that doll in my dream. But I didn't want to find it. Or else I couldn't, I just couldn't. Why, Steve? Why?'

She was so frightened she began to tremble.

# *Twenty-eight*

'If she just does what she did the other night,' Sam was saying, 'we might make it. We just might,' he added for emphasis, for he was most doubtful.

They were waiting in the lobby of the Ritz for Kit before they left for the airport and the final goal of their tour, New York. Broadway.

To Steve it seemed a lifetime since the first reading of his play. The first run-through now seemed years ago. Even New Haven was a distant memory. Time had no relevance to reality when one was on tour with a new play.

The limousine had arrived and was waiting. Sam urged, 'Steve, go up and see if she's ready.'

Once Steve left, Sam confided to Jeff, 'I got a call late last night. From Emil. He had bad news.'

'What?'

'The *Times* decided against running that interview.'

'After all those pictures? All the charm she laid on that little bastard?' Jeff asked indignant.

'Emil also said that the Shuberts are offering our theater for two weeks from now.'

'They can't!' Jeff argued. 'You've got a contract. The deposits are down.'

'They don't expect us to go beyond the week,' Sam said. 'And they're right. Either we get smash reviews or we close on Saturday. So the *Times* doesn't want to be caught with egg on its noble face. And the Shuberts don't want to lose a single week's rental.'

'You know, Sam, I've been thinking. We work so well together. And you're not chintzy with money where it helps a production, but you also know how to save a buck when you have to.'

'That's my job. I'm a producer.'

'So I was thinking if my new film keeps doing business, my agent says my next move is to set up my own production company. Not just a tax entity. But a real going production company. I've got no head for details, especially where money is concerned. So I'd want you to be my line producer. Handle the money. Keep costs in line.'

'What the hell do I know about picture budgets?' Sam asked.

'You could learn. I've got a very sharp accountant out there. And a shrewd lawyer.'

Sam stared at the younger man. 'Jeff, if you've got a sharp accountant and a shrewd lawyer, why do you need a broke old Broadway producer? But thanks, anyhow.'

'Sorry, Sam. I didn't mean to hurt your feelings.'

The air trip took only forty minutes. Sam's limousine was waiting for them at LaGuardia. The drive into the city was uneventful. It was a gray day, threatening rain. The streets were empty. It was a typical, disheartening fall Sunday in New York.

This time Sam insisted that Kit stay at the Algonquin. He had made the reservation without consulting her. He announced it to her when the car rolled up the Avenue of The Americas and turned right onto Forty-fourth Street. Kit did not resist. She had been noticeably silent all during the flight and the ride in. The others had had no clue to her mood. But Steve kept thinking of the dream that had haunted her most of her life. It was a wound no child should have had to suffer, an image no adult should be pursued by forever.

When they checked in, Steve found several messages. Two were from Melinda. Though it was past one o'clock, when he called he woke her. He could tell by the way she recognized his voice and spoke a sleepy 'Steve?' as she used to in the old days, which were less than a year ago.

'Got your messages. What's up?'

'Do you have a brunch date?' Melinda asked. From the sound of her voice, he could envision her stretching, naked, lithe. It was the first thing she did on awakening. Stretch – a long, easy, graceful catlike stretch. Sometimes it seemed to him she did that to take inventory of all her parts and make sure they were all there and functioning.

'No, I'm free. Unless Kit asks,' he admitted self-consciously.

'I wouldn't blame her if she didn't want to be alone today. When you know, call me. Meantime, if she doesn't have a good hairdresser in town, I'll send her to mine. She ought to be kept busy tomorrow. She can waste a good three hours at my beauty parlor.'

'Good idea,' he agreed. 'Call you soon as I know.' Then he asked, 'What did you mean, you wouldn't blame her if she didn't want to be alone today?'

'Steve, you might as well be prepared. The word is out. Kronheim came back and said it's beyond saving. There isn't a critic in town who hasn't heard. Someone will get word to her. You know how actors love gossip. Especially if its deadly.'

He called Kit from the desk, asked about her room, did she need anything from the drugstore, did she want to come down and have lunch, maybe walk up to the Gotham or the Plaza?

She sounded morose. He decided he had better go up and have a look. She was still dressed in her travel clothes. Her bags still stood, unopened, where the bellman had set them down. There was a copy of the Sunday *Times* on the couch. Intact, except for the Arts and Leisure section, which had been opened and lay abandoned on the floor. When he looked up from that to stare at her, she said, 'The first time . . . the first time the *Times* has ever ignored me.'

'Maybe the interview came in too late. This section is printed up days ahead of time.'

'They ignored me' was all she said, pathetic and frightened.

'Look, change clothes; we'll go out and get some brunch. Actually, you don't have to change. You look terrific just the way you are. Let's go.'

She did not move. Just stared, lost.

He felt the need to keep talking. 'Oh, by the way, Melinda called. If you don't have a hairdresser you like, she says use hers. He's terrific. Busy as hell, but she'll be able to get you a date for tomorrow. And we're not having our tech till five o'clock. Shall I call her?'

He had run out of things to say, things to ask, so he urged again, 'Let's go get something to eat.'

'I'll have something sent up,' she said. 'You go. I'll see you later.'

'You're sure?' he asked, lingering, fearful of leaving her alone.

'Yes, Steve, I'm sure.'

He kissed her tenderly. And though she submitted, she made no effort to cling to him. He stepped outside the door, waited, eavesdropping. He heard nothing. Feeling guilty, but having no choice, he went toward the elevator.

Alone, Kit Lawrence went to the phone. She gave the operator a number and waited.

'Dr Ross, please.'

'Who is calling?'

'Kit. Kit Lawrence.'

'Oh, yes, just a moment.'

Finally he came on. 'Kit?'

'Ross? Oh, Ross.' She broke down and wept.

'Kit, Kit,' he said, trying to comfort her. 'Compose yourself. Stop crying. Tell me what the trouble is.'

He waited patiently until she regained her voice.

'Ross?'

'I'm still here.'

'If I fail, will you take me back?' she pleaded.

'Does that mean you want to fail so you can come back?'

'Don't play analyst's games with me,' she begged, half in anger, half in fear. 'Just tell me. I have to know. Will you take me back?'

'If you do your best and fail, yes, I will take you back.'

She sighed in relief, wept softly for a few moments, then said, 'You don't have to love me – just take me back. Take me back?'

'I said yes,' he repeated in a comforting voice.

'I tried, Ross. Honestly, I tried. Up in Boston. I tried my best to play that scene. I fooled some people in the audience. But I didn't fool me. I pursued it, frantically, but I never was able to reach it. Do you know what I mean, Ross? Do you?' she pleaded.

'Yes, I remember your dream. The golden-haired doll with the white lace-trimmed dress,' Ross agreed, trying to retain his professional distance and conceal the painful sympathy he felt.

'It'll be the same. Wednesday night my doll will be muddy and broken.'

'That's only a dream, Kit. It has nothing to do with your opening Wednesday night. Nothing at all.'

'Then why does it feel that way?'

'We've been over that, Kit. Remember?'

They had covered that one disturbing dream many times. Kit knew its meaning almost by rote now.

'It isn't the doll. It's my mother I keep pursuing.'

'And?' Ross coached.

'When I find her I give vent to my hatred for her. That's why the one time I found her she was muddy and with her face smashed.'

'Why?'

'Because of what she did to me,' Kit answered, again as if by rote.

'And does it have anything to do with your performance?' Ross asked.

She did not answer at once.

'Kit,' he pressed.

'No,' she replied, because he expected it of her and she did not dare antagonize her doctor.

'Remember, just as you control your own dreams, so you control your own performance. You can do it, if you want to. You have to want to, Kit. Understand?'

'Yes, yes,' she agreed, not because she believed, but because she knew he could do nothing more for her.

Ross had no sooner hung up than he tried to reach Steve Brooks. He caught him as he was leaving to keep his brunch date with Melinda.

'Brooks? Do you have any sleeping pills or tranquilizers?'

'I always have some Seconal.'

'How many grains?'

'Five, I think.'

'Five grains is fine. Give one to Kit. See that she takes it. And make her take a nap. She's overtense.'

'How do you know?'

'She just called me.'

'Ross, are we pushing her too hard? Should we let her stop right now? Before the worst happens?'

'If we let her stop now, the worst will have happened. Give her that Seconal.'

He sat with her until she fell asleep. Then he slipped out of her suite to meet Melinda, who waited patiently at their old apartment. She was dressed in jeans and a blouse that he had always favored, but he knew his visit would be limited to brunch and business conversation. Else she would have worn a robe, and had her hair loose and flowing, instead of pinned up and severe.

He had not been in the apartment for almost a year. He was surprised at how much larger it seemed than it had when he had lived there. He used to feel cramped and unable to avoid her. Now the place seemed spacious and bright. He kissed her dutifully on the lips, but it sparked no emotion in either of them.

'How is she?' Melinda asked, while she mixed Bloody Marys.

'Sleeping.'

She brought out bagels and a platter of pink, thinly sliced Nova Scotia salmon, with mounds of white cream cheese. It was the same Sunday brunch they always used to enjoy with the *Times*.

'Just think, two one-hundred-percent WASPs, and what are we having for Sunday brunch? Wouldn't it be the final irony if the real melting pot was not America, but Zabar's? Do you know who are the second-largest consumers of bagels in New York after Jews? Blacks. I read that in *New York* magazine.'

She was pouring the fresh coffee when she asked, 'What are you going to do?'

'After the opening? Go West. Finish my novel.'

She did not ask what plans he had for his future life. Nor did he volunteer.

'Your publisher came up with an interesting idea for a new novel. Once the opening's over, he'd like to have lunch and discuss it. Would you?'

'I don't know. I get this feeling I'd like to take this play somewhere – some university, or local theater; say, Dallas or San Francisco – and try it out with another cast.'

'Another actress?' Melinda asked.

'I'd like to find out once and for all, is it her? Or is it my play? Or was the whole idea an impossible gamble from the beginning?'

They talked on. He ate without much appetite. The food turned plastic and tasteless in his mouth. He tried to wash it down with fresh coffee.

'You hear from your lawyer lately?' he asked.

'He called last week. The papers are all ready to sign.'

Suddenly he asked, 'Do you have . . . is there someone else?'

'I . . . I've been going out . . . but no one in particular.'

'Then what's the rush? Can't it wait till I finish my novel?'

'You know me. When I start to negotiate a deal, I like to have all the loose ends tied up and out of the way. My nature, I guess.'

'Is that what this is, Mel – a deal?'

'Please, Steve, don't,' she begged. 'It's not me who has ties to the past.'

He could not dispute her words.

'It would be like being married to someone who had cancer once,' she said. 'I'd keep looking for signs of metastasis. Always wondering, If our marriage survives two years, will it be clean forever? Or if I wait five years, will that do it? And what kind of chemotherapy is there for insecure marriages?'

'I don't know,' he admitted. 'After the opening, we'll see what happens to her; then we'll talk.'

He stood in the doorway, reluctant to leave, staring beyond her at the apartment, toward the windows, beyond which he could see the gold and red trees of fall in Central Park.

'We had good times here.'

'Yes, we did,' she agreed, making no effort to detain him.

'Will you come to the opening?'

'If you want me to.'

'I want you to.'

He stopped by Kit's door and listened. There was no sound. No radio, no television. She must still be asleep. Evidently the pill had done its work. He walked over to the theater.

The lights were on. The front of the house was dressed.

Huge portraits of Kit Lawrence. Smaller shots of the rest of the cast in action from the play.

Above the marquee, lights spelled out KIT LAWRENCE IN REUNION.

On easels there were mounted the few good quotes they had been able to extract from the uniformly unfavorable reviews out of town. Not very impressive.

He stopped by Kit's door again. This time he heard sounds. Her voice. It was animated. That encouraged him, though he could not make out any distinct words. He lingered. Then her voice disturbed him. For it was not conversation but a continuous outpouring of language, in a voice that had grown to sound not animated, but frenetic. It rose in pitch and excitement until it became a hysterical diatribe.

He pounded on her door. She was obviously asleep, under the influence of the drug. He raced down to the desk and persuaded the clerk to admit him to her room. On the way up in the elevator, frightening thoughts tormented him. Had she been able to secure other drugs, of which he was not aware? The synergistic effect could prove fatal. Or perhaps the reality of an impending Broadway opening had overwhelmed her and this was the final breakdown which Ross had warned about.

He dismissed the clerk and entered the suite alone. He heard her more distinctly now. She was weeping, babbling. When he reached her bedroom, she was thrashing about as if seeking to elude someone in the midst of a tangled mass of bedclothes dampened by a flood of her perspiration.

Her face was pale. It glistened with sweat. Her blond hair adhered to her damp forehead and her face. She breathed in deep, frantic, heaving draughts. She was in torment. She flailed out as if destroying something, pounding some imaginary object and repeating the only distinct word he could hear.

'Lie . . . lie . . . lie . . .'

He took her in his arms, forcibly restraining her from striking out. Finally she calmed and contented herself with being held. She was peaceful for a time. She woke, startled to find him. But she relaxed once she was sure it was he. She kept whispering, as if to comfort herself, 'Steve . . . Steve . . .'

## *Twenty-nine*

He had toweled her dry. He brushed her hair, washed her face. She submitted to his care like a patient too sick and weary to mount any resistance. She seemed barren of all feeling. She was too deeply immersed in the shock of her dream.

When he suggested food, she did not respond. He ordered dinner anyhow, for he remembered one of Ross's warnings. 'Make sure she eats. Physical debility can be as causative a factor in mental breakdown as emotional stress. Especially if the two are combined.'

He hand-fed her, like an infant. Steak in small bites. Baked potato. Milk in small sips. She was submissive, obedient. Thoughtful. Always thoughtful. She had seen a frightening vision that would live with her forever. He did not probe until he had made her consume what he considered enough food to sustain her.

Once he had pushed the food cart outside the door, and was sure they would not be disturbed, he asked, 'Do you want to tell me about it?'

She stared straight ahead, her legs drawn up, her arms locked around her knees. With her hair loose and flowing, she seemed a young, terrified girl.

'Kit?'

She tried to hide her face from him. But she did speak. 'This time . . . this time it was different.'

'What?'

'My dream was different,' she said softly, as if it were painful for her to make the admission.

'What dream?'

'The doll.'

'What was different about it?' he pursued. When she did not respond, he asked, 'You didn't find it? You chased and chased it, you searched and searched and never found it?'

She shook her head.

'Kit!' he commanded, forcing her to face him. 'What was different? What frightened you?'

She was evasive. 'It must have been your pill. What was in it?'

'It was only five grains of Seconal. Not enough to cause nightmares. Unless you took something else too. Did you?'

She shook her head. She sought to turn away; he held her by the arms. She struggled but was too weak for him. She contented herself with pressing her face against his chest so that she would not have to look into his eyes.

'Now, what was different this time?'

'I . . . I found it . . . In this dream I found the doll . . .'

'You found it once before,' he reminded her. Her strange aberration of memory forced him to consider the possibility that she was already in the first stages of a breakdown. 'Didn't you tell me that once in your dream you did find it?'

She nodded.

'Then how was this time different from that time?'

'This time it wasn't muddy . . . wasn't broken,' she forced herself to admit.

'You found the doll, the same doll, but this time it was whole and clean?'

'Her dress was clean, with white lace edges. Just like it was in the store window. When I used to stand outside and stare at it.'

'That's what you always wanted. Why did it frighten you? Kit? Why?'

She shook her head.

'Kit, what terrified you so?' When she did not respond, he said, 'Kit, when I came in, you were pounding something. Pounding. Beating. Destroying. What?' He waited, then asked, 'Were you destroying the doll?'

The fact that she had momentarily ceased breathing confirmed his suspicion.

This time she did nod.

'Why?' he asked.

'Because he lied.'

'Who?'

'I don't want to talk about it.'

'Who?' he insisted.

She was stubbornly silent. When she spoke she sounded vindictive, aggressive. '*He*. My grandfather.'

'What did he lie about?'

'The doll, of course!' she said impatiently, beginning to relive painful feelings she had experienced and buried years ago.

'How could he lie about the doll?' Steve asked, more puzzled now than before. 'How could he even know about it unless you told him?'

'He used to watch me. Standing in front of that store. Staring,' she recalled with considerable venom, as if observing her were a hostile act. 'He asked me. Over and over. About the doll. So one day I told him. I told him that my mother would come back and buy me that doll.'

'What did he say?'

'Nothing. Until Christmas morning. When I woke up. Under our scrubby little tree there was a big box. I opened it. And there was my doll. My doll!'

She embraced Steve Brooks as she had embraced that doll.

'My doll,' she said in fond and total recollection of the moment. 'I asked him and he said, yes, my mother knew I wanted that doll. So she had sent it. Because she wanted me to have it for Christmas.

'Even though it was one of those warm, sunny California days, I stayed in all day, playing with the doll my mother had sent me. Undressing her and dressing her in her gown with the white lace. Making her sit up. Combing her long golden hair.'

As she spoke, Kit Lawrence combed her own hair with her fingers.

'Combing and combing. Dressing and undressing. Putting her to sleep. Waking her up. Feeding her with the little toy bottle. I kept saying to myself, "I am going to be the best mommy in the world. The best mommy in the world" ...' Her voice trailed off.

'Kit?'

'That was when the thought first struck me. If she knew I wanted that doll, if she bought it for me, then she must have seen me standing outside that store window. And if she bought it, then she must have been in that store! Maybe she lived in this town! Maybe I passed her on the street a hundred times and never knew her!

'So the next morning, I went down to the toy store. I waited till the man opened it. Mr Copeland. I never forgot his name. He knew me. Because he used to see me outside his store. Very bright and smiling, he said, "Good morning, little girl!" As if he expected me to be bright and smiling too. I asked him:

' "The doll, the big doll with the blond hair and the lace-trimmed dress that was in that corner of the window – did you sell it?"

'He smiled and said, "If it isn't there, I must have sold it."

' "I mean, did *you yourself* sell it?"

'He became that special imitative way that grown-ups are with children. That they think is cute, but children hate. "Yes, *I myself* did sell it."

' "Then tell me about the lady who bought it. What did she look like, what did she say?"

'He stopped smiling. He didn't try to be cute anymore. Louder, I said, "I want to know about the lady who bought the doll! What did she say? Did she say anything about the little girl she was buying it for?"

'He wouldn't answer me, so I said, "If you don't tell me

I'll scream. I'll tear my dress. I'll say that you tried to do dirty things to me!"

'I terrified him. I have always been able to terrify people. So he said, "There wasn't any lady."

'And I said, "You're a liar!"

' "No, honest, little girl, I swear. There wasn't any lady."

' "There had to be!" I insisted.

' "No, believe me. Honest. There wasn't any lady!"

' "There was! There was! There was!" I kept insisting.

'He was practically pleading with me to keep my voice down. Then he said, "I'm sure there wasn't any lady. Positive."

' "There was," I insisted, "but she told you not to tell me who she was, or where I could find her. Well, you better tell me! You better!" He knew what I was threatening. "Tell me where she is!"

' "There wasn't any lady. I'm positive. Because that doll was so expensive, I only ordered one of them. So I know who I sold it to. And it wasn't any lady."

' "Then who?"

'He finally broke down and said, "It was a man. He made me promise not to tell anyone. It was supposed to be a secret. But it was a man."

' "What did he look like?" I asked, even though I had guessed. Of course he described my grandfather. "There never was any lady?"

' "No, little girl, I'm sorry. There never was any lady!"

'I went home, crying all the way. He wasn't there. He did part-time work, collecting refuse. And with Christmas just over, there were lots of wrappings and empty cartons and broken toys to pick up. I went into my little room. I picked up that doll. I took it outside and smashed it on the damp earth. Its face became muddy. I kept smashing until it broke into a hundred pieces. I tore its lace-trimmed dress, and I left it there, right outside the door. So he would see it when he came home.'

'And did he?'

She nodded.

'What did he say?'

'He was very angry. He wanted to know why. I told him, "You lied to me. It wasn't from her." He tried to make me understand that he only said that to make me feel better. But I wouldn't listen. He became angry. I remember his words: "Do you know how much that doll cost? When I gave up smoking it wasn't because any doctor said so. It was to save money to buy you that doll. And you destroyed it. You're vicious and destructive. You don't deserve to be treated like a child. You're a monster!"

'He started to beat me. But hard as he hit me, I wouldn't cry. I stood there and defied him: "You lied, you lied." He kept hitting me. Until he stopped, because *he* was crying.

'He may have done some bad things to me. But he wasn't all bad. And he did love me. He was right, too. I am vicious. Destructive. I destroy everything. I destroyed us. Steve, oh, Steve, send me back. Send me back to Ross,' she pleaded.

'Did you ever tell him about this?'

'About the dream, yes.'

'But not the rest?'

'No.'

'Why?' Steve asked.

'Because in my other dream when I found the doll it was muddied and broken. This time was the first time I found it whole.'

'That's still no reason not to have told him what actually happened.'

'I was afraid,' she said.

'Afraid?'

'That he would think I was so vicious that he couldn't help me. Or wouldn't want to help me. So I never told anyone. Anyone.'

Steve Brooks remained thoughtful.

'Why was my dream so different this time, Steve?'

'I don't know,' he replied, deeply troubled.

After a long silence she said, 'Maybe my dream was trying to say, just like my grandfather gave me that doll, you gave me your play. And I destroyed your play too.'

'It hasn't been destroyed,' he insisted halfheartedly.

'It hasn't been played, Steve. It hasn't been played,' she said wistfully. 'I may be mad. But if there's one thing I know, it's the people out there. I know when they love me. And when they don't. And they don't love me, Steve. Not this time.'

'They will,' he assured her. 'Tomorrow night we'll do our preview. You'll be among your own people again. And they'll love you again. Broadway is a whole different ball game.'

He could not detect whether she had gained any assurance from his words. He was comforted by the fact that she was sleepy again and drifted off.

It was past eleven o'clock at night before Steve Brooks could reach Dr Ross. Ross listened attentively while Steve related, in as much detail as he recalled, the entire episode about Kit's doll.

'Extremely significant,' Ross said, when he had heard it all.

'Is that all you can say – extremely significant?' Steve demanded.

'Her relationship with her grandfather was unusually involved and complex. She lied about him a number of times. She kept material about him from me more than once,' Ross was explaining when Brooks interrupted:

'Doctor, this isn't just material she kept from you! It is crucial! An episode like that could scar a child for life.'

'Brooks!' Ross corrected sternly. 'Let's not become melodramatic! It's only in books and plays that there is a single moment of shining truth which, once exposed, results in an immediate and miraculous cure.

'Sometimes I wish Freud had never had that first case where he made that crippled girl walk. It is never that easy. So let's not lose our heads.

'Now, even if we grant that the event happened exactly as Kit described, it is only one traumatic event among many. Her life with her grandfather was, to say the least, strange. The incestuous phase of it, the fact that she had neither mother nor father, that she had few friends, that she lived in a fantasy world most of the time all adds up to a very damaging history. So it is not going to be cured by a single revelation.

'The significant thing is that her dream, which had been a recurring one, has suddenly changed. That is new. And, frankly, very disturbing,' Ross admitted. 'Or helpful. We won't know till later.'

'Later will be too late. She may be on the verge of a total breakdown.'

'She has been on the verge of a total breakdown ever since I undertook her case. What is significant, and possibly hopeful, is that as she approaches the stress of a New York opening, material is beginning to emerge that has never come out before,' Ross said.

'And if it comes out and she can't handle it, as happened this afternoon?' Steve asked.

'But she did handle it.'

'Not well,' Brooks reminded.

'From what you describe, I think she handled it as well as could be expected. My advice is keep her occupied until the last moment. Don't give her a chance to panic at the thought of an opening. If she does, call me.'

'A lot of good that will do,' Steve Brooks said, but only after he had hung up.

# Part 7

# *Thirty*

Jeff was busy setting the lighting before the first New York preview. Sam was in a meeting with the theater-party brokers, vainly trying to line up a few last-minute benefits.

In accordance with a thoroughly discussed plan, Steve took Kit Lawrence out to an early dinner. All three men felt it was vital to keep her protected from friends, or enemies, who might feed her destructive gossip.

Instead of taking her to Sardi's, where she would run into actors and actresses who always ate early before their own shows, he took her to a small Italian restaurant on Forty-eighth Street. He avoided talking about the play, about her confession of the day before, about anything he suspected might cause her concern or torment.

His strategy proved transparent. Kit smiled. 'Poor Steve . . . trying to ad-lib the whole scene. And it isn't easy, is it?'

He could pretend no longer. He smiled too. 'It isn't easy,' he confessed.

'Someday,' she said, a slightly heroic smile on her face, 'someday *I* am going to be strong enough to protect *you*. *I* am going to take *you* out to dinner, tell *you* nice unimportant things, to keep *your* mind off the important things. *I* am going to smile until *my* jaws ache. All for Steve, who was so kind to me when I needed it.'

'And you will,' he said, reaching across the table to take her hand.

She shook her head slightly, but it betrayed the deep and cavernous fear that possessed her.

It was time to go. Half-hour was seven o'clock; the first preview was seven-thirty. Before she rose from the table she asked, 'Steve, you do believe I try, don't you? But somehow the harder I try the worse it is. Until I don't know whether to try or not. I work so hard at relaxing that I tense up. This morning I spent two hours doing all the acting exercises I could think of. Trying to dispel the knot.'

She placed her hand on her belly. 'It's in here. There is a second Kit Lawrence in here who is bent on destroying me. And I can't dislodge her.'

She glanced down at the table, then managed to say, 'Sometimes I think what's in here is really her.'

'Your mother?'

'My baby. I think maybe this is punishment for what I did. I always think of it being a girl. The little girl I might have had. For whom I would have done all the things that my mother never did for me.'

She looked up, searching his eyes.

'Steve, do you ever wonder what would have happened if we'd married, had the baby? Would I be like I am today?'

'No one knows the answer to that.'

'Not even Ross. Once I said to him, "Make me pregnant. Let me have her now. Maybe it will cure me." '

Steve Brooks realized that she had completely blocked out all memory of what the doctor had said years ago, that she could never have a child.

'Time to go,' he said.

People were already gathering out on the street in front of the theater. Steve steered Kit into the dark stage-door alley before any autograph hunters could spot her. He left her in her dressing room, then went out front to the house where Jeff, in shirt sleeves, was still belaboring the lighting technician about a shadow on the back wall of the set, and two dark areas where important moments were to be played.

Steve dropped into a seat alongside Jeff.

'Well, Steve?'

'She's like a fighter going into the ring sure that he's going to lose.'

'We'll know soon enough,' Jeff said – which was his way of giving up too.

'I've seen miracles before.'

Jeff corrected, 'I've *heard* of miracles before, but I've never seen one.'

Sam arrived. There was no need for him to report. The verdict was on his face. Influenced by the Boston reviews and Kronheim's negative report, the theater-party agents had turned him down cold.

'They even refused to come see tonight's preview' was all he said.

To divert his own mind from that and the dire financial consequences that flowed from it, Sam said, 'Christ, Jeff, downstage left looks like a dark cemetery scene in an English mystery. Get some light on there!'

As intent on avoiding discussion of their fate, Jeff said, 'You're right, Sam; we're working on it now.'

As if the lighting could affect the outcome, Jeff worked meticulously with the lighting crew until the house manager came down the aisle and said, 'We'll have to start letting the people in.'

'Okay, okay,' Jeff agreed, relieved not to have to continue the charade any longer. 'Take it down!' he called out.

The curtain was lowered. The audience began to file in. It promised to be a good-sized house, thanks to Sam's arrangement with several large insurance companies in New York which distributed free seats among their employees. It was most important that Kit be greeted with an ovation when she came on.

Kit Lawrence made herself up as she had done thousands of times before. Yet one thing was different. In previous times, previous shows, she had done it with excitement, with anticipation. Even with the most glowing out-of-town notices, she never took a Broadway audience for granted. There was always the excitement of the challenge. This time she felt no challenge. Only doom.

Twice she turned away from her mirror in panic and started to strip off her costume. Twice she barely managed to force herself to turn back. For Steve, she said. For Jeff. For Sam. Who had been so kind and loving and loyal. She stared at herself in the mirror and wished desperately that she could repay them. She knew she could not. Still, there was the ritual to carry out. Make up. Respond to 'Five minutes'. Come out at the call of 'Places, please!' But her hands trembled too much. She had to stop making up.

She stood up, took deep deep breaths. Tried to recall all the techniques Kronheim had taught her to achieve relaxation. The knot would not dissolve. Her hands would not hold still. She grasped the edge of her makeup table so hard that the tendons in her arms ached.

There was a knock on her door. 'Kit?' It was Steve's voice.

'Yes?' she called back, calmly as she could manage.

'Are you decent?'

'Just a minute.' She twisted about, managing to unzip the back of her costume. She seated herself before the mirror and made a pretense of finishing her makeup as she invited, 'Come in.'

She caught his diagnostic glance in her mirror.

'Zip me up?' she asked, smiling.

He did, kissing her on the shoulder at the same time. 'You smell great. You always smell great. If you didn't have to be onstage in five minutes I'd attack you right now.'

He's playing the game, to keep me going, she realized. God, she prayed, I hope I can do it for him. I hope I can do it.

'Five minutes!' came the stage manager's voice over the intercom.

'You want to be alone?'

'Please, Steve.'

He closed the door softly behind him. Jeff was coming down the corridor giving last-minute advice and encouragement to his cast. When he reached Kit's door, Steve shook his head.

Kit Lawrence was alone for five minutes that seemed forever. She tried desperately to summon the courage needed to go out and face them. She told herself what others had told her – Ross, Steve, Jeff, Sam: You've done it before, you can do it again. Just do what you did in your first play. Just go out there and be Kit Lawrence. It's not as difficult as you think. There's nothing to be afraid of. They love you out there. They love you. Just be the Kit Lawrence you were and they'll still love you. Just give them a chance. Just give them a chance. She sought strength through defiance by recalling what Kronheim had said to her in Boston and promising herself, I'll show that lecherous old fraud; I'll show him! In the end she asked herself, pitifully, I wonder if he's out there tonight – and what he'll think.

'Places, please,' came the stage manager's call. Trembling, she went out and waited in the wings. The curtain whisked up. She could sense the liveness of the audience.

The first line was spoken by the young pregnant girl. The play was on.

Steve and Sam stood in the back of the house. Jeff sat in a seat at the side of the house, whispering notes to his assistant.

When Kit came on, she was bright and beautiful. She received such applause that she had to wait many seconds before she could even attempt her first line.

'Good,' Sam whispered. 'There's some smart money in the house. I want them to go away feeling she hasn't lost her spell over audiences.'

Steve, Sam and Jeff mingled with the crowd during both intermissions. They chatted with friends they had invited, seeking frank opinions. All were optimistic.

The lights blinked to announce the curtain for the third act. They filed back into the house.

The third act started well. But once Maria Patrick entered, Kit did not speak her lines as written, but only approximated them, robbing Maria of proper cues. The older actress had to anticipate when Kit's speeches ended, had to rephrase her own lines to make them flow in context with Kit's improvisations.

The enthusiasm that had been building during the first two acts slowly began to dissipate. The audience, keyed up to expect a highly emotional resolution, witnessed only a slow diminuendo, robbed of dramatic impact. The play limped to its end instead of rising to a climax.

Though there was polite applause, Kit did not remain onstage for her solo call but hurried to her dressing room, slamming the door.

Steve found her, head down on the table, weeping softly. He put his hands comfortingly on her shoulders. 'Kit. Kit?'

'Don't touch me,' she begged.

'Kit, please?'

'You gave me your beautiful shiny play and I broke it.'

Her choice of words disturbed him. One never spoke of a play as being broken.

'Kit?'

'He gave me that beautiful shiny doll with the golden hair, and I ground it into the mud, shattered its face. And I did the same to your play, Steve – the same.'

He resorted to the usual placebos theater people invent to explain their failures: 'It's a different house, different acoustics. It'll take getting used to. And you know New York audiences. Everyone is a critic.'

He lifted her to her feet. 'Come, change; we'll get something to eat. I'll bet you haven't had a good Chinese meal in months. Years.'

She stayed pressed against him, her face on his shoulder as she kept repeating, 'You gave me a doll and I broke it, you gave me a doll and I broke it.'

When they returned to the hotel the clerk handed him several messages. He did not stop to look at them until he had seen Kit back to her suite and safely into bed. When he left her, she was going over her battered script trying to relearn the third-act lines she had once known so well.

He went up to his own suite and looked at his messages. Melinda. Ross. Barnes, Dean of the School of Creative Writing back at the University.

He called Melinda first. It was a brief conversation. How did it go? The same. What did he think? The same. What could she tell his publisher? He would be back on his book in a week.

'And how is she?'

He confessed, 'This time I feel sure she will do something drastic to herself.'

'Steve, no!'

'Something is going on in her that no one can reach. Come Wednesday night, when it doesn't go well, God knows what she'll do.'

'Could a woman help? Would she talk to me?'

'No,' he said simply. 'I have to call Ross back.'

'If there's anything I can do, Steve, let me know.'

'I will,' he promised meaninglessly.

'How did it go?' Ross asked.

'Worse.'

'Did she say anything afterward? Was she aware of what she'd done?'

'Yes, she kept saying, "You gave me a beautiful doll and I broke it." '

'I've been thinking about that,' Ross confessed. 'We should work on it.'

'When? After she flops on Wednesday night, there won't be anything left to work on, Doctor!' Steve warned. 'I've seen her before when she tried it. I can't give you any symptoms, but I have the same feeling.'

'Look, I'll call a pharmacist I know in New York and have him send over some sedatives. They'll have your name as patient, so you can dole them out to her. I don't want her getting her hands on a full bottle.'

'Okay.'

Ross had hung up. Steve undressed, climbed into bed, lay on his back in his dark room, listening to sounds of late-night taxis racing up the Avenue of the Americas. He wondered if he should have stayed with her until she fell asleep. He would have, if there had not been those calls to return. Without being aware, he drifted off to sleep.

His phone rang. It could have been hours later or minutes. It was still dark. He reached, without turning on the light. He knocked the phone off the night table and had to grope on the floor to find it. He was leaning over the side of the bed when he said, sleepily, 'Yes?'

'Sorry, Mr Brooks,' the hotel operator apologized, 'but there's a doctor on the line and he says it's an emergency.'

Steve sat up sharply. She had done it! Or she had sneaked out of the hotel, gone on a bender and been picked up drunk somewhere. Or perhaps she had done again what she had done in Boston.

'Yes, Doctor?' he asked grimly.

'Brooks, sorry to wake you.' It was Ross.

'Have they called you? What happened?' Steve asked urgently.

'Has who called?' Ross countered.

'Never mind,' Steve said, once his worst fears had been allayed. 'What time is it?'

'Quarter to four,' Ross said. 'I haven't been able to fall asleep since we talked. I've been working on what she said to you.'

'About the play I gave her and how she smashed it?'

'Brooks,' Ross said suddenly, 'how long does it take to rewrite a scene?'

'Doctor, this is Monday! Tuesday morning, to be precise. And we open Wednesday night. What the hell do you mean, how long does it take to rewrite a scene?'

'Just that!' Ross said. 'How long would it take to rewrite the last scene of your play?'

'Do you realize what you're asking? Rewriting is only part of it. It has to be learned, staged, rehearsed, polished. Played before an audience. You can't open cold with a scene that's never been played before. Actors have to be sure of what they're doing. You once told me, psycho-analysis does not produce miraculous cures. That only happens on the stage or in films. Well, the same goes for theater. We don't do miracles either. The understudy does not become a star overnight. Except in other plays and films.'

'Is it possible to delay the opening by a few days?' Ross asked.

'Doctor, there isn't one dollar left in the budget for anything but to open. Sam can't even afford an opening-night party,' Steve confessed.

'I see,' Ross said, pondering.

'What was your idea about the rewrite?'

'Ever since I talked to you I've been thinking of what she said, about your play, and breaking it. I related that to what she confessed about the real-life episode. How she coveted the doll, but when she got it and found it wasn't from her mother she destroyed it. Something became clear to me. The real problem in the final scene.

'From the start, she has insisted on using that scene to purge herself of the hatred she has always harbored toward her mother. And it sounded very therapeutic to me. If she could unleash that enormous hostility, and at the same time enjoy the love from the audience, she would gratify her two most important drives. And become functional in the process.'

'Only it didn't work that way,' Steve rebuked.

'Remember what I once told you about screen-defenses?'

'The patient avoids facing certain painful feelings by screening them with other feelings.'

'And sometimes suffering areas of amnesia as a result,' Ross reminded him. 'Such as Kit avoiding until the other day having been given a clean new doll and destroying it herself. Well, in working on that, it came to me not more than an hour ago that her strong need to hate her mother may be a screen. That there is nothing she would rather do, even now, than find her mother and receive from her the love she has been searching for all her life.'

'Doctor, are you asking me to rewrite the final scene so there is a real reunion, not the ironic one in the title?'

'I don't say it will work. But it might. Can you possibly do it? There's too much in her as a human being to waste. Try, Brooks, try!' Ross pleaded.

Weary, sleepy, Steve climbed out of bed and found his script. The first thing he did when someone suggested a significant rewrite was to read through from the beginning and see what effect the change would have on the rest of his play.

Rewrites, he lamented, as he began to read. The world was composed of two kinds of people. A small, tough, brave band of authors. And everyone else: producers, directors, actors, critics, audiences and now doctors, all of whom knew how a script should be rewritten.

When he reached the final scene, he had convinced himself of one encouraging thing. The last scene could be rewritten without doing violence to the rest of the play.

Now, he reminded himself sarcastically, all that remained was rewriting seventeen pages of dialogue, building to a new and totally different ending. From long, harrowing experience, Steve Brooks knew if he wanted to avoid angry protests from other guests, he had better not use his typewriter. He began the slow, laborious job of rewriting by hand.

# *Thirty-one*

Sam, Jeff and Steve were sitting in a corner of the Stage Delicatessen, the first three customers for breakfast.

'Take apart the end of the play? Forty-eight hours before we open?' Sam Rogers demanded in a combination of outrage and amazement. The frustrations and defeats of the past two months had taken their toll. For the first time in their long and friendly association, Sam turned on Steve fiercely. 'You must be crazier than she is! Or have you been getting into the sack with her? I thought we agreed at the outset, no screwing around! I didn't go for my last dollars just to make it possible for you to start that old business all over again! I didn't . . .'

He did not complete the thought. Instead he looked away, saying, 'Sorry, Steve. I didn't mean to blow my top. It's not me talking. It's the strain of the last few years. All my life I have been able to make things happen my way. I was a doer. I made plans. Built skyscrapers, shopping centers, homes, where there was only raw earth before. But the last two years with Bertha, I have been frustrated, defeated, ground into the dust. For the first time in my life I ran up against the word "impossible."

'Now with Kit, the same thing. Talent couldn't do it. God knows, you and Jeff tried your damnedest. Money couldn't do it. I did the best I could. I guess that's what growing old means: discovering the word "impossible." '

Jeff and Steve were both embarrassed at the sight of Sam's teary eyes once he had mentioned his beloved Bertha.

Sam grew more temperate, more fatherly, as he said, 'Steve, forgive what I said about you and Kit. Let's just be hardheaded theater men. You know what happens. You take an act apart and try something new. Always thinking to yourself, What's the harm in trying? If it doesn't work we can always go back to the old scene. But after that, the old scene somehow never works either and you wind up with a shambles. Everything goes to hell.'

'So what do we do?'

Sadly, Sam said, 'We face reality. We open. We play the best show we can. We take our lumps. And we close Saturday night. Frankly, if I thought it would make it easier on her, I wouldn't even open.'

Steve looked at Jeff, his eyes demanding, for God's sake, do something, say something!

Jeff stirred the remains of his cold coffee. 'Steve, I haven't put this much effort into anything in years. It doesn't work. Let me be more honest about it: *she* doesn't work. So I say, Sam is right. We ought to consider very seriously not opening.'

'We have to open,' Steve said.

'To what end? To get murdered by the critics? To cut my price on the Coast? To make it tougher to get your next play financed? How can it help her, if we open and get blasted? And don't forget, that's why we all came together. *To help her*. Well, we failed.'

'But Ross thinks—' Steve started to say.

'Oh, yes, Ross,' Jeff interrupted bitterly. 'Tell me more about our dear Dr Ross. Who got us involved in this insanity. Besides, how can we suggest a whole new scene to Kit at this late date? It would throw her completely.'

'Boys, there might be a way to handle it without upsetting Kit,' Sam said thoughtfully. 'But it would have to be done carefully. Very carefully. What if I were to say . . . well, I say Josh Logan was at the preview last night . . . or Kazan . . . or some other director Kit respects. And I talked with him after the show. And Logan said, if we could rework the end of the third act we'd have a good shot. So I got hold of Steve last night. And talked to him. He said, Okay, I'll take a crack at it. This morning he comes in with a new ending. So if she and Maria Patrick will try it, we'll see if Logan was right.'

'So she tries it, and then what?' Jeff demanded.

'Then what?' Sam echoed. 'Then I give you my word, if it doesn't work, I will not open the show. We just play out the week as previews. We never get reviewed in New York. We walk away with as little damage as possible.'

'Except for your last building on the East Side,' Jeff reminded him.

'What the hell,' Sam said. 'I've got a nephew I set up in the real estate business years ago. I can always go in with him.'

It did not sound as convincing as Sam intended.

'Well, Jeff?' the producer asked.

'I came this far; another forty-eight hours can't kill me,' Jeff relented. 'Let's see those pages.'

Steve gave Jeff his handwritten pages. Jeff started to read, passing each page to Sam as he finished it. As he passed the last page to Sam, he said, 'This completely changes the staging of the scene. Nothing we had before will work.'

'I know,' Steve said.

Sam turned down the last page. 'You think she'll play this?'

'Ross thinks she might,' Steve said.

Sam shook his head dubiously. 'Jeff, do you think you can get it out of them?'

'Sam, you know actors; they can do anything they have to.'

'Will you give it a try?'

'On one condition,' Jeff said.

'I promised you if this doesn't work we won't open.'

'Cancel the preview tonight.'

'But we've sold tickets; there's cash in the till,' Sam protested.

'Cancel the preview. Give me all day today. And all night if we need it.'

'Okay,' Sam agreed finally.

They reached Maria Patrick at Lou Lattimer's. They did not have to wake Kit. She had been up since dawn. Rehearsal of the new scene was called for eleven. The rest of the cast and crew were barred from the theater. The box office was instructed to tell anyone who called that there would be no performance tonight.

They assembled in the set. Steve was ready with half a dozen copies of the scene which had been hastily typed. Sam was ready to make his little speech. Jeff sat in the armchair in a corner of the set, pretending to be relaxed and casual, but actually studying Kit Lawrence, who sat on one end of the couch as far from Maria Patrick as she could. Maria was more curious than tense. A veteran of many plays, most of which had failed, she knew these last desperate measures that were always resorted to, and always proved futile. It was part of the job. Actors, like captains, went down with the ship.

'Well,' Sam began, making an effort to sound as cheerful as possible. 'We had an unusual stroke of luck last night! It happens that my lawyer is also Josh Logan's lawyer. So he asked Josh to drop by last night and take a look. Josh called me later. What he feels is that we end a little too downbeat. He thinks that a play as touching as this, and a performance as magnificent as Kit's, needs to end on a hopeful note – uplifting, inspiring. How did he say it, Steve?'

As prearranged, Steve took over. 'Josh said that an audience which has lived with this character for three acts, which has loved her, sympathized with her all through her search for her mother, is not going to go away satisfied with anything less than her finding the love she's missed all her life.

'Well, at first, as authors do, I resisted. But early this morning I thought about it. And I said, What the hell, I'll give it a try. So I wrote a new scene.'

Maria Patrick interrupted, 'You're going to ask us to learn a new scene and open tomorrow night?'

'One step at a time,' Steve said. 'First, we read the scene. We try it on our feet. Then we decide what to do.'

Having evaded Maria's objection momentarily, he continued: 'I wrote the new scene. I liked it. But by five o'clock in the morning an author likes anything he writes. So I called Sam. He read it. And he liked it. So we dared to wake Jeff and ask him to read it. After all, he is only the toughest bastard in the world when it comes to new material. And what did he say?' Steve turned the meeting over to Jeff.

'It was like being struck by lightning,' Jeff declared. 'I said, "That's what we've been needing all along!" And it took a shrewd old genius like Josh to point it out. I said, By all means, we have to try it!'

Jeff had been a fairly good actor before he turned director.

'So these are the pages. Look them over a time or two and then we'll read them out loud.'

Steve gave a copy to Maria, a copy to Kit, who took hers with undisguised hostility. She did not attempt to read the pages at once, but stared off, as if thinking. Finally she let her eyes scan the first page.

While she read, Sam, Jeff and Steve exchanged furtive looks, wondering how she would react. Maria finished reading long before Kit. She said nothing. Kit read slowly, very slowly for an actress who once had been able to scan a page and say, 'Okay, let's wing it.' This time as she came to the end of a page she went back to the middle to read down again. The longer she took to read, the more tense the atmosphere became on that stage. Sam began to sweat. Jeff kept glancing impatiently at Steve, whose eyes pleaded for forbearance.

Finally Kit lowered her pages and said, 'I don't feel it.'

'Darling, what do you mean, you don't feel it?' Sam asked anxiously.

'I mean the woman I have been playing for two and a half acts would not do or say the things that are in these pages. This is crap. Sheer unadulterated crap! And I won't do it!'

'But Josh said—' Sam tried to argue.

Kit interrupted viciously: 'Josh said nothing! He wasn't even here!'

'What do you mean he wasn't here?' Sam asked, appearing as indignant as he dared.

'If you look in this morning's paper you will see a photo of Josh, taken last night at a charity ball at the Waldorf,' she said. 'Don't lie to me,' she exploded. 'God, if there's one thing I can't take it's people lying to me! No matter what I've done . . . the drinking . . . the screwing around . . . signing to do things and never showing up . . . being mad . . . and I am . . . I am! But I don't deserve to be lied to.'

She turned upstage and began to sob as she said, 'I have enough trouble with the truth. Don't add lies to it. Don't . . . please . . . please . . .'

At a sign from Sam, Jeff moved upstage to put his arms around her.

'Kit, darling, listen to me?' She did not relent. Nevertheless he continued: 'There is no one on this stage who wants to harm you. If we told you a lie, it was a constructive lie, or so it was intended. The truth is, the bare, honest truth is, we all think this change would help. Would help the play. Would help us. Would, most of all, help you.'

'But I can't do it,' she pleaded, still in tears.

'You don't know. You haven't tried yet.'

'I can't, I can't, I can't,' she kept repeating, believing it more the more she said it.

'Would you at least read it out loud once with Maria?' he pleaded.

Steve called to her, 'Please, Kit? Darling? For me?'

She turned back, her blue eyes moist. 'For you? All right, Steve, for you.'

Without returning to the couch, still facing away from

Maria Patrick, Kit began to read her lines. Maria read hers. It was a stiff, stilted reading, lacking any interplay or rapport. There was no emotion, no conflict. Only an aloofness that Kit insisted on by her approach to the scene. Once done, she scattered her pages across the couch and said, 'See? I told you it wouldn't work.'

'Let's try it on our feet and change what doesn't seem to work,' Jeff suggested. 'Or if you'd rather, we can just improvise the scene. Let's see where that takes us. Kit?'

'The first week of rehearsal you improvise! Not the day before an opening!' Kit exploded. 'And tonight – what about tonight?'

Sam interceded, 'There will not be any performance tonight, darling. We are going to work on the scene. All night if we have to.'

'No performance tonight?' Kit asked, surprised.

'Before I let you open to those Broadway vultures we call critics, I want you perfect. They are not going to see a Kit Lawrence who is less than perfect.' He took her hand and kissed it. 'Try the scene, please? For Sam?'

'Sam, it won't do any good.'

'That's all I ask. Try it.'

Jeff said, 'Okay, let's read it once more. From the top.'

Kit read the scene, not giving herself to it more than the first time. But Jeff, with a sly signal to Maria, urged her up off the couch so that the women were closer together than before. Without realizing it, Kit Lawrence turned slightly toward Maria. There was beginning to be a semblance of connection in the scene.

'Okay, fine!' Jeff said. 'Now let's try to block it roughly. If the lines get in your way, ad-lib them. If you feel the urge to say something a little different from what is on the page, I'm sure Steve won't mind. We can polish the lines later. Now we are searching for the truth of the scene. Let's start.'

It was always a difficult, treacherous process, undoing something actors had been doing for weeks. It was as if one asked the actor to remake his entire personality and character in the process.

New pages in hand, Kit Lawrence and Maria Patrick put themselves at the disposal of Jeff Warrener.

'Okay, let's start from the top of the scene, from the moment when the stage manager has told you a woman is waiting to see you. Kit, darling, you know she's your mother. We out front, we know that. Only Maria doesn't. Before the scene is over you're going to let her know. You're going to show her what she gave up when she deserted you. Let's go from there! Stage manager exits. There is a knock at the door. What's the first thing you do, Kit?'

Instinctively she responded, 'Make a move to the door. Then stop.'

'Why?' Jeff asked. 'Now that the crucial moment has arrived, are you afraid?'

Kit looked down at Jeff Warrener, who sat alongside Steve. She shook her head a bit sadly, then smiled. 'Jeff, and you used to direct women so well. Any woman would stop, turn back to her mirror to make sure of how she looked and *then* answer the knock.'

'Good! Try it. Let's see how it looks out here. Okay, stage manager exits. Maria!'

Offstage, Maria Patrick knocked on the door. Kit turned to face it, took half a step in that direction, stopped, caught a glance at herself in the mirror, brushed back an imaginary strand of hair and drew herself up to a posture that conveyed all her expectations, all her hostility. It set exactly the right tone for their confrontation.

'Yes?' she read her line sharply. 'Come in!'

The door opened tentatively. Maria Patrick entered, hesitant, acting the part of the confused and nervous woman who had been summoned to this unexplained meeting in a star's dressing room. She stared at Kit, then paused and for a slight instant, as the direction in Steve's new pages indicated, she half-turned to flee. But Kit's single-word line pinned her: 'Wait!'

Maria turned back to look at her. Glancing at their scripts to catch fragments of their new lines, and roughing out the moves, they continued with the scene. Jeff interrupted only infrequently, making mental notes of awkward or constricting moves that he would eliminate or polish later. The important thing was that Kit was beginning to be less hostile to the new scene. She had not embraced it. She only played it on a single level of dramatic interest. She resisted certain of the lines, discarding them after trying them, then improvising new lines.

Jeff nudged Steve each time he felt that one of Kit's lines was more natural for her than the one Steve had written. Slowly the scene moved on – a ragged, jerky piece, half written, half improvised, cluttered with false and new attacks, lacking any semblance of pace or unity. Thus far it was hardly a scene but a succession of lines and actions, without the force of a single driving emotion.

A dozen times in the course of it, Kit hurled her pages to the floor. 'I can't do it! It won't work! It's wrong! Can't you two idiots sitting out there see that it won't work?'

Meantime, out in the box office, Sam Rogers was arguing with the house manager.

'I am not going to face a lobby full of people and say there's no performance tonight!' the manager declared. 'I'm not! That's it! Finish!'

'Larry, Larry, how many shows have I had in this theater in the last twenty years? Have I ever asked you to do anything unless it was absolutely necessary?' Sam pleaded.

'You know what'll happen. In half an hour the word will be in at Sardi's. Kit Lawrence is on a bender again. So there's no performance. Or she's had another breakdown. Think what that'll do to your show. *If* you've even got a show!' Larry Markowitz said.

Sam Rogers glared at him.

'Sam, I always considered you a gentleman producer, but a smart man. But how the hell did you ever get involved in this? I watched this play yesterday in the run-through and last night in the preview. It runs downhill like a dollar watch with a broken spring. I don't know what your friends have told you, but I'll tell you the truth. You open this show with that nothing ending and they'll crucify you. Critics don't hand out awards for past successes. They only know one thing: *Show me now*!'

Larry Markowitz reached out to pat Rogers on the shoulder. 'Sam, even in a two-bit poker game, when you haven't got it, the smart thing is throw in your hand. I tell you this as a man who respects you and always has.'

Sam Rogers said firmly, 'I don't care what the rumors are. We do not play tonight.' Before the manager could resume the attack, Sam left the office and went back into the house.

Kit and Maria were just feeling their way through the middle of the scene, in which Kit, bitter and vengeful, was revealing to her mother their true relationship. The lines also gave Kit a chance to vent much of the hostility she felt toward Steve and Jeff for forcing her to try a new scene. She became sharp, tense, combative. She played it as though inflicting physical punishment on Maria.

Jeff nudged Steve. It was a sign of hope. Kit seemed to be accepting the scene more fully than he had hoped, for a first run-through. Knowing all he knew, having had conversations with Ross about her dreams and destructive impulses, Steve was far more cautious in his optimism.

Sam sat behind them. He leaned forward, whispering, 'At least she's trying.'

Steve watched; his hands were cupped around his eyes so that he focused on Kit and only on Kit. The treacherous moments in the scene were yet to come. When she would have to contend not only with the new ending, but with her own inner conflicts as well. If she failed there, the entire scene failed and they would have only the original discredited scene left.

They had stopped for the fiftieth time so that Maria and Kit could make notes in their script to indicate their moves, pauses, reactions. Steve suspected that that was only a diversion on Kit's part to avoid confronting the crucial climax.

Finally it could no longer be avoided. They reached the last three pages, the beginning of the final drive of the scene and the play toward the curtain.

Kit became more uncertain. She found excuses to delay. She had trouble reading in the faulty light. She misread several of her lines. She began facing away from Maria, as she used to in the first days of rehearsal. Steve could see her early hostility reasserting itself. They reached the dramatic moment when Maria turned to go. The lines called for Kit to cry out, 'Mama, no!' It was her first use of an endearing word in the entire play. Maria fed Kit her cue, turned to the door, started to move, expecting to be called back. Kit did not call out. Maria slowed her move. She waited. She was at the door. Finally, giving up, she opened the door and exited.

'Kit?' Jeff called out, 'you have a line there. The most important line in the play.'

Instead of responding, Kit Lawrence ripped the wrinkled pages in half, then into quarters, and flung the pieces out into the house.

'I told you it wouldn't work! Because it's false. The whole idea is dishonest. It isn't life. It's a playwright's version of what life ought to be like. Well, it's a lie! A big lie!'

'Kit, just try. . . .' Jeff pleaded.

She overrode him in a vicious attack. 'And you! What the hell are you trying to do to me? Destroy my performance? Go back to Hollywood where you belong! Make your great big multimillion-dollar monuments to junk! That's all you're fit for now. Whatever talent you had is gone. Gone! Well, I am not going to permit you to destroy my talent. Did you hear me? Did you hear me?' she cried out.

She started to tremble; she turned away. Steve saw her fingers move in a strange crablike action. He remembered that long ago one of her early breakdowns had been preceded by such bizarre activity.

Since Sam was the only one she had not attacked, Jeff whispered, 'Sam! Go up there. Talk to her!'

For a man his age, Sam Rogers moved with unexpected agility. He came out of his seat, leaped up on the stage, crossed to her, gently placed his hands on her arms.

'Kit, darling . . .' he coaxed softly.

She turned on him, her eyes glaring with almost maniacal anger. 'Take your hands off me, you Jew! You're no better than Ross! You two Jews conspired together. Trying to make money off me because I have talent and you don't!'

Sam Rogers stood motionless.

'Oh, God,' Steve whispered.

For a moment there was dead silence in the empty, cavernous theater. Sam Rogers, his eyes blinded by unshed tears, crossed the stage and leaped down to the orchestra floor. He started up the aisle. Steve pursued him, pleading, 'Sam, Sam, she doesn't know what she's saying. She's in a crisis. Ross warned me she might be. Don't blame her. Please! Try to forget what she said.'

Sam faced him. Even in the darkness Steve Brooks could read the pain in his eyes.

'Sam, if you can't forget, can you at least understand and forgive?'

'I . . . I . . . I need a little . . . a little fresh air,' the older man said, and continued toward the street.

Steve retreated down the aisle. It appeared to him as if a tableau had been staged. No one had moved. Jeff was still slumped in his seat. Kit was still staring catatonically as she had been when she had vented her unreasonable fury on Sam.

The door on the set opened timidly. Maria Patrick appeared. In an effort to dissipate the bitterness and the hurt that filled the air, she spoke in a soft, apologetic voice: 'May I say something?'

'Why not?' Jeff replied hopelessly.

'Steve, if you don't mind my saying so, I think Kit's right about the scene. It's written from the wrong angle. Oh, I think there should be a reconciliation. For the play's sake, for the audience and for the characters. But is it possible the impetus is wrong? Maybe I should be the one to make the first move toward a reunion. The title *Reunion* should not be ironic but genuine. That way, as Kit says, it would be truthful, honest.'

'Steve?' Jeff Warrener deferred to the author.

Realizing what Maria intended to accomplish, Steve played along willingly. 'It's worth a try. Let's walk it and see.' Trying to lure Kit out of her catatonic state, he asked, 'Kit? Did you hear that? Maria agrees with you. So let's try it the other way. The first overtures come from her. Just wing the lines; let's see what happens.'

He did not expect Kit to respond easily, so he prodded, 'Maria, darling, how do you feel it?'

'Kit sends me off. I start to go. But I'm carrying a lifetime of guilt. Don't forget that all the while she has been struggling with her past, my desertion, her lonely childhood, so have I. When she longed to be held, I longed for someone to hold. When she wanted to be loved, I longed for someone to love. We are actually two parts of a single emotion. Well, since I am the one who feels the guilt, I think it's up to me to make the first move. So I stop. . . . Wait, let me show you!'

Maria Patrick took up her position on the stage. She started her exit, stopped, turned, looked back and adlibbed, 'Before I go, would it be asking too much if I just . . .'

She did not finish the line, but crossed to Kit, giving every evidence of intending to embrace her and kiss her.

Just as she reached her, Kit spoke out vehemently, 'Don't touch me! I can't stand for you to touch me. I felt that way from the first day of rehearsal. Ask them! Ask Jeff! Ask

Steve!' She turned to them. 'Didn't I say, I hate her? I hate her! And now you want me to let her *touch* me! Never!'

Maria Patrick stared down at Jeff Warrener, accusing him of lying to her in those early days. His guilty face made no defense, only pleaded for understanding.

Kit Lawrence continued to vent her sick fantasies on them all. 'You made me do this play! I never wanted to. You conspired, all of you. With Ross! You fooled me. You always planned to change the ending. But you knew I wouldn't do it. So you waited till the last day to spring it on me.'

She glared viciously at Steve. 'You had these lousy pages written all the time! You were waiting, just waiting till we got close to opening. When you thought I'd have no choice! I don't have to open; I've walked out on shows before and I can walk out on this one! And that's exactly what I intend to do! Bastards! You're all lying, cheating, conniving bastards! Well, you may need me. But I don't need you. Not any of you! Not any of . . .'

She broke into tears and sank slowly to the floor. She covered her eyes with one hand. With the other she began to draw lines on the carpet, parallel lines.

Remembering what Ross had said, Steve rose from his seat. He stared at Kit, then at Maria Patrick. He raised his hand slowly and with a single sharp gesture he ordered Maria Patrick to approach Kit.

Maria hesitated, then slowly moved to Kit. She sank down beside her. Because it seemed the only natural thing to do, she embraced the tormented young actress. For a fleeting instant Kit drew back hostilely. Then, slowly, she relented, surrendering herself to the older woman, pressing her face against her breast and weeping, not in torment but in relief.

Soon, interspersed with weeping, a single word began to emerge. 'Mama . . . Mama . . .'

In all the years Steve Brooks had known Kit Lawrence, it was the first time he had ever heard her utter that word. Until now it had always been a severe and vitriolic 'Mother', usually preceded by obscene adjectives. Now it was simple, childlike, warm, beseeching. Steve said nothing. Jeff said nothing. In a while Kit Lawrence was no longer crying. She was silent, content to rest in Maria Patrick's arms.

Jeff looked to Steve for a clue. Steve signaled for forbearance. After a long silence, Kit spoke softly, 'Maybe . . . maybe it could work. . . .'

'Shall we give it a try?' Jeff asked gently.

'Let's . . . let's try it. Once. To see if it can. . . .'

'From the top of the scene?' Jeff asked.

'No, just near the end. If . . . if the end works, it will all work,' Kit said, with a sense of trepidation. She was aware of the risks to herself and the play if she could not make it work now.

'Okay, Maria,' Jeff asked, 'pick it up a few lines before you start to exit?'

Maria assumed her place on the stage.

'Kit?' Jeff asked.

'I seem to remember that I was here . . . looking away from her . . .' She asked Maria, 'Is that right?'

'Yes, dear, that's right.'

'Okay, girls, let's go from there,' Jeff said. 'Wing the lines. Just go for the emotions.'

Kit took time to re-create the mood. When she was ready she nodded to Maria. Maria fed her her cue. Kit responded, approximating the line Steve had written. Maria rephrased her line to fit with Kit's. Working in concert, aware of each other's ad libs and inventions, they pieced the lines together until the moment when Maria had made her plea. Then, rejected, she turned to leave. With a calculation born of instinct and experience, Kit waited until the last possible second and then uttered a half-stifled 'Mama!'

It was barely more than a whisper, but it filled the empty house with the kind of emotional magic that creates memorable moments in the theater. Maria Patrick paused for a beat, then turned. It was a turn of exquisite slowness, which externalized all her guilt, her uncertainty, her hope, her doubt that she had been forgiven until she could see her daughter's face. The permission to stay would have to be etched there. Kit's lovely and forgiving face gave her that assurance. Maria started toward the young actress. They embraced as Kit whispered, 'Mama, Mama, Mama . . .'

Softly, almost reverently, Jeff said, 'Slow curtain and end of play.'

Steve recalled Ross's admonition in one of their early meetings: 'Actors are actors because it allows them to achieve onstage the satisfaction denied them in real life.'

Now, if Kit could only do that again and again.

For fourteen straight hours, with only a single break when Sam insisted on sending in sandwiches and coffee, they improvised, staged, restaged, wrote and rewrote the scene, trying to endow it with the ascending emotional power demanded of a climactic scene.

The audience for the preview arrived and refused to be sent away. But Sam stood in the lobby and staunchly announced, 'Miss Lawrence is sick, and I'm sure you wouldn't want to see an understudy. So exchange your tickets for another performance. The box office will be glad to cooperate. Or, if you wish, you may have a refund,' he promised, wondering if there was sufficient cash in the till to make good. They finally dispersed, but not without much grumbling.

Inside the house, rehearsal continued. Kit and Maria, both near exhaustion, had shed their shoes to relieve their tired feet. Steve was writing changed lines on the backs of old script sheets so he would have a copy to give the stage manager for the opening.

At quarter past one o'clock in the morning, a weary Jeff Warrener said, 'Let's run it again to make sure you're secure. After all, tonight's an opening.'

They ran the scene one more time, from the moment

when Kit was left alone onstage to receive her mother until the final curtain, which found the two women in each other's arms.

When they were done, Jeff said, 'Tomorrow we'll run the whole act twice before the complete run-through. And then we should be ready for those bastards,' he said, a bit too optimistic.

He leaped up onto the stage to kiss Kit as a reward for her superhuman effort during a long and arduous rehearsal, filled with great emotional pain for her. She evaded his embrace only long enough to look around him at Maria Patrick, who was leaving the stage exhausted, carrying her shoes in one hand, trying to straighten her tangled hair with the other.

'Maria?'

Maria Patrick looked back.

'Sorry' was all that Kit could say. 'Sorry.' But for Maria it seemed to be enough.

Steve waited in the wings. Maria Patrick practically walked into his arms. He held her for a moment as he whispered, 'I'll never forget what you did for her and for us tonight.'

'I did what I felt I had to. But we're not out of the woods yet,' she warned.

'I know,' he agreed. 'Get some sleep. We've got a tough day ahead. And an even tougher night.'

Jeff interrupted them: 'Steve, take Kit back to the hotel?'

'Of course.'

Jeff Warrener found Maria Patrick in her dressing room getting ready to leave.

'Maria, darling, if I weren't already in love with you, I would have fallen in love with you today. I am going to watch this opening from the second balcony. Like I used to in the old days.'

Maria blushed slightly.

'Jeff, what do you think? *Really* think?'

'When you're too tired to think, you hope. I hope she'll make it.'

When they arrived back at the hotel, Steve made sure Kit undressed and got into bed. He turned out the lights and was at the door when she called out, 'Steve, don't leave me? Please?'

'Okay,' he agreed. He lay down on the couch in the living room, kicked off his loafers and settled down for the night.

He fell asleep before she did. She could not find a comfortable position. Tonight, the bed seemed hard and unfriendly. It fought her at every turn. She lay awake, exhausted, yet unable to sleep. Something tormented her. It was like nights at Silvermine, when she could not sleep and they refused her any sedation. She would toss and turn and go the whole night sleepless. Only to discover the next morning, in her session with Ross, that what had kept her awake was guilty material she was unconsciously fighting to keep secret. It felt that way now.

After almost two hours it came to her. Sam. What she had said to Sam was tormenting her. She must make amends. It could not wait till morning. She must do it now. She could hear Steve's even breathing in the living room. She slipped out of bed, silently closed her door, turned on the light to look among the collected bits of notepaper on her nightstand for Sam's home phone number.

She gave it to the operator, who diplomatically reminded her it was past three-thirty. Kit insisted, 'I have to make this call. It's an emergency!'

Aware of Kit's condition, as was the entire staff at the hotel, the operator complied. 'Of course, darling.' She dialed the number and listened in, fearing the emergency was more than could be resolved by a telephone call.

She heard a suddenly wakened Sam Rogers answer with a frantic 'Yes? Hello? What is it? What's wrong?' For an instant it was the same alarm he used to feel when Bertha was near the end and he lived with unexpected phone calls, and nights of little sleep and only troubled drowsing.

'Sam?' Kit asked timidly.

'Oh, Kit . . . yes?'

'Sam, I'm sorry. I never felt that way. Never thought of you that way. Never. I swear to God. I'm sorry . . . sorry . . .'

'I know,' he said, trying to conceal his own pain.

'Say you forgive me?' she pleaded.

'I forgive you, Kit. You were under great strain. You didn't mean it. Believe me, I wasn't hurt. Wasn't hurt at all. And I do forgive you.'

'Thanks, Sam.'

'Kit, darling, get some sleep. Do you know what time it is?'

'Late,' she said. 'Maybe too late,' she managed.

'You'll be great tonight, great!' He tried to encourage her. Before he might break down himself, he said, 'Get some sleep' and hung up.

# *Thirty-two*

Jeff Warrener was one of those directors who believed that you kept a cast working or preparing throughout the entire day of an opening. He put Kit and Maria through their scene four times. Then he called the entire company onstage for the final run-through before the only fateful and decisive night in the history of any play.

During the run-through he deliberately managed to find a dozen places that he decided needed a brushup as soon as the run-through was over. He kept them totally occupied until two of the actresses in the company had to remind him that they had appointments with their hair-dressers so that they could look their best for tonight. He relented, knowing that he had kept them sufficiently engrossed to get them past the most nervous hours.

Kit had to be reminded to go off to the hairdresser. Maria went with her to make sure she would manage. Kit went without great excitement or enthusiasm, but out of a sense of duty. It was what every actress did on the day of an opening. She did it as she used to do sense-memory exercises at Max Kronheim's insistence. In those old days, beneath the tension she had felt defiance, confidence. She used to look forward to openings.

Today, whether it was the accumulated weariness of weeks of rehearsing and playing or being battered from without by reviews and from within by her own torment, Kit Lawrence felt none of the old excitement. She felt narcoticized, as she used to when Ross would wake her from a pentothal session. Conscious, alive, but not truly part of the real world. She would go out there tonight, move as she had been directed, speak the lines she had learned. But the real

Kit Lawrence would be in the wings watching the other one perform, and disapproving of her. She had never before had that feeling on opening night.

Maria stayed with Kit throughout her session at the hairdresser's. To keep Kit from brooding, Maria pretended she was still insecure with her new lines. She prevailed on Kit to cue her. They ran the scene endlessly. When the beauticians had finished, Maria insisted they have an early supper so that they could both snatch a nap before half-hour.

Kit would not sleep unless Maria stayed with her. Finally, Kit fell asleep from exhaustion. Maria watched her jerk frenetically in her sleep, tortured by dreams that she would not recall when she woke.

Finally, blessedly, it was time to go to the theater.

In the lobby, the opening-night audience was beginning to arrive. Like the father of the bride at a wedding, Sam Rogers waited out front, greeting friends, critics and inveterate first-nighters – mainly agents, producers, directors and authors who had come prepared to witness a disaster. The gossip that had preceded the show into town had been confirmed by the cancellation of last night's final preview. The smart money was saying, That's Kit Lawrence for you.

Sam detected their skepticism, but remained outwardly cheerful and gracious, exuding as much optimism as possible under the circumstances. If he fooled some of them, he did not succeed in deceiving them all.

Backstage, the cast was going through the usual first-night flurries. They exchanged little gifts and mementos. They tried to make jokes. They made frequent trips to the lavatories. They drove themselves to mount the proper degree of excitement for an opening night. They were tense, yet not sufficiently on edge, as actors with confidence should be. Instead of being ready for an opening, they were only playing being ready for an opening.

In her dressing room, Kit Lawrence was brushing her long

golden hair, staring in the mirror at her face, which to her would never be truly beautiful but only a mask to cover all the ugly things that had happened in her life. She was impervious to the false excitement being generated just outside her closed door. Her hair long, loose and flowing, she began to make up. It was her usual painstaking ceremony, except that anticipation was lacking, as it had been in New Haven and Boston.

If only she could recapture the feeling of bygone openings. But that was half a dozen years ago. She stared at herself as she worked meticulously on her lips, making them full, rich, red, to contrast vividly with her golden hair and pale skin. She stopped, suddenly overcome by the feeling that it was all useless. Panic was beginning to set in. She must escape this place. She must flee. Back to Silvermine. Or anywhere. She must not let them see her with all her naked anxieties and terrors. She must have been insane to let herself become involved in this production. That was her real insanity.

The new scene, which had seemed to work in the early hours of morning when they had discovered it, was suddenly false to her. She could never do it before an audience. Though the dramatic feeling might be honest, she could never let the whole world know her secret. She had to go on believing, or pretending, that she hated her mother and always would.

It was a huge lie. The scene and everyone involved in it. They had tricked and deluded her into doing it. They had lied to her when they said it was a better scene. They had coached Maria Patrick to pretend to really be her mother and seduce her into forgiving her. She felt no forgiveness, she needed no love from a woman she had hated all her life. The scene was a fraud! She could not play it. Feelings, confusing and contradictory, raged within her mind in a battle in which she was the enemy and the victim.

Her panic became so intense that her hands trembled and she smudged her makeup badly. She hurled her lipstick case at the mirror, shattering a corner of it. She leaped up and started out, hoping to escape the theater without being seen. She was reaching for the door when there was a knock.

She stopped, tense, breathless, the pain of panic a knot just under her breasts.

'Five minutes, Miss Lawrence, five minutes.'

'Yes,' she whispered in a voice so weak and low it could not be heard.

The discipline of the years took command of her. She sat down again and in the remaining moments tried to complete her makeup. Good or bad, truthful or fraudulent, she would have to go out and give her performance out of loyalty to the rest of the company. To Steve, and Jeff, to Sam, whom she had hurt so badly. She would try to do it this once, for them. Then she would be ready to go back to Ross and Silvermine, where she would be safe forever behind those quaint rock walls, amid the peaceful, protective New England countryside.

There was another knock at the door, and a familiar voice. Steve was asking, 'Kit?'

'Come in,' she managed, trying to conceal her panic. In her mirror, she watched him enter. She could tell at once he had caught sight of the corner of shattered mirror. 'My hair was tangled. The comb slipped out of my hand,' she explained.

He pretended to believe her. 'We'll have it fixed first thing tomorrow.'

'Yes, please,' she said, playing along.

He stood behind her as she applied the last touches to her face.

'You used to be a pretty girl. You are now a beautiful woman.' He reached for her hand, ostensibly to lift her to her feet, actually to diagnose her condition. Her hand was tense, as he had feared.

'Kiss you?' he asked.

'Would you?'

'Remember the first time I kissed you on an opening night, I almost ruined your makeup? I know better now.'

He kissed her on the cheek, avoiding smearing her lipstick or disturbing her pancake make up. She clung to him for a brief, terrified moment.

'You'll be great, Kit. Great!'

She smiled sadly. 'Have I ever been less than great to you, Steve?'

'Never,' he said, smiling back.

'The new scene, Steve – tell me how right it is?' she asked, like a child begging for the security of a familiar fairy tale.

'It's right. It's true. It's honest. That's why it hurts so. Why you're so frightened now.'

She glanced up at him. She had not succeeded in fooling him.

'Go out there. Share your feeling with them. Don't be ashamed of it. What you've felt for all the years, this may be the night to realize it. Pretend she *is* out there; let *her* know how you feel.'

'Places, please,' the stage manager's voice came over the squawk box just outside her door.

'I'll try, Steve, I'll try,' she promised, trying even now to mean it more than she actually did.

Jeff Warrener sat in the first row of the second balcony, damp right through his dinner jacket. He arched his fingers over his nose and leaned forward, tensely, as the house lights began to come down.

Sam Rogers sat in his aisle seat in the fourth row. Beside him an empty seat, a tradition he had observed ever since Bertha's death. His own show or someone else's, he always reserved two seats even though he went unaccompanied.

He had tried to maintain an air of confidence as long as others could observe him. Now that he sat hidden in the dark he slumped, exhausted from the strains and pressures of recent months. God, he kept saying to himself, let it come out right for that girl, that girl . . .

At the rear of the house, Steve Brooks stood behind the last row, his accustomed place for opening nights. He could see Melinda in the aisle seat he had reserved for her. The house was hushed and dark. That quiet moment before curtain rise was always magical and nerve-racking. A door opened behind him, allowing the lobby lights to intrude on the darkness. He turned to rebuke the latecomer. 'Damn it,' he whispered angrily, 'shut that door!'

'Sorry I'm late,' he heard Ross say. 'All trains from Connecticut are late.'

Ross took his place beside Steve Brooks.

'How is she?' he whispered.

'We'll know soon, soon,' Steve said as the curtain warmers began to glow.

The first light broke across the apron of the stage. The curtain started up. The play had begun.

The set received its opening-night due. The cast started off brisk and bright. The first act was going well. On her entrance Kit received an ovation, to which she pretended to be impervious. To acknowledge it would prevent her from completing what she must do to survive this terrifying night.

When she played her first moments with the pregnant young girl, she was warm, solicitous and motherly, realizing every value Steve had written into them. It ingratiated her character with the audience and created an empathy which must last throughout the night. To Steve she appeared to be warmer and more endearing than she had ever been. Still, the audience did not exude that unreserved feeling of having been completely won over. The cancerous gossip had obviously done its damage.

The response at the end of the act was polite. The talk in the lobby was mainly in terms of condescending surprise. They had not expected a play that started so well. But they reserved judgment.

Ross kept asking, 'You know about these things, Brooks. How is it going? What's your guess?'

'Nothing matters except the last scene.' Steve was reserving his judgment too.

Kit played the second act with more bite and determination than she had evidenced before. Her every motivation was sharper through the scenes involving the search for her mother. Her determination to punish and demean her mother grew stronger, clearer. She was preparing herself to fulfill a lifelong vow of vengeance when they finally met. When the word came that her mother had been found, Kit Lawrence was as menacing as an enraged empress as she dominated the stage at the second-act curtain.

The audience did not stream up the aisles so quickly this time. Many remained in their seats. Those critics who did venture up the aisle seemed more thoughtful and engrossed than they had been at the end of the first act.

A feeling of expectation was beginning to pervade the theater. It imposed an even heavier burden on Kit. If she could fulfill it, she would have come back in magnificent style. If she failed to realize the promise she had shown in the first two acts, the rumors and the disastrous predictions would be doubly confirmed. There would be some pretense at sadness that a career which had once shone so brightly had sputtered and died out. But the reviews and the reactions, no matter how benignly phrased, would be fatal. There would be no next time. Not for Kit Lawrence. Steve did not want to speculate on what awaited her if she failed now.

He recalled the fantasy she had recently described, of being an old gray-haired lunatic roaming through empty corridors, calling out for help, and no one to hear her.

The image chilled him.

The house sat quiet and expectant, waiting for the third-act curtain to go up. There were a few tense coughs from scattered spectators in the audience. Audiences sometimes coughed out of boredom or discomfort. Sometimes because the subject of the play disturbed them deeply. Steve chose to believe the latter was the case tonight.

Once the curtain went up, all coughing ceased. The third and final act was on.

The mood built well, Kit apparently in control all the way. If there was any criticism Jeff could have made to this point, it was that she was too strong, too vindictive, betraying no hint of the vulnerability that would make the ending more credible. He was willing to make allowances for that, as long as she seemed in possession of her performance and the scene. He was leaning forward so intently that he did not even attempt to brush away the trickle of sweat that traced its way down the side of his face.

In the rear of the house, Steve shared the same feeling. Had she gone so far in her portrayal of hatred that she could not possibly reverse it without making the ending seem false and contrived? Nothing would offend the critics or the audience more.

With a sudden foreboding of disaster, he recalled that she had said it wasn't truthful, honest. Was she now so bent on proving it that she would destroy her performance, which had been a jewel of perfection thus far? Actresses more stable than Kit Lawrence had been known to do that. Nowhere does self-fulfilling prophecy work with such inexorable effect as on the stage.

Maria Patrick made her entrance. The two women had the stage to themselves now and until the end of the play. Maria was properly contrite and sympathetic as she tried to justify her past sins. Kit was even more adamant and rigid in her refusal to be moved. Finally Maria's lines became halting, vague pleas, incomplete sentences, phrases, single words, till she was silent, as the scene called for her to be.

There was a long pause, complete silence, total absence of movement. Maria turned to leave as Kit had commanded her to do. She started towards the door, unsure as to how Kit

Lawrence would finish the scene. By the time Maria's hand was on the knob, she felt terrifyingly certain that at the last moment Kit had decided to revert to the original ending.

Steve suddenly felt the same surge of panic. Up in the balcony, Jeff rose out of his seat. For this was the moment when Kit should be turning to Maria, calling out 'Mama . . .' Maria was already opening the door. Slowly Kit turned – not to Maria but downstage; staring out not at the audience, but beyond it. Far into space, far into that wide limitless world in which her real mother must be.

She whispered the single word, 'Mama . . .' In the hush onstage and in the house, it recaptured that powerful but subtle and penetrating quality she had once possessed. Maria Patrick turned. Instead of Kit's holding her position onstage, as they had rehearsed, she had become the more eager of the two. She started toward Maria Patrick. They embraced, mother and daughter. Kit Lawrence wept as the curtain started down slowly.

The impact of her performance was so profound that there was a reverential silence as the curtain touched the stage. Then applause erupted in an explosion accented by bravos. People rose in their seats and cried out to her. The cast took their curtain calls in the manner Jeff had rehearsed. But the audience kept demanding Kit.

Steve Brooks and Dr Ross had raced backstage. They found Kit still wet-eyed and trembling.

'Kit, go on out!' Steve urged. 'They want to tell you how much they love you!'

Kit pleaded, 'Ross? How was I? Do I deserve it?'

'You deserve it, Kit. You deserve all of it.'

She started out to take her first solo bow. She walked erectly, like a goddess; she partook of their applause as if it were her eucharist, her bread and wine.

'This is where she lives,' Ross whispered. 'This is her reality.'

Steve watched from the wings, elated and relieved. He felt someone behind him. Jeff was beaming.

'You sonofabitch, we did it! We did it!' Jeff whispered, as if hardly daring to believe they had carried it off.

Eight curtain calls followed. People crowded down the aisles to the edge of the stage. Men and women blew kisses to her. They reached up, trying to touch her. One of the daily critics, who should have departed the instant the curtain started down, was still there, cheering.

Jeff said, 'We'd better get her off and to her dressing room. They'll never let her go.'

He signaled the stage manager to bring the curtain down for the final time. He went out, embraced Kit and led her to her dressing room, through the crowd that already filled the corridor.

Sam was trying to direct traffic, calling out to the visitors, 'Please! Give my little girl a chance to catch her breath. We will see all of you at Sardi's. Upstairs! You are all welcome! So please, we'll meet you over there!'

Meantime, Jeff Warrener had shepherded Kit through the crowd and into her dressing room. He shut the door. Finally the crowd started to disperse.

Steve found Kit Lawrence seated before her dressing table, staring into the mirror as if seeing her own face for the first time. Her eyes caught Steve in the mirror. Behind Steve was Ross.

'Tonight, for the first time, I felt it. Really felt it,' she said softly. 'And it felt so free. So free, after a long, long time of being locked away.'

She turned to Ross. 'Am I free?'

'As free as you want to be,' Ross said.

She smiled. Impetuously, Steve reached out his arms, enfolded her and kissed her full on the lips. She clung to him. As she did, Melinda appeared in the doorway. The smile on Melinda's face froze, then dissipated slowly. She became restrained, and quite professional as she said, 'It's a hit. You were marvelous! Never better. You'll run two years. More if you want to.'

Sam tried to ease the moment by urging, 'Come on! Get changed, Kit, darling. We've got a mob waiting for us at Sardi's.'

'All right,' she said. 'Clear out, all of you. I want to change.' As they turned to leave, she asked Melinda, 'Would you stay and help me?'

'Of course,' Melinda said, politely but unenthusiastic.

The men waited outside in the corridor.

Jeff asked, 'Sam, where the hell did you get the money for such a big party at Sardi's?'

Self-consciously, Sam confessed, 'I offered to put up my limousine as security. But Vincent said my credit was always good there. "Besides," he said, "it wouldn't be Sardi's if Sam Rogers' limousine with SIR on the license plate didn't roll up a couple times a week. It gives the place class." Yes, there are nice people in this world. Even in show business.'

Jeff, Steve and Sam laughed. Ross did not appreciate it. He was too engrossed in his own thoughts. Without any seeming provocation he said, 'Brooks, I want a word with you. Later. Alone.'

'Of course, sure.'

Inside the dressing room Kit Lawrence was behind the screen slipping into an after-theater gown. She had had no assistance from Melinda, nor did she need any. But once she was behind the screen she asked, 'Did I . . . did you ever get a note from me?'

'Note, yes,' Melinda said.

'I'm glad. Because I could never decide was it a fantasy or did I really write that note and send it.'

'I received it. It was very touching,' Melinda said, realizing Kit had no memory of her answer.

'You know, Steve is very dear to me.'

'I could see that,' Melinda said, referring to the sight that had greeted her when she opened the door.

'That's why I wanted to talk to you. Alone.' She came out from behind the screen in a short bright red cocktail dress. 'Zip me?' she asked.

As Melinda came around behind Kit, both women were staring into the mirror.

'Being dear and being in love are not the same,' Kit said.

Their eyes met in the mirror.

'Steve might think so. Especially after tonight. He'll recall the old days. And how it used to be. Well, it wasn't. He only remembers what it might have been.'

Melinda stared questioningly into the mirror. Kit turned to her so that they were eye to eye. 'What Steve couldn't understand, or wouldn't accept, is that no one man can love me enough. I didn't understand that myself till Ross. I need people. I need them like they were tonight. Loving me. Cheering me. Approving of me. And then tomorrow more of them, and more. Every night. More and more.'

'Do you want me to tell that to Steve? You don't think he'd believe me, do you?' Melinda asked.

'No. But don't turn him out. He needs one woman to love who can love him back. I can't.'

It was a sad confession.

'And you?' Melinda asked.

'Me?' Kit reflected. 'As long as there are plays to play, and I can manage to play them, I'll get along.' She broke the mood suddenly by laughing. 'I used to threaten Ross, "If you cure me I'll never be able to act again." Well, I guess he didn't cure me. Because here I am acting again.'

'You were fantastic!' Melinda said, with complete honesty and respect.

'I'll tell you something, if you promise never to tell anyone. Not Steve. Especially not Ross.'

'Promise.'

'Just before the curtain, when I turned to look out, I really wanted, really hoped, that she would come out of that audience and . . . and claim me.'

When they entered Sardi's, Kit Lawrence received a standing ovation. Sam and Jeff swept her up the stairs. Ross, Steve, and Melinda followed.

Upstairs, on sets strategically placed around the large room, the first television reviews were coming in. They were unanimous in their praise of the play, ecstatic over Kit Lawrence and her triumphant return. Each fresh review was greeted with more cheers, more applause.

The phone was ringing. Jeff, Steve and Sam knew what that meant. Emil Bernstein was phoning in the first word of the morning reviews. The message was terse. '*Times*, fantastic. *News*, terrific. *Post* – even more enthusiastic!'

When an opening goes badly, celebrants disappear with the first bad reviews. With tonight's success they stayed on, eating and drinking, joking and laughing. Dr Ross had no time for such celebration. His first patient was at nine o'clock in the morning, and he had a long ride back to Silvermine tonight. Once the reviews were in, he found Steve Brooks and took him aside.

'Can we find a place to talk?' he managed over the chatter and the laughter.

Steve led the doctor down the stairs and out onto Forty-fourth Street.

The late-night traffic had dwindled down to a few empty cabs. The cold air was an invigorating change from the smoke-clouded celebration.

'Brooks, at a time like this it is very natural to be misled. To engage in undue optimism. We would all like to congratulate ourselves tonight. I know I feel a certain self-righteous pride. It was my idea to call on you and Warrener to help make her functional again. And surely you must feel that your play had a great deal to do with it. It did. And she will be fine. So long as the pressures don't overwhelm her. So we should all feel smug and self-satisfied.

'But let me point out to you that she groped her own way to her solution. The dream that opened the door to the right ending for your play, that was *her* dream. She was trying to tell us something. And once she did, it began to work. The most constructive thing is that she finally exhibits a will to recover.'

Ross turned more grave. 'There may be regressions, periodic crises, panics. But this is the first definite affirmative step for her. I hope it lasts. It may not. But I'll keep hoping. As I told you once, in my business, unlike yours, we don't perform miracles.

'Well, it's late and I have to leave,' the doctor said, changing subjects suddenly. 'Oh, by the way, Brooks, let her go. She can function now. Don't feel responsible for her any longer. And don't thrust any burdens on her.'

'What burdens could I thrust on her?' Steve demanded.

'Don't fall in love with her again. Please? For her sake.'

Ross kissed Kit Lawrence on the cheek.

'Ross,' she whispered into his ear, 'can I come and see you?'

'Anytime you feel a need to.'

Ross was gone. The guests, even the most exuberant and the drunkest, began to depart.

Kit Lawrence, Steve Brooks, Melinda, Jeff and Sam walked east on Forty-fourth Street from Sardi's toward the Algonquin. Sam's huge black limousine paced alongside. But this was a night for walking.

Nothing was said. There was nothing left to say. All the jubilation had been poured out. All that was left was the silent shared feeling of the struggle being ended, the triumph having been achieved.

In the lobby of the Algonquin a few late theater-goers were still having supper. They applauded when Kit entered.

There was already a fistful of telegrams waiting for her at the desk. The night manager had secured copies of the *Times* and the *News* and had them open to the reviews.

Fearing Kit might become overtired and overtense, Steve took charge of her. 'Come, Kit, I'll take you up.'

'No, Steve.'

'It's late. It's been a long day. And even longer night,' he insisted.

'Oh, I'm going up,' she agreed. 'But Steve, your wife is waiting.'

She stepped into the elevator, turned, smiled at them as the door closed.

At Steve's side, Sam said softly, 'My little girl. I only wish Bertha had been here tonight.' Then to dispel his own mood, Sam brightened and said, 'My car's outside. Can I give anybody a lift?'

'If it's not out of your way,' Melinda said. 'I'm up on Madison in the sixties.'

'Not out of my way at all. I'd be delighted, my dear.' Sam offered Melinda his arm and they started for the door.

'Sam . . .' Steve called after them.

Sam looked back.

'Got room for one more?'

Melinda turned to stare questioningly at Steve.

'Mel?' he asked. That single syllable was a plea for understanding and an apology for all the past and painful events in their marriage.

She hesitated. Then she admitted with a tearful smile, 'It's what I've always wanted. My own Author-in-Residence.'